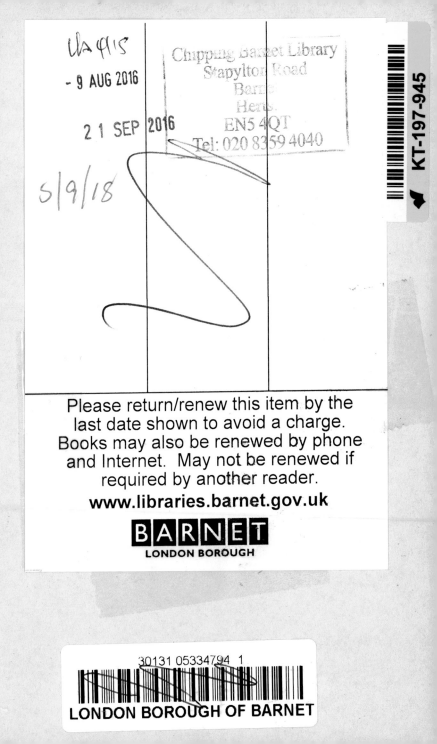

Also by Tamara McKinley

Ocean Child
Savannah Winds

Available in ebook

Jacaranda Vines
Matilda's Last Waltz
Undercurrents
Dreamscapes
Windflowers
Summer Lightning

FIRESTORM

Tamara McKinley

First published in 2013
This paperback edition published in 2014 by

Quercus
55 Baker Street
7th Floor, South Block
London W1U 8EW

A CIP catalogue record for this book is available
from the British Library

PB ISBN 978 1 84866 867 6
EBOOK ISBN 978 1 78206 963 8

10 9 8 7 6 5 4 3 2 1

Printed and bound in Great Britain by Clays Ltd, St Ives plc

Typeset by Ellipsis Books Limited, Glasgow

Long before the white man came to Australia, the Aborigines understood the importance of fire, for it cleanses and clears away the debris of old vegetation to regenerate, propagate and nurture the circle of new life in the bushlands of the Outback.

And yet, when a firestorm threatens an isolated and perhaps divided community, it brings not only devastation and fear, but binds those people in one purpose – to overcome and survive. In the aftermath of such a fire comes the chance to set aside old enmities, past regrets and sadness and to begin rebuilding their lives and nurture what matters most. For in the ashes of the past lie the dormant seeds of new beginnings, and hope for a future unclouded by what had come before.

1

Brisbane, 1946

He knew he must cut a strange, solitary figure in the ill-fitting suit someone had kindly given him, but he had money in his pocket and army discharge papers in his kitbag. To all intents and purposes, he was a free man.

But it wasn't just the glare on the water that brought the tears to his eyes as he looked out across the Brisbane River, and as they rolled down his thin face he unashamedly let them fall. He'd waited so long to return home to Australia, had held the scents, sights and sounds in his head and heart like a sweet promise to sustain him throughout the horrors of jungle warfare and the privations of the Japanese prisoner-of-war camps. But he'd found no redemption in this homecoming, for despite the long months of care in the hospital, he was still haunted by his experiences, and now had to face a new battle against another, far more invincible enemy.

He was thirty-four, and had seen things no man should ever see – had survived the worst of man's inhumanity, only to discover that his weakened, battered body had been invaded by cancer and that he was going to die anyway. The irony of his situation hit him hard, and he raged silently against the cruelty of Fate as he dashed away the tears and struggled for composure.

Once he felt ready to face the world again, he hoisted the

kitbag over his bony shoulder, turned his back on the river and headed for the train station. He'd discharged himself from the hospital this morning against doctor's orders, but he had a feeling the surgeon understood his need to use whatever time was left to him to embrace this momentary freedom and seek some kind of peace.

He slowly made his way through the bustling city, awed by the new buildings and the sense of purpose in the people around him. It was daunting to be free after so many years of following orders and being under the lash, and he was disconcerted by the traffic noise and the swirl of people hurrying past him. The city had changed during his absence – but then so had he – and now he was a stranger, invisible to those around him, a thin shadowy figure spared not even a glance.

Their lack of curiosity didn't touch him as he continued on his way, for his heart and his mind were focused on a place far from here – a place where the silence is broken only by the sough of the wind in the eucalyptus – where the enormous sky stretches above endless plains of rich red earth and scrubby pastures, and the clear, bright light falls on the old wallaby tracks that would eventually lead him home.

The deep rumbles of thunder rolled over the Outback plains, the sky darkening with roiling clouds as forks of lighting flashed over the hills, reflected in the depleted rivers and billabongs. The heat was intense, the very air electric with the powerful storm that was building to the south-west of Morgan's Reach. And, as the desperate farmers looked up at those threatening skies from their parched land, they prayed that this time the storm would break and that after three long years of waiting the rains would finally come.

Morgan's Reach exists only because of the natural spring that flows even in the driest years. The tiny settlement of less than twenty dwellings lies deep in the Queensland Outback, far from the highway at the end of a meandering dirt track. The main street is half a mile long and wide enough to accommodate a team of oxen, but it leads only to the cattle trails and ancient Aboriginal and animal tracks that traverse the surrounding bush. There are no signposts to Morgan's Reach, for the people who live and work on the vast sheep and cattle stations that surround it know where it is and, because of its geography, it remains hidden from outsiders unless they have business there.

Rebecca Jackson's grandfather, Rhys Morgan, was a doctor of medicine, explorer, adventurer, benefactor and eccentric who stumbled across this remote oasis back in 1889. Having discovered what he considered to be the perfect location for a bush hospital, he'd celebrated his fortieth birthday by digging the foundations of the hospital and giving the settlement his name. All he needed then was a wife.

Gwyneth Davies was twenty and feeling stifled by her parents' ever-pressing desire to see her married off to a man they thought could elevate their position in Brisbane society. Her resolve was beginning to weaken when she literally bumped into Rhys Morgan on the boardwalk outside the drapers' shop. In the time it had taken to gather up her packages and accept his offer of a cup of tea in a nearby cafe, Gwyneth had fallen in love.

Despite her genteel upbringing, Gwyneth was of tough Welsh stock, and not easily daunted by the prospect of living out her life in the back of beyond and, with this exciting, driven man at her side, she knew she was in for an adventure.

Yet she was a woman of strong opinions, and when she caught her first glimpse of the brushwood and tin hovel her new husband expected her to live in, she'd made it very clear that she had no intentions of doing so. Rhys, rather awestruck by this forceful young woman he'd married, quickly realised that if he was to keep her, he must build her a proper home. Gwyneth had overseen the work with a judicious eye to detail, and when she was satisfied that it suited her she'd moved in the furniture she'd brought with her, rolled up her sleeves and got on with her new and challenging life.

Over the decades that followed, Gwyneth worked at Rhys's side, tending the sick and comforting the dying. She endured the flies and the dust in this most primitive of surroundings, and learned to survive fire, flood, heat and drought as she raised her six children and bullied the School Board into sending a teacher to the small school she'd had built in the centre of town.

Rhys had become close to three of his grandchildren, Millicent, Rebecca and Terence, and had lived long enough to meet his great-grandson, Danny. He'd reached the grand age of ninety when in the spring of 1939 he finally succumbed to the harsh environment and the pressures of his far-flung practice. Gwyneth had lost not only a husband, but her dearest, closest friend, and she mourned him still. Yet she gave thanks that he'd gone in peace, safe in the knowledge that his eldest son, Hugh, would carry on his lifetime's work, and that Hugh's wife, Jane, and daughter, Rebecca, would be at his side.

The bush hospital had changed since those very early days, and the facilities it offered now were far more sophisticated. In place of the old tumbledown shack there was a single-storey wooden building that stood back from the road in a large plot, its deep verandas and green painted shutters offering shade on the hottest of days and a view down the dirt track that eventually met the main highway. There was a single ward, an isolation room, a consulting room with a small operating theatre tucked behind it in case of emergencies, a kitchen and a proper indoor bathroom and lavatory. The medical stores were kept under lock and key behind a sturdy door, and the two-way radio was linked to the one in the homestead next door where Rebecca and her nine-year-old son, Danny, now lived with her parents.

Rebecca had closed all the shutters to keep out the fierce noonday sun, so the ward was dim and should have been relatively cool. But the squeaking ceiling fan wasn't doing much to alleviate the heat and, as she walked down the ward to check on her six patients, she made a mental note to get it oiled before it drove everyone mad.

Her starched apron crackled as she moved quietly past the beds in her rubber-soled shoes. It was unusual to have every bed occupied, but none of the cases had been serious enough for the Flying Doctor to whisk them away to the main hospital in Brisbane, and most of them would go home the following day. Satisfied that they were comfortable after their lunch, she left them to doze and went out onto the veranda.

The heat shimmered on the wide dirt road and the air was still and heavy, laced with a tang of copper that heralded an electric storm. Eucalyptus trees wilted by the depleted waterhole, and the birds were silent as the sun beat down on the corrugated iron roofs and patches of yellowing grass. There had been no rain worth mentioning for over three years now, and the likelihood of fire was growing by the day as the farmers on the outlying cattle and sheep stations struggled to feed and water their dwindling stock.

Rebecca unfastened the top button of her blue-and-white striped dress, thankful she didn't wear starched collars and cuffs as she'd had to during her training in Sydney. She checked the watch pinned to her apron bib, glanced up at the dark clouds gathering to the west and then surveyed the deserted road that ran through the small settlement. There was no sign of Danny, even though she'd told him in no uncertain terms to

5

be back here by twelve. At this rate, she thought darkly, he was in danger of missing out on his birthday party tomorrow.

She chewed her lip, fretful at the memory of how he'd refused to listen to her this morning when she'd tried to explain yet again that his father, Adam, was dead and that there was no hope of his ever returning – and how he'd stomped off, slamming the screen door behind him. Her son's habit of disappearing into the bush was worrying – not least because of the reason he kept doing it. She had hoped that now he'd started at boarding school in Brisbane he'd grow out of this obsession and realise it was a childish fantasy born of a deep longing – but it seemed that nothing had changed, and that this school holiday would follow the same pattern as all the others.

Rebecca had thought long and hard about how to deal with Danny – had even driven the sixty miles north to Killigarth Station to seek advice from her best friend, Amy Blake. Their circumstances were very similar, for Amy was a war widow too, her husband John killed in Malaya just like Adam. She lived with her parents on their cattle station so, like Rebecca, had the love and support of her family to help her through the painful mourning period and to raise her son, George, who was the same age as Danny. But even the wise and gentle Amy couldn't help, and it made Rebecca feel very alone sometimes.

Impatient that she was beginning to feel sorry for herself, Rebecca left the shade of the veranda, pushed through the outer screen door and went down the steps and into the glare of the sun. She was used to the vagaries of the Outback weather, for she'd been born and raised in Morgan's Reach and had spent nearly every one of her thirty years here, but it was sad to see how badly her mother's lovely garden had been ravaged by the long drought.

She crossed the dying lawn, noted her father's old utility

was parked by the homestead steps and pushed through the fly-screen doors that sheltered the veranda and the house. Nothing much had changed since her childhood, for the furniture had always been battered, the curtains and rugs faded by the sun, but it was home – a refuge she and Danny had returned to when it was clear that Adam would not be coming back from the war.

Her parents, Hugh and Jane, were sitting in the shabby kitchen, the remains of their hasty lunch scattered on the table. Hugh looked exhausted, with dark shadows under his eyes, but Jane looked as cool and elegant as ever in her nurse's uniform

'Have you seen Danny?' Rebecca asked.

Hugh shook his head. 'I've only just got back from Warratah Station, and didn't pass him on the track. Why? You lost him again?'

Rebecca nodded and headed back to the door. 'I'll go and see if he's with Gran,' she said.

'You worry too much over that boy,' said Hugh through a vast yawn. 'He'll be ten tomorrow, and he knows his way around the bush.'

Rebecca and her mother exchanged knowing looks, for they shared the same worry over Danny – and it had very little to do with his familiarity with the bush and its dangers. 'That's as maybe,' she replied, 'but he's running wild, and it's time he learned to do as he's told.'

She left the homestead and crossed the deserted main street to the house on the corner. Granny Gwyn lived in a neat one-storey wooden stilt-house which faced the hospital but backed onto the bush, and Danny loved going over there to help look after Gwyneth's menagerie of sick and abandoned animals, and to listen to her many stories about the old days. If he wasn't there, then she'd have to go and see Sarah at the native shacks on the far side of the town to see if her son, Billy Blue, had disappeared too. The pair of them were always going off together, and she wouldn't mind betting they were up to some mischief or other.

As she was about to unlatch the gate she heard the unmistakable roar of a fast-moving truck. Turning, she realised it was Ben Freeman, the local fire chief, and as he screeched to a halt beside her he covered her in a cloud of dust.

Despite her pleasure at seeing him, she greeted him with a frown. 'Thanks, Ben,' she muttered, trying to shake the worst of the dirt from her apron and dress. 'These were clean on this morning, and now I'm going to have to change before I go back on the ward.'

'Sorry, Becky,' he drawled as he swung out of the utility and ambled over to her.

He didn't look a bit sorry – not with that stupid grin on his face. But it was a grin that made her heart flutter and sent a thrill right through her, so she supposed she would have to forgive him. 'What's the rush anyway?' she asked, shielding her eyes from the sun as she looked from the boots and moleskins, past the check shirt straining across the broad chest and up to his face.

'I wanted to catch you on your lunch break,' he replied, his very blue eyes regarding her from beneath the broad brim of his bush hat. 'I wondered if you and Danny might like to come up to my place for some tucker this evening?'

'That would be good, Ben, but Danny's gone walkabout again, and when I do find him, he'll be confined to his room for the rest of the day.' She smiled up at him to soften her refusal. 'I'm sorry. Perhaps another time?'

He tucked his hands into the pockets of his moleskins as he leaned against the utility and crossed his long legs at the ankle. 'I reckon I can wait a while longer,' he said softly, 'but it's been almost a year, Becky. I was hoping we could make it a more permanent arrangement between us.'

She let him take her hand and draw her towards him. 'We will, Ben, I promise,' she replied. 'But Danny has to get used to the idea, and he's not ready yet. Please be patient.'

'I'll try, Becky, but it ain't easy,' he murmured.

His eyes were mesmerising as he gazed down at her and she could see the fine lines across the tanned flesh of his face. At thirty-five, Ben was a handsome man, and the knowledge that he loved her and wanted to marry her and take on Danny made her feel a warmth that had little to do with the blazing sun.

'I'm sure we could manage a few quiet minutes together while Danny's party's in full swing tomorrow,' she said softly. 'And then there are the picnic races next month. Perhaps we could all go and make a day of it?'

'Yeah, that'd be good. Want me to pick you up?'

She thought about it and then shook her head. 'It's probably better if we meet you there.'

'You're not having second thoughts about us, are you?' His expression changed and his eyes clouded with doubt.

She glanced quickly along the street and lightly kissed his cheek. 'Not for a minute,' she assured him. 'You're the man for me, Ben Freeman,' she added softly, 'and I have no intention of losing you. But you know how gossip starts out here – let's keep it to ourselves a bit longer, eh?'

He grinned down at her. 'Reckon that'll have to do for now,' he said.

She giggled. 'Reckon it will. Now, I really do have to go.'

'Catch you later then,' he said wistfully. At her nod, he tipped his hat brim over his eyes and opened the utility door. 'I'll keep an eye out for Danny,' he reassured her, 'and if I come across him, I'll bring him home.'

Rebecca watched as he drove off, raising yet another cloud

of dust in his wake. Poor Ben had been badly hurt once before, receiving a 'Dear John' letter from his fiancée while he was fighting Rommel's army in Egypt – and it was clear that he'd begun to wonder if Rebecca was really serious about their relationship.

She gave a deep sigh as she walked down the path and headed towards the back of her grandmother's house for, in their different ways, they'd both been damaged by the war. And yet time was indeed a great healer, and now they were ready to commit to a new future together. But Danny was the sticking point, and she could do nothing to further this burgeoning relationship until her son would accept that his father was dead.

Gwyneth was feeling every one of her seventy-seven years today, but was damned if she was going to let a few niggles stop her getting through her many chores. She ignored the ache in her knees and shoulders as she finished feeding the last of the orphaned kangaroo joeys and tucked him firmly down into the pillowcase that she'd tied to the veranda railings. There were four pillowcases in all, each bulging with its long-legged cargo, and it had become quite time-consuming to look after them all when she had so many other things to attend to. It was at times like this that she missed Danny, and she fleetingly wondered where he'd got to this morning.

'G'day, Gran. Is Danny with you?'

Gwyneth turned and her welcoming smile faltered as she noted Rebecca's worried expression. 'I haven't seen him since he came to feed Wally last night,' she replied. 'Why? Has he gone off with Billy Blue again?'

Rebecca chewed her lip. 'It looks like it,' she muttered crossly, 'and when I get hold of him he'll get a clip round the ear for disobeying me.'

Gwyneth shrugged in an attempt to lighten Rebecca's worry. 'He's a little boy,' she replied, 'and boys rarely do as they're told. I shouldn't worry, Rebecca. He knows the bush well enough and will be back when he's hungry.'

'That's not the point, Gran, and you know it.' Rebecca's blue eyes glistened with unshed tears as she tucked her light brown hair behind her ears. 'I thought it would be different now he's away at school so much of the year. But it seems he's still unable to accept . . .' She blinked rapidly and folded her arms tightly about her waist. 'I tried talking to him this morning, but he stormed off, refusing to listen. It's as if he's punishing me every time he goes bush, and I don't know what to do for the best, Gran,' she admitted softly.

Gwyneth had her own ideas about that, but knew Rebecca was in no mood to listen to some straight talking. In many ways, Danny and his mother were very alike, for they didn't appreciate good advice, no matter how well-meant it was. And yet Rebecca had been through a lot these past years, and she deserved all the help she could get. 'I'll try to have a word with him again,' she murmured, 'but don't expect miracles, Becky. It's a big thing to come to terms with.'

'George Blake is the same age, but he's accepted that John won't be coming back. I had hoped that now they were at school in Brisbane together, Danny would follow his lead,' she replied with a watery smile.

'He's a bright little boy who thinks too much,' said Gwyneth drily, 'but eventually he's going to have to accept the way things are. And he will, Becky. I promise.'

'I hope you're right.' She sighed. 'This has gone on long enough, and every time he disappears into the bush it just brings it all back – and I need to put it behind me now – start again.'

Gwyneth eyed her granddaughter fondly. 'Then that is what

you must do,' she said briskly. 'You're still young, and Ben Freeman seems to be a good man.'

Rebecca blushed. 'How do you know about Ben?'

Gwyneth chuckled. 'I might be getting on, but I'm not blind, or daft. I've noticed how he's been coming into town more regularly – and the way you are with him.'

'I'd better get back,' she said, the blush still colouring her cheeks. 'Dad's worn out from being up all night, Mum has some house calls to make this afternoon, and there are still a hundred and one things to do for Danny's birthday party. If you see that young larrikin, tell him to get his skinny backside home, or suffer the consequences.'

Gwyneth watched her leave, then brushed back the stray wisps of grey hair from her sweaty face, rubbed her grubby hands down her trousers and tugged at the hem of her loose cotton shirt. She'd never been a woman who'd set much store in fancy clothes or make-up, and living out here all these years meant it was practical and comfortable to wear sturdy boots and old, scruffy clothes worn soft with use. But she was feeling the heat today, could taste the copper in the air and the weight of the gathering storm – not only from the elements, but within her family.

With her thoughts still troubled by Rebecca's unhappy situation, she grabbed her walking stick and broad-brimmed hat and went carefully down the veranda steps to check on the rest of her menagerie.

The chicken run and aviary had been set up in the shade of the trees at the bottom of the garden where the bush slowly encroached on the settlement and the feral goats grazed. The pens beside the runs were for the injured and orphaned animals that people always seemed to be bringing her, and she spent hours every day cleaning them out and tending to them.

There was a lorikeet with a broken wing, a pair of orphaned

possums, several lizards of various types and with various injuries, a rock wallaby recovering from a nasty abscess and a wombat joey that had been born, unusually, during this long drought, and which would have died of starvation if she hadn't found him cowering in the abandoned burrow.

The lorikeet was almost ready to be released, and the possums were thriving. The lizards were asleep in their hollowed-out tree branches, so it was difficult to tell how they were, and the tiny rock wallaby's abscess was healing nicely. She nodded with satisfaction, glanced about her and realised Wally, the wombat joey, had escaped from the burrow she'd made for him under the veranda. No doubt he was around somewhere, getting into mischief – just like young Danny.

She fed the chickens and stood in the shade of the overhanging trees, relishing the brief respite from the sun as she regarded her surroundings. Morgan's Reach might be isolated, the population scattered – but it was a tight-knit community that had not escaped the dark, tragic clouds of two world wars.

Two generations of young Australian men had heard the call to arms from England – the land they still considered their 'mother country' – and they had rushed to enlist, eager to fight and prove their courage. They'd left the rural stations to the women, their Aboriginal stockmen and those too old, too young or too unfit to be drafted into the services, trusting that there would be something to come home to when it was all over. But, like Rebecca's Adam and Amy Blake's John, many had not returned, and their loss was still sorely felt by everyone.

She experienced the now familiar pang of sadness, but didn't allow it to linger for it did no good to anyone, and turned her attention to a much earlier past. Morgan's Reach had grown since she and Rhys had come here all those years ago, and Gwyneth's lips twitched with a wry smile as she remembered how shocked she'd been to discover Rhys's paradise was in fact a ragtag collection of ramshackle wooden houses, dubious tin shacks and wattle-and-daub humpies.

The bush hospital that Rhys had so proudly expounded upon turned out to be a one-roomed wooden shack on stilts with a veranda and a sagging roof – and their proposed home wasn't much better. There was no door or window, the floor was compacted earth and she'd been expected to cook on a camp oven which had been set outside next to a washtub and mangle. It was a far cry from the comfortable home she'd had in Brisbane, and she'd told him in no uncertain terms that she wouldn't live there.

Gwyneth chuckled. Poor Rhys. He hadn't quite realised then how strong-willed she was, but over the years he'd come to admire her spirit, and she could look back on a long and happy marriage.

Morgan's Reach in those days had a tiny church, a pub and a general store which stood beside the single dirt track that had been widened to accommodate the mobs of cattle and sheep the drovers brought through to water at the spring on their way to market and the bullock teams that passed through laden with bales of wool and supplies.

It had been a rough sort of place, especially for the few women settlers, for the itinerant shearers, ringers, bullockies and drovers would come in to drink their wages and fight among themselves before they moved on. The small local tribe of Aborigines had been suspicious of everyone, and very few ventured into town, preferring to keep to the old ways by living in their traditional camp in the bush and often disappearing for months on walkabout.

Gwyneth's expression was wry as she thought about the changes that had been slowly wrought over the last fifty years. The drovers and shearers still came into town to drink and fight, but it had become quite respectable now, for there were more women, and the sturdier houses that lined the main thoroughfare had picket fences and painted fly-screens.

The simple one-roomed church that stood at the northern end of the street was the same, with a few battered pews and an old kitchen table for an altar. But the vicar no longer had to live in a tent, for a fine house had been built by his parishioners just next door to the cemetery. It was just a shame that the Reverend Algernon Baker, the latest incumbent, was a dour, unsociable man whom no one liked, despite the best efforts of his timid little wife, Frances, and the impish charm of their twin boys. But then that charm often led to trouble, and the boys were fast earning a reputation for mischief.

Gwyneth turned her thoughts to the schoolhouse which sat in the next large plot, and was ably run by young Emily Harris, who lived in the small cottage behind it. The old church hall had long burned down, so the school doubled as a dance hall and meeting place at the weekends.

The general store was fronted by a boardwalk shaded by tarpaulins, and further along were several small wooden cottages and a blacksmith's forge where Charley Sawyer held sway and continued to argue ferociously with his spinster neighbours over his randy old dog. The police station was opposite – though to call it by such a grand name was a little ridiculous, for Jake Webber ran the office from his front room, and the prison cell was a lean-to at the back of the house.

A few Aborigines still followed their traditional ways, but most of them now lived in shacks on the northern edges of the settlement, where the old bush camp had once been. They'd slowly integrated into the community by working as jackaroos and drovers on the cattle stations and, after a great deal of cajoling from Gwyneth, sent their children to the school.

Bert and Sal Davenport who ran the Dog and Drover hotel, which was handily placed near the church, were not allowed by law to serve the natives in the pub, but the ever-wily Bert got around this by selling them beer from the back window. Unfortunately this led to some quite serious fights, for the natives had a low tolerance to alcohol, and now the townspeople were beginning to badger Jake to do something to stop Bert. Not that it would do any good, thought Gwyneth with a wry smile, for they'd discovered how to make a lethal hooch of their own from the berries and leaves they foraged from the bush.

She turned her attention back to her home. The original homestead had burned down long ago, and its replacement was destroyed by termites. In their place now stood a sturdy wooden house on concrete pillars which had been topped and tailed with beaten metal to deter the white ants. A veranda ran around the house, offering shade on the hottest day and a relatively cool place to sleep at night behind the fly netting, which had been firmly nailed in place.

Danny and his friend George Blake loved sleeping out there during school holidays, but Gwyneth suspected they often went walkabout at night, and that worried her. The bush was a dangerous place in the dark no matter how well you knew it, and even though they were usually accompanied by their Aboriginal mate, Billy Blue, Gwyneth couldn't rest easy until she heard them return.

She gave a deep sigh. It was good to have young kids about the place again, for five of her other children had flown the nest years ago and were scattered all over Australia. She rarely saw them, and the only real contact she had was with Bethany's daughter, Millicent, who'd recently moved to the area with her husband to work on Carey Downs Station.

Hugh, her eldest son, was the only one who'd come back after training as a doctor, but he was in his mid-fifties now, and Gwyneth knew that, despite the Flying Doctors' Service and the unstinting help from Jane and Rebecca, he was beginning to find it all too much. There had been some hope that his son, Terence, might perpetuate the family tradition once he'd qualified, but Gwyneth had strong doubts that he would, for she'd met his wife, Sandra, and a woman like that wouldn't fit in here at all.

Aware that she was wasting time wool-gathering, she nevertheless continued to lean on her walking stick and enjoy the cooling shadows cast by the trees. The garden wasn't up to much, she thought, as she eyed the ragged tufts of grass, the bare patches of red earth and the encroaching lantana and weeds. It was a far cry from the lush lawns and heavily scented rose garden she could just remember from her childhood – but then this wasn't Wales, and the amount of rain they'd had these past three years wouldn't have filled a teacup.

At the thought of tea, she headed back to the house and, as she passed the large birdcage which always sat beside the screen door, she was greeted by her late husband's sulphur-crested cockatoo.

'G'day, g'day, g'day,' he squawked, his bright yellow crest bristling as he bobbed up and down on his perch.

'G'day to you too, Coco,' she replied as she replenished his water bowl and fed him a few seeds.

'Pretty boy, pretty boy. Arrgh.' Coco shuffled back and forth on his perch, lost his balance and just managed to cling on as he swung upside down and flapped his wings. He was aptly named, for he was a complete clown.

'You're just a silly old show-off,' she muttered affectionately. 'But I haven't got time to stand about watching you all day. I've got a birthday cake to make.'

She opened the screen door, letting it clatter behind her as she entered the gloomy interior and headed for the kitchen. She'd closed all the shutters to keep out the sun, but she didn't need light to see where she was going, for she knew every dusty corner of this cluttered house.

Rhys had travelled the world before they'd met, and had been an enthusiastic collector of artefacts and curiosities. Gwyneth regarded them as mostly junk and not worthy of houseroom, but she hadn't had the heart to get rid of any of it after he'd passed away, and they'd become so much a part of her life she now barely noticed them.

There were warrior shields, spears and shrunken heads from Africa; wooden carvings from India and the South Sea Islands; an elephant tusk, a rhino horn, stone figures from Egypt, and a thousand and one books, magazines, old maps and diaries. Drawers and boxes were stuffed with a plethora of meaningless souvenirs, and his desk remained as cluttered today as it had been on that morning seven years ago when he'd sat back in his old leather chair and fallen asleep for the last time.

Gwyneth wound her way through it all into the kitchen. The range was lit, making the little room like a furnace, and she opened the shutters in the hope there might be a bit of a breeze to cool the place down. As the light poured in she discovered to her dismay that Wally had found his way into her larder and was happily snuffling through her last sack of sugar.

'You're a naughty boy,' she scolded, avoiding his lethal claws and grabbing him by the scruff. 'No wonder you're getting so fat.' She couldn't help but grin as he eyed her solemnly and continued to lick the sugar from his nose and paws with relish. She carried him to the back door and dumped him on the veranda. 'Shoo,' she hissed.

Wally eyed her mournfully and then wandered off in a huff, his bandy legs so pigeon-toed it was a wonder he didn't trip himself up.

'Right,' she said forcefully. 'Now, perhaps I can get on.'

She returned to the kitchen, her mind busy with plans for

the birthday cake. Danny was her delight, and when he was away at school she missed his cheeky smile and his endless questions. But a part of her did wish he was more like John Blake's boy, for George was a quiet, unquestioning child, who had easily accepted the truth about his father's demise.

Gwyneth sighed as she weighed out the cake ingredients. She could only hope that Danny's long absences from Morgan's Reach, and his friendship with George, would eventually make him see sense, but after the scene Rebecca had described to her earlier she was beginning to have serious doubts – and that worried her deeply.

2

Ben Freeman's thoughts and emotions were confused as he drove out of Morgan's Reach and steered the utility along the dirt track that would lead through the bush and up to the house he'd built on the tablelands.

He'd known Rebecca all his life. His parents owned Wilga Cattle Station to the west of Morgan's Reach, and he and Rebecca had attended the same school, the same picnic races and get-togethers over the years. But he hadn't given her much thought back then, for she was just another annoying girl, and of no interest whatsoever. He'd left to finish his education in Brisbane as most of the Outback children did, and stayed on after college to work for the fire service.

But the lure of the great empty plains and the magic of the bush drew him back home, and on his return to Morgan's Reach he'd heard through the gossip that Rebecca was now training as a nurse in Sydney, and engaged to a veterinary student called Adam Jackson. Even then he hadn't taken much notice, for he was in love with Maggie Wheeler, gossip was for housewives and he could barely remember what Rebecca Morgan even looked like. And then, in September 1939, war was declared and Ben had left Morgan's Reach to enlist along with his mates, thinking it would be a great adventure and a chance to see the world.

Thinking back, Ben grimaced. It had been a gut-wrenching,

terrifying and bloody experience, and far from an adventure. The last letter from Maggie had extinguished the one glimmer of hope he'd kept burning through those endless enemy bombardments in the North African deserts – compounding the horrors of war and the reality of being so very far from home.

He steered the utility through the trees, the flickering light filtering through the canopy on to the dusty, scratched windscreen making it hard to see where he was going. But he'd come this way so often he barely had to concentrate, and his thoughts returned to his dilemma.

He'd survived the war and come home to discover that his mate John Blake hadn't been so lucky – and neither had several others. Maggie had long since married and moved to Darwin, but time and distance had healed the hurt, and when he met Rebecca again the attraction was instant, and he was amazed at how quickly she'd got under his skin.

And yet he was wary. He didn't want to get hurt again, and Rebecca was still fragile after losing Adam. He'd tried not to rush things, tried to understand that she and Danny needed time to adjust to a new commitment, but it was getting harder to stay patient, and despite her reassurances, he was beginning to suspect she was having second thoughts.

A movement amid the shadows caught his attention and he glanced across just in time to catch a glimpse of bright red hair and two small figures darting through the trees.

'Gotcha,' he murmured as he continued along the track as if unaware of the two boys. Billy Blue and Danny were heading for the caves on the side of the hill – a favourite hiding place for generations of boys. He'd let them settle in and think they were secure before he hauled them back home.

He drove past the almost invisible track that led to the caves and waterfall and continued on up the steep, winding slope to where he'd cleared a broad plot of land to build his house on the brow of the flat-topped hill. It wasn't a big house, but he was proud of it. The walls were tightly packed tree trunks he'd taken from the bush, the chimney made from the black rocks that lay scattered across the hillside, the corrugated iron roof low over the windows that gave an unrivalled view across the bush canopy to the sweep of surrounding plains and distant hills.

The kitchen and two bedrooms led off from a large central sitting room, and although he didn't have the luxury of an indoor bathroom, he could sit in the old tin tub outside, up to his neck in hot water from the copper boiler, and gaze at that fantastic view, safe in the knowledge he couldn't be seen and wouldn't be disturbed. After the noise and the horrors of the war it was his refuge, and he could think of nothing better than to share it with Rebecca and her son.

He parked the utility and climbed out, heading not for the front door but for the tall stone watchtower he'd built at the side of the house. He'd left Django in charge while he rushed into town, and although he trusted the Aboriginal elder to do his best, he also knew the man had a short attention span if left to his own devices for too long.

Django's broad brown face split into a wide grin as Ben reached the high wooden platform. 'All clear, boss,' he said cheerfully. 'Plenty storm coming in though. Reckon be here by tonight.'

'Thanks, mate. Go and get some tucker while I'm here, but don't be too long – I've got a couple of larrikins to round up and take home.'

'Them boys up to no good again, eh?' His amber eyes glinted with humour as he pulled the sweat-stained hat over his bushy hair. 'Sarah gunna give that Billy Blue a whopping, I reckon, but it dun do no good. He wild, that boy. Wild as his hair is red.'

He was still shaking his head and chuckling as he headed down the ladder and went into the house in search of food.

Ben picked up the binoculars and surveyed the panorama spread beyond the canopy of trees. The atmosphere was heavy and still, the thunder grumbling in the distance as lightning forked over the far hills. Dark clouds were building all around, casting deep shadows across the plains and the rocky outcrops. But there was no sign of fire – not yet anyway.

He turned the powerful binoculars onto the bush canopy and found the caves above the trickling waterfall which Django's tribe had once used as shelter and which still had ancient paintings on the walls. Billy Blue and Danny had crawled inside, but their legs were dangling over the ledge as they competed to throw their stones into the water that splashed over the rocks from the underground spring and eventually ran into a large pool at the bottom of the hill.

He grinned as he remembered how he and his mates used to hide in the same place when they wanted to dodge lessons or the endless round of chores. 'Sorry, boys,' he murmured, as he reached for the two-way radio he'd rigged up to the generator. 'It's time to go home.'

The radio crackled and whined through the headset as he gave his call sign and waited impatiently for Jake Webber to answer. Jake was either courting Emily Harris in her little cottage behind the school, or more likely dozing in the hammock on his front veranda, oblivious to everything. There was very little crime in the area, and although he also acted as an assistant fireman, Jake had far too much time on his hands.

Ben was about to cut the connection when Jake's sleepy voice broke through the static. 'G'day, mate. You gotta problem up there?'

'Nothing serious to report, Jake. But Rebecca's been looking for Danny, and I've just spotted him and Billy up at the caves.

23

Could you tell her he's fine, and that I'll be bringing him home?'

'No worries, mate.'

'Thanks. And Jake, try to stay alert. The storm's brewing and I'll need you on fire-watch tonight.'

'No worries,' he drawled again. 'Catch you later.'

Ben cut the connection, took one more look at the distant bank of black cloud and reluctantly left the tower. He and Jake were in for a long night of surveillance if that storm didn't break, for the bush was as dry as tinder and it would only take a single bolt of lightning to start a serious fire.

'I'm off to get the boys,' he told Django, who was lounging on the couch with a doorstep mutton sandwich and a mug of tea. 'Stay close to the radio until I get back. Should only be about half an hour.'

'Righto, boss.' Django settled more comfortably into the cushions and slurped his tea.

It was probably unwise to leave Django sated with sandwich and tea for too long, for experience had taught him that the man could fall asleep at the drop of a hat. But Becky needed to know her son was safe – and the bush was no place to be during an electric storm.

Ben hurried across the clearing, his loping stride eating up the distance as he headed for the jumble of basalt known to the locals as Eagle's Head. The black rocks balanced precariously against each other, emerging from the surrounding mulga scrub and spinifex like a giant prehistoric bird preparing for flight. They looked as if the merest puff of wind would bring them tumbling to the forest floor, but they'd been there for thousands of years, carved by the elements to stand sentinel over the dreaming place the local tribe called Namardol – Wedge-tailed Eagle.

The army had taught him well, and Ben carefully made his way down through the rocks, his boots making no noise as he tested each foothold and avoided disturbing the shale, which could come loose and give him away. Slowly easing over the last boulder, he stepped silently on to the ledge, effectively blocking off the boys' escape.

Both boys were so absorbed in their play they didn't notice him. Barefoot, in scruffy shirts and shorts that revealed skinned knees and elbows, they were of similar height, with the gangly limbs and soft faces of childhood. Danny's paler skin had browned in the sun until he was almost the same dark caramel as Billy – who'd inherited his colouring from an itinerant, red-headed drover, name and whereabouts unknown.

Billy Blue was the first to see him, and he nudged Danny before scrambling to his feet. 'We done nothing wrong,' he said defensively, his wild mop of red hair glinting in the sun as his amber eyes darted back and forth in search of another escape route.

'I know that, mate,' Ben said. 'But it's time to go home now.'

Danny's hands were clenched at his sides as he eyed Ben belligerently through the lick of brown hair that flopped over his forehead. 'You can't tell us what to do.'

'I just have,' he replied mildly. 'There's a nasty storm coming and your mothers want you home.'

'I don't wanna go home,' Danny objected, 'and you're not my father. I don't have to listen to you.'

Ben regarded the boy thoughtfully, noting the defiant stance and tilt of his chin. But his brown eyes held the hurt he was keeping at bay, and Ben knew that for all his bluff and bluster, Danny was just a small boy struggling to deal with what life had thrown at him. 'Sorry, mate,' he drawled, 'but I'm in charge up here, and like it or not, you can't stay.'

'Betta go,' muttered Billy Blue, his chin dipping so his gaze avoided Ben's. 'Mum gets plenty crook if I'm late for tucker.'

Danny shuffled his feet, unwilling to give in, but knowing he had no choice in the matter. 'We can't leave until you get out of the way,' he mumbled.

Ben stepped aside, leaving them no option but to climb up through the boulders. 'You lead the way, Billy. Me and Danny will follow.' He had no qualms about making the boys clamber up that jumble of rock – they were as nimble as lizards – but he suspected that the minute they reached the top, Danny would try to make a run for it.

Billy began the climb and Ben followed closely behind Danny, ready to grab him the minute his feet touched the summit. Danny put on a sudden spurt as he neared the top, but Ben was faster and, as they breached the hill, he clamped a large hand into the seat of the boy's shorts.

'Let go of me,' the boy shouted furiously as he kicked out and tried to wrestle from the man's grip.

'Not until you're in the truck,' replied Ben. 'And if you don't stop kicking me, I'll put you over my shoulder, dump you in the flatbed and tie you in like a cattle dog.'

'I'll tell my mum,' he yelled, his face red with fury.

'You do that, mate,' he said, 'but your mum asked me to get you home, and that's what I plan to do.'

He held on to the boy, his gaze steady and determined as the struggle weakened and the fight went out of him. But he didn't let go even then, for he didn't trust him. 'That's better,' he said softly. 'Now why don't you show me how good you are at driving the ute?'

The brown eyes widened above the freckled nose as Danny looked up at him, and Ben could see the reluctant excitement in his small, dirty face. 'Really?' Danny breathed. 'You'll let me drive?'

Ben nodded and released his grip on the boy's shorts before climbing into the passenger seat after Billy. 'It can be your turn next time, mate,' he said to the Aboriginal boy, who was looking a bit put out.

Danny clambered into the driver's seat and yanked it forward so his bare feet could reach the pedals. Like most Outback children he'd been taught to drive while still very young, for no one could ever predict the sort of emergency that might call for this skill one day, and it was always best to be prepared.

The journey back into Morgan's Reach was hairy to say the least, but they made it in one piece to find Rebecca and Sarah waiting for them outside the hospital with expressions that didn't bode well for either boy.

Billy scampered off and just managed to duck Sarah's clip round the ear, but Danny wasn't as fortunate. Rebecca hauled him out of the ute, slapped the back of his legs and ordered him indoors.

'Thanks, Ben,' she said with a distracted smile. 'I'm sorry they put you to so much trouble. Do you want to come in for a cuppa?'

'Better not,' he replied regretfully. 'I need to get back and keep an eye on that storm.'

'I'll see you tomorrow afternoon then.' She kissed his cheek and thanked him again before hurrying indoors to deal with Danny, and Ben drove back to his eerie on the tableland warmed by her smile and the soft touch of her lips.

Hugh Morgan was used to being watched by the native children who seemed fascinated by the hospital and the things he and his family did there, and although they chattered away like galahs and often got in the way, he didn't mind one bit.

Mary's brood was no exception, and the six youngest ones clustered around her as he finished taking the glass out of her foot and began to dress it. Short and stout, with skinny legs and arms and skin so dark it didn't reflect the light, Mary was

Billy Blue's aunt. Her eyes and tangled hair were tawny, her broad features etched with tribal markings and the deep lines of hardship. He had no idea how old she was, and neither did she, but she was clearly still able to bear children, for there was yet another on the way, which he reckoned would make about twelve in all.

He eyed her sternly. 'You've got a nasty cut there, so you're to keep the bandage clean and come back tomorrow so I can check up on it.'

Mary grinned and waved her bandaged foot about so the children could admire it, and then looked back at him. 'Me alonga walk stick?' she asked.

He eyed her bare feet and nodded before reaching into a nearby cupboard. She would have been better off with a pair of crutches, but they'd all gone missing and the new ones hadn't arrived yet. He selected two sturdy walking sticks and handed them over. 'I want them back, Mary. Don't go giving them to the kids to play with.'

'Me alonga keep sticks,' she replied, regarding him with mischief in her eyes. 'Good to beat kids, keep old man in place when he want gig-gig.' She shrieked with laughter and the kids, who were used to her raucous humour, giggled along with her.

Hugh helped her up, and the children swarmed around as she carefully balanced on one leg and tested the sturdiness of the sticks. He watched as she swung onto the veranda and then made her way down the steps and into the late-afternoon glare.

Her children did a fair impression of her awkward progress as they followed her, and she swung one of the sticks at them good-naturedly before making her way across the clearing and out of sight.

Hugh smiled wearily and, thankful there were no more patients, turned back to tidy up the surgery. The day had dragged by and he'd been unable to catch up on his sleep because of the heat. Now the pain in his chest had returned and he ached for his bed.

There was a hesitant knock on the door. 'Sorry, Hugh, am I too late?'

He looked around to find Sal Davenport on the doorstep, dressed in her usual bright skirt and pretty blouse, her hair spilling from beneath her straw hat and over her shoulders. His smile of welcome faded as he saw the nasty gash on Sal's cheekbone and the angry swelling around her eye. 'Come in, Sal,' he said resignedly. 'You know the drill.'

Sal and Bert had taken over the Dog and Drover when her parents retired to a bungalow on the east coast twenty years back. She was a slender, bustling little woman in her early forties, who dyed her tangled black curls with red streaks, wore jangling jewellery and was rarely seen without a smile – even when she bore the evidence of Bert's latest bashing.

Hugh liked her immensely, for she never seemed to run out of energy even though she did all the work at the pub while Bert got drunk with his customers on the other side of the bar. But for all her straight talking and defiance, Sal had been one of Hugh's regulars over the years and he wondered, for the umpteenth time, why such a feisty woman had even contemplated marrying such a nasty piece of work as Bert Davenport – let alone stayed with him.

'I fell over and hit my head on the bar,' she said to forestall his questions.

'You seem to do a lot of falling down and bumping into things, Sal,' he murmured as he gently cleaned the cut and checked to make sure her cheekbone hadn't been fractured again. 'Perhaps you should get your eyes tested?'

'Nothing wrong with my sight, Hugh,' she replied drily. 'I was just born clumsy.'

Hugh didn't bother to argue, for he knew she would never

29

admit that Bert bashed her. He checked her vision as best he could through the swollen eyelid and put iodine on the bruises. 'I'm going to have to stitch this cut, Sal, otherwise you'll end up with a scar.'

She winced as he injected anaesthetic into the cut to numb it. 'Makes no difference,' she said. 'I've never been a beauty queen, and at my age no one will notice.'

He pulled the stool closer and carefully began to stitch the wound. 'You're still an attractive woman, Sal,' he murmured. 'And young enough to start again.'

'Hmph. And where would I go, eh? My parents left me that pub and I've invested too much time and effort in it to just walk away.'

'You could sell up,' he suggested.

'No one wants a place all the way out here,' she replied. Her brown eyes regarded him steadily as he finished stitching. 'Bert and I get along fine,' she said. 'He has his funny ways, and I have mine. When things get me down, I take myself off for a bit of a breather. He's not all bad, y'know.'

Bert didn't have a redeeming bone in his scrawny body, but Hugh said nothing as he placed a square of lint over the wound, fixed it with a sticking plaster and pushed back the stool.

Sal rose rather unsteadily to her feet and fiddled with her hair until it hung over her battered eye. Fixing it firmly in place with her broad-brimmed hat, she caught him watching her and gave him a wan smile. 'It hides my face so the busybodies don't bother me with questions,' she said flatly.

'It rather suits you,' he murmured.

She ignored his flattery and placed the exact number of coins needed to pay for the treatment on the table. 'Catch you later, Hugh – and try to get some flaming sleep, mate. I might look crook, but you look like death warmed up.'

Hugh was still smiling as she swept out of his surgery, her

scarlet skirt swinging round her knees as her bracelets jangled and her hair bounced down her back. She looked like a Gypsy, and perhaps many generations back she'd come from Romany stock – for she would often disappear for days in her battered old utility.

In a small place such as Morgan's Reach, everyone knew everyone else's business, but despite the rumours and gossip no one had yet discovered where Sal actually went – or what she got up to during her mysterious disappearances.

'Good on you, Sal,' he muttered as she drove away from the hospital in a cloud of dust. 'Wherever you go, I hope you find the peace you so obviously deserve.'

He finished clearing everything away and took one of his pills before closing the window and locking the door. Rebecca was looking after the patients on the ward, and Jane would take over from her during the night, so his duties were finally done for today – as long as there wasn't another emergency. He yawned as he shoved the keys in his pocket and made his way to the hospital kitchen to make sure everything there was going smoothly.

The hospital at Morgan's Reach was blessed by additional help from two local spinster sisters, Louise and Enid Harper. They been nurses there until retirement, but had soon found they didn't really like being idle and had become permanent fixtures to be relied upon in any emergency.

Enid was the bossier of the two, but Louise held her own and refused to be bullied even under the sternest of glares. When not occupied at the hospital they tended their neat little cottage garden and took their fluffy lapdog, Sweety, for long walks in the bush. Most evenings they would sit on their porch and watch the world go by as they kept a wary eye open for Charley Sawyer's disreputable old mongrel which had a nasty habit of trying to mate with their precious Sweety.

Tonight, however, they had stayed on to oversee the cooking of the patients' evening meal so that Jane could have a few hours' respite. It was their opinion that the native women who worked in the hospital kitchen could be a bit slapdash, their ideas of hygiene not always acceptable, and they aimed to make sure everything came up to their high standard.

Hugh saw that the meals were almost ready to serve and, after saying goodnight to everyone and thanking the Harpers, he left them to it and went home in search of a cup of tea and an early night.

It had been a long, very hot day, and as he crossed the yard to his house he could feel the electricity in the air which heralded one of those fierce dry storms that didn't produce a drop of rain but made the earth tremble and cower with its ferocity.

Jane was standing at the kitchen window in her striped nurse's dress, starched white cap and apron, a cup of tea in her hand, the smoke from her cigarette drifting out through the fly-screens. The fan was sluggishly stirring the humid air about, but at least it didn't squeak any more; he'd had all the fans oiled this afternoon.

Hugh never ceased to be amazed at how cool and elegant Jane always looked, with her girlish figure and her fair hair rolled into a chignon. As he kissed her cheek he was once again reminded of what a beauty she was, and how lucky he'd been to meet her at medical school all those years ago and persuade her to be his wife. Most Outback women were quickly aged and lined by the dry heat and harsh conditions, but at fifty-five Jane had maintained the creamy complexion of her Nordic ancestors, and there were only a very few silver strands glinting amid the gold beneath her starched cap.

Her blue eyes regarded him with concern as she placed the plate of hot food on the table in front of him. 'You look tired,

Hugh. Why don't you eat that and get to bed? Becky and I can cope tonight.'

He avoided her searching gaze, sat down, eyed the plate of roast mutton and potato without much relish and poured himself a cup of tea. 'That's exactly what I plan to do,' he said wearily. 'Has Danny turned up?'

She nodded. 'Becky gave him a good talking-to and sent him to bed early without supper – for all the good it will do,' she added. 'Poor Becky, she doesn't know which way to turn.'

Hugh was so tired he didn't have much energy to think about anything but the lure of his bed. 'He needs a firm hand, that's for sure,' he said on a sigh.

She didn't look convinced, but said nothing as she continued to smoke her cigarette.

Hugh really wasn't very hungry, but the pill he'd taken earlier had eased the tightness in his chest, so he ate what he could and then pushed away the plate. 'That was lovely,' he lied, 'but it's too hot to eat.'

'I wish you'd at least *think* about retiring soon,' she replied softly. 'This is all getting too much for you.'

Hugh's gaze slid away from her as he ran his fingers through his thinning brown hair that was now liberally sprinkled with grey. This subject had been broached before and he was in no fit state to reiterate all the old arguments. 'This is our home, Jane,' he said wearily. 'We have Mum and Becky and Danny to consider. We can't just walk away from Morgan's Reach.'

Jane stubbed out her cigarette rather forcefully in the tin ashtray. 'That's all very well,' she said flatly, 'but your dad worked until he literally dropped dead at his desk – and I don't want that happening to you.'

'He was ninety years old, Jane – hardly a spring chicken.'

She shrugged this off. 'Your mum will probably never leave this place, but Becky and Danny would have a better life away from here. And I want to retire to that house you promised me by the beach, and see a bit of the world before it's too late.'

'I know, I know,' he murmured, once again regretting that rash promise he'd made all those years ago. 'But until I can get someone willing to replace me, we aren't going anywhere.'

'The people out here are a special breed, Hugh. The youngsters don't want to be tied to this sort of life – especially after coming through a war.'

Hugh thought about the conversation he'd just had with Sal about the pub. Giving advice was so much easier than taking it. 'Ben and Jake came back, and they've settled down just fine,' he said stubbornly.

'They were born in the Outback – it's what they know and understand,' she retorted. Then she gave a deep sigh. 'I don't want to fight with you, Hugh, but you must see that you can't go on for much longer. It's wearing you out.'

'It's not as bad as it was,' he protested wearily. 'The Flying Doctor Service sees to the more remote stations and—'

'It's a godsend, I know,' she interrupted. 'But you're here – on the ground – and year by year the number of patients is growing. It's too much for one man.'

Hugh silently agreed with her, but wasn't about to admit it. 'Perhaps Terence will change his mind and take over,' he suggested.

'Our son has never shown the slightest inclination to come home and practise here. And after being away at sea during the war, I expect he just wants to settle back down with Sandra and try to pick up the pieces.' Her expression saddened. 'It can't be easy for either of them after what happened, and I suspect he's having a bit of a hard time of it with Sandra. She always was brittle.'

Hugh finished the cup of tea and shrugged off the white

coat, slinging it over the back of the chair. 'You're probably right,' he sighed. 'You usually are.'

'Just promise me you'll think about retiring,' she said urgently, reaching for his hand. 'I love you, Hugh, and I can't bear the thought of you working yourself into the ground.'

He looked into her lovely blue eyes and tried not to show how reluctant he was to make yet another promise he doubted he could keep. This was his home and his life's work, and although it would probably be the death of him, the prospect of leaving it all behind for some anonymous retirement bungalow by the sea was unbearable.

'I'll think about it,' he hedged as he kissed her cheek. 'Now let me go to bed, or I'll be fit for nothing tomorrow.'

It was too hot to sleep indoors, and after he'd washed and changed into pyjama trousers and singlet Hugh headed for the back veranda. The daybed was beneath a canopy of mosquito netting, the veranda shaded by the drooping branches of a pepper tree, and he sank on to the rather moth-eaten mattress with a sigh of relief.

Jane was right, he admitted silently. He was deathly tired and beginning to find every day a trial. He'd been up most of the previous night with a drover whose horse had kicked out and shattered his leg. The Flying Doctor had been busy on an even more remote property and it had been almost dawn before he could hand his patient over and begin the long drive home.

Hugh turned on his side and stared beyond the mosquito netting into the cool shadows of the pepper tree his father had planted so many years ago. The angina was a warning, but how could he heed it when so many people relied on him? There were times when he really envied Sal Davenport – for how nice it would be to get in the ute and drive away, to find some spot far from the cares of Morgan's Reach and to just be.

He closed his eyes. The answers to all the things that

plagued him would not be found among the lime-green fronds – or in the muddled mind of an exhausted man. Perhaps after a good sleep he would be able to think more clearly about his future.

Darkness fell swiftly in the Outback, and although it was barely six o'clock, Becky had turned on the lights in the ward and closed the shutters. She had been distracted since Ben had brought Danny home, and it seemed her patients had noticed this, for after failing to engage her in the usual round of gossip, they'd left her alone.

Worrying about Danny was giving her a headache and, as it was hard enough to concentrate on anything in this awful heat, she turned her attention to the practicalities of tidying the linen cupboard and writing up her patient notes.

She had just closed the last folder when her mother came into the ward. Becky rose from her chair and stretched. 'Everyone's settled for the night,' she said, 'but they're all complaining of this heat.'

Jane smiled and took the notes. 'There's nothing we can do about that, but pray the storm will break,' she replied softly. 'Now, you get back to that boy of yours. Just don't disturb your father. He's snoring fit to bust on the back veranda.'

Becky nodded and reluctantly gathered up her book and knitting, for she knew the day was far from over, and that she had to have a long and serious talk with her son before she could get to bed. 'How is Danny?'

'He's still sulking and refusing to have a wash or get changed for bed. I left him to stew.'

Becky sighed. 'I'll see you in the morning then, but if there's an emergency . . .'

'I know where you are, and I'm sure we can both cope without your dad for one night. Now shoo. I promised to read

Mrs Philips the last instalment of her Agatha Christie murder mystery.'

Becky kissed her mother goodnight and ambled out into the stifling heat of a stifling evening. The thunder was still distant, but it rolled relentlessly as the sky flickered with flashes of lightning and ominous clouds hid the moon and the stars. The air was charged with electricity and carried the scent of sun-baked dust and dying pastures from the great heart of the Outback.

Becky glanced across at Granny Gwyn's house and waved to the figure sitting in the deep shadows of her screened porch. Granny loved storms, but she also loved keeping an eye on everyone, and that dark corner was a perfect lookout.

She quietly closed the screen door behind her, kicked off her shoes, and entered the big square room which was the centre of the house. Walking past the three sagging couches which were placed around the stone hearth, she dumped her book and knitting on the cluttered coffee table and went through to the kitchen area.

A collection of mismatched cupboards hid the china; cooking pots and pans hung from hooks above the stone sink and wooden draining board, and a kerosene fridge hummed in the corner by the scarred table and chairs. The range belted out a furnace blast no matter the season, for it was their only means of cooking.

She peeled off her apron and cap, leaving them carefully on a chair before she opened the fridge, took out the remains of the roast mutton joint and made a pile of sandwiches. Adding a cup of tea and a glass of milk to the tray, she steeled herself for what was to come and carried it through the lounge and along the corridor to Danny's room.

'I thought you'd probably be hungry by now,' she said as she entered.

Danny's expression was surly as he looked up at her from his untidy bed. He was still in his grubby shorts and shirt, and his filthy feet had marked the clean sheets she'd put on that morning. He gave a shrug as if he didn't care, but Becky noticed how his eyes kept flitting to the pile of sandwiches.

She set the tray down next to the lamp on the low cupboard beside his bed and reached out to brush the lick of hair from his forehead. 'We've had a bit of a day, haven't we?' she asked softly.

He shrugged again, refusing to look at her.

Becky handed him the plate and perched on the end of the bed to drink her cup of tea while he devoured three sandwiches and half the glass of milk. She nibbled a sandwich, found she had little appetite and waited for Danny to finish his supper. She'd lost count of the times she'd ticked him off about going bush, making it clear that his behaviour wasn't acceptable and that it upset everyone – and this afternoon had been no exception. But had he really listened this time?

She regarded the open cardboard box with a heavy heart, for it spilled out photographs and letters, mementos of her marriage and Adam's short and tragic involvement in the war. Sifting through the black-and-white photos that littered the bed, she tried to maintain a calm expression and steady voice.

'You're growing up to be just as handsome as your dad,' she said softly as she selected a photo of Adam standing with his back to Sydney Harbour.

She swallowed the lump in her throat as she looked down at the dark-eyed man who was laughing back at her from that frozen moment by the harbour. She could remember that day so well. They'd been young and in love, with the whole of their lives stretching before them, their dreams and hopes within touching distance as they'd celebrated his veterinary degree.

He'd asked her to marry him that evening, and she'd been so happy she'd burst into tears and couldn't speak for ages.

She gave a soft smile as she remembered how Adam had understood and taken her in his arms, holding her until she could accept his proposal and tell him how very much she loved him. 'I miss him just as much as you do,' she murmured.

Danny shifted on the bed until he was leaning against her arm, his head resting on her shoulder. 'It's all right, Mum,' he murmured. 'He'll be back soon and then you—'

'No, Danny,' she said firmly as she tilted his chin up to look him in the eyes. 'Daddy was killed in Malaya.'

'No, he wasn't,' he protested, trying to squirm away from her. 'He'll come back, I know he will.'

She held him tightly, willing him to understand and accept. 'Danny, he won't,' she said evenly, her heart aching for the pain and the futile hope he was clinging to. 'And deep down you know it's true, because I've told you how he died, and I would never lie to you.'

'That's what you say,' he muttered as he squirmed away. 'But Dad promised me he'd come back – and a promise is forever. You said so.'

'Sometimes we make promises that are impossible to keep,' she replied softly, drawing him to her again. 'Daddy wanted to come home, but in a war things happen that we can't control.' She reached into the box and pulled out a letter. 'You've seen this from his commanding officer, and there is absolutely no doubt that your daddy was killed. One day, when things settle down and we can afford to make the journey, we'll go to Malaya and see the place where he and all those who died with him are buried.'

Danny shook his head furiously as he scrambled away from her. 'I've seen the ships arriving in Brisbane, and there are still hundreds of men coming home from Thailand, Burma, Malaya and Singapore. Our teacher showed us the newspapers, and they say that lots of those men were supposed to be dead, but they were alive all the time and no one knew – not even their families.'

Becky silently cursed the teacher for perpetuating this awful obsession that seemed to have Danny in its thrall. 'Darling, I know how much you want your daddy to come home – but it's just not possible, and you have to accept that.'

'He will,' he said stubbornly, the tears sliding down his grubby face.

Becky eyed him solemnly. 'No, Danny. Not ever.' She reached for his hand, but he snatched it away from her and shuffled further up the bed. 'Those men who've come back were prisoners of war. They'd been captured and put into very remote camps deep in the jungles and no one knew they were there until the Allies liberated them. Your daddy was with his regiment, behind his own lines in the field hospital when the Japanese attacked.' Her voice broke as the tears welled. 'There was no mistake, Danny – absolutely none.'

'You're only saying that cos you want to kiss Ben,' he retorted, his small fists balled on his knees, his freckled face distorted with conflicting emotions.

Becky was shocked by his vehemence – and by the fact he must have seen them together despite the care they'd taken to keep their burgeoning romance to themselves. 'I kiss Ben because he's a nice man and he—'

'Jake's a nice man, but you don't kiss him,' he threw back.

'I don't like Jake the same way I like Ben,' she replied softly, desperately trying to think of a way to get through this quagmire of accusations and anguish. 'And I like Ben very much, Danny. He's become very special to me.'

'But you still love Daddy, don't you?' he asked plaintively. 'And if he was here you wouldn't kiss Ben, would you?'

'Not if Daddy was here, no,' she replied. 'And I will always love him, no matter what. But he's been dead for nearly three years, Danny, and although I miss him, and wish with all my heart things could be different, I know for certain that he won't be coming back.'

He curled up on the bed, his scabby knees drawn to his chest, his hair flopping over his tear-streaked face. 'But he might,' he muttered. 'He might just be lost somewhere and trying to get home.'

'Oh, darling,' she whispered through her tears as she curled round him and held him close. 'You're breaking my heart with all this. Please don't keep going off trying to find him. He's not out there – and he never will be.'

Danny didn't reply as he turned away from her and buried his face in the pillow.

Becky lay beside him, her emotions in turmoil. Her little boy was hurting so badly and there seemed to be nothing she could do to ease his pain. And yet his tears told her that he was beginning to believe the truth – that the hopes he'd clung to so fiercely were slipping from his grasp, and that he was frightened to let them go after so long.

'Daddy wouldn't want you to be sad, Danny,' she urged. 'He would want us to learn to live without him, to look to the future and make the best of things – not always looking behind us, wishing things were different.'

She eyed the scattered photographs and the letters that catalogued her all too brief time with Adam. They had lived in a Sydney suburb after they were married, and Adam had joined a small veterinary practice while Becky completed her nursing training. Their lives had been made complete when Danny had been born. But Becky had been missing her family and wanted Danny to get to know them better, and Adam was the son of a local cattleman and always intended to return to the Outback, where his skills were sorely needed. So they'd begun to plan a move to Morgan's Reach, where they would be closer to both their families.

But then the war in Europe had changed everything.

Danny had been five when Adam had enlisted in 1941, and she'd used the contents of that box to keep his memory alive for their small son as they waited for him to come home. But she could see now that those photographs and letters had perpetuated the close bond Danny had forged with his adored father – had become his reality. No wonder he was finding it so difficult to face another, far bleaker truth.

Becky listened to the mutter of thunder and the cracks of distant lightning as Danny finally fell into an exhausted sleep. She had found solace in returning to the family home after Adam's death, and although she yearned to begin again with Ben Freeman, it seemed there was to be no escape from the past – or what might have been.

Her tears blinded her as she drew the sheet over Danny, collected the scattered mementos and closed the box. It was time to put it away – and although Adam would never be forgotten, the memory of him would sustain them as they stumbled towards what she hoped would be a brighter future.

3

Sal Davenport had left Morgan's Reach several hours ago and, as the ancient utility whined and rattled its way over the rough track, she at last began to feel lighter in spirit. Her face was hurting, and her left eye had almost swollen shut, but the sense of freedom and the knowledge that soon she would be in her special place made up for the discomfort.

She carefully negotiated the ruts, potholes and tree roots as she drove further and further from Bert, the pub and the claustrophobia of life in a small town where everyone knew your business. There wasn't far to go now, and as long as the storm didn't break too soon, she'd reach her destination before the sun came up.

A particularly loud crack of lightning startled her, and the ute swerved alarmingly. She gripped the steering wheel to get it back under control, staring determinedly through the windscreen as the headlights wavered over the track and gave her a fleeting glimpse of the black basalt mountain that loomed ahead of her. This was a lonely place, far from civilisation, where a snakebite or venomous spider could kill within minutes and a breakdown or accident would leave her stranded. But she was well aware of the dangers, had a healthy respect for this remote, sprawling emptiness, was prepared for most eventualities and was not afraid to be alone out here.

She'd first taken this track on one of her many escapes

from Bert – had followed it out of curiosity and found her sanctuary. Now she rejoiced in the solitude, her pulse quickening in anticipation as she steered through the steep, narrow mountain pass.

The high walls of black rock closed in on both sides, the headlights rising and dipping as the utility rumbled over scree and around the scattered boulders which could snap a crankshaft or puncture a sump. The thunder was rolling overhead, the night sky lit by forks of jagged lightning giving her flash-bulb glimpses of the panorama before her as she left the mountain behind and began the long, steep descent to the heavily forested valley.

Startled wallabies and kangaroos bounded out of the headlight beams, brightly coloured birds rose from their night roosts with sharp cries and the beating of a thousand wings as a boobook owl watched, unafraid, from a nearby tree branch, its big yellow eyes following her progress solemnly as it continually shrilled its double hoot.

Despite being in a hurry to reach her hiding place, Sal slowed the utility to a crawl as she reached the valley floor. The track was overgrown and much narrower now, the darkness more profound beneath the forest canopy, and she knew that a moment's carelessness could cost her dear.

The spare tyres, spade, chains, ropes and petrol and water cans rattled beneath the tarpaulin that covered the flatbed as the utility negotiated tree roots and anthills. Low-hanging branches scraped the roof and foliage brushed against the windows as Sal edged the ute along the almost invisible track that wound tortuously through the bush.

She knew she was very close now, for suddenly the trees didn't encroach on the track, and as she took the last bend she came to the edge of the clearing and gave a sigh of pleasure and relief. Letting the engine idle, she could now hear the sound of a dog barking furiously. Brandy had probably heard her coming from miles back.

She ignored the dog's racket and smiled as she drank in the sight that always restored her. The trees surrounding the wide clearing were tall and slender, their silvery trunks reaching for the light beyond the bush canopy and the rocky outcrop that soared skyward. The craggy sides of this outcrop were almost hidden by the giant ferns and clinging lantanas nourished by the trickle of water that had once been a torrent – splashing over the black rocks and racing down to a narrow stream which fed the river that ran through the bush. The long drought had depleted the fall and the stream, and Sal suspected the river was no more than a dry shale bed.

She drove slowly into the clearing towards the log cabin where a rusting utility was parked by the woodpile, and a pair of shaggy, hobbled ponies eyed her with suspicion. Switching off the engine, she grabbed her overnight bag and clambered down, already reaching for the sugar lumps she'd stowed in her pocket.

The ponies whickered with pleasure as they recognised her and, as she stroked their soft noses and gave them the sugar lumps, the cabin door opened and a large red setter came tearing towards her, his furious barking turning into fawning yips and whines as he licked her hands and rolled over to have his tummy rubbed.

Sal obliged, but her attention was soon diverted from Brandy to the man who'd emerged from the cabin and was quietly watching her from the veranda.

He was of indeterminate age, with long, silver-streaked brown hair, deep-set hazel eyes and the weathered skin of someone who lived mostly out of doors. Dressed in dark brown moleskins, khaki shirt and scuffed tan boots, it was as if he was hewn from the colours and textures of his surroundings.

He said nothing as he leaned heavily on the gnarled walking stick, his gaze fixed angrily on her swollen eye and bandaged cheek. But that gaze warmed as he looked into her eyes, and there was welcome in the soft curving of his lips.

'Hello, Max,' she said, the joy of seeing him making her voice unsteady.

'Welcome home, Sal,' he replied in his deep, musical voice as he opened his arms to her.

'It's good to be back,' she sighed as she moved into his familiar embrace, her undamaged cheek pressed against his chest, the drum of his heart soothing and restoring her. She had fallen in love with him the moment they'd met, but she had never told him – Max was a solitary man and would shy away from such strong emotional entanglements.

He kept his arms about her and rested his chin on her head. 'Then stay a while and keep me company,' he murmured into her hair. 'You look like you need a refuge, and I've missed you.'

Sal drew strength from his words and his embrace, for despite his own demons Max offered her shelter and solace – had encouraged her to find her real self beneath the hard shell she hid behind, and to explore the talents she'd allowed to wither during her marriage to Bert.

As they stood in that peaceful clearing and heard the storm gathering in ferocity all around them, Sal felt a renewal of hope that, one day soon, she would find the courage to leave Bert and tell Max how she really felt.

Gwyneth was of an age when she didn't need much sleep. Rather than tossing and turning in her bed, she preferred to doze in her rocking chair on the front veranda with Wally tucked up in an old dog basket at her feet. There was always something to watch, something to think about and mull over

46

as she sat there keeping an eye on things, for life in Morgan's Reach might be slow, but it was never dull.

There had been a fight in the pub earlier and Jake had hauled the drunks apart and thrown them into his makeshift jail to sleep it off and cool down. Louise and Enid Harper had left the hospital after seeing to the evening meals and returned to their little wooden cottage which backed on to Charley Sawyer's forge. Within minutes of their arrival they'd harangued Charley over the fence about his shaggy, lovesick mongrel having sex on their lawn with their yapping ball of fluff.

It was an ongoing feud and this particular episode had been most amusing. Charley had towered over the two old harridans, waited for them to say their piece and then let them have his viewpoint on the matter at the top of his great booming voice. They'd snatched up their silly dog, retreated into their cottage and slammed the door, and Charley had whistled to his randy old dog and gone stomping off to the pub.

Emily Harris seemed to find an inordinate number of things to do which would take her past Jake's police house, and from the silly smile on his face, it seemed Jake was quite happy with this arrangement, and Gwyneth hoped something would come of it. Jake needed someone like Emily to pull him up by the bootstraps and make him see there was more to life than sleeping in a hammock all damned day.

Annie and Sean O'Halloran had had one of their usual furious arguments on the boardwalk outside their general store, and he too had gone stomping off to the pub – but would no doubt get it in the neck from Annie when he wove his way home again. Annie's small, round, motherly appearance hid a fierce temper, and although Sean could shout as much as he liked, Annie always got the better of him.

But the shenanigans hadn't stopped there, for the Reverend Baker's twin boys had untied the horses from the hitching post outside the pub and scattered them into the bush. This piece of mischief had earned them a heavy clip round the ear from one of the furious drovers and, Gwyneth suspected, a beating from their stern-faced father who'd marched them home. Algernon Baker was a strict disciplinarian who bullied his ineffectual little wife and preached hellfire and damnation to his parishioners every Sunday. Peter and Mark were fourteen, under threat of expulsion from their school in Sydney and rebelling against their upbringing.

One of these days their mischief risked taking a more serious turn, and Gwyneth decided to have a word with Ben's father out at Wilga Cattle Station to ask if there were any jobs going. A good dose of hard work never killed anyone, but it might turn those twins from the destructive path they seemed determined to follow.

She rocked back and forth as the lightning flashed above the hills and the thunder rumbled ever closer. The electricity in the air made her scalp tingle and lifted the hairs on her arms, but it also sharpened her anticipation. She loved a good storm, and this one was threatening to be a monster.

She settled back into the cushion and watched the lights go out one by one in the houses. People had always fascinated her, and there wasn't much she didn't know about the residents of Morgan's Reach, for she'd become almost invisible as she aged – part of the scenery, and of little interest to the younger ones. She gave a wry smile. None of them suspected she had sharp hearing and a keen eye and, as they went about their daily lives unaware of her presence, she gleaned their secrets, and sometimes even managed to quietly solve their problems without them even realising it.

She rocked back and forth, fanning her hot face with an old

magazine as she thought about Sal's short visit before she'd left this afternoon for her hideaway in the bush. Gwyneth was probably the only person in Morgan's Reach who knew where she went, for Sal had always confided in her.

Poor Sal, she didn't have much joy in her life, but Gwyneth thought she understood the younger woman's reluctance to leave Bert – for over the years her sense of worth had been beaten out of her, and Sal had almost certainly come to the conclusion that it was better to stay with the devil she knew, rather than risk one she didn't. And Max had enough demons to deal with without the added responsibility of knowing how Sal felt about him.

Gwyneth sighed. Life was complicated at the best of times, and even though she had few worries of her own, she knew her family were struggling to cope with things. Hugh was certainly not the man he'd once been, and she had the deep suspicion that he was hiding some sort of health problem. Jane was itching to leave for a retirement on the coast, and their son Terence was of absolutely no use whatsoever.

Gwyneth understood how worried Jane was about Hugh, but there was the practice to consider as well as Becky and Danny's future. She had no qualms about the family leaving Morgan's Reach, and although she would miss them even more than she missed the rest of her brood, she had no intentions of dying anywhere else but in this house. But the future of the hospital was in jeopardy unless someone could be found to replace Hugh – and she knew this was only part of the reason why Hugh was reluctant to throw in the towel.

The crash of thunder directly overhead made her jump, and the echo of it trembled in the boards beneath her feet and in the walls of the house. The corrugated iron roof vibrated with it and the birds roosting in the nearby trees and among the reeds surrounding the precious waterhole rose in an answering thunder of wings and cries of alarm. Wally scrabbled deeper into the nest of old blankets in the dog basket, and Gwyneth could hear Coco screeching furiously from beneath his covered cage on the back veranda.

Jagged lightning pierced the ominous black sky, blinding her with its intensity as another crack of thunder shook the earth and rattled the shutters and screens. Gwyneth shivered, for she could now hear the rusty turn of the weathervane on top of the nearby bore-water pump, but the wind that turned it wasn't cool and pregnant with rain – it was hot, dry and deadly.

'I told you it was stupid to come all this way with the weather like this,' snapped Sandra Morgan as she lit another cigarette and furiously puffed smoke out of the car window. 'What if there's a flash flood and we're caught in the middle of it?'

Terence's expression was grim as he kept his eyes on the road ahead. 'Give it a rest, Sandra,' he retorted. 'And mind what you're doing with that cigarette. It's as dry as tinder out there.'

Sandra slumped back into the soft leather seat of the imported sedan and continued to flick ash out of the window. 'I don't know why you want to bury us out here,' she muttered. 'We had a good life in Sydney.'

'Yeah,' he replied drily. 'So good you drank a double gin before you even got dressed in the morning, and by mid-afternoon you were so drunk you didn't care what sort of fool you made of yourself – or me, for that matter.'

'Oh, well, we can't have that, can we?' she said nastily. 'Your precious reputation has to be preserved regardless of how *I* feel about things.' She took a deep drag on her cigarette, blew a stream of smoke into the car and tapped her long nails on the armrest. 'It's no wonder I need a drink to get me through the day when I have to put up with you whinging on about everything and laying down the bloody law.'

Terence had heard it all before and was sick of it. Sandra was well on the way to becoming a drunk, but she didn't fall asleep in a corner or become flirtatious and silly; she became loud and aggressive, speaking her mind and sometimes lashing out if anyone tried to calm her down. It was the reason he'd handed in his notice before he was asked to leave the prestigious practice in the heart of the city – the reason why they'd rented out their beautiful house overlooking the harbour and were making this long and exhausting drive to Morgan's Reach.

He drove on in a heavy silence. The atmosphere was poisonous, the weather outside threatening and, after the endless furious rows they'd had over the past few weeks, he was exhausted, and suddenly not at all certain that this was a good idea.

'I'm bored, Terry,' she said a while later as she fidgeted in her seat. 'And I need to pee. Is there a roadhouse coming up?'

Terence was half blinded by the flashes of lightning as he concentrated on the road. The storm was definitely gathering momentum and getting closer, and although they'd already been on the road for a week they still had over a hundred miles to go. 'We passed the last one three hours ago,' he said. 'If you're that desperate I'll pull over so you can go in the bushes.'

'Not bloody likely,' she said with a glower at the offending trees that grew thickly on both sides of the single-lane highway. 'Apart from the fact I have no wish to bare my backside to snakes and creepy-crawlies, I wouldn't trust you not to drive off and leave me there.'

Terence fleetingly wished he had the nerve to do just that. It would certainly make his life easier. But despite everything, he could still remember why he'd fallen in love with Sandra, and sadly understood all too well the reason behind her drinking. He just hoped that his spur-of-the-moment decision to return home to Morgan's Reach would not only rescue Sandra from her drinking, but also save his marriage.

'We'll have to stop soon anyway,' he said. 'It's not wise to be driving after dark. But you don't have to go into the bushes, Sandra. You can use the storm drain at the side of the road. I'll watch out for creepy-crawlies.'

'I'll hang on,' she said grimly.

'Then why don't you put the seat back and try to catch some sleep?' he said softly.

'I don't want to sleep,' she replied, vehemently stabbing out her cigarette in the dashboard ashtray and lighting another immediately. 'I want a drink.'

'There's a flask of coffee in the glove box, and some water in the—'

'Not coffee!' she spat. 'I want a proper drink.'

'I know you do,' he said with infinite care, 'but we agreed you'd try to go without for a while.'

'*We* didn't agree to any such thing,' she retorted furiously. '*You* told me I had to stop drinking and forced me to leave my lovely home in Sydney for some *dump* in the back of buggery.'

He winced at her vulgarity. 'You agreed to give it a go,' he said with determined calm, 'and Morgan's Reach isn't a dump – it's a nice little town in one of the most beautiful parts of Australia.'

'Yeah, right,' she sneered, 'and I'm the flaming tooth fairy.'

Terence ignored her sarcasm knowing it was her need for a drink that was making her sour and jumpy. And yet he was uneasy at the thought of her at Morgan's Reach, for although the family would be there to support him, there would be very little for Sandra to do – and a bored Sandra went in search of alcohol, which then led to trouble.

He'd been so desperate to get her off the booze and away from the reminders of what had happened during the war that he hadn't thought things through properly when his father's latest pleading letter had arrived. The chance to get out of Sydney and away from the awkward situation at the practice – to give Sandra time and space to deal with her demons and find herself again – had seemed like the answer to his prayers. But the daunting reality of this homecoming was beginning to dawn on him and, as they left Sydney further and further behind, he wondered if he was making the biggest mistake of his life.

With Sandra chain-smoking beside him in venomous silence he tried to concentrate on the road ahead as the storm gathered in strength and black clouds roiled across the skies, driven by a hot and deadly wind. Born in the Outback, Terence was all too aware of the havoc such a dry electric storm could cause after a long drought. If it did break, the rain would be torrential, and a flash flood was not a possibility – it was a certainty.

The sudden crash of thunder and whip-crack of hissing, jagged lightning made them both jump.

Sandra screamed and threw herself across Terence, making him momentarily loosen his grip on the steering wheel.

The sedan swerved alarmingly towards the gravelled edge of the highway and the deep storm-water run-offs.

His pulse was racing as he battled to shove Sandra out of the way and keep the car on the road. But they'd been going too fast and the tyres spat gravel as they skidded ever nearer that storm ditch.

'We're going to die,' she screamed, still clutching his arm.

Terence yanked on the steering wheel as the rear of the car threatened to fishtail over the edge. The tyres found enough purchase to carry them away from the gravel, and they spun out into the middle of the road, coming to a halt on the other side. The sweat was cold on his back, his heart was hammering and his hands were trembling so badly he could barely manage to turn off the ignition.

They sat in stunned silence as the overheated engine ticked beneath the car bonnet and the lightning continued to rip through the skies. 'Don't ever do that again,' he said with cold fury. 'You could have killed us both.'

Sandra was shaking, her face white with shock. She crept back into his arms and huddled there like a frightened child. 'I'm sorry,' she said tearfully, 'but I'm terrified of thunderstorms, and that was so loud and much too close.'

He forgave her instantly and cupped her face in his hands, softly kissing her lips and eyelids to ease her fears and reassure her. 'It's all right,' he murmured as she looked back at him with green eyes still sparkling with tears. 'The storm will move away soon.'

She jerked away from him suddenly, her eyes wide with fear as she looked over his shoulder. 'What was that?' she said sharply.

He glanced back but could see nothing in the profound darkness beneath the closely packed line of trees. 'You're imagining things,' he replied wearily. 'It's probably just shadows cast by the lightning.'

She pointed with a bright red fingernail. 'Over there, look,' she hissed impatiently. 'There's someone hiding in those trees.'

Terrence bit down on his own impatience and turned to look properly at where she was pointing. He had keen eyesight, but could see no sign of anyone lurking in the shadows. 'I can't see anything out there,' he said flatly.

'There's a man,' she retorted. 'I saw him watching us. Get us out of here, and quick, Terry. I don't like it.'

'We're miles from the nearest town, and no one in their right mind would be wandering about out here in this.'

'That's my point exactly,' she shouted. 'It's a madman, and if we don't get away from here, he'll . . . he'll . . .'

'Oh, for heaven's sake,' he sighed with exasperation as he turned the key in the ignition and wearily resumed the journey. 'You're jumping at shadows. There's no one out there.'

He'd left the train earlier than planned, discarding the suit for the more familiar and comfortable faded camouflage trousers and shirt he'd been given by the Brits when they'd liberated the camp. The worn army greatcoat was rolled up in his kitbag in case the weather turned or he needed a blanket to lie beneath in the chill of an Outback night.

It had been the camouflage that had masked his presence from the man as he'd melted deeper into the shadows – but the woman had seen him, and his pulse was still racing from the shock of that strange and unexpected encounter as he waited for the tail lights to disappear into the distance.

Memories of hiding in the jungle returned full force. Of hearing the enemy searching for them, seeing their lights and smelling their sweat as they jabbed the thick foliage with their bayonets and hacked their machetes at the vines that grew as thick as a man's arm. He could feel his own sweat trickling down his face and back as he slid down the rough bark of a tree trunk and tried to banish those images as he waited for his pulse to steady.

Reaching into the kitbag with trembling hands, he pulled out the tin of tobacco, box of matches and a slim packet of rolling papers. The ritual of making a cigarette finally calmed him and, as he struck the match and lit it, he breathed in with a sigh of pleasure. It tasted so good after the dried grass and thin lavatory paper they'd smoked in the camp and he wanted to savour this sweet moment of victory, for the enemy was conquered and, for now, so were his fears.

The storm still raged, but the wind was picking up, its hot breath reaching him even in the cooler, dark shadows of the surrounding trees. He'd been walking for almost a week now and would have liked to stay here, to rest his head on his kitbag, the soft, dry forest floor a perfect mattress for his tired body, the canopy of trees the only roof he would ever need. But he was still many miles from his destination and he didn't know how long he had before the gnawing pain in his gut became unbearable and his meagre strength ran out.

He leaned against the tree, relished his cigarette and let his thoughts drift with the smoke. Freedom was a precious gift, and he'd yearned for the simple things as he'd struggled to survive the Jap camp. Things like the scent of pine and eucalyptus on the wind; the wide open spaces where a man could ride for days without seeing anyone; and the soft, piping warble of the magpies and currawongs. But there were even more precious needs: like that for a loved one's smile, the sound of a child's laughter and the deep contentment to be found in the place where he truly belonged.

He clenched his fist as anger swept through him. His freedom had come at a terrible price, and in a way he was still confined within the unseen but impregnable prison walls of Fate. For his family thought he was already dead, and it was better for everyone to keep it that way. There would be no joyous homecoming – no happy ending – just a covert glimpse to reassure himself that they were safe and happy before he left them for the last time.

And then, in the wide open spaces of the land he loved so well, he would try to seek redemption for his failure to save those he'd sworn to protect. And in that redemption he hoped to find the peace he so sorely needed to face the inevitable and embrace it.

His eyelids fluttered, heavy with sleep, and he forced himself to crush the cigarette beneath his boot and get to his feet. With the kitbag slung over his shoulder, he turned his back on the road and headed deeper into the bush, his inner compass guiding him home.

4

The triangular rusting iron frame of the windmill had stood sentinel for decades over the vast open ranges of Wilga Station. When the wind blew, the weathervane would swing away from it and the thin metal sails would begin to turn, pumping the lifesaving water from a deep borehole into cooling tanks and then into the cattle troughs. The ground surrounding the troughs and windmill had been trampled by hundreds of thirsty animals, and when it rained, the whole area quickly became a quagmire.

But the mud had long since dried to a fine dust which lifted beneath the restless hooves and drifted like an ochre veil across the dying plains. There was only a trickle of water in the bottom of the troughs, and the sails were still and silent in the heavy air as the clouds thickened and rolled ominously over the land. The cattle could smell the approaching storm, and they bellowed and snorted as they shifted uneasily in the tightly packed huddle they'd formed close to the windmill.

It was close to dawn, and the lightning still flickered above the distant hills as the thunder reverberated with menacing intent. And as the hot winds came from the west the rusty weathervane began to waver. The sails screeched as they moved sluggishly in that first hot breath, and then, as the wind strengthened, they began to spin.

As the first gush of water came out of the pipe the cattle

jostled to drink, their fear of the storm forgotten in their terrible thirst.

The lightning bolt cracked a jagged rent across the black sky, hit the windmill and bounced off the metal troughs with a deafening bang that resounded across the empty miles and killed two of the cattle. The survivors fled as the electricity spat blue sparks and sizzled the length of the old landmark, momentarily lighting it up like a beacon before it died out.

But the lightning bolt had rebounded from the trough and hit the barbed wire of a nearby fence. There was no one to witness the spark that dropped into the parched, brittle clump of grass that clung to the fence-post, no one to notice how the first tendril of smoke delicately wove through the under-growth – or how the hot wind blew on that spark and fanned it into a flame.

Becky had slept fitfully, troubled not only by the stifling heat and the crashing thunder, but by the almost impossible situation she was in. Danny had made her feel disloyal to Adam for loving another man, and it was clear her son was nowhere near accepting Ben as a surrogate father. And yet she'd finally come to terms with Adam's loss and stepped through the fog of grief to realise he wouldn't have wanted her to mourn him forever – that life had to move on. But until Danny could see beyond his pain and bewilderment, any future she might have with Ben was in doubt. Would he wait? Did he love her enough to understand the awful quandary she was in and be patient? She simply didn't know.

She realised she must have finally fallen asleep when she opened her eyes to find it was almost dawn and the heavenly smell of frying bacon was drifting throughout the house. Her mind was sluggish as she washed and pulled on fresh underwear and the thin cotton uniform dress. What the day

59

would bring, she had no idea, but as it was Danny's tenth birthday, and there was a party planned for this afternoon, she hoped he'd woken in a more positive mood and that nothing would spoil it.

She gathered up the card and the neatly wrapped present she'd ordered from a catalogue several months ago and went into the kitchen.

Her mother had finished her night duty on the ward and was sleepily drinking tea. She'd cooked breakfast for her patients and had left the three Aboriginal women to do the washing-up and the cleaning under the watchful gaze of the two Miss Harpers, who were sticklers for discipline and cleanliness.

Hugh was making a great show of industriously wielding a frying pan over the hotplate as the bacon spat and the eggs sizzled. He liked to dress up for these special occasions and if his patients could see him now they would wonder if he'd gone mad. This morning he was wearing an eyepatch and one of Danny's old Red Indian headdresses, the remaining feathers sticking to his sweating face. His feet were clad in bright yellow striped socks and his shirt and trousers were covered by a voluminous flowered apron which had 'Mum' inexpertly embroidered on the bib. One of his sisters had made it at school many years ago for their mother, and Hugh had found it in the back of a kitchen drawer and deemed it perfect for Danny's celebratory breakfast.

Danny was wearing fresh shorts and shirt, his face, knees and hands scrubbed clean, his hair still damp from his bath. His eyes were bright with excitement, his freckled face alive with expectation as he sat at the table. 'Grandpa's cooking me a special breakfast,' he said, allowing his mother to kiss his cheek and ruffle his hair. 'We've got bacon and eggs this morning.'

Becky's relief was immense, for Danny had clearly made

up his mind to enjoy his day, and the mood of the previous evening had been banished. It was amazing how resilient and changeable children could be. 'A special breakfast for a special boy,' she replied as she handed him her gift. 'Happy birthday, darling.'

'Thanks, Mum. What is it?'

She chuckled. 'Open it and see.'

He ripped back the paper, saw the picture of the train on the Hornby box and stared at it in awe. 'Cor,' he breathed. 'It's the engine and freight trucks I wanted to complete my set. Thanks, Mum.'

She caught her father's eye as he placed the large plate of food on the table, swept the irritating feathers from his face and adjusted his eyepatch as he tipped her a wink. 'You and Grandpa can have fun with that while I go to work and Grandma Jane catches up on her sleep,' she said.

Danny ran his fingers lovingly over the die-cast models. 'Only if Grandpa promises to let *me* do the signals for once, and lay out the track the way *I* want,' he muttered.

Becky giggled as her father pulled a face. 'I'm sure he will. Now eat your breakfast. That's the last of the bacon until the supply truck comes in.'

'I hope the storm doesn't break until it gets here,' said Jane through a vast yawn. 'The shop's out of almost everything, and if the rains come, the road will be impassable.'

'We need the rain,' Hugh solemnly reminded her as he tucked into his breakfast.

'We need sugar, tea, flour and a thousand and one other things,' she replied, 'and if the road train can't get through, we'll be living on fresh air.'

'I miss the days when the Afghans used to come by with their camels loaded up with supplies, their harnesses decorated with brightly coloured tassels and tinkling bells. These modern army trucks that pull up to three nineteen-foot trailers aren't half as romantic.'

His gaze became dreamy and Becky exchanged a knowing look with her mother. Dad was off on one of his reminiscences, and although they'd heard his stories a dozen times, he still made them interesting and Danny loved them.

'We called them Afghans, but not all of them were,' he recalled. 'Some were from Baluchistan, Kashmir, Egypt and Persia . . . exotic names of faraway places we could only read about, that brought to mind spices, palm trees, palaces of gold and the long journey of those three wise men who followed a star to Bethlehem.'

He leaned back in his chair, his breakfast forgotten. 'I remember when I was a boy that we used to run out into the street and watch in awe as they slowly and majestically came into town. They were a strange and mystical sight, those dark-skinned, keen-eyed men dressed in long flowing robes or loose trousers that ballooned to the ankle. In the earlier days they had curved daggers tucked into the sashes round their waist, the jewels on the hilts glinting in the sun – and we boys would have given our eye teeth to possess one, if only we'd had the nerve to ask those fierce-looking men.'

He smiled at his audience and picked up his knife and fork. 'Some of them wore embroidered caps, others had brightly coloured turbans, their dark beards flowing to their waists. But we dared not go near the camels because they were nasty-tempered and would spit at you and try to bite.'

Danny looked up at him with a knowing grin. 'You're telling stories, Grandpa. We don't have camels here. They're all in Brisbane zoo.'

'Ah,' said Hugh, waving his fork about, 'that's where you're wrong, young Danny. Camels were once used for all sorts of things. They were practical, you see, able to carry heavy loads across the harshest of terrains, and go without water and food for weeks on end. They helped the men build the roads and railways – which was their nemesis, of course, for with the coming of the trains and trucks, the Afghans and their camels were no longer needed. In some parts of Australia there are huge mobs of feral camels roaming about.'

Danny still didn't look convinced, but obviously decided not to voice his disbelief just in case his grandfather was actually telling the truth. The three of them ate in companionable silence as the sun began to rise to reveal a clear and untroubled sky. The storm had passed, but it was already hot and there was still no promise of rain.

Becky had eaten her fill and was sipping tea when the front screen door clattered and Gwyneth stomped into the room, followed by Wally. 'Happy birthday, Danny,' she said cheerfully as she plonked herself down in the chair beside him and hooked her walking stick over the edge of the table. 'How does it feel to be ten?'

He grinned back at her, trying to hide the disappointment that neither she nor his grandparents had brought him a present. 'I dunno,' he replied. 'I haven't been ten for very long yet, and it might take some getting used to.' Smearing away the milk moustache with his arm, he slid from his chair to make a fuss of Wally, who was snuffling about under the table in search of crumbs.

'I suppose,' she said with a twinkle in her eyes, 'that as you've finished your breakfast, you might like to see the surprise me and your grandparents have got for you.'

His doleful expression brightened immediately. 'Too right,' he breathed. 'What is it?'

'Well, that would rather spoil the surprise, wouldn't it?' she said drily. 'Why don't you go over to my place and look on the back veranda?'

He shot out of the kitchen, clattering the screen door behind him, his bare feet thudding down the steps.

'It's good to see he's cheerful today,' said Gwyneth as she accepted a cup of tea. 'I hope that now he's ten he'll forget all this nonsense over Adam and get on with things.'

'He's unlikely to just forget his father overnight,' protested Becky.

'He never will if you keep talking about him and letting him go through that box,' she retorted. 'It's been almost three years, Becky, and time to put the box away and look to the future. There's no good to be had in living in the past, and Ben Freeman isn't going to hang about forever while you dither.'

'There's nothing between me and Ben,' she said firmly, in answer to her parents' questioning looks.

Gwyneth snorted. 'And there never will be unless you stir your stumps and do something about it, instead of pandering to that boy's obsession.'

'Mum,' Hugh protested softly. 'Don't start – not today.'

She glared at him. 'I speak as I find, Hugh. Always have and always will.'

Becky swallowed her anger with some difficulty. 'Danny's my son and I'll deal with things my way,' she said flatly. 'And I'm not pandering to his obsession, as you call it – just trying to ease him out of this terrible mourning without doing any further harm.'

'All this modern talk is stuff and nonsense,' she snorted. 'He's ten, and quite old enough to listen to some straight talking.' Gwyneth folded her arms and regarded her granddaughter evenly. 'If this continues, and you don't do anything decisive to put an end to it, then I will.'

'I love and respect you, Grandma Gwyn, but you will do no such thing. This is my business, and I'll handle it as I see fit.'

'It's not just your business,' she snapped. 'This is affecting all of us.'

Becky was saved from answering by the clatter of the screen door.

Danny didn't seem to notice the brittle atmosphere as he came into the room wheeling the shiny black bicycle. 'It's a beauty, Granny Gwyn,' he breathed, barely able to contain his excitement. 'And it's even got a special toolkit in a leather pouch – and a bell – and a light.'

'Glad you like it,' said Gwyneth, who was still clearly in a bit of a huff.

He beamed back at them as he repeatedly rang the bell Hugh had attached to the handlebars. 'Billy's going to be green with envy,' he declared, his little face becoming solemn. 'But I'll let him sit on the crossbar if he wants.'

'He won't need to do that,' said Hugh. 'I fixed up your old bike for him – gave it a new mudguard and chain and a lick of paint.'

'Oh, ripper, Grandad,' Danny yelled. 'We can have races when George comes over.' He forgot he was ten and all grown up, threw his arms round each of them and gave them a sticky kiss before he manoeuvred the bike back towards the door. 'See ya later,' he shouted as he pushed his way outside, bumped the bike down the steps and was gone.

'We won't see either of them until they get hungry again,' murmured Becky. 'Thanks, Dad, for doing that for Billy.'

Hugh shrugged. 'He's a nice kid and I thought it was time he had a bike of his own.'

'It's not just the bike, Dad,' she replied with heartfelt warmth. 'It's seeing Danny smile again – being a little boy.'

'Long may it last,' muttered Gwyneth.

As the storm had moved on and the hot wind had dwindled, he began to hear the birds begin their dawn chorus. He smiled at the kookaburras' squabbling, their cackles echoing through the trees as a bellbird chimed her single note and the currawongs piped their melodies. Darting zebra finches flitted back and forth as brightly coloured parakeets squawked, wagtails hopped through the undergrowth in search of a juicy worm and the tiny blue wren watched with sharp eyes as he passed by.

There were glimpses of a pearl-grey sky above the trees now and, as he reached the forest boundary and looked out at the great sweep of open country before him, he saw the first glimmer of the sun as it breached the horizon in a blaze of orange and red.

He gazed in awe at the magnificent sight of that giant, glowing orb slowly gilding the empty miles of pale grass and isolated stands of trees. The enormous sky was shot with streaks of pink and peach as the sun rose majestically, shimmering as if it was molten lava. It took his breath away, and brought tears to his eyes as he experienced a deep and abiding affinity with the scene before him – for this was what he'd fought for, this was Australia, his country and his home.

He stood there in the calm silence of dawn and let the peace wash over him before he hitched the kitbag over his shoulder again, left the shelter of the trees and continued on his way. There was grandeur out here, a timeless beauty that probably hadn't changed since the first men walked across it, a silence and sense of antiquity and spiritual presence that had never failed to awe and inspire him.

But it was a harsh life for those who dared to live here and, for the greater part of his life, he'd been a witness to the struggle to survive the heat, dust, fires, droughts and floods that were endemic to this remote part of this vast island. And yet it was in his heart and in his blood, and as he tramped along he drew strength from it.

*

The single railway track ran through the sweeping ochre plains to disappear in a mirage of shifting haze on both horizons. There was precious little shade now, and the foraging kangaroos had fled for cover as the sun climbed higher and the heat intensified. The sky was bleached of colour, the silence almost absolute but for the caw of a single crow and the sibilant hiss of the innumerable insects that lived among the rocks and termite mounds that were dotted amid the clumps of spinifex and wilting gum trees.

He stepped into the meagre shade of an isolated stand of eucalyptus, dropped his kitbag, drank some of the water from his leather pouch and looked along the two iron rails. Some might call this a lonely place, for the nearest settlement was many miles away. But these rails were the link between the wide open spaces of the Outback and the rest of Australia.

He tipped the slouch hat brim over his eyes as he sat on the kitbag and chewed on some of the dried beef jerky he kept in his shirt pocket. These rails had taken him to boarding school in the city when he'd just turned ten, and had brought him back briefly as a young man. And then the war had come and another train had carried him far from home and everything he knew to the military barracks where he'd had to forget all he'd ever stood by and learn to kill.

He tugged at his hat brim and absent-mindedly waved the annoying flies away from his face as he continued to gaze out at the expanse of red earth and bleached grass. The ache for all that he'd lost was still there, buried deeply until moments like this, and it took him a while to regain his composure.

Once he felt ready to move on he reached for his kitbag and began to follow the railway lines northward, his boots now crunching on the red gravel that lay strewn across the parched earth. He needed to find some decent shade so he could rest during the worst of the day's heat, or he'd be fit for nothing tonight. And if he remembered rightly, there was a shepherd's hut a few miles from here, where, as it wasn't lambing season, there would be no one from Wilga Station to stop him bedding down until sunset.

And then he smelled something that made his heart skip a beat and his skin crawl with fear.

He stood very still and keenly surveyed the area, his senses alert as he sniffed the air and listened. His sharp eyes trawled over the rusting windmill that was screeching as it turned in the warm wind, and caught the wisps of smoke curling up from a clump of spinifex that grew close to a barbed-wire fence. There was the flicker of flames licking at the fence-post and more racing through the grass, spreading to other clumps.

He began to run, the kitbag bouncing against his back, his boots thudding across the hard ground. Yanking the bag open, he tipped everything out and unrolled the greatcoat. The flames were catching a tighter hold on the post and the nearby grass, their tentacles reaching out greedily for more fuel. But the fire must have just started. It was still manageable – but only if he was quick.

He was sweating as he smothered the flames with the coat, stamping on it to make sure every last spark was extinguished. A fire out here could rage for miles, and Bob Freeman, who owned the land, would lose everything.

His greatcoat was charred and burnt through in places, but that didn't matter. He flung it aside and continued to stamp on the blackened grass until he was certain it hid no glowing embers, But the post was still hot, for the burn had gone deep into the wood and found the ancient creosote that had been painted on it when it was new. One puff of this warm wind would stir the fire into life again.

He scrambled between the barbed-wire strands, filled his hat with water from the trough and quickly doused the post and the grass beneath it. He did this repeatedly until he was absolutely sure everything was safe. Exhausted by his efforts, and almost depleted of strength, he thrust his head beneath the trickling pipe that fed the trough and then shook himself like a dog before slumping to the ground.

The two dead cows had already attracted a swarm of flies and were beginning to stink in the growing heat. He eyed them grimly and struggled to his feet. He couldn't stay here – or he'd end up like the cows.

The barbed wire tore his shirt and scraped his back as he clambered between the strands, and there was the acrid scent of fire lingering in the air and in his coat as he repacked his kitbag. Fire was his enemy, for it evoked the worst memories of all – memories of being helpless, of hearing the screams and seeing . . .

Turning his back on the windmill, he hoisted the bag over his shoulder and stumbled away. He was wasting his energy by recalling those scenes, for they did no good to his spirit and he couldn't turn back time to stop what had happened. With his boots kicking up dust and the pain gnawing at his insides, he slowly and wearily continued to follow the rails.

Terence had finally been forced to pull the car off the road by Sandra's desperate need to empty her aching bladder. A short while later he almost fell asleep at the wheel and so stopped again to snatch some much-needed rest.

This unscheduled delay had caused yet another row with Sandra, who'd refused to share the driving and was vitriolic about sleeping in the car in the middle of nowhere. But her ranting did her no good, for Terence fell almost immediately into a dead sleep and didn't hear a word of it.

He'd been startled awake by the sharp prod of her finger in

his ribs, and he eyed her blearily, confused momentarily by the unfamiliar surroundings.

Sandra looked a mess, with her fair hair in a tangle and her mascara smudged under her eyes, the inevitable cigarette filling the car with its noxious smoke. 'The sun's up and you've had enough rest,' she snapped. 'I couldn't sleep a wink, knowing we could be murdered at any minute, and you snoring like a litter of hogs didn't help.'

He ran his fingers through his light brown hair and yawned. 'I need a pee and a cup of coffee first,' he replied. He clambered out of the car, stood on the lip of the storm run-off, unbuttoned his fly and sighed with pleasure as the seemingly endless stream darkened the red earth. Adjusting his clothing, he opened the passenger door and reached past Sandra for the flask of coffee in the glove compartment.

'It's all right for you men,' she muttered as she swung her long legs out of the car and stood up. 'You can pee anywhere.'

'There's nothing to stop you here, and I won't look,' he replied, savouring the warm, sweet coffee.

'It's getting lighter by the minute,' she growled through a stream of cigarette smoke. 'Anyone could come past and see me.'

'I doubt it. We haven't seen another vehicle since yesterday morning. Sort yourself out, and then we can get going.' He moved away from the open car door, turned his back on Sandra, who was still grumbling, went round to the other side and sat on the running board.

The soft croon of the magpies drifted on the warm air as the sun rose into a clear pale sky, and Terence was soothed by the beautiful melody. He'd forgotten how peaceful it was out here and, as he gazed along the deserted road that wound its way through pristine forests and mile upon mile of rolling, empty country, he was surprised at how deeply it affected him.

He'd left Morgan's Reach sixteen years before to attend medical school and had never really returned but for a week or so in the early years. The city had offered everything he'd thought he'd wanted then, but the war had taken away the gloss, and before he'd realised it he was thirty-five and just another worker in the anthill of Sydney, always in a rush, never stopping to listen to the birds or appreciate a sunrise.

He finished the coffee and tipped the dregs on to the tarmac. Perhaps this hadn't been such a bad idea after all; it wasn't just Sandra who needed a change of scenery and a chance to catch her breath. There was a bit of poetry he'd learned at school and he was trying to remember it, for it suited the occasion perfectly. But the only phrase he could recall was something about standing and staring. '"What is this life if, full of care, / We have no time to stand and stare?"' he murmured, pleased that he hadn't forgotten it completely.

'You're talking to yourself, Terry,' said Sandra through the open window.

He gave a sigh as he checked the oil, water and petrol, replenished the fuel tank from one of the two cans in the boot and climbed back behind the steering wheel as some more snatches of the little poem came back to him.

'"No time to see, in broad daylight / Streams full of stars, like skies at night,"' he breathed. '"A poor life this if, full of care, / We have no time to stand and stare."'

She raised her eyes to the roof and tutted impatiently before continuing to fix her make-up. 'Just get us out of here, Terence.'

Ben had spent an anxious night listening to the chatter that went back and forth between the outlying stations on the two-way radio. He'd stayed up in the tower watching the storm until midnight, when Jake arrived to take over. But they both had needed to stay alert and, after a long night of endless pots of coffee, they were not only exhausted, but jumpy from all the caffeine.

As Ben returned to the house after preparing for the day, he found Jake gathering up his things. 'I'd better get back and give those blokes in the lock-up some breakfast,' he said through a vast yawn. 'Then I promised Emily I'd help to paint the schoolroom and put a new coat of varnish on the floor.'

Ben grinned and ran his fingers through his dark brown hair. 'She's got you on a string, mate. You wanna watch it, or before you know it you'll be walking up the aisle.'

Jake's answering grin was sheepish. 'Yeah, well, worse things happen at sea, mate.' His dark eyes met Ben's. 'And you're no better,' he added. 'You've been chasing Becky for months. Ain't it time you let her catch you?'

'I wish she would,' he admitted. 'But she's got Danny to think about, so we can't rush things.'

Jake nodded thoughtfully as he buckled on his gun holster and adjusted the belt. 'I know. It's always difficult when there's kids involved.'

Ben regarded him with a wry smile. His friend knew nothing of the sort, for he'd always been a love 'em and leave 'em man, and any hint of a complication usually had him running for cover. Until he'd met the very determined Emily. 'So,' he teased, 'when are you going to admit that Emily's the girl for you?'

Jake almost dislocated his jaw with another yawn. 'Look, mate, she does the running, and when I decide the time's right, I'll let her catch me. A bloke has to have some dignity.' He rammed his police hat on his head and tugged at the brim. 'You going to the picnic races next month? How's about the four of us driving over together?'

'I'm meeting Becky there, but yeah, we could join you.' He shot Jake a grin. 'As long as Emily hasn't made other plans for an intimate little picnic. We wouldn't want to intrude.'

Jake tried to look disgruntled at the thought and failed miserably. 'Reckon the races ain't no place for that sort of carry-on,' he muttered. 'I'll see you later.' He loped out of the house and down the steps and climbed into the utility truck provided by the Police Authority of Queensland.

Ben took a breath of the warm, still air and surveyed the skies as Jake headed back into town. The storm had moved on, but another threatened over in the south, with dark tendrils of cloud already streaking the pale blue.

He went back into the house, tidied the blanket and pillow away from the couch where he and Jake had taken it in turns to listen to the two-way and began to wash the dirty crockery of a long night's vigil. There would be precious little sleep for any of them until the rains came.

He was just about finished when the two-way crackled into life. 'This is Bob Freeman out at Wilga Station. You there, Ben?'

'G'day, Dad. You all right out there?'

His father was a thoughtful, slow-talking man who was rarely known to panic about anything. 'Well, we've had a bit of a burn on the south-western corner by the old windmill,' he drawled. 'Strangest damned thing I ever saw.'

Ben frowned. 'What do you mean, Dad?'

There was a long pause. 'Well, there must have been a lightning strike, cos two of my bloody cows are dead and the rest have gone hell west and crooked. A fire started in the scrub by the fence, but someone must have seen it cos it's been put out. But who the hell would be out there I don't know – and it certainly wasn't any of my men. I kept them close to the homestead paddocks last night.'

'Probably a swagman,' said Ben. 'Or one of Django's lot gone walkabout.'

'I dunno,' murmured Bob. 'I had a look around out there and found some fresh tracks of what look like army-issue boots, and

73

a few shreds of camouflage cloth caught in the barbed wire. Don't reckon it to be a black fella.'

'Just be thankful that whoever it was caught it in time, Dad.'

'Too right, but I don't like the thought of some stranger on my land, no matter if he is a good Samaritan. I've had enough trouble with Big Mac Mackenzie's men over the years. Lost too many clean-skins to their poddy-dodging – and I've warned him I'll put buckshot in the arse of the next man I catch.'

Ben smiled. Carey Downs Station was almost a hundred miles away and shared a long northern boundary with Wilga, and his father and Big Mac had carried on a feud ever since he could remember. Accusations of stealing unbranded calves had flown back and forth over the years, and it seemed they would never come to an armistice. 'I'd be careful, Dad,' he said. 'Shooting people is against the law.'

Bob Freeman cleared his throat. 'That's as maybe, but it's every man's right to defend his property, and Mackenzie has a very free idea of what boundaries mean.' He paused for a moment. 'I don't suppose you or Jake know about anyone new coming into the district?'

'There haven't been any reports so far,' he replied. 'And as long as there's no damage done, I can't see there's a problem.'

'Fair enough,' Bob muttered at the other end of the crackling line. He cleared his throat. 'By the way, I've had Gwyneth Morgan on the two-way this morning, asking me if I'll take on the reverend's boys during the school break. What do you think?'

Ben chuckled. 'They're a couple of larrikins, but I reckon a few weeks of hard work among tough men might put them right. You know what it's like, Dad – their father's a bully, they have too much time on their hands and they're bored and rebellious. It's no wonder they get up to mischief.'

'There'll be no bloody mischief here,' he rumbled. 'I'll have a word with the reverend and, if he's willing, I'll take them on a week's trial at basic rate. But if they step out of line even once, I'll send them home again.'

'Sounds fair to me, Dad.' Ben smiled. His father stood no nonsense, but he had a kind heart under all that grumpiness.

'Good to talk to you, Ben,' his father drawled. 'Yer ma sends her love and says she'll see you at the races. Over and out.'

Ben was still smiling as he pushed back from the radio and reached for his hat. Gwyneth Morgan was a wise old bird, and her continued watch over the residents of Morgan's Reach meant that she quite often had a solution to their many problems. It would do the twins good to get away from their father, and to see what life was really like on the vast expanse of Wilga Station, where toughness didn't come with the strike of a belt against a backside, but with the discipline and knowledge learned in a harsh environment. The men who worked those thousands of acres earned respect from their mates by working as a team, and the twins were bright enough to catch on quickly and put their energies into something useful for a change.

5

As they left the single-track highway and the car bounced over the potholes and ruts in the narrow bush track Terence could feel the tension rising in Sandra. He glanced across at her and saw the forlorn expression on her face as she stared out at the surrounding trees. 'We're nearly there,' he said softly.

'I want to go home,' she replied, her voice hitching as a single tear sparkled on her eyelashes.

Her sudden vulnerability struck at his heart and he stopped the car and switched off the engine. 'Oh, Sandra,' he murmured as he took her in his arms. 'It won't be so bad, really it won't.'

'I can't bear it,' she spluttered. 'Please, Terry, take me home.'

He held her close as she clutched at his shirt, dampening it with her tears. 'Don't cry, my love,' he soothed. 'Think of it as a new beginning – a chance for us both to recover and look at things afresh.'

Her mascara was running down her cheeks as she looked up at him. 'I don't want to start again,' she rasped. 'I want to be in Sydney, close to where little Michael is buried so I can go and talk to him.' Her voice was rising as the hysteria took hold. 'How the hell do you expect me to just forget him when he's in my thoughts every hour of every day? Why do you think I need to drink? It eases the pain, Terry – blots out the memories of him lying so still in that awful coffin – of seeing it lowered into the ground, knowing I'll never hold him again.'

Her words twisted his heart. 'I mourn him too,' he replied, his own voice strangled by the lump in his throat. 'He will never be forgotten,' he added softly, 'but it's time to accept that he's gone, and that there's nothing we can do but be thankful we were blessed to have him, if even for such a short time.'

He pulled a handkerchief from his pocket. 'Dry your eyes, darling, and try to look to the future—'

'That's easy for you to say,' she interrupted, snatching the handkerchief from him. 'You didn't give birth to him. You weren't there when he got sick and . . .' The words petered out as her emotions overwhelmed her.

'I came home as soon as I could,' he said, reaching for her again.

She jerked away from him, blew her nose and dashed away the tears before lighting a cigarette with trembling hands. 'It was too late, Terence. Much too damned late.'

He hung his head, the sadness and guilt a weight on his soul that was almost unbearable. 'There was a war on,' he objected. 'I couldn't get back.'

She glared out of the window as she continued to smoke. 'How very convenient,' she snapped.

'That's not fair, Sandra – and you know it. I was in the middle of the bloody Atlantic Ocean when your telegram came. Of course I wanted to be with you.'

She shrugged, but Terence could see she knew full well how unreasonable she was being, but was reluctant to admit it.

Terence climbed out of the car and slammed the door. His patience was at breaking point, and he knew from past experience that words hastily said in such moments could be regretted for years to come. He stared out at the surrounding trees, his sight blurred by his tears as he thought of the little son he'd barely had time to get to know.

Michael had been born in the January after war had been

declared, and Terence had received his call-up papers eight months later. Posted to a Royal Australian Navy hospital ship, he'd been at sea for almost two years when that awful telegram had been relayed to him, and although he'd been desperate to return home to Sandra, his circumstances had made it impossible.

Terence swallowed the lump in his throat and took a deep breath. He very much wanted things to be right between them again – and although another baby could never replace Michael, he had hoped Sandra would agree to at least trying for one. But she had undoubtedly suffered some sort of nervous breakdown during his long absence and he'd realised very quickly that another baby wasn't the answer at all. Not that there was much hope of one all the while she refused to sleep with him.

He blinked back his tears. It seemed that, even now, she couldn't forgive him for not being there when she'd needed him most – and he couldn't really blame her, for his own guilt haunted him even though he'd had no choice in the matter.

The past eighteen months had been fraught with difficulty, and this journey to Morgan's Reach was his rather desperate last attempt to get things back on an even keel. If it didn't work, then he'd failed – and Terence was not a man used to failure. He walked round the car and opened the door, prepared to try yet again to appease her.

Sandra was looking more composed and had even begun to repair her make-up. 'Unless you've come to tell me we're going back to Sydney, then you can save your breath,' she muttered.

'I do understand how difficult you're finding this trip,' he said softly. 'But we both know how important it was to get out of Sydney – to look at things with a clearer eye and begin again. You won't be alone, Sandra. I'll be right here beside you every step of the way, and we'll get through this together.'

She closed her powder compact with a snap and returned it

to her handbag. Her gaze was challenging. 'You promised on our wedding day that you'd never leave me,' she replied evenly, 'and look what happened.'

She would try the patience of a saint, he thought wearily. 'I love you, Sandra' he said simply. 'Please don't be like this.'

'I want a drink,' she said flatly.

He took a deep breath as he stood and closed the passenger door. 'All I can offer is coffee or water,' he said wearily.

'But I need a proper drink if I'm going to have to face that family of yours,' she retorted. Her expression became artful as she reached for his hand. 'Come on, Terry,' she wheedled. 'I know you must have a small bottle of something hidden away. Just a little sip won't hurt.'

Terence thought about the bottle of whisky he'd hidden beneath the spare tyre in the boot. Sandra clearly hadn't found it yet, but as it was a gift for his father it would stay hidden and unopened.

He rounded the car and climbed back behind the steering wheel. 'You've done really well so far,' he murmured. 'Eight whole days without a drink is quite an achievement. I'm very proud of you.'

Sandra glared at him and folded her arms tightly round her waist. 'Don't patronise me, Terence. I'm not a kid.'

'Then stop behaving like one,' he said mildly as he turned the key in the ignition.

She glowered out of the window at the surrounding gum trees and the narrow track they were following, her hostility almost tangible in her heavy silence.

Terence tried his best to ignore her as they bounced and jolted over the ruts and half-buried tree roots. He was concerned about the damage such a rough track might inflict on his treasured car, for it was never meant to withstand such a journey, and the last thing he needed now was to break down and have to force Sandra to walk the rest of the way in those ridiculous shoes.

As the engine whined and the suspension complained Terence fought the steering wheel in an effort to keep the car on the track and away from the encroaching trees, which threatened to scratch the immaculate black paintwork or snap the heavy straps that held the pile of suitcases on the roof.

Then, at last, the track began to widen, and he could see a glimmer of white ahead. 'We're almost there,' he said excitedly. 'Look, Sandra, there's the hospital and Granny Gwyn's side porch.'

She shrugged, making it all too clear she didn't care one bit about the hospital or anything else to do with Morgan's Reach.

Terence came to the end of the track and let the engine idle as he drank in the sight of his boyhood home.

The broad main street was almost empty, but for the police-department utility parked outside the police house and the few dozing horses tied to the hitching post outside the pub. Smoke streamed from the forge where a mongrel dog sat guard by the neighbours' fence, a couple of women were gossiping in the shade of the boardwalk outside the general store and a group of small boys was haring about on bicycles, kicking up the dust in the road as they executed sliding twists and turns.

He noted the neat but yellowing gardens, the white picket fences and the rusty windmill which had stood sentinel over the town's waterhole long before he'd even been born – nothing much had changed during the years he'd been away; it was as if he was a boy again.

Terence began to relax for the first time in ages as the sight of this wonderfully familiar place warmed his heart. For this was home. This was where he belonged, where he would be welcomed back into the heart of his family and given the chance to put things right again.

'Is this it?' said Sandra with scorn. 'You've brought me all this way for this . . . this *backwoods slum*?'

Her words shattered the pleasant glow of his homecoming. Without bothering to reply he drove the car to the other side of the road and parked it outside the Morgan homestead, where a graceful coolibah tree gave some meagre shade. He looked at the dying garden and the familiar green shutters and screens, then searched for and found the deep indent scarring one of the veranda posts. He'd been five or six when he'd crashed his scooter against it, but he could still remember sailing over the top of that railing and landing with such a thud on the grass he'd had the wind knocked out of him.

He gave a wry smile as he fingered the small crescent-shaped scar on his forehead that was a memento of the occasion. It had bled profusely, he remembered with a touch of the same pride he'd felt all those years ago, and had been quite something to boast about to his mates.

'I don't see what you've got to smile about,' said Sandra crossly. 'This place gives me the creeps. Turn the car around, Terence. I want to go home.'

'I'll do no such thing,' he replied quietly, his gaze fixed on the elderly woman emerging from the house opposite. 'This is our home now for a while, so just behave yourself and be nice. You're about to get reacquainted with Granny Gwyn.'

She followed his gaze and scowled. 'Once was enough, when your family came down for the wedding. Horrible old trout – picking holes in everything, and turning up her nose at my friends.'

'Well, try your best to be pleasant,' he said firmly. 'She's an old woman and deserves a bit of respect.'

Terence climbed out of the car before Sandra could reply, and met his grandmother in the middle of the almost deserted street. He embraced her gently and did his best to mask his dismay at how much she'd aged since he'd seen her last. 'G'day, Granny Gwyn,' he said. 'You're looking as sprightly as ever. How ya going?'

'Good,' she replied, looking up at him. 'Which is more than I can say for you. You look like something the cat dragged in.'

He grinned and ran his fingers through his hair. 'Thanks, Gran. I always knew I could rely on you to speak as you find.'

She eyed him thoughtfully. 'Well, this is a surprise, I must say. Never thought you had it in you to realise where your responsibilities lie. But your father will be delighted to have some help at last. He's getting old and past it, just like me.'

'Didn't Dad get my letter?' he asked, running his fingers through his hair. 'I posted it just before I left Sydney.'

Gwyneth shook her head. 'The mail takes its time getting here, Terence. You should know that.' She glanced across the street to the car. 'I see you brought Sandra with you,' she muttered with a distinct lack of enthusiasm. 'How long are you *actually* planning on staying?'

'For a while,' he replied vaguely. 'Perhaps longer if things work out. Sandra and I need a break from the city, and Dad's been asking me to come out here ever since I got demobbed.' He looked down at her, knowing his smile was tense. 'I know you and Sandra didn't get along very well when you came down for the wedding, but give her a chance, Gran,' he pleaded quietly. 'She's been through such a lot and is still not well.'

'A good dose of hard work and clean country air will sort her out soon enough,' she said briskly. 'These city girls are spoilt and soft, but we'll soon have her pulled into shape.'

'Go easy on her, Gran,' he murmured. 'She is my wife, after all, and if we're to settle here, she needs to feel welcome.'

Gwyneth gave him a glance of derision that spoke volumes, before tucking her hand into the crook of his arm and leaning on her walking stick. 'You'd better come to my place for a cuppa,' she said as they approached the car. 'Jane and Rebecca are busy at the hospital and your father's had to go out to one of the stations to see to a difficult birthing. But they'll all be home soon enough. It's Danny's birthday today, you see, and we're having a tea party at the school later.'

There wasn't time to ask about his sister and her boy, for Sandra had climbed out of the car and was waiting beside it, the broad-brimmed sun hat casting a soft shadow over her features. Considering how upset she'd been only minutes before, she looked amazingly calm and collected in her pretty cotton dress and white high-heeled shoes, and Terence noted that she'd even managed to plaster on a rather stiff little smile.

'Nice to meet you again, Mrs Morgan,' said Sandra, holding out her hand, her gaze steady and almost challenging.

Gwyneth shook hands with her, her gaze returning that challenge. 'Welcome to Morgan's Reach,' she said with a ghost of a smile. 'I hope you don't find us too dull after all the excitement of Sydney – but as humble as it is, it is home, and I hope you don't find it too hard to get used to our funny ways.'

'Thank you,' she replied flatly. 'I'm sure Morgan's Reach will prove adequate for the short length of time I intend to be here.'

Terence noted how the two women eyed one another with steely intensity and, with a sinking heart, realised that the first challenge had been made and that Granny Gwyn was all too capable of taking up the gauntlet and throwing it back.

Sal woke to the melodic sound of birdsong and the delicious smell of freshly brewed coffee. Despite the fact she and Max had spent what was left of the night eating and drinking and catching up on the months they'd been apart, she had slept dreamlessly and felt refreshed and eager for the new day as she stretched luxuriously and kicked off the sheet.

The small travelling clock she'd brought with her told her it was past eleven, but there was no rush, not here, and she lay a moment longer to absorb her surroundings.

The steeply pitched roof kept the sun from shining directly into the windows, but the dappled light that came through the nearby trees, danced on the wooden walls and up into the high, bare rafters. Max had built this one-roomed cabin log by log, had crafted the sturdy hearth and chimney from the dark red stones that lay scattered throughout the bush in these parts, choosing each of them for their colour and the veins of black, blue and grey that streaked them. He'd planed the wooden floor and polished it to a gleam, cut each wooden roof tile and placed it with care, and even refurbished the ancient cooking range.

Sal eyed the few pieces of furniture and the rudimentary kitchen which consisted of a stone sink, two lines of shelves and a mesh meat safe hanging from a nearby hook. There was the sagging couch where Max slept when she was visiting, a handcrafted table and two chairs and the bed she lay upon, which had been built into the niche beside the hearth. On cold nights she could lie here warm and cosy, watching the flicker of firelight on the walls – but on this hot, sultry day the heat from the range was almost unbearable.

There was no running water or electricity, and certainly no bathroom. The vast copper boiler out the back had to be laboriously filled by hand with buckets carried back and forth from the river, the bath was a big tin tub and the dunny a hole in the ground sheltered only by canvas walls strung from a nearby tree. It was primitive and isolated, but Max's tender care showed in every glowing beam and neat dovetail – and to Sal it was the most beautiful place in the world.

Unable to bear the heat any longer, or resist the smell of the coffee, she swung out of bed and dragged on her skirt and blouse. She brushed her hair, put on her earrings and bracelets and felt ready for the day. Her face was still painful, but not bad enough to distract her, and the swelling had gone down around her eye so she could see properly again.

Having used the dunny, cleaned her teeth and scraped a damp flannel over her face, she poured a large cup of steaming black coffee and padded barefoot out to the veranda and into the dazzling sunshine.

The ponies were grazing beneath the trees on the far side of the clearing, and the still, almost breathless air was full of birdsong. Brandy thumped his tail in greeting as he sat at Max's feet, but he didn't get up as Sal approached. Man and dog were settled in front of the easel that had been set up in the clearing and probably had been since dawn. Which wasn't surprising, for Max liked to paint in the clear early light. The concentration on his face was absolute as he added tiny darts of yellow oil paint to the canvas, making the bush landscape spring into life as if the sun had awakened it.

'You make it look so easy,' she breathed. 'I wish I could do that.'

He turned from the easel and smiled. 'Well, good morning, sleepyhead,' he said. 'What time do you call this?'

She grinned back at him. 'Not everyone wakes with the sun, and I'm on holiday, remember?'

'You've missed the best light if you wanted to paint today,' he replied, turning his attention back to his canvas. 'There's another storm coming in.'

Sal watched the streaks of purple, grey and blue twist within the thickening clouds. It was dramatic and powerful and she was suddenly impatient to paint it. 'I'll get a better view from up there,' she said, pointing to the top of the trickling waterfall. She finished the last of her coffee and threw the dregs into the undergrowth.

'It's been a while,' he reminded her. 'So don't get impatient if you can't get exactly what you want at first. Just keep working at it. It'll come.'

'Thanks, Max.' She kissed him lightly on his cheek, resisting the deep need to embrace him.

He grinned back at her from beneath the brim of his hat. 'You know where everything is,' he drawled. 'I've kept your brushes supple, and there are new canvases, and the fresh paint tubes are in the dresser drawer.'

She raised her eyebrow. 'Don't tell me you've actually been shopping?'

His smile was suddenly shy. 'I had a visitor,' he admitted, 'and he very kindly brought me everything I needed.'

This was indeed surprising news, for Max strenuously avoided human contact as much as possible, and she was fully aware of how privileged she was to be here. 'You can't make that sort of statement and not expect me to be curious,' she said. 'Come on, Max. Spill the beans.'

Max cleaned his palette knife with a bit of old rag, clearly playing for time and trying to work out how much to tell her. 'He was a mate of mine from way back,' he said eventually. 'We lost touch after . . .'

He cleared his throat and shook his head as if to dismiss the memories that Sal knew had been invoked by those words. 'Anyway, he tracked me down a few years ago, and sent a letter to my mailbox in Windorah. As I only make the trip a couple of times a year, it had sat there for months.'

'But that's wonderful news,' said Sal without thinking. Then she frowned. 'Wasn't it?'

He shrugged. 'I didn't know if I wanted to see him again after everything we'd been through, so I didn't reply for a while. Then I reckon curiosity got the better of me and I wrote back.'

Sal could see that Max was finding it difficult to reveal so much of himself, for he was a private man, with a history that even she had been unable to fully uncover. 'It's all right, Max,' she soothed. 'You don't have to tell me anything more.'

His gaze remained fixed on his unfinished painting. 'I reckon you need to know,' he said softly, 'because his visit here concerns you too.'

'Me?' She looked at him in horror. 'But you promised never to tell anyone about me coming here. Oh, Max, how could you?'

His weathered face creased in concern. 'He doesn't know your name, or where you come from, Sal. I didn't break my promise.'

'Then why should his visit concern me?'

He cleared his throat and again concentrated on cleaning his palette knife. 'Sam Butler was an artist when I knew him before. Quite a good one, actually. Now he owns a gallery in Sydney and comes out once a year to have a look at what I've been doing.'

'Strewth, Max,' she breathed. 'You've kept that quiet.'

He shrugged again. 'It wasn't anyone's business but my own,' he murmured.

'Has he taken any of your work to exhibit?'

His smile was bashful and he couldn't quite meet her eye. 'He's shown a few over the years,' he admitted shyly, 'and people seem to like them enough to pay top quid for 'em.'

She gazed at him in awe. 'You're a famous artist, and I never knew.'

He clucked his tongue impatiently. 'I paint under a pseudonym, so you're not the only one,' he said. 'Fame ain't all it's cracked up to be, Sal. I had a shot at it once before – and it did me no good at all.' He dumped the knife alongside the clean brushes in a jam jar and stood up. 'Which is why I live out here – far from the madding crowd – and under my own terms.'

'But if you're earning top quid, you could at least afford a few comforts.'

'I have all I need right here,' he said softly as he stroked Brandy's head. His hazel eyes met her brown ones and he smiled. 'I reckon you'd better get on if you want to paint that storm,' he said. 'If it starts to thunder then the top of those rocks is no place to be.'

She grasped his hand. 'Max, you haven't told me why this Sam Butler's visit concerns me.'

He frowned in his vague kind of way and shuffled his feet. 'He followed me into the shed where I store the canvases and saw some of your work. He got very excited and wanted to take a couple of them back with him. But I wouldn't let him,' he said quickly. 'Not before I talked to you first.'

'Bloody hell,' she breathed. 'He liked my work? Really?'

'Yeah, that's about the strength of it.' He tugged his hat brim. 'But don't let it go to your head, Sal. These things have consequences, and I don't reckon you're ready for that sort of exposure.'

Sal's pulse was racing as her thoughts and emotions whirled. Yet, as she stood in that sunlit clearing with the storm clouds gathering beyond the canopy of trees, she knew Max was right. There was indeed a great deal to think about – for her secret had been carefully guarded over the years and, like a mother giving life to her children, such precious and private treasures were not something to be easily shared with strangers.

'I did do the right thing, didn't I, Sal?' he asked tentatively.

She smiled back at him and nodded. 'I'm not ready to make that leap of faith yet – and you, my darling Max, are a wise mentor and good friend. I don't know how I would survive without you.'

He reddened and stuffed his hands into his trouser pockets.

'Fair go, Sal. There's no need for all that soft talk. Go and paint your storm.'

She almost skipped to the shed that had been attached to the back of the cabin. Her secret was safe with Max until she felt ready to reveal it – but the confirmation that her passion had not been misguided, and that she did indeed have a talent which had been recognised by such a man, was intoxicating.

Greeted by the wonderful smells of turpentine and oils, she gathered up everything she would need and then clambered barefoot up the rocks to settle down and watch the storm rolling in.

When she had watched her fill, she began to mix the paint on her palette. Imbued by the majesty and power of those cloud formations, she was soon lost in a world of her own – a world where nothing mattered but the colour and energy she needed to translate that sky on to the canvas.

Down in the clearing, Max picked up his sketchbook and a piece of charcoal. Sal was perched above the waterfall, her skirts fluttering to reveal long tanned legs, the blouse slipping from one sweetly curved shoulder where her dark curls lay ruffled by the wind. His heart thudded painfully as he noted how the sun gilded her skin and winked fire in her earrings and bracelets. In that moment he loved her more than ever, for she was as beautiful and as untamed as her surroundings.

His hand trembled a little as he tried to capture her on the paper, for he knew in his heart that this Gypsy girl who'd come into his life so unexpectedly was unattainable to a man such as he, and must never know his true feelings.

Night had fallen swiftly, but there was no let-up in the heat, and the whine of mosquitoes accompanied the soft battering of moths against the screens that protected the back veranda. The house was silent; everyone else had gone to bed, but Becky knew that her grandmother would be on her own porch, watching and waiting for the storm to arrive.

She sat beside her brother as she smoked her one cigarette of the day and watched the lightning flash in the distance. 'I still can't believe you're here,' she said. 'It's been so long since we did this.'

'Too long really,' he sighed. 'I didn't realise until today just how much I've missed this place.' His smile was wry in the shadows cast by the kerosene lamp. 'We all come home eventually though, don't we?'

'It's our healing place,' she murmured in agreement. She looked at her brother's profile, so handsome in the soft light, and yet so weary. She reached for his hand. 'Sandra will get better,' she assured him. 'Just give her time to adjust.'

He squeezed her fingers. 'As long as everyone keeps her away from the booze she'll be fine,' he said. 'I'll go and have a word with Sal in the morning – she is still at the pub, isn't she? Only I didn't see her at the party this afternoon.'

'Sal's gone off for a while to lick her wounds and find some peace. Bert's in charge at the moment.'

'Damn,' he hissed. 'I was hoping to get Sal's cooperation.' He looked at his younger sister. 'He's still bashing her then?' At Becky's nod, he glowered. 'Men like that should get a taste of their own medicine,' he growled.

'Undoubtedly. But as long as Sal keeps coming back, he'll keep on bashing her. There's nothing anyone can do about it.' She decided the conversation was getting a little morbid and changed the subject. 'Danny's party went well,' she said lightly, 'and it was a good way for you and Sandra to get to know Jake and Annie and Sean and catch up with everyone – although I think Sandra found it a little disconcerting to be surrounded by Sarah and her sister's mob.'

'She's not used to seeing the black fellas,' he agreed, 'and was definitely a bit alarmed at the way the women kept pawing at her clothes. But the kids are all so cheeky and mischievous she couldn't fail to be drawn to them.' He grinned. 'Despite her reluctance, I think she actually enjoyed herself.'

'Mary, Sarah and the other women meant no harm,' she said. 'They were just in awe of her hat and shoes.' She chuckled. 'I thought at one point they'd run off with that hat, but she took it all in good part.'

He was still smiling as he nodded. 'It was good to catch up with Ben after all these years. We had quite a few boyhood escapades to reminisce over, and when I look back I realise we must have been a right couple of larrikins.'

'You were,' she said drily. 'Teased the life out of us girls and got into all kinds of scrapes.'

'He's a good bloke, and obviously smitten with you,' he observed with a teasing smile. 'And I can't believe how big Danny is now. It can't be easy for you, but you've done a good job there, Becks, and should be proud. He's a bonzer kid.'

'He has his moments,' she murmured. She smiled with pleasure at his praise, but she was very aware of how hard it must have been for Terry and Sandra to be surrounded all afternoon by Danny, George and the other kids; their own poor little boy would have been six by now if the scarlet fever hadn't taken him.

'Granny Gwyn told me about him going bush to look for Adam, but he seemed quite all right today.' He squeezed her fingers again. 'He'll come right, Becks. Just as we all will eventually.'

'Yeah, I know.' She stubbed out the cigarette in the metal ashtray and gave a vast yawn. 'I'm for bed. Talking of which, are you and Sandra all right in the back room? It must be a bit of a squash with those two beds pushed together and all those cases you brought.'

He grinned back at her. 'I'll clear out Dad's clutter tomorrow morning and make some space. I'm actually looking forward to sleeping in my old room again. Do you know, I even found a few of my toy cars hidden behind those cardboard boxes of medical books?'

She chuckled. 'I suspect you'll find a whole lot more treasure before the week is out. That room has been used as a glory hole since you went to medical school.'

He caught her hand as she prepared to go indoors. 'Thanks for making Sandra so welcome today,' he murmured. 'I know she can be prickly, but she wasn't always like that.'

Becky smiled back at him. 'I like her,' she said simply, 'and I understand how very vulnerable she must be feeling right now. We might be the only family she's got, but we're strangers and she's clearly out of her depth here.'

'Yes,' he sighed, 'but I had to get her out of Sydney.' He scrubbed his face with his hands. 'She was starting to make a nuisance of herself at the surgery, coming in drunk, demanding to be taken out to lunch or driven somewhere. When she made a scene in the middle of a busy clinic, accusing me of having an affair with our practice nurse, I knew it was time to leave.'

Becky eyed her brother sharply. 'Was there any truth in her accusations, Terry?'

He shook his head, his expression grim. 'None whatsoever.' His gaze met Becky's. 'I'm hurt you should think I'm that shallow,' he said.

Becky took his hand. 'I never thought you shallow,' she replied, 'just a man driven to the very edge of his patience. I wouldn't have blamed you if you had sought some sort of comfort elsewhere.'

'Well, I didn't,' he muttered, 'though God knows I was tempted at times. But I love Sandra – I always have – and all I want is for things to get back to how they were before Michael died.'

She heard the crack in his voice and squeezed his fingers in sympathy. 'Mum and I'll keep an eye on her, no worries. And when she feels ready, we'll find her a uniform and put her back to work on the wards. She needs to be busy, and we need all the help we can get. It would be a shame to let those years of training go to waste.'

'She was an excellent nurse,' he agreed, 'and as Dad will no doubt keep me on my toes, it would be good to see her back on the wards again. But don't rush it, Becks,' he warned softly. 'She's had her confidence knocked and it could be a while before she's ready.'

He stood and embraced her. 'Thanks, Becks,' he murmured into her hair. 'You're a lifesaver.'

'Little sisters do sometimes have their uses,' she teased. 'Now go to bed before you fall down. Dad will want you up and ready for work first thing, and you know what a stickler he is for punctuality.'

They parted in the long corridor that led to the four bedrooms and she peeked in on Danny. He was asleep, exhausted by his exciting day, his beloved bicycle propped against the end of his bed. Becky closed the door and went to her own room.

Lying in bed some time later, she listened to the thunder as the flashes of lightning threw shadows on the walls and the heat intensified. Terry's surprise arrival had given her father a new lease of life, and her mother's smile hadn't faltered all day. Granny Gwyn had done her best to hide her disapproval of Sandra, her pride in her grandson shining through as her gaze followed him everywhere. And Danny had found a new playmate all too willing to let him set out his railway lines just the way he liked them and lie on the floor with him for hours shunting trains about.

All in all it had been a very good day – made even better by the kisses she and Ben had managed to steal behind the schoolhouse while the birthday party was at its peak. Becky closed her eyes, the smile of contentment still on her lips as sleep claimed her.

As the stars disappeared behind the ominous roiling clouds and the thunder boomed with deeper menace, the residents of Morgan's Reach lay asleep behind shutters and windows closed tightly against the dust that would soon sweep through the town as the hot winds came out of the western desert.

It was now two o'clock in the morning. The street was deserted, with every house in darkness as the windmill started to clatter and the first coils of fine red dust began to spiral down the tracks and trails.

Gwyneth had long since left her watching post on the front veranda, for there was nothing to see now the town was asleep, and she was very tired after the long, hot day. But if she had stayed for just a while longer she would have discovered that not everyone in Morgan's Reach was asleep – and perhaps could have prevented the single act that, once achieved, set in motion a series of random events that would ultimately have tragic consequences.

6

He'd reached the shepherd's hut shortly before noon. It was standing forlornly in the meagre shade of two wilting gum trees – a tumbledown collection of roughly hewn logs covered by a rusting sheet of corrugated tin. There were no windows, and the door was just a rough opening so low he'd had to crawl through it and pull his kitbag after him.

It was dark, musty and as hot as Hades in that cramped space. Flattened earth provided the floor, on which was strewn ancient straw that smelled of decades of sweat, lanolin and dirt. The makeshift bed was a plank of termite-ridden wood balanced on rickety piles of crumbling stones, and someone had left the remnants of a hessian flour sack as its only mattress. The hut had been abandoned even by the snakes and spiders, for which he'd been grateful, but the flies had come from nowhere, buzzing around him, drinking his sweat and settling around his eyes and mouth. He'd been so exhausted he'd barely noticed them and, throwing his charred overcoat over the filthy straw, he'd used his kitbag as a pillow, pulled his hat over his face and was asleep almost instantly.

He'd been woken by the sound of thunder and the sharp rent of lightning and, as he stared blearily at the luminous dials on his watch, he realised it was late evening. The heat had intensified and he swept his fingers through his damp hair and grimaced at the sour smell coming from his body. It was like being back in the camp again.

Not wanting to dwell on such thoughts, he swallowed the pills his doctor had given him with the last few drops from his water-bag, packed away his coat and tied his bootlaces. His stomach clenched with hunger, but the rest of the dried beef was not enough to take the edge off it, and he realised that if he was to reach his destination, he would have to risk going to a homestead to ask for food.

The thought made him nervous, for he was getting closer now, and although his appearance had changed radically since he'd been here last, there was still the danger that he'd be recognised.

He crawled out to discover that the wind was blowing harder, swirling the dust of those dying acres into thick, rolling clouds that veiled the horizon. But at least the pain in his gut had eased, giving him the strength to carry on. Pulling his hat brim down, he tucked his chin into the collar of his army issue shirt and headed into the gathering storm, his gaze fixed to the rails which would lead him safely northward.

His boots rapped along the wooden ties that lay across the gravel bed and were bolted to the sleepers. It was easy to ignore the hunger pangs, for he'd had plenty of practice in the camps, but his thirst was becoming more difficult to contain. He stopped, selected a small smooth pebble from the rail-bed and wiped it as clean as he could with the inside of his shirt. Tucking it between gum and cheek, he tasted the grit and dust, but the precious saliva was already soothing his parched mouth. It was an old survival trick and it wouldn't work for long. But it would have to do until he reached the cookhouse at Wilga Station.

With the dust billowing round him, he could barely see more than a couple of feet ahead, and if he hadn't looked up when he did he would have missed the unmistakable sight of an old army truck and three trailers parked at the side of the highway. This was a chance too good to miss, and he couldn't afford to ignore it.

He stepped away from the rails and climbed the steep incline until he was several yards in front of the truck, but still hidden by the dust. It was facing north, the cab softly lit by the flickering of a kerosene lamp and the glow of two cigarettes. As the dust shifted and swirled he caught sight of the men in the driver's cab and guessed they were probably jumpy enough without him suddenly appearing out of nowhere.

He thought about how best to approach the situation, and once he had a plan firmly set he spat out the pebble and reached into his shirt pocket. Pulling out his tobacco tin, he plucked out a cigarette he'd rolled earlier and took a few steps towards the truck. With the match cupped in his hands, he waited for their reaction as he let the flame glow on his face long after his smoke was lit.

Both men sat up and peered through the truck windscreen. The headlights were switched on and a window wound down. 'Who the bloody hell is that?' came a rough voice over the rumble of thunder.

He shielded his eyes from the blinding glare and took another tentative step towards the truck. 'John Miller,' he shouted – though that was not his name.

'Get your arse in here, mate. This flaming dust is getting everywhere.' The window was wound back up again, but the headlights stayed on.

He tugged his hat down and hitched the kitbag over his shoulder as he walked against the wind and the choking, sharp grains of dust that stung his face. He reached the truck and looked up at the grizzled face of the driver. 'Jeez, am I glad to see you blokes!'

The driver jerked his thumb towards the other side of the truck. 'Better climb in next to me offsider,' he said, his hard eyes narrowed and suspicious.

He trekked around the truck to discover that the offsider was even older and just as grizzled and wary. The door was opened and he clambered up the high step and sank into the battered leather seat, the kitbag between his legs. The windows were tightly shut and the stiflingly hot cab stank of old cigarettes, musty clothes and sweat. 'G'day,' he said to both of them as he blinked the grit from his eyes and offered his hand.

The offsider nodded his welcome, his muddy brown eyes still suspicious. But the driver's handshake was firm as his gaze took in the army-issue clothes. 'The name's Frank, and this is Jim,' he said. 'I reckon you was lucky to find us, John. We don't usually stop here.'

'Where are you heading?' he asked, trying not to keep looking at the steaming cup of tea resting on the dashboard and the half-eaten meat pie lying beside it. The smell was masking the other odours and making his mouth water and his stomach growl.

'Wilga and then Morgan's Reach and up country to Killigarth and the other northern stations. We should have been this far up a couple of days ago, but the truck broke down and we had a fair old job trying to flamin' fix it. What about you, John? Where you heading?'

'South,' he lied, 'and then east.'

The trucker eyed his army boots and clothes. 'Still fighting the war, are ya?'

He shook his head and his gaze returned once more to the half-eaten pie that was oozing rich dark gravy on to the greaseproof-paper wrapping. 'Going home, mate.'

The eyes widened. 'Strewth, you've taken yer time. Most of the blokes I know have been home for months.'

He winked. 'I had things to attend to,' he replied.

Jim sniggered and Frank grinned, revealing a mouthful of bad teeth. 'Yeah,' he said with a leer and a nudge, 'and we all know what kind o' business that might be.'

'Too right, mate,' he replied with another wink. The effect was rather spoiled by the loud rumbling of his aching stomach.

'Sounds like you ain't eaten in a while,' said Frank. 'Jim, get the tucker box down while I pour the tea. This bloke's got less meat on him than a scrawny chook.'

The tucker box was duly dragged from the back shelf and opened with a flourish to reveal more food than he'd seen for weeks. Handing Frank his tin cup, he took one of the pies and unwrapped it almost lovingly. The first bite made him close his eyes in rapture, for the meat was tender, the gravy as rich and thick as he remembered his mother's had been.

Frank poured the steaming tea, his gaze now softened by something that could have been pity. 'Here you go, mate,' he murmured. 'And have another pie. My missus made 'em, and there ain't none better this side of the Blue Mountains.'

He didn't want to reveal how hungry he was, but he couldn't help himself, and he gobbled up three pies and two cups of tea as Frank told him his life story and Jim sat dumbly staring out of the window at the dust clouds. At least he didn't have to reciprocate, for Frank seemed quite happy to talk, and showed a remarkable lack of curiosity about this unexpected visitor. Perhaps the other man had an inkling that he wasn't quite all he seemed and had decided not to probe. After all, a man's business was his own out here, and if he didn't want to talk about it, then that was all right.

Sated, he finally leaned back and rubbed his tight midriff. 'Your missus deserves a bloody medal.' He sighed.

'Reckon she does,' Frank replied thoughtfully. 'How long you been on the road, John? When was the last time you ate?'

He smiled ruefully. 'A while,' he replied, 'and I've a ways to go yet.'

'It's a shame we ain't goin' the same way, cos we could have given you a ride – though it's not strictly allowed.'

'Na, you're right, mate. I like walking.' He glanced at his watch and reached into his trouser pockets for some money. 'I'd better get going – it's easier walking at night.'

'You can't go out in this,' Frank protested. 'And I don't want yer money neither. You blokes fought a war for us. The least we can do is give you a bit of tucker.'

He put the money back in his pocket. 'Thanks for everything, mate. It was a pleasure getting to know you, but I need to keep going if I'm ever to reach home.'

The silent Jim reached into the tucker box and pulled out two more pies, a packet of biscuits, another of tea and a paper screw of sugar, which he carefully packed into the kitbag. 'Reckon these might come in handy,' he drawled, 'and you can fill your water-bag from the container strapped to the side of the truck.'

He shook their hands and clambered down from the cab into the furnace blast of windblown grit. Having filled his water-bag to the brim, he tipped his hat in farewell and headed down the road, past the three long trailers as if he was going south. Once he was sure he was out of sight in the swirling dust, he carefully made his way down the slope to the railway line, turned his back to the wind, and continued his journey north.

'Mum, Mum – Uncle Terry's car's gone.'

Becky was shaken roughly awake by Danny's urgency. She eyed him blearily, not really taking in what he was saying. 'What?'

'The car's gone,' he said impatiently. 'Wake up, Mum.'

'Uncle Terry probably parked it round the back under the

lean-to,' she muttered, settling back into the pillows. 'It'd be out of the dust there.'

Danny shook her again, determined to make her take notice of him. 'I checked there, and over at Granny Gwyn's. It's gone, Mum, and I bet I know who took it.'

Rebecca was now wide awake. She threw back the sheet and reached for her thin cotton dressing gown. 'You mustn't throw those sorts of accusations about,' she said distractedly. 'You can't possibly know who took it.'

'Bet I do,' he said stubbornly. 'The Baker twins were eyeing it up all afternoon, and Uncle Terry even opened the bonnet so we could all look at the engine.'

'Every man, woman and child pored over that car yesterday. That's enough,' she said sternly.

She hurried down the passage and, despite the very early hour, found the rest of the family staring out of the screen door to the dust-laden garden and street, and the to empty space by the kerb. Terry's face was tight with fury, her father's was confused, and her grandmother's was set in the sort of expression that boded ill to everyone.

'I'll get Jake on the two-way,' Becky said. 'He'll soon—'

'He's up with Ben on fire-watch,' said Hugh, running his hands distractedly through his thinning hair. 'I spoke to him as soon as I saw what had happened, but Ben's only just gone to sleep after a long night, Django's nowhere to be found and Jake can't leave the two-way. The storm last night did a fair bit of damage to some of the outlying stations, with two reports of lightning strikes. They've been dealt with, but the situation is too tenuous for him to leave his post.'

'I never thought I'd see the day when a man's car can be stolen from right outside his house,' muttered Terry. 'Things must have changed drastically since I was last here.'

'It was that man. It had to be,' said Sandra, who was still in her lacy nightdress and negligee, her hair pinned up in rollers, her face smothered in some white lotion.

'What man?' asked Hugh.

'A man I saw hiding in the bush on the way here. I knew he was up to no good – he looked furtive.' She folded her arms and glared as if daring them to contradict her.

Everyone turned to look at Terry, the questions clear in their eyes.

'I didn't see anyone,' he admitted, 'but Sandra's convinced someone was out there the other night.' He turned to his wife. 'But even if there was,' he said tightly, 'it was miles back, and if he was on foot he couldn't possibly have made his way here in such a short time. I really think we should consider the fact that our thief was a local.'

'It was the Baker twins,' piped up Danny.

'You don't know that for certain,' admonished Rebecca. She turned back to Terry and Sandra and explained about the twins. 'But I'm sure they wouldn't have done such a thing,' she finished, giving them the benefit of the doubt. 'They're not thieves by nature, and their pranks are often annoying, but quite harmless.'

'I'm more interested in this mysterious man Sandra thought she saw,' said Jane.

'I didn't *think* anything,' snapped Sandra. 'I know what I saw.'

'And *I* think we should all take your observations very seriously,' Jane soothed. She glanced at Terry and silenced his objection with a wave of her hand. 'I happened to be listening to the chatter on the two-way yesterday morning and heard Bob Freeman talking to Ben about a fire that'd been put out by someone on the far south-western corner of his property.'

'Did he say what the man looked like?' asked Sandra eagerly.

Jane shook her head. 'He didn't see him, but he knows for certain it was none of his men. He found clear tracks of heavy

102

boots and a remnant of cloth that could have been army-issue camouflage – not something worn by Django's mob or swagmen.'

'It was him,' she said excitedly. 'The camouflage explains why Terry couldn't see him. He shifted back into the shadows as soon as we made eye contact, but I'll never forget that moment.' She looked at each of them triumphantly. 'You see – I *was* right.'

'Where was the fire exactly?' asked Gwyneth.

'By the old windmill and cattle troughs just east of the railway line and Nine Mile Creek,' replied Jane.

Gwyneth leaned on her walking stick and looked thoughtfully out of the screen door. 'That's a fair way,' she muttered. 'Too far for a man on foot to get here by now.' She looked at Sandra and nodded with approval. 'It seems you have a keen eye,' she said, 'and the man you saw could very well have been the same one who put out Bob's fire. But I don't think he's our thief.'

'Then who?' said Terence with a rasp of impatience.

'I think it's time I went and had a word with Reverend Baker,' she said sternly.

'See, Mum, I told you,' shouted Danny.

'You will keep your opinions to yourself, young man,' snapped Gwyneth. 'Calling a dog by a bad name is one thing – accusing him of a crime without proof is quite another. Go and eat your breakfast and leave this to me.'

'I should come with you,' said Terence. 'After all, it's my car.'

'You'll stay here and help your father,' she replied firmly. 'There has been an outbreak of food poisoning, and half the male population of Morgan's Reach is making its way to the hospital.'

She pushed through the screen door and went out on to the dusty veranda. She turned just before she had to negotiate the steps. 'By the way, Terry, did you leave the spare petrol cans in the boot?'

He groaned and nodded. 'Two – and one was full.'

'Then I doubt you'll see your car again for a good long while,' she declared. 'With that much fuel they could bloody well drive to Darwin.'

The settlement had been covered in red dust. It lay thickly on the roofs, gardens and verandas, and weighed down the slender branches of the gum trees. Gwyneth eyed the scene with displeasure and stomped up the road, her walking stick tapping in time with her steps. Her shoes and trousers were already stained by the dust that swirled up with every step, and she could taste it on her tongue and feel its grittiness on her skin. At least the wind had stopped, but the heat was already intensifying and it was only just dawn.

She reached the large house the townsfolk had built thirty years before for the lovely old vicar and his family. They had long since gone, and the Reverend Baker had proved to be far less likeable than the previous incumbent – but they were stuck with him until he retired or was moved on by his bishop.

Gwyneth had no compunction about knocking on someone's door at this time of the morning. The sun was breaching the horizon and only sinners and drunks lazed in bed at this hour.

Frances Baker opened the door a crack and peered through nervously, her grey eyes and wan little face bearing the shadows of a sleepless night and perhaps a deep worry. 'Mrs Morgan,' she breathed, clutching her dressing gown to her meagre bosom. 'Is something the matter?'

'Yes, there is,' said Gwyneth, 'and I'm not prepared to discuss it with you on the doorstep. Is the reverend in?'

Frances's expression sharpened and her eyes became fearful.

'He's dressing,' she said nervously, 'and it is far too early to disturb him.'

Gwyneth was not to be deflected from her mission, and although she felt sorry for this dowdy little woman, she was also impatient with her lack of backbone. She placed her hand on the door, pushed it open and, before the other woman could stop her, she was standing in the wide square hall.

Frances clutched her dressing gown as if her life depended upon it. 'Please, Mrs Morgan, Gwyneth, don't upset him. He's not feeling his best this morning.'

'Why? What's the matter with him?'

'I'll deal with this, Frances. Go and finish preparing breakfast.' The Reverend Baker cut a fine and imperious figure as he came down the stairs in his black suit and highly polished shoes. He was in his late forties and his humourless grey eyes regarded Gwyneth from beneath bushy eyebrows as he plucked the pocket watch from his waistcoat and rather pointedly looked at the time.

'You can stop putting on airs and graces,' snapped Gwyneth. 'I'm not impressed. Are your boys at home?'

The eyes narrowed and there was a hint of something wary in them. 'Why do you wish to know the whereabouts of my sons?'

'Are they here or not? It's not a difficult question.'

'I have no intention of answering any of your questions, Mrs Morgan, and I would appreciate it if you'd leave immediately.'

'Did Bob Freeman get in touch with you yesterday?' she asked abruptly.

'He did, and I'll thank you not to meddle in my business again. My sons have not been educated to the highest standard to have them working as farmhands.'

'So you turned his offer down?' She didn't wait for his answer – she could see it in his eyes. 'You bloody fool,' she muttered.

'Those boys are getting out of hand and a good dose of honest labour might have been the making of them. Where are they now?'

'They've gone,' said Frances timidly from the kitchen doorway. She stood there with her dull hair hanging in wisps about her face as she twisted her hands in the folds of her dressing gown.

'Hold your tongue, woman,' roared the reverend.

'But their beds haven't been slept in,' she dared to continue, 'and with that terrible storm last night, I fear for their lives. We should at least call Jake or—'

Reverend Baker grabbed his wife by the arm, making her wince. 'Be silent, woman! I will not have our business discussed like this.'

'There's no need for that,' said Gwyneth sharply as she rapped her walking stick on the polished floor. 'Bullying your wife won't make things any better for you or your boys.'

He let go of his wife's arm and turned on Gwyneth. 'Get out of my house!' he shouted, two high spots of colour reddening his pale cheeks, his eyes alight with fury.

'It is not your house,' she replied calmly. 'It is owned by the community. And I will leave when I'm good and ready.' She held his furious gaze. He didn't frighten her, and if he dared to lay a finger on her, she'd hit him with her walking stick.

Like all bullies, Reverend Algernon Baker had no stomach for his own medicine. His pomposity and rage withered beneath her glare. 'What business is it of yours where my sons have gone?'

'They seem to be missing – along with my grandson's car. With two cans of petrol in the boot, I suspect they're already miles away. Jake has been informed about the car, but not about your boys. I will leave that up to you. But if they were my sons, I would be very worried about them. Car thieves or not, they're out there somewhere, and this weather isn't fit for a dog, let alone two fourteen-year-olds.'

Frances burst into tears and her husband grimaced in disgust. 'My sons are not thieves,' he said evenly. 'They're probably hiding out in the caves out of rebelliousness. I expect them to return in due course.'

'Let us hope they do,' said Gwyneth. She patted Frances's arm in sympathy. 'Come and have a cup of tea with me later,' she murmured.

'My wife has parish duties to attend to today,' Algernon said pompously. 'She does not have time for cups of tea.'

Gwyneth eyed him with loathing and reached for the door handle. She had nothing else to say to this cold-hearted man. She stepped out into the hazy orange light of that dusty dawn and headed for Jake's police house. She would leave a note telling him about the boys' disappearance; she could bet a penny on the pound that the reverend wouldn't do it.

After Terence and Hugh had left for the hospital, Jane went to bed and Sandra locked herself in the bathroom.

Becky dressed quickly. She should have been on the ward twenty minutes ago, and the spinsters would no doubt give her a ticking-off. She saw that Danny was settled at the table with cereal and toast, distractedly kissed the top of his head and raced out of the door. The dust was everywhere, which meant the day would be spent cleaning.

Her father came out on to the veranda as she approached the hospital. 'We've got eight men with food poisoning,' he said, 'and I suspect there'll be more before the day's out. Every one of them ate at the pub last night and, as Bert's doing the cooking, he's probably infected half the Aborigine camp as well.'

'That's all we need.' She sighed.

'Indeed,' he agreed as he glanced up the dusty road towards the vicarage. 'No sign of Ma, I suppose.'

Becky shook her head. 'I would have liked to be a fly on the wall during that conversation,' she said with a wry smile.

Hugh nodded absent-mindedly. 'I've got Sarah and the other women cleaning up, and Terence is dealing with the surgery this morning. I need you to keep an eye on the men and help the Miss Harpers get more beds ready. We'll have to use the back veranda, so I'll pull down the big blinds and get it swept as soon as possible.'

Becky eyed the piles of dust that had sifted into the corners and stained the wooden floor. It would be a mighty task to undertake with eight men vomiting and needing bedpans every few minutes. The joys of nursing were often overrated – and this was a prime example.

Danny came out of the homestead, unseen by the women who were bustling about in preparation for the expected influx of more patients. He stood there for a long moment, his expression thoughtful as he gazed up and down the street. Then he hitched the haversack over his back, carefully wheeled his new bike down the steps and quickly cycled away towards the shack in the bush where Billy Blue lived with his mother.

The light in his eyes would have told Becky that he was on a mission. But Becky was otherwise occupied.

7

Gwyneth had seen to the joeys in their pillowslips and released a few of the lizards as well as the bird whose wing was now mended. Wally had taken himself off somewhere to hunt for food and Coco was shouting for attention from his cage on the veranda as the two young native women tried to sweep away the accumulation of dust that lay like a pall over everything.

Gwyneth kept a close eye on the pair of them, because they preferred to lean on their brooms and gossip, and their idea of actually using a bit of elbow grease was more of a lacklustre swipe with a damp cloth and a dab here and there with a duster which merely spread the mess about and made things worse.

She finally had the place as clean as it would ever be and, once the windows and doors were tightly closed and the shutters bolted against any further storms, she sent the girls over to the hospital to help there and went to see to the goats.

They were mostly feral, but had become used to being around Gwyneth and were quite happy to be milked occasionally. They'd come closer to the homestead during the storm and were huddled in a bleating mob under the trees at the bottom of the garden. Gwyneth could tell by their skittishness that they could feel the onset of another storm and she chose to milk only the most docile of the nannies.

She was perched on a low three-legged stool, her cheek resting against the warm, hairy flank as the milk squirted into the bucket, when she heard the unmistakable sound of the reverend's car grinding its way down the road. No doubt he'd decided to round up his two boys before Jake became involved, and Gwyneth silently wished him luck. The boys were probably nearer to Darwin than to Morgan's Reach, and their father was in for a long drive.

The explosive bang of the car backfiring made Gwyneth jump and the goat kick out. The sharp little hoof caught her just below her arthritic knee and, as she gasped in pain and tried to keep her balance on the stool, the car backfired again – just beyond her hedge – and the terrified goat kicked up her back legs, catching Gwyneth squarely on the jaw.

As the goats raced helter-skelter into the bush, Gwyneth toppled off the stool into the puddle of milk that had been spilled from the upturned bucket. She lay there winded and shaken, staring up at the ochre clouds that were scudding across the murky sky and wondering what the hell had happened.

As the shock began to wear off the pain took hold. Her knee throbbed, but her jaw felt as if it was on fire, and she hoped to goodness it hadn't been broken. She warily ran her finger over her teeth, relieved to discover they were all still where they should be. But even this simple act was painful, and she could taste blood and feel loose flaps of skin as she gingerly touched her face and tried to move her jaw, which seemed to be stuck at a strange angle.

Her light movements sent the agony ripping through her, and she closed her eyes, her old heart thudding like a steam train as she tried to address her situation. There was little doubt she was in trouble, for no one could see her lying here, and the rest of the family were occupied with all those cases of food poisoning. She doubted very much if Frances Baker would call even though her husband and his damned car had left the settlement, and if she did she'd probably be worse than useless. But Gwyneth knew she couldn't just lie there and wait to be found – she was losing too much blood.

'Ups-a-daisy,' shouted Coco from his perch. 'G'day, g'day, g'day.'

Gwyneth groaned as she slowly sat up. Every movement shot a salvo of red-hot agony through her face and into her head and, as she attempted to use her good knee to winch herself up, she could feel the deep throb start in her other leg. Grabbing the stool, she used it to lean on and, bit by bit, managed to get her behind on to it.

She sat there for a long moment, trying to get her breath back, all too aware of the blood pouring down her chin and the wound from beneath the tear in her old trousers. If she didn't get across the road to the hospital she'd soon pass out, and it could be hours before anyone came.

'Ups-a-daisy,' yelled Coco again. 'Aarrgh. Pretty boy.' He swung from his perch with one claw and flapped his wings.

She found it was too painful to tell him to shut up and mind his own flaming business, so she made a sort of grunting sound in her throat and concentrated on reaching her walking stick. It was annoyingly just out of reach, so she tentatively reached out her good leg and tried to draw it towards her with her foot.

The process exhausted her and seemed to take an age, but she finally managed to hook it in, and she sat again for a long while catching her breath and working up the energy to get to her feet.

She discovered that as long as she didn't move her head, the pain in her jaw could be controlled. Leaning heavily on her stick, she took a step and gasped at the knife of agony that shot up from her injured knee. But she couldn't stay here.

She had to keep going. And yet that short walk she'd taken so many times around her house and across the street seemed to stretch before her like a marathon.

As she reached the front corner of her side veranda she had to stop again for a rest. She clung to the railing and looked anxiously up the street for a sign of anyone that could help her. But it seemed the residents of Morgan's Reach were busy cleaning up after the storm, for the street was deserted.

She took a deep, shuddering breath and hobbled on, the blood slowly soaking through her shirt and trousers. She was beginning to feel light-headed now, and her hand trembled as she reached the gate and tried to unfasten the latch.

A flicker of movement caught her eye and she blinked blearily towards it. Sandra had come out on to the homestead veranda, elegant in well-cut slacks, crisp white shirt, delicate sandals and broad-brimmed hat. But she seemed intent upon something at the other end of the street.

Gwyneth couldn't call out, and the desperate keening in her throat was too soft to be heard from such a distance. She took a tight hold of her walking stick and began to crash it against the metal panels of the garden gate.

Sandra finally turned towards her, shielding her eyes from the low sun with her hat, clearly wondering what on earth Gwyneth was doing.

Gwyneth waved her stick in the air and began to bash the metal gate again. To her frustration, Sandra seemed to be horribly slow on the uptake, and it felt like an age before she stepped down from the veranda and ambled across the street.

Her eyes widened as she came nearer, and her last few steps were at a run. 'Gwyneth, what on earth's happened?'

She looked up at her and made a sort of gurgling noise in her throat. She was feeling faint and she fought against it, unwilling to collapse in a pathetic heap at Sandra's daintily shod feet. She waved her stick towards the hospital.

Sandra opened the gate and put an arm round Gwyneth's waist. 'Lean on me,' she said quietly, 'and don't try to rush. I'll get you there.'

Gwyneth felt like an old fool as she hobbled across the road, but she was grateful for Sandra's sturdy support, and the fact that she didn't seem to mind that her pristine blouse was now smeared with blood.

'Terence!' bellowed Sandra as they approached the steps. 'Terence, I need some help here. Now!'

Gwyneth was of the opinion that Sandra could have made an excellent sergeant major, with a commanding voice like that. It had certainly provoked a reaction.

Terence was just one of the crowd that appeared on the veranda. He took one look at Gwyneth, pushed his way through the others and carefully swept her up in his arms to carry her into the treatment room. Gently placing her on the examination couch, he began to snap orders at Sandra.

'Basin, hot water, lint and scissors – then needle, thread and shot of morphine for the pain.' He jerked his head towards the locked cupboard and handed her the keys. 'You'll find everything in there.'

He didn't touch Gwyneth's face, but his expression was solemn. 'I'll deal with that in a minute,' he said. 'What on earth have you been up to, Gran? You look as if you've gone ten rounds in a boxing ring.'

Gwyneth felt as if she had. She watched through a haze of pain as Sandra moved efficiently about the treatment room. It seemed she hadn't quite forgotten her skills, for as Terence cut away her trousers and dealt with the wound on her knee, Sandra always had the right instrument to hand so that the treatment ran seamlessly.

113

'You're lucky the bone wasn't broken, Gran,' he murmured as he cleaned the wound. 'A couple of stitches should sort it, but it'll be bruised and swollen for a while, and you'd do best to rest it.' He tenderly felt her knees. 'Looks like you've got a touch of arthritis there as well,' he added.

She shrugged. Arthritis was something she'd learned to live with and, as Sandra handed Terence the hypodermic, she closed her eyes and waited for the soothing numbness to flood through her. But when Terence had finished stitching and bandaging her knee he touched her chin, and her eyes flew open as she cried out with the pain.

'Sorry, Gran,' he said. 'That looks as if it's dislocated, but we'll need an X-ray to make certain there are no fractures. I seem to remember we had one years ago, but it was never that reliable.' He turned to Sandra who was quietly and methodically clearing up. 'Can you have a look in the operating theatre? It's just off the ward.'

Sandra was about to leave the room when Hugh came in. He took one look at Gwyneth and went pale. 'I'm sorry I didn't get to you straight away, Ma, but I've been on the two-way to Cloncurry.'

He nodded as Terence asked about the machine. 'We've still got it, but it's ancient and unreliable, and if her jaw's broken she'd be better off being flown down to Brisbane.'

'Then that's what we must do,' Terence replied. 'At Gran's age we can't afford to take risks.'

Hugh ran his fingers agitatedly through his hair. 'I wish it was that easy,' he replied. 'But I've just been on to the Flying Doctor Service about another case. They can't fly today, not with the dust storms building up.'

'So what do we do?' Terence mirrored his father by ruffling his own thick mop of hair.

'We'll have to operate here if it's necessary,' he said with a worried frown. 'Or at least, you will. I've got to get to Carey Downs Station. One of Big Mac's kids has been badly burned and she needs urgent attention.'

Gwyneth eyed the pair of them and tried to convey her frustration at them talking over her as if she was a bit of furniture. But she soon discovered it was far too painful to express her fury, so she flapped her hand at Hugh to shoo him out to the child that needed his attentions far more than she did, and glared up at Terence. She had no idea how skilled he was at surgery, and didn't really care one way or the other – she just wanted to be free of this awful pain.

Hugh seemed to understand, for he grabbed his medical bag and kissed her on her forehead. 'Be good, Ma,' he murmured. 'And I'll see you when I get back. Terry knows what to do, so you're in safe hands.'

She flapped at him again and closed her eyes.

Algernon Baker was an angry, frustrated man. Life had become nothing more than a battle against a series of crashing disappointments, and today he was at breaking point.

It hadn't always been so, as an ambitious young man he'd carefully considered the career options open to someone who'd been born and raised in the Sydney slums and who had little education. He'd been drawn to the Church for the theatrical ritual of the services, the rich vestments of the bishops and the way a clever orator could hold an audience enthralled as he stood in the high pulpit like a biblical prophet. For a man who'd held secret yearnings to go on the stage, it seemed the perfect solution.

Religion had never really come into it, but it was a means to an end, and once he'd taken Holy Orders he actually began believing in the message he preached, but that hadn't stopped him from meticulously planning how to forward his career.

He'd thought that by marrying a bishop's daughter he would quickly be promoted to richer, more important parishes, where he would be noticed by those who mattered in the church hierarchy.

And for a time it had been so. But his ambitions had been thwarted by those who hadn't approved of his eloquent, dramatic sermons, and by his father-in-law, who made it clear he despised the way he ran his household. After a particular incident which resulted in Frances sustaining a black eye, he'd been banished from his well-to-do Sydney parish to this hole in the ground called Morgan's Reach.

After eight years the humiliation still rankled, but today his rage was focused on his sons, on his witless, whining wife, and on Gwyneth Morgan – who'd had the temerity to stand up to him with her aggressive accusations. The weather wasn't helping his mood either and, as the wipers ineffectually smeared the dust over the windscreen, making it almost impossible to see further than the car bonnet, he cursed this isolated godforsaken place and the people who lived here.

In his opinion, the blacks were little more than savages, the rough men who worked the stations weren't much better and the townspeople of Morgan's Reach were an ignorant bunch of country bumpkins who sang out of key on Sundays and only came to his services because it was an opportunity to exchange the latest gossip.

He gripped the steering wheel and peered through the murky windscreen. It was unbearably hot, and he didn't like the look of those dark clouds which were gathering overhead. Another storm was brewing, and the last place he wanted to be was out here, but he had no choice. He had to find those boys and get them home before they brought any more disgrace to the family – and when he did, he vowed silently, he would beat the sin out of them and lock them in the storage cellar beneath the house until they were suitably repentant.

He finally reached the end of the track and the turn-off to the highway and sat there pondering his options as the exhaust pipe burbled and backfired. He rarely left Morgan's Reach unless it was with Jake or one of his parishioners and had absolutely no idea which way to go. With the storm closing in, either way was hazardous. If Gwyneth was right, then the boys had taken off in the middle of the night and could be miles away by now. But there was just a chance they might have sat out the storm and were only in the next shire.

He seethed with fury as he tried to make up his mind. 'Oh, Lord,' he shouted to the lowering skies, 'show me a sign and guide me on to the right path.'

The response was a roll of thunder and the stuttering flashes of sheet lightning to the north. Taking this as confirmation that God had heard his plea and was guiding him away from the worst of the storm, Algernon turned the car to the south, coaxing the reluctant and badly maintained engine to greater effort.

He would drive until the fuel in the tank was used up, and then refill it from the spare can in the boot and go back home. The dread of being stranded out here made him go cold and, if he failed to find his sons, then he would have to rely on God's good grace to protect them. Not that they deserved it, he thought bitterly.

The broad white blinds had been pulled down to give added shade and protection from the dust and heat on the verandas, for the original eight patients had become eighteen, and if the situation worsened then more beds would have to be found and the other verandas utilised.

As Django's female relatives did their best to clean away

the dust that lay on everything, Becky and the two spinsters had their hands full. Their male patients threw up repeatedly, groaned like stuck bulls and constantly demanded bedpans and bottles. Bert, who'd been the cause of this influx, was the worst patient, of course, and he'd kicked up a fuss at having to share the veranda with the natives who'd also been struck down by his dubious meat pies.

Hugh had told him in no uncertain terms that if he didn't like it he could go back to the pub and suffer on his own. The family had always believed medicine was for everyone, regardless of creed or colour, and they stood firm on that.

Becky had been occupied with Bert when Sandra had brought her grandmother in, and it was a while before she could leave the ward. She'd been shocked at how frail and pale Gwyneth had been, but knew better than to let the old lady see even a glimmer of sympathy or pity in her expression.

Realising there was little she could do to help, she'd returned to the ward mildly surprised at how efficient Sandra had looked. She hoped that this was her first step to recovery. There was nothing like being dropped in at the deep end to see things more clearly.

As food was the last thing any of her patients needed, Becky had put Sarah and her sisters to work in the laundry; they would soon run out of linen at this rate. The Harper spinsters were thoroughly enjoying themselves now they had eighteen helpless men to boss about, and when Charley Sawyer came in they took particular delight in stripping the blacksmith's clothes and wrestling him into ill-fitting hospital pyjamas.

Charley was a big man and his feet stuck out past the end of the bed where his mongrel dog whined and tried to lick his toes. To a subdued but enthusiastic chorus of disapproval, the women finally caught the dog and tied it to the front veranda post with a bowl of water and two digestive biscuits.

Becky had watched the kerfuffle with a wry smile. The two old dears were efficient and their years of nursing experience were a godsend, but she did wish they'd show a bit of sympathy for those poor men.

She was in the sluice scrubbing out bedpans when her father appeared in the doorway.

'I'm off to Carey Downs,' he said. 'Terry and Sandra will look after Ma, but you'd better be on standby in case you're needed. Sandra looks as if she's coping, but you never know.'

'How is Gran?'

'She'll be fine,' he said with a distracted smile. 'Her jaw looks as if it's only dislocated, thank God, but it'll be the devil's own job to stop her from talking for a few days so it can rest.'

'I'll find her a pad and pencil when I've got a minute,' she replied, relieved that Gwyneth had done no serious damage.

She glanced out of the window at the lowering skies. It was ominously still and the heat was unbearable despite the many whirling ceiling fans. 'Do you have to go, Dad? It looks like we're in for another storm, and Carey Downs homestead's a long way out.'

'Polly's only four. She knocked over a kerosene lamp and her dress caught alight. By the sound of it she's suffering from very serious burns. I have to go, Becky.'

She saw the look in his eyes and understood that despite the fact it was unlikely the child would survive such a terrible accident, he was needed and would go anyway. 'Of course you must,' she replied, putting her hand on his arm. 'Take care out there, Dad. And give us a call on the two-way so we know you've arrived safely.'

'I'll go and wake your mother before I leave,' he said as he packed clean bandages into his bag, alongside the jars of ointment, and phials of morphine. 'You'll need all the help you can get over the next couple of days.'

Becky gave him a hug and kissed his cheek. 'If you see Danny, tell him not to wander too far.'

He nodded, then rammed his hat over his thinning hair, picked up his precious bags of medical equipment and left the hospital.

Half an hour later, Becky recognised the sound of his utility making its way down the main road and eventually fading into the distance. She looked out of the window and saw the trail of dust he'd left behind, then up to the sky where much darker clouds were gathering. Carey Downs homestead was at least four hours' drive away along some of the most isolated and barely discernible droving tracks, which could soon become obliterated in a dust storm. She sent up a silent prayer that he would come home safely, and then returned to her patients.

The dark clouds rolled ominously over the land as they hid the sun and spat jagged forks of lightning across the skies. There was a heavy silence, and all was still. It was as if the earth was holding its breath, poised for the moment when all that harnessed power would be unleashed in an explosion of fury.

Birds fluttered nervously as they sought their roosts; kangaroos, emus and wallabies left the open plains and found shelter within the trees; and the Outlanders looked up at those threatening skies and wondered if, at last, the rains would come and rescue them from penury.

Algernon had been driving for several hours when the needle on the fuel gauge showed it was very nearly empty. He'd almost fallen asleep several times and was virtually in a stupor as he pulled off the road, the car bumping over the clumps of tough dry grass that were dotted along the edge of a vast and empty pasture.

Seeking the meagre shelter of a stand of wilting ghost gums, he switched off the engine and clambered out of the car in search of refreshing cooler air. But there was little respite, for the heat was searing even in the shade.

He grimaced at the unpleasant way his shirt and trousers clung to his sweating body, and how his hair was wet beneath the broad-brimmed hat. He'd long since discarded his suit jacket and waistcoat, for his enforced imprisonment in the car was like being slowly boiled in a tin can.

There had been no sign of his sons, or anyone else for that matter. The barren road had stretched ahead of him in a haze of shimmering heat, becoming narrower and rougher as he went on. The only sign of life had been a few scavenger crows tearing at the carcass of a kangaroo.

He took a long drink from his water-bag, dampened his handkerchief to mop his face and neck and put his hat back on. The miles of emptiness stretched away from beneath those rolling thunderous clouds, the distant waterhole a dry clay pan, the bleached bones of long-dead cattle gleaming against the unforgiving red of the earth.

Algernon shivered despite the heat. A man could die out here if he wasn't well prepared with enough fuel and water to see him home.

He adjusted his hat against the glare and went to unlock the boot. There was a strong smell of petrol in that hot, enclosed space, and congratulating himself on being a wise traveller he reached for the can.

He experienced a rush of terror. The can was light – much too light.

With trembling hands he drew it from where it was wedged in beside a spade, a coil of rope and the spare tyre and unscrewed the cap, which he let fall to the ground. Muttering a passionate prayer, he looked inside. It was empty.

He stared at it in disbelief. He remembered filling it only the other day. And then he noticed the rust on the bottom

– and the tiny holes. He ran his fingers over them, detecting the unmistakable oily dampness – and then he knew why the boot had smelled so strongly. Everything was soaked in the precious, lifesaving fuel.

The fear was a living thing squirming in the pit of his stomach. With a cry of anguish he threw the useless can into the field and watched it bounce away until it settled beneath a clump of mulga scrub. He kicked the metal cap after it, looked in despair at his surroundings and stepped out into the road in the faint but desperate hope that someone might appear.

But the heavy stillness seemed to wrap itself around him, the leaden skies pressing down with ominous intent as the heat hummed in the gravel beneath his feet.

Algernon stood in the middle of the deserted track as the thunder growled ever nearer. He had no idea where he was, only that Morgan's Reach was many miles to the north, and the only way he had to get there was on foot.

He was muttering feverishly, half-prayer, half-curse, as he returned to the car and fetched his jacket, pocket watch and the two water-bags. One was only quarter full, but surely, surely he'd be rescued before they were both empty?

He checked the time. It was just past noon, but fortunately the sun was masked by the clouds, the half-light murky in the eerie silence. Tying his jacket round his waist, he hitched the bags over his shoulder and turned his back on the car. There was little point in locking it, and the open boot would allow the stink of petrol to disperse.

As he slowly began to walk down that lonely track, the only sounds that accompanied him were the rasp of his boot-heels on gravel and the beating of his anxious heart.

Ben was snatched from a deep sleep by Jake roughly shaking his shoulder. He looked blearily at the clock on the wall and realised he'd slept for barely four hours. 'What now?' he groaned.

'Sorry, mate, but I've had the reverend's wife on the phone in a panic, and I need to go back to town.'

Ben yawned and ran his hand through his hair. 'Bloody hell,' he muttered as he swung his legs off the couch. 'What's the matter with the woman?'

'It looks as if the twins have nicked the new doctor's car and their father has gone after them.' Jack wedged his hat firmly over his dark hair and adjusted his belt. 'But that's only the half of it. The bloody hospital's full of the poor bastards that ate Bert's old meat pies last night, and I have to go and inspect the kitchen, lock up the pub and write a report.'

Ben shot him a wry smile. 'Just another quiet day in store for you then?' He gave a vast yawn. 'How's the weather?'

'Building up to a right ripper,' he replied with a grimace. 'It's as black as your hat out there, with the wind picking up and the heat rising. I don't like the look of it at all.'

'You'd better get off then, mate. I'll keep an ear open on the two-way. I don't suppose there's any sign of Django, is there?'

'Nah, mate. He's in the hospital, so don't expect him back for a couple o' days at least.'

Ben gave a sigh of exasperation and headed for the coffee pot that was simmering away on the stove. 'What are you going to do about the boys and the reverend?'

'I've put out a call on the two-way for any sightings, but as Mrs Baker doesn't know which way they went, I don't hold out much hope. There's not much more I can do but patrol up and down the main road for a bit. They could have ended up in a ditch somewhere – but on the other hand, they could be off the road altogether and out on the tracks.'

'They won't get far in that fancy car,' muttered Ben as he hunted out a clean cup and the last of the tinned milk and sugar. 'I'll put a call in to Dad. They might be heading for Wilga.'

'Already thought of that. He ain't seen 'em, but he's sending some of his jackaroos out to check the tracks that lead off the highway.' He snatched up his tin of tobacco and stuffed it into his shirt pocket. 'If the bloody reverend had let those boys take the jobs out at Wilga, none of this would have happened.'

'I'll catch you later, mate. Best of luck.' Ben grimaced as he tasted the bitter, stewed coffee. 'And if the road train comes through, give us a shout. I'm out of everything.'

'Will do, mate. See you later.' Jake pushed through the screen door, leaving it to slam behind him. Within moments he was driving back down the track through the bush.

Ben sipped the coffee that had the taste and consistency of tar and went to the two-way radio to call Becky. It took a while for his call to be answered, and when she finally came on she sounded harassed. 'I just wanted to see how you're coping down there,' he said. 'Jake tells me Bert's cooking is up to its usual standard.'

'He's blaming Sal of course, and making a terrible fuss about everything. How are things up there?'

He peered out of the window to the black clouds and the haze of red dust that was coating the canopy of trees. 'Hot, dusty and getting darker by the minute. I'll try to get down to see you this evening, but I can't promise anything.'

'That'd be good,' she said distractedly. 'Sorry, Ben, can't talk now. I'm needed. Catch you later.' There was a click and the line was abruptly disconnected.

Ben sighed with frustration. There was always something keeping them apart, but then the hospital was always busy, and with this storm brewing, he just couldn't take the risk of leaving the two-way unmanned. Perhaps, if Jake managed to get back up here later, he could take an hour off to go and visit her.

He finished the disgusting coffee, made toast and went up to his watch-tower. Even with the binoculars he could see very little through the veils of dust which were swirling to meet the lowering clouds. The temperature had reached a hundred and fifteen degrees and the wind was like a furnace blast searing his skin, not only with the heat, but with the minuscule particles of sand that blew with it.

He narrowed his eyes against the assault, tugged his hat brim low and reached for the two-way. 'This is Ben Freeman, your fire chief, calling all stations,' he said, cutting through the usual chatter. 'The weather conditions are worsening, and the risk of fire is at the highest level. Be alert. Be alert. Stay off this channel unless it's an emergency. I'll keep you informed.'

He thought about saying something regarding the reverend and his two boys, but as Jake had already done so, he didn't want to overload the listeners with information. 'Over and out.' He broke the connection and picked up the binoculars again.

It was almost impossible to make out anything at all through the roiling clouds and the thick layer of red dust, but as he made a final sweep over the canopy and down into the valley, something caught his eye. Gripping the binoculars, he clenched his jaw. Those damned boys were at the caves again.

Just as he was about to rush down and haul them out of there, they emerged from the cave, scrambled down the rocks and collected their bicycles. He watched as they pedalled expertly through the hazardous trees and undergrowth until they were out of sight. At least they were heading for home, but something in their manner intrigued him and, although he couldn't pinpoint what it was, it kept niggling at him as he went back down into the house to monitor the two-way in more comfortable conditions.

He sat by the radio, replaying that little scene repeatedly in his mind until he couldn't stand it any longer. Those boys had been up to something – he just knew it.

Grabbing his hat, and pulling a neckerchief over his mouth and nose, he snatched up his powerful torch and ventured out into the gathering maelstrom. The hot wind plucked at his shirt and hat as he picked his way swiftly down the boulders beneath Eagle Head Rock, but as he reached the relative shelter beneath the canopy the sting of dust lessened.

He stepped on to the ledge which led into the largest cave. It was dark and gloomy inside, and at first he could see nothing different. And then he switched on his torch.

Danny and Billy Blue had been busy. There was a neat pile of twigs and screws of paper placed on the floor at the back of the cave, with a box of matches and a billycan beside it. A can of corned beef, half a loaf, a bottle of beer, a screw of tea and two blankets were set to one side of the cave on a low natural shelf in the rock – and under a sturdy stone there fluttered a piece of paper.

Ben squatted down and picked it up. Letting the beam from his torch play over the childish writing, his spirits sank. He finally understood exactly what the boys had been up to, but that knowledge had given him a real dilemma.

The blades of tinder-dry grass began to brown and shrivel where they touched the hot exhaust pipe of the abandoned car. As the charring began to travel downward to the tightly packed clumps where the grass sprouted, the first wisps of smoke began to rise.

It was very slow at first – almost a lazy meander of brown that travelled deep into the heart of those clumps where it could gather strength and begin to spread. But the fumes of petrol coming from the boot were a deadly haze, drifting about the car waiting for the first spark to ignite it.

As the heat increased in the dry embrace of those pale fronds they wilted and charred under the assault. And then the first flame flickered to life.

Within moments it was joined by others, finding the dribble of petrol that traced the path of the metal cap kicked into the field – and racing to feed upon it. The narrow stream voraciously engulfed the petrol-soaked cap and became a much larger, hungrier flow, extending its reach, moving inexorably towards the can that lay shimmering in the half-light.

But there were other flames lapping hungrily at the overheated undersides of the car. The air shimmered like a living thing as the birds rose from the surrounding trees with shrill cries of alarm and the hot wind began to blow across the empty landscape.

The first explosion sent the remains of the petrol can into the air – feeding the fire – widening its reach.

The second was much bigger, and blew the car apart. Boot, bonnet and doors were flung into the undergrowth beneath the trees as the windscreen shattered and the leather seats began to burn. One of the tyres was tossed across the track in a cartwheel of flame to land in a welcoming bed of dead leaves and twigs that lay on the edge of the forest that covered several thousand square miles and led to numerous homesteads and stations.

The flames engulfed the car now, and still they multiplied, reaching out with greedy fingers to consume everything in their path as the hot wind strengthened. The overhanging trees were already blossoming with flame as the fire raced up the slender white trunks in search of more fuel. And there was fuel aplenty in the eucalyptus oil that emanated from their leaves.

As the fire claimed the trees on both sides of the narrow track the heated breath of the wind stoked the flames to greater fury. There was little chance of anyone seeing it in time to stop it spreading further. The low clouds masked the smoke, a range of mountains stood between it and the fire-watch station at Morgan's Reach, the nearest homestead was over a hundred miles away – and Algernon Baker had been mistaken when he'd thought he was on the main road.

8

It had been a long tussle of wills, but Becky had finally managed to give the blacksmith an injection in his hairy backside. 'There,' she said, giving the spot a brisk rub to ease the sting, 'that'll stop you being sick.'

'I hate needles,' Charley muttered as he pulled up his pyjama trousers. 'When can I get outta here?'

'Not for a while yet. The medication has to work.' She poured a glass of water from the jug that stood on the table between him and Bert. 'Drink as much of this as you can, Charley. It will rehydrate you.'

He eyed the water as if it was poison. 'Can't I have a beer instead?'

'No,' she said firmly, and handed him the glass. She waited until he'd drunk all of it and then poured more. 'I want to see that jug empty within the next two hours, Charley,' she said, trying to appear stern. He was the biggest man in Morgan's Reach, but he was acting like a wilful toddler.

The sound of heavy footfalls made her turn. Jake was striding towards her, his expression grim. Her spirits plummeted. 'You're not ill too, are you?'

He took off his policeman's broad-brimmed hat and shook his head, his gaze drifting over the beds. 'I'm here on official business,' he said. 'I need to have a word with Bert.'

'Best of luck,' she replied. 'He's been in a foul mood all day.'

'He'll be in a worse one when I've finished with him,' retorted Jake.

Becky and her patients watched as Jake strode over to Bert's bedside. This was clearly no social call, and could turn out to be interesting. Bert might be married to the landlady of the only pub within a hundred miles, but he'd never been popular – and after this episode with the pies his standing in the community was lower than ever. Perhaps he was about to get his comeuppance.

'Bert!' Jake snapped. 'Bert, don't pretend you're asleep, cos I know you're not.'

Bert opened one bleary eye and grimaced. 'What you want?'

'I've come to tell you I've closed the pub until further notice. The kitchen's a pigsty, most of the food is rancid and I found animal droppings and vermin everywhere.'

Bert shot up in his bed, his ratty face scarlet with fury. 'You can't shut my pub,' he shouted.

'I already have. And until you get the place cleaned up, it stays shut.'

'It's Sal's fault,' he yelled. 'If the bitch hadn't shot through I wouldn't have had to cope on me own.'

'You can shout all you like, mate, but the pub stays shut until you sort it out.'

'How can I when I'm stuck in here?' he whined. 'What kind o' mate are you, to do such a thing when a bloke could be dying?'

Jake regarded him with loathing. 'I'm not your mate,' he said evenly, 'and you're about as dead as those maggots I found crawling in your old meat pies. It's only sheer luck no one was killed.'

He gave a glance round the room at Becky and Jane and the patients who'd come on to the veranda with the Harper sisters to listen avidly to this exchange. 'You've got two weeks, Bert, and if it isn't sorted, then the pub will have a contamination order slapped on it and be closed for good.'

There was a murmur of protest from across the veranda, but Jake ignored it as he handed over a slip of paper. 'I'm giving you this order in sight of witnesses, and will inspect the pub two weeks from today.' With that, he settled his hat on his head, nodded to Becky and her mother and strode off the veranda.

'I'll flamin' kill Sal when I finally get hold of her,' Bert growled.

'You lay one hand on her and you'll have me to deal with,' rasped Charley Sawyer from the next bed.

'Yeah, you and whose army?' snarled Bert, his eyes narrowed.

Charley sat up and raised his enormous fists, the muscles bulging in his arms. 'These are all I need, you mongrel,' he growled. 'And they're itching to wipe that sneer off your ugly mug.'

Becky and her mother exchanged worried looks. The last thing they needed today was a fight. But before they could do anything, the moment was defused by Danny and Billy Blue bursting on to the veranda.

'The road train's here,' Danny shouted.

'Yeah, and it looks like they'll be staying,' added Billy. 'The weather's getting real crook out there.' He ran over to Django and leaned on his bed to chatter away at him like a small parakeet.

There was a stirring among the men, and the short spat between Bert and Charley was forgotten as those who felt well enough began to clamber out of bed.

'You'll all stay exactly where you are,' said Jane firmly. 'Especially you, Sean O'Halloran,' she said, grabbing the Irish-born storekeeper by the arm. 'You're still far too weak, and Annie's quite capable of coping without you.'

'But she can't lift—'

'She won't need to,' she interrupted. 'The drivers will do that.' She efficiently got the grey-faced Sean back into bed and tucked in before he realised what was happening. 'Right,' she said, turning to Becky, 'I think it's time you had a bit of a break. The other ladies and I can cope here.'

'Thanks, Mum. I won't be long.' She managed to grab hold of Danny, who was about to race away with Billy again. 'Where have you been all day?' she asked.

'Nowhere,' he said, avoiding her gaze.

It was the standard answer of a boy who probably hadn't really been anywhere or done anything in particular, but who'd been very busy nevertheless. 'Well, I need you to stay close to home now. With the storm building up, it'll be dangerous out there.'

'But I wanna go and hear Frank tell his stories,' he protested. 'Then me and Billy wanna—'

She silenced him by tilting up his chin so he had to look at her. 'Granny Gwyn's had an accident and would appreciate a visit. How about we go together?'

His petulance disappeared immediately. 'What sort of accident? She's not real crook, is she?'

'She's dislocated her jaw and hurt her leg, and she's feeling rather sorry for herself, but she'll be right. Come on. We can visit for a little while and cheer her up before you go and sort out her animals and watch Jim and Frank unload.' She picked up a notebook and pencil and nudged him off the veranda towards the isolation room.

Gwyneth was lying in solitary splendour with her bandaged leg resting on a pillow. But she didn't look too happy about the white crepe that was tightly bound under her chin and over her head, and she glowered at them as they came into the room. 'About time,' she managed to mutter.

'Don't try to talk, Gran,' said Becky. 'Look, I've brought you these so you can write down whatever you want to say.'

Gwyneth eyed the notebook and pencil and set them aside. She glared at Danny, who seemed fascinated by the head bandages. 'I know I look like some ancient nun in a wimple,' she said through her restricted jaw. 'Don't you dare laugh.'

'But you do look funny, Gran,' he replied, scrambling on to the bed to get a better look and leaving smears of dirt on the pristine sheets.

'At least I'm clean,' she retorted. 'You look as if you've been dragged through a hedge backwards. And mind my leg,' she added sharply as Danny shifted on the bed. 'I've had stitches.'

'Cor,' said Danny. 'Let's have a look.'

'You'll do no such thing,' said Becky sharply. 'And get off the bed, Danny. Your feet are filthy.'

He slid to the floor and leaned his elbows on the counterpane, his gaze fixed to his grandmother's bandages as if by sheer will he could see the scars beneath them. 'Does it hurt, Gran?' he asked. 'Was there lots of blood and stuff?'

'Gallons of it,' said Gwyneth.

Rebecca sighed in exasperation. 'If you keep talking, you'll dislocate that jaw again. Please, Gran, do as you're told for once and use the notepad.'

Gwyneth flapped her hand at Rebecca in dismissal as Danny began to bombard her with questions.

As Gwyneth haltingly supplied all the gory details, Becky gave up trying to give advice and after a few moments decided to leave them to it and go in search of a much needed cup of tea.

Apart from the chaos of so many men going down with food poisoning, the surgery had also been busy. One of the Aboriginal kids had fallen out of a tree and broken his leg; Mrs Baker had been so distracted by the disappearance of her boys she'd sliced through her finger as she'd been chopping up meat for a stew, and the heavily pregnant Mary had gone into labour.

Mary had arrived accompanied by the rest of her large brood as well as several aunts, her grandmother and mother-in-law. Birthing was women's work, so there was no sign of her husband. Terence had had to shoo them all out when it became apparent it would be a breech birth, and as he delivered the baby, he and Sandra could clearly hear their chanting from the veranda.

'Talk about being thrown in at the deep end,' said Terence as they left mother and baby contentedly tucked up in bed on the side veranda, well away from the sick men. 'You coped brilliantly, Sandra.'

'Is it usual to let them light a fire on a bit of tin and have the whole family camp out beside the patient?'

'It's their way,' he replied. 'In the old days we had willow and daub humpies set out in the garden for them – they were suspicious of our white man's building. They'd light a small fire in front of the openings so they were kept in touch with their Ancestor Spirits, and the rest of the family would stay until they were well.'

'Extraordinary,' she murmured.

'Yes, it is rather, and you'd be amazed at how quickly they recover too. If they're sent away to hospital in Brisbane, it's as if distancing them from their spiritual ties weakens them, and they take much longer to recuperate.'

'Well, I need to get changed and have a proper wash,' said Sandra, grimacing at the stains on her blouse and white apron. 'Isn't there any fresh water in this place?'

'Only from the spring and the rainwater tanks, but with the levels so low, that's strictly for drinking. Everything else is taken from the bore.'

Sandra wrinkled her dainty nose. 'It smells,' she said. 'Even after my bath this morning, I didn't feel clean.' She picked up her hat and sighed. 'I knew it was primitive out here, but I didn't expect to have to wash in swamp water.'

Terence realised this was not the moment to give her a lecture on the mineral-rich bore water and changed the subject. 'It was lovely having you working with me today,' he said softly. 'Quite like old times.'

She smiled wearily back at him and tucked stray wisps of fair hair behind her ears. 'I'd forgotten how exhausting nursing was. I feel as if I've been run over by a steamroller.'

'You look marvellous,' he said, kissing her hot brow. 'And I'm very proud of the way you mucked in like that. You did really well.'

She pulled a face. 'Don't expect too much of me, Terry. Today was an exception, and I'm really not in the right frame of mind to cope with this day in and day out.'

Terence took her hand and squeezed her fingers. 'Why don't we go and have a quick look at the road train?' he suggested. 'I'm sure I can be spared for a few minutes now things have quietened down.'

'Strewth, Terry,' she breathed as she rolled her eyes, 'is the arrival of a road train what passes for entertainment out here?'

'Not entertainment exactly. But certainly an event. They only come in about once a month, and we rely on them for almost everything. Besides, Frank Hawkins always has a great yarn to tell, and it's as close to theatre as you can get out here.'

She looked up at him quizzically. 'You really love this place, don't you?'

He nodded. 'I haven't always appreciated it, but now I'm here . . . Well, this is home, and these people are my family. That's what makes it so special.' He drew her close and kissed the top of her head. 'I know you're finding it all very strange and primitive after Sydney. But give it a fair go, Sandra, and you might be surprised at how good it can be.'

She drew back from him with a wry smile. 'I doubt it,' she said. 'I'm a city girl, Terry, used to noise and bustle and proper shops and bathrooms. But without your car it seems I'm stuck here whether I like it or not.'

Terence didn't want to think about his lovely car which, no doubt, had been smashed to bits by those two young hooligans. 'So, you'll come and listen to Frank's yarns with me?'

'I've got a better idea. Let's go to the pub and have a drink. We've both earned it.'

'By the sound of that ruckus earlier on, Jake's shut the place until further notice,' he said, doing his best to keep the relief out of his voice. 'But I'll treat you to a glass of Annie O'Halloran's home-made lemonade.'

Sandra's eyes narrowed and her lips formed a thin line. 'I'm a grown-up, Terence. I don't drink sticky cordials.'

'Come on,' he coaxed. 'It'll be worth it, I promise.'

'But I need to bath and wash my hair before I go anywhere,' she replied. 'I must look a fright.'

'Nobody will notice, not out here – and with the weather being like it is, you'll only be wasting the water.' He smiled hopefully at her. 'Come on, Sandra. You'll enjoy it, really you will.'

She reluctantly stripped off the apron and followed him out of the surgery, waiting on the heavily screened veranda while he fetched his jacket and locked the door. It was only mid-afternoon, but the clouds were thick and black, the half-light eerie.

'It looks a bit fierce out there,' he said as he came to stand beside her and they looked out to the street. 'But this is nothing compared to some of the dry storms I've seen.'

Her expression was grim as she took in the dust which was

being spun into willy-willies – tiny whirlwinds – that twisted down the wide dirt track and deposited heaps of sand on every surface. 'And you expect me to walk out in that?'

'It might sting a bit, but you'll be right if you wear my jacket.' He helped her into it and kissed the tip of her nose before tugging her hat well over her eyes and taking her hand. 'Hold on tight, keep your head down and think of it as an adventure.'

They clattered through the outer screen door and were immediately buffeted by the hot wind and the stinging grains of sand that came with it. Sandra clung to his side and battled to keep her hat on as they were virtually pushed down the street. Terence held her close. It was hardly the most romantic of outings, but as Sandra, stumbling alongside him, actually burst out laughing, he revelled in this all too rare moment of intimacy.

The road train was parked outside the general store. The old army truck was high off the ground on enormous wheels, the three vast metal trailers strung behind it, each covered in dusty weathered tarpaulin. The driver and his offsider were sitting at leisure on the bench that stood outside the general store in the lee of large canvas blinds that had been pulled down to shield the boardwalk from the worst of the wind.

'That's Jim and Frank,' said Terence as they drew near. 'They've been on this run since I was a kid.'

'They certainly look ancient enough,' she muttered in reply.

He was about to protest when he saw the gleam in her eye that made his heart miss a beat. She was teasing him – and she hadn't done that since before the war. He grinned back at her and led her through the gathering on the boardwalk. He knew everyone there, but this was no time to stand and talk, for Frank was holding court while Jim sat in morose silence and watched the willy-willies spiralling down the street.

They walked into the gloom of the general store, which

welcomed them with the heady scents of leather and hessian, of flour, sugar, oil, kerosene and dried goods. Sacks and boxes had already been stacked on the wooden floor, and the long counter at the back was covered in bolts of cloth, hats, gloves and the flat-heeled boots worn by the men who worked on the stations.

'Well now,' said Annie, as she wiped her hands down her big white apron 'if it's not the young doctor and his wife. How's that daft old fool of a husband of mine?' Annie's Irish accent was still strong after almost thirty years in Australia.

'He'll be better by tomorrow, Annie,' he replied.

'That's a shame to be sure,' she said crossly. 'I've enough to do without him getting under me feet, so I have. Coming home late and—'

Not wanting her to begin a long diatribe over her husband's failings, Terry interrupted. 'We've come for a glass of your famous lemonade, Annie. I hope you still have some.'

'To be sure, and I always have a supply for me special customers,' she said, her temper restored with a beaming smile. She reached into the kerosene fridge and poured them both a generous glass. 'If that no-good husband of mine stuck to my lemonade and good home cooking, he wouldn't be half the bother,' she observed cheerfully.

Terence made no comment as he paid for their drinks and steered Sandra back out on to the boardwalk before she could spot the boxes of spirits and the crates of beer that were stacked behind the counter.

Frank still held his audience in thrall. 'Yeah,' he drawled, 'the trip's been eventful, you might say, and I reckon we'll be stuck here for a bit.' The weather's closing in all around – just like it did the other night when we had what you might call a strange occurrence.'

He surveyed his audience like a seasoned performer. 'Me and

Jim had parked up for the night. No good pressing on when the dust kicks up like that.' He paused just long enough to build the tension. 'The wind was blowing and the dust was rising, and we couldn't see a damned thing out o' the window. Then there was a break in the dust clouds and this bloke was suddenly standing there in the middle of the bloody road. Cool as ya like, lighting a smoke.'

The gathering leaned towards him, and Frank's eyes gleamed. He was renowned for his yarns and liked nothing better than a rapt audience. 'Fair put the wind up Jim, who thought he were a ghost.' He shook his head and gave his audience a rather superior smile. 'But of course I knew he weren't.'

'Ach, bejesus, Frank, you do spin things out,' sighed Annie, who'd come to sit beside him. 'Will you be after tellin' us who he was?'

Frank grinned, clearly enjoying his moment. 'Well now, Annie, that's the mystery,' he replied. 'He said his name was John Miller, but I don't reckon that was the truth.'

There was a general muttering before Annie said, 'Why not?'

His gaze became distant and thoughtful. 'I dunno,' he admitted finally. 'But there was something about him that didn't ring true.' He looked back at his audience. 'I could be wrong – but my instincts rarely let me down.'

Terence felt Sandra snatch her hand away, and before he could stop her, she'd pushed her way through the crowd. 'What did this man look like?' she asked.

Frank regarded her for a long moment. 'He was a skinny sort of tall youngish fella,' he replied. 'With eyes that looked as if they'd seen too many things a bloke shouldn't see – and a hunger that told me he hadn't eaten in days.' He cocked his head, his expression thoughtful. 'He looked like a man who was still fighting his own personal war – and was about to lose it,' he finished.

Sandra hesitated as she suddenly realised every set of eyes had turned her way. 'I think we might have seen him too,' she said, looking to Terence for support.

Terence simply nodded, uncomfortable at being the centre of attention.

Frank was busy rolling a smoke and his tone was casual. 'Oh, yeah? When was that?'

'Three or four days ago,' she replied. 'We were coming up from Sydney and had just gone through Bourke.'

Frank shook his head. 'Nah, missus, it can't be the same bloke, cos we saw him somewhere around Wilga Station and he was heading south.' He frowned and became thoughtful. 'At least, that's what he said.' He turned to the silent Jim. 'What you reckon, mate?'

Jim took a deep breath and pondered the question. 'I dunno,' he drawled after a while. 'Seemed like a nice young bloke to me, and a bit down on his luck after leaving the army. But it ain't none of our business anyways.'

'How did you know he'd been in the army?' piped up Annie.

Frank pursed his lips. 'He was wearing service camouflage and carrying a kitbag. Said he was on his way south back to his wife.' He brought an end to his performance by rising from the bench and placing his hat back on his head. 'Reckon we'd better finish unloading this lot before it gets too dark. As the pub's been shut, Annie, is there any chance of a bed for the night, and some tucker?'

As Annie set a price for the night's bed and board, the crowd began to disperse and Sandra turned to Terence with a gleam of excitement in her eyes. 'That about proves it,' she breathed. 'It's got to be the same man.'

'So what if it is?' he replied, weary of this obsession Sandra seemed reluctant to let go, and yet rather intrigued all the same. 'He's doing no harm.'

'I never said he was,' she replied impatiently. 'But don't you find it just a bit odd? What on earth is he doing out there – and why so secretive?'

Terence had had the same thoughts but decided not to voice them. Sandra was already far too caught up in this piece of fantasy, and it would do no good to encourage it. He looked down at Danny, who'd been standing beside him for the past few minutes. 'I think Frank just tells a good yarn. What do you reckon, mate?'

Danny shrugged. 'I reckon it's time for tea,' he said nonchalantly. 'I'm starving.'

Terence laughed and was about to ruffle his hair when he remembered how much he'd hated people doing that to him at that age, so clapped him on the shoulder instead. 'Come on, mate. Let's see what there is in the fridge. Then we'll go and see to Gran's menagerie.'

The three of them walked back down the street, heads bent against the hot wind that seemed to have strengthened during the past half-hour. To an observer they would appear to be entirely focused on reaching shelter from the gathering storm But in the heart and mind of the small boy there raged a very different tempest – one of overwhelming hope that battled against gnawing doubt and common sense. It was a struggle he knew he had to keep to himself if he was ever to discover the truth.

Knowing how far he had to go, and all too aware of the approaching storm, Hugh had pushed the utility to the limit as he'd headed south-west to Carey Downs Station. Now it was dark, and the storm was rapidly closing in as the thunder crashed overhead and the lightning flickered over the mulga trees and clumps of spinifex.

He still had at least another hour's driving before he reached

141

the homestead, which had been built on a low hill right at the heart of the property which sprawled over several thousand square miles of thick bush and open pasture. His headlights picked up the faint track that he'd followed so many times before, but as the dust blew across it he was finding it increasingly difficult to spot the usual landmarks.

He was beginning to have serious doubts as to the wisdom of trying to carry on in the dark when he saw a rider emerge through the dust clouds.

'G'day, Doc,' said the black tracker as he leaned down from his stock horse to speak through the window. 'Boss said alonga you. Big storm wipe out track.'

'Thanks, Jimmy. Much appreciated, mate. How's the leg?'

Jimmy grinned as he held on to his hat. 'You make betta, plenty good.'

'And how's the lovely Delilah – still keeping you on your toes?'

Jimmy grinned at the mention of his wife. 'She good too, Doc. Plenty kids, but she alonga good tracka like me.'

Hugh was still smiling as he wound the window back up against the whip of the dust-laden wind and followed the slender figure hunched in his saddle. Jimmy and Delilah were regarded as two of the best trackers in the district. A couple of years back Jimmy had broken his leg in two places when he'd been thrown by his horse, and he was glad the man had come through so well; Jimmy was just the man to have at your side in conditions like these.

Just over an hour later they saw the lights of the homestead and the anxious figures waiting for them on the veranda. Hugh thanked Jimmy again, reached for his medical bags and hurried up the steps. He was dreading what he suspected he would find.

*

Algernon's hat had been whipped away by the wind some time ago, and he trudged along the track with his jacket over his head to shield him from the scour of the sand that was being blown at him from all sides. He'd thought he'd heard muffled explosions far behind him some time ago, but had dismissed them as thunder. The storm was clearly building, and he was feeling very vulnerable in the middle of nowhere, with no sign of shelter and no hope of rescue.

His legs felt as if they were made of lead, and his head was pounding from the deep pain that blurred his vision and made him nauseous, but he didn't dare slake his terrible thirst, for he had no idea how long he would be out here. His thoughts skittered from one thing to another as he kept his gaze on the track and tried to overcome his terror. He couldn't see his watch in the darkness, but it felt as if he'd been walking for hours.

Algernon's discomfort and fevered thoughts merely stoked his confusion and fear. He'd been positive that the highway had been metalled, and although he vaguely remembered driving over this rough track, he was sure it had only been for a few miles. But where was the bitumen – surely he should have reached it by now?

The next great clap of thunder was right above him. It made him stumble and his heart missed a beat as his ankle twisted and he was sent sprawling on to the unforgiving ground, jarring his shoulder and hip and skinning his elbow. He curled into himself, his heart pounding, his back against the assault of the wind, the precious water-bags clutched to his chest as the lightning cracked overhead and the thunder continued to boom.

Caught in the maelstrom of noise and whipping sand, the darkness closed in as the banshee wails of the wind howled around him and clawed at his clothes. In his tortured mind he was experiencing the Armageddon he'd so often described from his pulpit – and he cowered beneath its ferocity, certain he was about to die.

An eternity seemed to pass before the thunder rolled away to grumble in the distance as the lightning stuttered between the billowing black clouds. He waited there, curled on the ground until the desperate need for water stirred him. His fingers fumbled with the stopper on the lighter bag. 'Not too much,' he muttered. 'I must be strong and not drink it all.'

The water was tepid, but that first taste was nectar. He held it in his mouth and felt it soothe his dry tongue and lips. He swallowed it greedily and took some more, feeling the pain ease in his head as the nausea ebbed. Tipping back the bag for what he promised himself would be the last time he felt only a trickle land on his tongue. Staring at it in bafflement, he shook it and tried again. But it was empty.

Throwing it away in disgust, he curled once again away from the wind, clutched the last precious bag of water to his chest and closed his eyes. He would rest until daylight.

The man who had called himself John Miller had found sanctuary from the storm in the deep dry riverbed that wound through the bush. There was little danger of flood-water rushing down, for the storm carried no hint of rain.

Sheltered by the overhanging trees, he'd made a circle of stones and lit a small fire. With the billy boiling merrily, he threw in some of the tea, added a eucalyptus leaf and chewed on one of Frank's last few biscuits as he waited for it to stew.

Staring into the flames, he wondered what stories Frank and his offsider would be telling now. It had been a risk to approach them, but with no water or food he'd had no other option. No doubt the townsfolk of Morgan's Reach would be on the alert for a stranger passing through – and that had to be avoided at all cost. But it wouldn't be so hard; it was well off the beaten track, and he knew the lie of the land that surrounded it.

He poured the billy tea into his tin cup and breathed in the fragrant steam as his thoughts turned to the man whose identity he'd used for that brief encounter with Frank.

John Miller had been a good mate, and they'd shared the rigours of training, the terrors of jungle warfare and the deprivations of the camp. But John had not survived the starvation, the beatings and the repeated bouts of malaria, and he'd been buried in the makeshift cemetery behind the camp's bamboo huts.

He finished the tea and rolled a smoke, then lay back on his coat, his head resting on the kitbag. There had been too many deaths – too many young men like John whose families had been left bereft by their passing – and he knew without a doubt that his own family had suffered when they'd received the dreaded telegram.

But in the confusion and chaos of war mistakes had inevitably been made, and it was only because Dr Philips had been an understanding man that he'd agreed to keep his survival a secret from the authorities. Better for the family to mourn him and continue to receive his army pension than to be faced with a walking dead man and have to go through losing him again.

He threw the last of his cigarette into the fire and damped down the flames by kicking dust over them. Pulling his coat round him, he tugged his hat over his face and closed his eyes so he could conjure up the images of those he loved.

The thought of home soothed the ache in his belly that always seemed to be with him now and, as sleep claimed him, the lines of weariness and pain were softened in a smile.

The fire raced across the mulga scrub and through the parched detritus that littered the forest floor. Driven by the hot wind, it feasted on the carcasses of dead animals, gobbled up the termite-ridden wood of shepherds' huts and makeshift shelters and headed inexorably north-west. Towards the distant pinpricks of light that came from Carey Downs Station.

But there were two rivers of fire – and the second was rapidly spreading the other way, north-east to where Morgan's Reach huddled in the valley beneath Eagle Rock.

9

The wooden cabin was cosy in the flickering light of the lanterns Max had placed around the single room. The atmosphere was in sharp contrast to the fury of the storm which raged outside, for the wind howled and rattled the shutters, the thunder drummed in the rafters and, as the lightning sizzled all around them, the dust and debris hit the outer walls with all the force of machine-gun bullets.

As a rule Sal loved storms, but this one was right overhead and, as she finished washing the pots and tidying up after supper, she felt suddenly very vulnerable. One strike of lightning could start a fire in the dry tinder on the forest floor and they would be trapped. For the first time in her life she wished she was in Morgan's Reach, where there was at least a remote chance of escaping.

She looked across at Max, seeking comfort and reassurance, but in that single glance she realised his fear was far greater than any that possessed her.

Max was huddled into the corner of the couch, his face ashen, his eyes haunted as he ignored the whining dog and shivered and cringed at every crash of thunder and clatter of shutter.

Sal swiftly crossed the room and drew him into a tight embrace. 'It's all right,' she said above the awful noise. 'The storm will pass soon.'

He clung to her as the dog continued to whine and paw at his leg. 'The noise,' he moaned. 'I can't stand the noise. Make it stop. Please make it stop.'

She drew him closer, feeling the tremors run through him as he clutched at her and buried his face in her neck. She didn't know what to say or what to do, for Max had always been so calm, so at ease with his solitude and his surroundings. He'd been her rock, her steadfast mentor and friend – the only man she'd ever truly loved. And now he was like a terrified child, fighting demons that only he could see.

Yet his vulnerability strengthened her, made her forget her own terrors in her need to soothe him. 'It will pass,' she murmured into his hair. 'Soon it will be all over and—'

'That's what they said back in 1914,' he gasped as a particularly loud crash of thunder shook the very foundations of the cabin. 'All over before Christmas. But it went on and on and on . . .' He curled into her, his strong fingers digging in, his whole body trembling. 'They're coming,' he rasped. 'I can hear the guns – the mortar fire – the screams of the dying in the mud. Oh, God, have mercy.'

Sal felt her own hot tears course down her face as she held the terrified man and tried to imagine the scenes that must be playing in his mind as the thunder continued to rock the very earth beneath the little cabin. She knew so little of his past, but those few words had given her some idea of what must be haunting him. Max was of an age to have been in the so-called 'war to end all wars'. Had he been on the front line at Gallipoli and Ypres – a witness to the horrors of the trenches like so many young Australians of his generation?

Wherever he'd been, it was clear he was reliving something so terrible it was sending him to the very edge of sanity. And she didn't have the words to comfort him, had no experience of dealing with such crippling terror. All she could do was hold him, and pray that the storm would soon be over.

Ben had given up trying to keep watch from the tower. Now it was dark it was impossible to see anything through the heavy clouds and the swirling dust.

He'd settled in an easy chair by the two-way, but found he couldn't relax. The night was too wild, the storm too ferocious to sleep or read – or even make something to eat from his depleted store. At least the weather would keep Danny and Billy at home but, come tomorrow, Ben knew he would have to tell Becky about the camp they'd made in the caves.

The static from the radio was accompanied by the howl of the wind, the deep mutters of thunder and sharp lightning cracks. For once the homesteaders weren't cluttering up the radio channels with their usual chatter, but that empty crackling hiss was almost as unnerving as the fury raging overhead.

He was contemplating making a cup of tea and a mutton sandwich when something came through the static. The voice was faint, and at first he thought he'd imagined it, but as he tweaked the dials and listened hard, he realised he'd not been mistaken.

'I hear you, Jake,' he shouted above the howling wind. 'What's the news?'

'No sign of the twins or their father,' he replied, his voice sharpening and fading through the static. 'But the road train's in, and will be here at least until this storm dies down. I've put in your usual order with Annie, but if you want anything else you'll have to come in.'

'Thanks, mate. I would appreciate it if you could get up here tomorrow though. Can't go without sleep much longer.'

'Too right. Will come up as soon as possible.'

'How's Django doing?'

'Still crook, but on the mend. Should be right by morning.'

They exchanged a few more words and broke the connection, aware that the storm could be causing havoc out in the Never-Never, and someone might be trying to get through.

For want of anything better to do, Ben sauntered into the kitchen area and started to make a pot of tea – he couldn't face the coffee which was stale and bitter, but he needed something to keep him awake.

He'd just finished making his sandwich when the static was interrupted again. 'This is Wilga Station calling. You there, Ben?'

He hurried to the radio, his mouth suddenly dry, his pulse picking up a beat. 'Yes, Dad. What is it?'

'Couple of my trackers found them boys,' he replied. 'Bloody young fools got lost on the tracks and ended up driving into a ditch. Bloody lucky they weren't killed.'

'Do they need medical assistance?'

'They'll be right,' he drawled. 'Which is more than I can say for the car. We'll keep 'em here until the storm blows over.'

'How's it going out there?'

'Wind, dust and electric storm. We've battened down the hatches, and the last of the cattle we could reach were brought into the pens. Any still left on the plains will just have to get on with it. Over and out.'

After contacting Jake about the twins, he drank his tea and chewed on the sandwich. Mrs Baker would rest easier tonight knowing they were safe. As for the reverend, he would have to take his chances along with Bob's scrub cattle.

Becky was exhausted. It was barely seven o'clock, but it had been a long fraught day, and by the look of the weather, they were in for an even more tempestuous night.

'I don't see why I can't go home,' said Gwyneth crossly. 'The animals need feeding and . . .'

'You'll stay where you are,' Becky replied firmly. 'Terence and Danny are seeing to the animals, and you need to stop talking and rest that leg.' She took her grandmother's hand. 'It really is for the best, Gran,' she said with a soft smile, 'and Mum, Terry and I are sharing the night shift, so you'll have company if you need it.'

Gwyneth grunted and flapped her hand towards the clattering shutters. 'I shan't sleep with all that racket going on,' she muttered.

Becky gave her a glass of water and two tablets. 'These will ease the pain and help you sleep,' she said. She waited as her grandmother swallowed the pills and then kissed her cheek. 'Goodnight, Gran. I'll see you in the morning.'

Gwyneth slid down the pillows, pulled the sheet to her chest and closed her eyes, but Becky could tell from her expression that, despite her grumbling, she was glad not to be out in this awful weather, but safe and snug in her comfortable bed, the pills already beginning to work on the pain.

Turning off the light, Becky left the door ajar and went along the veranda to check on Mary and her new baby daughter. The entire family was asleep on the floor surrounding her bed, the small, smoky fire still smouldering in the tin tray. No one stirred as she tiptoed between them to take a peek at the baby.

The little mite was sleeping soundly in the cot, wrapped like a chrysalis in a white sheet, her tiny lips moving as if at the breast, her fists bunched sweetly beneath her chin.

With a smile of contentment, Becky turned away and headed back to the ward. The day might not have started well, but it had not been all bad. There was a new life to celebrate, Sandra had proved to be far more efficient than she'd ever expected, and the Harper sisters had shown some charity for Charley's poor mongrel by taking him home with them.

No doubt it would be locked in the outhouse, well away from their silly little lapdog, but at least he would be well fed and out of the storm until Charley was able to go home.

Jane was sitting at the desk in the middle of the ward, the light from the small lamp spilling over the paperwork. She looked up and gave Becky a weary smile. 'As if we didn't have enough to do, Jake's asked me to fill this lot in so he can do a full report on the state of the pub and the effects of Bert's cooking,' she said with a sigh.

Becky looked around the ward and out through the door to the crowded veranda where the men were talking or reading old newspapers. 'They all seem fairly settled and on the mend,' she said. 'Why don't you come back with me and have a rest for a couple of hours?'

Jane's blue eyes widened. 'And leave this lot to their own devices? Becky, really. You know as well as I that the minute I turn my back someone will be off to fetch enough beer to sink a battleship. Then it'll be games of two-up, followed by a fight.' She grinned despite her weariness. 'That lot are worse than a bunch of troublesome monkeys, and need watching at all times. I'll stay here until Terence comes back.'

Becky kissed her. 'I'll tell him to come over the minute he's had his tea,' she promised. 'See you later.'

As she reached the outer screen door that shielded the front veranda from the worst of the weather, she put her cardigan over her head and battled against the wind to get to the house.

The lightning was flashing, turning the small settlement into a series of sepia snapshots as the hot wind whipped up the stinging dust and bent the trees. The rusting sails on the windmill were clanking and squealing at the onslaught, and anything that wasn't tied down tightly was caught up in the maelstrom and carried away into the darkness.

Having narrowly missed being hit by wooden crate that had

come bowling out of nowhere, she pushed through the screen to the homestead veranda with a sense of utter relief at having made it safely. Removing the cardigan, she took a deep breath. She felt battered and bruised, and every aching part of her seemed to be coated in red grains of abrasive sand.

Shaking out the cardigan, she ran her fingers through her gritty hair and opened the inner screen door, which led into the heart of the house. She would have a quick bath and then eat before snatching a few hours sleep and going back on the ward. But as she stepped into the living room she came to an abrupt halt and all her plans for the evening fled.

Sandra was alone in the untidy kitchen. Surrounded by unwashed pots and dishes, she sat at the table in her dressing gown, a bottle of whisky and a glass before her.

Becky dropped the cardigan on the nearby couch and slowly approached the table, noting with relief that the bottle had yet to be opened. She sat down opposite her sister-in-law and folded her hands in her lap. 'It's been a long, trying day, hasn't it?' she began.

Sandra nodded, but her concentration was fixed on the bottle before her.

'You and Terry undoubtedly saved Mary's life, and that of her baby. That alone must make you realise just how good a nurse you are – and just how much we need you here.'

Sandra's gaze drifted up to meet Becky's. 'Not good enough to save my own baby,' she said flatly. 'Go away, Becky.'

'I'm not going anywhere until you decide what you're going to do about that whisky,' she replied firmly.

Sandra shrugged and her gaze returned to the bottle as her hands fidgeted on the table. 'It's none of your business,' she muttered. 'If I want a drink, then I'll have one.'

'Go on then. Open the bottle. Fill the glass and gulp it down. But before you do,' she added quietly, her hand reaching for those nervy fingers, 'think how well you've managed without it since you left Sydney. You don't need it, Sandra. You've already proved that today.'

'What do you know?' she retorted, her expression one of mixed emotions. 'It helps me to forget. Stops the pain.'

'But only for such a short while,' said Becky, her soft heart going out to this poor tortured young woman who seemed so lost and alone.

'It's better than nothing,' she retorted.

'Is it? Then what are you waiting for?' She squeezed the twitching fingers. 'I think you're already having doubts, aren't you? You know that if you open that bottle you'll be giving in – and you're stronger than that, Sandra.'

Becky's gaze never left Sandra, who was clearly battling with the temptation of the whisky and the knowledge that one sip of that drink would send her back on the slippery path she'd begun to slowly and painfully conquer.

Sandra seemed aware of her scrutiny, and she snatched her hands from Becky's grasp and tightly clasped them in her lap. 'I'm not strong at all,' she stuttered, the tears glistening on her lashes. 'I'm weak, and a failure – a failed mother, wife and nurse. You don't understand,' she murmured as she dashed away the tears and tried to remain in control. 'Nobody understands.'

'You're neither weak, nor a failure,' Becky replied. 'And I do understand, Sandra, really I do. When I lost Adam I thought I'd never get over it – and although it was the hardest thing I've done, I managed to come through. And you will too. I promise.'

'Easy for you to say,' she retorted. 'You can get another husband. It's not the same as losing a child.'

Becky experienced a pang of something approaching anger at this heartless response, but she knew Sandra wasn't really thinking straight, so managed to contain it. 'Of course it isn't the same,' she soothed. 'But you're not alone, Sandra. Terry is grieving too, and has to carry that awful burden of guilt at not being with you at the time.'

Sandra dipped her chin and didn't reply.

'He loves you, Sandra,' Becky continued. 'Don't push him away.' She watched the emotions flit across the tear-streaked face and knew that her words were being absorbed. 'We are your family, Sandra, and we care about you. We'll help you through this – but you have to help yourself. Why don't we put the bottle away and have a nice cup of tea instead?'

Sandra pushed back her chair, her expression obdurate. 'Don't treat me like one of your idiot patients,' she hissed. 'I'm perfectly capable of dealing with this without you or anyone else sticking their nose into my business.'

Becky was about to reply when Sandra snatched the bottle from the table, turned on her heel and marched out of the kitchen and along the passage to her bedroom, slamming the door so hard it rattled the pictures on the wall.

Becky gave a deep sigh of anguish. She'd handled the situation badly, and now Sandra would probably work her way through that damned bottle. Poor Terry. No wonder he'd needed to come home for family support.

But where on earth had she found the whisky? All the alcohol had been locked away at Gwyneth's place to ensure Sandra couldn't find it and, with the pub shut and Annie O'Halloran warned not to sell her any, Sandra must have been very enterprising to sniff it out.

Her troubled thoughts were disturbed by the slam of the screen door and the appearance of her brother and son. Danny was carrying a screeching Coco in his cage, which he deposited on the already cluttered kitchen table. Terence would have to be told about Sandra, but it would have to wait until Danny was out of the room.

'G'day,' squawked Coco as he bobbed up and down on his

perch and regarded them with a beady eye. 'Pretty boy. Ups-a-daisy.'

'The animals are all fed and locked in for the night,' said Terence through a vast yawn. 'Wally the wombat seems to have gone into hibernation under the back veranda, but Coco was kicking up such a racket we thought it best to bring him here out of the weather.

'Well, you can get the cage off the table for a start,' she said briskly. 'Lord knows how many germs he's spreading about.'

'Aw, Mum. He'll be right. Just needs a bit of company.'

Becky lifted the cage and put it on the floor. She was tired, hungry, in need of a bath and in no mood to argue. 'I see you've both had your tea,' she said, waving towards the pile of dirty dishes. 'Is there anything left in the larder?'

'Sorry, sis,' said Terence as he shed his coat and dumped it over the back of a chair. 'I meant to clean up after Dan and I sorted the animals out, but it took longer than we expected.' He opened the larder and peered inside. 'There're tins of corned beef and some onions and spuds. Want me to make you a hash? It's my speciality.' His smile was rueful as he looked back at her.

She took pity on him and shook her head. 'I'll make egg on toast after I've had a bath,' she replied. 'But don't forget you've got to relieve Mum. She's been on the go all day and needs some sleep.'

'I'll clean this lot up and get over there. No worries.' He gave a deep sigh. 'And here's me thinking I'd have a quiet, easy life as a country doctor. Is it always like this?'

She smiled back at him. 'Thankfully, no. But it's never easy, Terry, even on the quiet days – which is why Dad is so delighted you came home.'

Coco broke the solemn moment by going into his clown routine and misjudging the distance between perch and claw.

Despite her weariness, Becky giggled as the ridiculous bird

landed on his back in his water bowl with a cry of outrage and a flurry of feathers. 'You'd better put the covers over him, Danny, or he'll have us up all night,' she said.

Danny reached into the cage and coaxed Coco to clamber on to his hand. 'I'll put him in my room,' he replied, stroking the damp white feathers as the bird edged up his arm to his shoulder and began to nibble his ear.

'It's not healthy to have a parrot in your bedroom,' said Becky. 'And don't let him do that, Danny. He'll have your ear off.'

'He's never done it yet,' said Danny as Coco delicately plucked at his earlobe and brushed his sulphur crest against Danny's cheek. 'And I don't see why he can't sleep in my room. It's not as if he'll be in my bed.'

Becky gave up and went to put the kettle on the range. 'Just clean up the mess he's made on the floor, Danny, and then refill his water bowl.'

'Have you heard from Dad?' asked Terence as he made a start on the washing-up.

'He radioed in while you were over at Gran's,' she said, keeping her voice low so Danny couldn't hear. 'The little girl's badly burned, and the prognosis isn't good. Big Mac is trying his best to hold it together, but his wife, Maeve, is on the point of collapse. Dad said he'll stay until the end – it's all he can do for them.'

Terence paused in the act of scraping the plates clean. 'If only they weren't so far out we might have been able to do something. What a tragedy.'

'It wouldn't have made any difference, Terry,' she said sorrowfully. 'The burns were too extensive and too deep. You know as well as I that the shock would be enough, but with the complication of nephritis to the kidneys, there's nothing anyone could have done.'

'I'm going to bed,' said Danny, the bird still happily perched on his shoulder.

Becky looked at him in astonishment. Danny usually had to be forced into bed at the end of the day, and it was still quite early. 'Are you feeling crook?' she asked, reaching to feel if he had a temperature.

He dodged her hand and concentrated on lifting the cage. 'Nah. I just want to get Coco settled and then finish the new comic George gave me for my birthday.'

'You'll have a bath first,' she said sternly. 'I've never seen such a dusty, dirty boy.' She grabbed him before he could run off and, wary of Coco's sharp beak, planted a kiss on his grubby cheek. 'I'll come in later and turn out the light,' she murmured.

Danny looked embarrassed as he muttered goodnight and hurried off to his bedroom with bird and cage.

'He's getting a bit too old for kisses,' said Becky wistfully, 'but I can't resist doing it. To me, he's still my little boy.'

Terence finished stacking the clean dishes on the drainer, poured them both a cup of tea and joined her at the table. 'He's at a funny age,' he said. 'Give him another ten or fifteen years and he won't mind a bit.' He stirred his tea. 'Sorry about the mess. I was rather hoping Sandra would sort it out, but it looks as if she's gone to bed.'

Becky remembered and reached for his hand. 'She's certainly in the bedroom,' she said softly, 'but I doubt she's asleep.' She noted the startled look in his eyes and hurried on. 'I'm sorry, Terry, I should have told you earlier – she's found a bottle of whisky.'

'Oh, God,' he groaned. 'How the hell did she do that?'

Becky shrugged. 'All I know is she was sitting here staring at the bottle – but she hadn't opened it, Terry. She hadn't had a drink.' She squeezed his fingers in empathy. 'I tried talking to her, but she didn't want to listen, and I just hope I haven't made things worse.'

'I must go to her,' he said, scraping back his chair.

'Be careful, Terry. She's tired and emotional and not in the mood for any kind of confrontation.'

Terence nodded and traipsed out of the room and along the narrow corridor. Becky heard the click as he closed the door and hoped with all her might that Sandra had resisted opening that bottle.

He awoke to a strange stillness that was broken only by the first few croons of sleepy birds. As he opened his eyes and looked up at the canopy of dust-laden trees, he realised it was almost dawn, and that the storm had once again come to nothing.

Having slept well, he felt stronger, and if it hadn't been for the deep-rooted pain that twisted in his belly, it could have been like old times. There had been many a night spent out in the bush, sleeping in a bedroll, his saddle for a pillow, the night sounds his only companions. But there was no stock horse to carry him on the final stage of his journey, just his will to reach his goal while he still had the strength.

He washed down the doctor's pills with billy tea, chewed on a biscuit and finally clambered out of the deep ditch that had been his shelter. The forest floor was littered with freshly broken branches and twigs that had been ripped from the trees during the storm, but the creatures were already busy searching for food, Vast ants marched like soldiers from their conical hills, beetles crawled over fallen leaves and spiders were weaving intricate webs that trembled at his passing. If there had been a dew they would have sparkled like jewels, but there was no moisture in the air this morning, just dust-laden, gritty heat.

As he left the bush and headed out into the open country he found himself enfolded in the thick haze of red dust that still hung over the landscape. But as the haze shifted and shimmered, he could see the distant black basalt hills of

Morgan's Reach silhouetted on the far horizon. He was almost home.

Algernon Baker opened his eyes and stared into the yellow demonic orbs of some prehistoric spiny creature with a forked tongue and long tail.

He scooted backwards with a yelp of fright and the creature hissed furiously at him before skittering off in a puff of dust. It was only one of those lizards, he realised, but it was probably poisonous, like most things out here in this godforsaken place, so he'd had a lucky escape.

His heart was still pounding as he did his best to clean his sore, itching eyes and look round warily for any other slithering, hissing creatures. It was well known that snakes liked nothing better than to share a warm bed with a human. But it seemed the storm had sent them scurrying for safer shelter, and with a sigh of relief he took in his surroundings.

The dust was a shimmering red pall that floated all around him, but as it shifted and lazily swirled like smoke he could see no sign of a homestead – or of the tarmac road. He tried to quell the fear, but his heart was thudding painfully and he was finding it difficult to breathe, or even to think. He knew only that he was lost, and that his thirst was greater than ever.

He reached for the last water-bag and carefully rationed himself to one precious mouthful. He held it on his tongue, feeling it absorb into dry gums and cracked lips until he could no longer resist swallowing it. It might taste warm and musty, but it was nectar, and it took all his willpower not to drink more; his hands trembled as he determinedly replaced the cap. This was all he had to see him home, and although there would doubtless be boreholes and troughs along the way, he knew the mineral-rich water that came up from the depths of the earth would cause stomach cramps, sickness and diarrhoea – and he was weak already.

The sun was only now breaching the horizon, but it shed very little light through the haze, which he thought smelled strangely of wood-smoke and eucalyptus. He dismissed the idea as fanciful – an aberration due to his unfortunate circumstances and an overactive imagination.

He fumbled in his jacket pocket in search of the large white handkerchief he always carried, and tried his best to clean the grit and mucus from his eyes. The handkerchief would do to cover his mouth and nose, for the dust was making it difficult to breathe. But without his hat, there was nothing he could do about his swollen eyelids or the raw scratching every time he blinked.

Algernon balled the now-filthy handkerchief in his fist as he shifted on the stony ground and tried to stand. A gasp escaped through his cracked lips as the arrow of pain shot up his leg. The ankle he'd twisted last night had swollen, and he could barely put any weight on it. He looked down at his foot in despair, the ready tears of frustration and anguish rolling down his face. It was unfair. He didn't deserve this. Why, after everything he'd gone through, was he being punished?

He licked the tears from his lips, tasting bitter salt and grit – at least they had brought some relief to his tortured eyes, but how could he hope to find the road if he couldn't walk? He knew then that God was testing him – testing his resolve and his strength – asking him to prove himself and show what he was made of.

Algernon's pride wouldn't allow him to be defeated. He sniffed back his tears and gingerly got to his feet. The pain in his ankle was bearable, but he suspected it would worsen once he began to walk over this rough ground and in the heat the swelling would no doubt increase. He looked about him for something he could use as a walking stick. There was nothing. Just miles of unfenced emptiness, and a profound silence that seemed to worm its way to his very core.

He could see no tracks of his boots on the ground, just drifts of sand, but he was certain he had been facing north when he'd fallen. But he'd moved since then – turned and twisted to look for snakes – shifted again to take in his surroundings and hunt for something to lean on. The panic was raw as he tried desperately to think what to do.

And then it came to him, and he hastily fumbled in his pocket for his watch. Holding the dial parallel to the ground he turned it until the hour hand was pointed towards what he hoped was the rising sun. It was difficult to tell exactly where it was in the thick haze, but he was sure it didn't matter too much if he was just a bit out. He peered at the dial, saw it was four in the morning and calculated that north had to be at two o'clock.

He smiled with satisfaction as he returned the watch to his pocket and tied the handkerchief over his mouth and nose. He'd always prided himself on his ability to remember things, and that skill had been taught to him long ago by an old seaman he'd once met in Sydney docks. It had certainly come in use today. The main road couldn't be too far away now.

As Algernon hobbled painfully along the rough track he was completely ignorant of the fact that his watch had stopped – that he'd walked in a wide circle – and the glow that he'd thought was the sun was in fact the swiftly advancing bushfire. And he was heading straight towards it.

10

Sal had comforted him through the storm, and as it had passed, and Max's fears were quelled, she had finally fallen asleep in his arms.

She was now in that soft, languid half-world between sleep and wakening and was reluctant to stir from it. His warmth enfolded her, the hard length of his body stretched alongside her as she breathed in rhythm with the drum of his heart. The very nearness of him made her feel safe and cherished, and she burrowed into his embrace, her face lifted towards his yearning for the kiss that must surely come.

'Sorry, Sal, but my arm's gone dead.' Max gently disentangled himself and sat up on the sagging couch.

Disappointment surged through her and she opened her eyes. 'I was enjoying that cuddle,' she reproached him softly.

He didn't look at her, but scrubbed his face with his hands and got stiffly to his feet. 'The sun's up and the storm's passed. I have to let the dog out and see to the horses.'

Brandy was whining by the door, and Sal watched as Max picked up his walking stick and slowly crossed the room. As he opened the door the dog shot out and the light flooded in, and she could see the hobbled ponies waiting patiently by the veranda.

Feeling rejected and rather cross, Sal swung her legs off the couch and realised in horror that her blouse had slipped off her shoulder to reveal most of one naked breast, and her skirt had been hitched up to her knickers. No wonder he'd shot off like a scalded cat, she thought, the humiliation making her crosser than ever. He must think I'm a wanton tart.

She tied the drawstrings of her blouse, yanked her skirt down and got off the couch. Max had behaved like a complete gentleman, and although he must be as embarrassed as she, she wished with all her heart that he'd taken advantage of the situation. She wanted him to ravage her, to make love to her with the passion she knew he possessed – wanted to feel his hands and lips on her skin and the driving urgency of glorious, liberating sex with the man she adored.

Her hands were trembling as she reached for the coffee pot. Her senses were alive, her pulse was ragged and her body ached for fulfilment, but she knew she must pull herself together before Max returned – for if he suspected for one minute that she was in love with him, he would shy away from her. He was such a solitary man – a troubled man – and burdening him with her feelings would probably put an end to the lovely relationship they shared. And nothing must endanger that.

Having made the coffee and heated up the big pot of porridge he always had standing by the range, Sal washed quickly, found clean underwear and had her emotions under control by the time he came back into the cabin. 'I thought I'd go down to the river to paint today,' she said with studied casualness as she sat down at the table.

He concentrated on his porridge. 'There's not much to see down there,' he muttered. 'River's all but dried up.' He spooned some of the porridge into his mouth, his gaze firmly fixed on the bowl. 'Reckon it might be better if you go back to Morgan's Reach now the storm has passed over.'

She looked at him from across the table, her heart thudding. 'Don't send me away, Max,' she pleaded softly.

He looked at her then, his expression unreadable. 'Best you go,' he replied. 'With more storms due, things could get rough, and I don't want a repeat of last night.'

'But I want to stay,' she said quickly. 'I can't bear the thought of you going through all that on your own, and if I can help, even a little, then—'

'I don't need your pity, Sal,' he said sharply. 'I just want to be left alone to deal with things the way I know best.' He gave a deep sigh as he abandoned the cooling porridge. 'I'm sorry,' he mumbled, 'but I hate you seeing me like this. Go home, Sal.'

She blinked back her tears. 'There's nothing for me in Morgan's Reach, Max. I want to stay here and look after you the way you've always looked after me.' She reached for his hand, holding it firmly as he tried to pull it away. 'You know everything about me, Max, but I hardly know anything about you – and I want you to talk to me – to tear down those high barriers you've built around yourself and let me in.'

He hung his head, his silver-streaked tawny hair drifting around his face. 'You're just a girl. You wouldn't understand.'

'I'm forty-two – hardly a girl,' she said with a wry smile. 'And I want to understand. Please, Max, let me share whatever it is that troubles you.'

He drew his hand away and sat back in his chair, his hazel eyes studying her with an intensity that told her he was struggling to decide what to do. She waited, willing him to overcome his natural reticence and put his trust in her.

'I'm almost sixty,' he said eventually. 'An old man, set in my ways, half crippled and inclined to fits of blinding, overwhelming terror. I choose to live alone out here because I've come to despise the cruelties of what man can do to man. I hate their noise, their numbers and their bloodlust for war, and it's only here that I can find peace.'

Sal could see that he wasn't finding this easy, but she felt instinctively that he needed to talk, to open the floodgates on all that horror and fear he'd been holding on to so that he could be healed. 'I found peace here too,' she murmured, 'and the chance to be myself – but only because you let me into your world and gave so generously of your warmth and compassion. Now I want to give you the same chance to unburden your troubles – and I think you're ready to do that, Max. I really do.'

He bowed his head and the dog nudged his elbow and licked his hand as if it understood Max was struggling to deal with some deep and forceful emotions.

Sal watched those strong, capable fingers run over the dog's head and silky ears. She longed to be the one to comfort him, to hold him close and tell him she loved him and couldn't care less about his age or his crippled leg. But she said no more, simply waited for him to come to a decision.

The long silence stretched between them, and Sal was beginning to wonder if the struggle Max was going through had proved too hard. She was about to say something when he lifted his head and looked at her, his expression full of pain, his hazel eyes shadowed by memories.

'I was a struggling artist in 1914, working as a reporter for the *Sydney Times*. Like so many young fools I thought going to war would be an adventure – a chance to see a bit of the world, prove what a brave man I was, and come home covered in glory.'

He grimaced as he looked down at the dog and continued to fondle his ears. 'My skills meant I was sent as a war artist – to record the glorious scenes of heroic battle,' he said with heavy irony. 'Because of this I was close to every front line, every rat-infested trench and water-filled bomb crater. I saw things no man should witness, and they live with me to this day – just as the constant barrage of the guns and the gnawing fear return every time I hear a loud noise.'

He dipped his chin, his voice becoming softer as he relived those experiences. 'That fear was tangible, and touched all of us – and yet we dared not show it because it was called cowardice, punishable by firing squad.'

Sal felt the ache for him in her heart and wondered whether she was right to have insisted upon him dredging up these images – but it seemed that, once started, he couldn't stop.

'Our senses were heightened by the knowledge that every moment could be our last – that the next bomb-blast might blow us to smithereens just as it had to the mate who'd been standing right beside us. No man was safe – except for the generals who sat miles behind the lines in the safety of their comfortable billets and used their men as cannon fodder.'

Sal heard the bitterness in his voice as he continued to talk of the horrors he'd witnessed. As an artist he had the eloquence to describe the scenes with graphic clarity, but he did so with very little emotion – as if by living through it he'd had to distance himself from it to stay sane. She'd been only ten in 1914, but she'd seen the newspapers at the time and had been mature enough to be horrified by the seemingly endless lists of the dead and wounded that appeared each week. But those who returned from that war rarely spoke of what had really happened – and now she knew why.

'I was one of the lucky ones,' he said much later. 'I got what the Poms called a "Blighty wound" and was sent to England to recuperate. Flying shrapnel put paid to my calf muscle and most of my ankle, and trench foot lost me two toes. I survived the flu epidemic that killed more people than had been lost during those four terrible years, and was shipped home in 1921.'

He looked sourly down at the discarded bowl of porridge. 'I discovered that my drawings as a war artist had made me famous, and I was inundated with offers of sponsorship and exhibitions. But I didn't want any of it, so I packed my things and took to the road.'

Sal watched as the tension seemed to lift from his shoulders and his expression softened.

'I had no idea what I was searching for,' he continued. 'I knew only that I needed solitude and silence so I could put all the ugliness behind me. When I found this place I knew it offered everything I needed – and so I stayed.'

He looked back at her then and the shadows were gone from his eyes as he reached across the table for her hands. 'I treasure these rare moments we have together, Sal – and you will always be welcome. But friendship is all I can offer, my dear. Please don't expect more.'

Sal's face was burning with embarrassment. 'I don't,' she stuttered. 'I didn't . . .'

He put his finger to her lips. 'Don't deny it, Sal – your love is too precious a gift. But it is not to be wasted on a man who is incapable of returning it.'

She could feel the hot tears rolling down her face as she silently pleaded with him to take back his rejection.

'You are a beautiful, talented young woman with a great deal to give, Sal,' he said as he rose from the table and drew her to her feet. 'And a life that, as yet, is unfulfilled. Go back to Morgan's Reach, take your leave of Bert and have the courage to find your destiny. It's out there, waiting for you, Sal. You just have to believe it.'

She closed her eyes as his thumbs gently brushed away her tears. She felt the soft touch of his lips on her forehead, and leaned into him. 'Please . . .' she breathed. 'Please don't send me away.'

He moved from her and picked up his walking stick. 'It's time for both of us to face reality,' he said. 'I have work to do and you have a long drive ahead of you.' He opened the door and, before he stepped outside, turned back momentarily. 'I'll never forget you, dearest Sal. Godspeed.'

Sal stood there for a long moment after he'd closed the door. She felt abandoned and bereft as her tears blinded her – but there was finality in his words and in his demeanour that she could not ignore. And, as she stood there, the silence enfolded her as her long-held dreams shattered like fine glass.

It was some time before she could summon up the strength to gather her few clothes and stuff them in her bag. The hardest part was going into the shed at the back and collecting the paintings she'd done over the years. Each one evoked a memory – a time when they'd laughed and talked – of long, companionable silences in the surrounding beauty of this forest glade.

There was no sign of Max or his dog as she loaded everything into the ute. She gave the last of the sugar to the ponies, her tears dampening their shaggy coats as she rested her cheek against theirs and said her last goodbye. Then she climbed into the ute and, after a final, yearning look at the little shack in the woods, she drove away.

Becky had been on the brink of sleep when she'd heard Terry quietly leave the house to take over from their mother. Glancing at the bedside clock she'd been surprised he'd left so soon, but as there had been no raised voices or sign of trouble, she assumed everything was all right.

As the first rays of sun lightened the sky she clambered out of bed, and prepared for another busy day. The heat was intense despite the hour and she dressed slowly, her hair cool and damp from her bath. She was still tired despite several hours of deep sleep, and she hoped that most of the patients could be discharged today. Once Gran was back home and settled then perhaps they could all take a bit of a breather. Not that it would last for long, she thought wryly as she fastened her starched cap over her damp hair. The storm had no doubt left tons of sand everywhere and the cleaning would have to be done all over again.

She tiptoed down the hall, aware that her mother and Sandra would still be asleep, and stopped to peek into Danny's room. There was very little light coming through the curtains, but she could make out the untidy lump in the bed and the shape of the parrot cage on the table beside it. Not wanting to disturb boy or bird at this time of the morning, she closed the door and, after a hasty breakfast of toast and tea, headed for the hospital.

The dust was everywhere, lying in heaps on verandas and roofs, coating the trees and shutters and hanging in red clouds over the entire settlement. Becky sighed as she climbed the steps to discover great drifts of it along the veranda. It would take hours to clear it all away.

She was about to head for the ward when Terry emerged from the hospital kitchen looking harassed. 'Whatever's the matter?' she asked.

'Those women are worse than sergeant majors,' he muttered as he distractedly ran his fingers through his hair.

Becky grinned. 'Oh dear,' she sympathised. 'You've had a run-in with the inestimable Harpers.'

He eyed her ruefully. 'I only wanted a fried slice and an egg – and you'd have thought I was asking for the crown jewels.'

'Never mind,' she soothed. 'If you go down to Annie's she'll have most of our order waiting to be picked up. If you're lucky, you'll have bacon to go with the eggs – but be warned, one whiff of frying bacon usually has Danny at the table in double time, so you'll have to cook for him too.'

'I'll leave you to it then,' he said as he smothered a yawn. 'Sandra will be waking up soon and I want to spend a bit of time with her before I catch up on my sleep.'

'How did it go last night?'

'It didn't,' he replied, his expression hardening. 'She'd had at least half that bloody bottle and was out cold. I poured the rest out of the window and left her to sleep it off.'

'Oh, Terry,' she sighed. 'I am sorry.'

'Yeah, so am I.' He gave her a wan smile. 'I'd better go and get those supplies before she wakes up. Sandra's inclined to get edgy when she's hungover, and I don't want Mum to have to deal with it.'

'But you need to rest, Terry,' she protested.

'How can I when she's likely to go off hunting for more booze?'

'Send her over here,' said Becky rather briskly. 'There's plenty to keep her occupied, and we can keep an eye on her at the same time.'

He gave a great sigh of relief. 'Thanks, Becks, you're a star.'

She watched as he hurried down the street towards the general store. Poor Terry – he was clearly at his wits' end to know what to do about Sandra, and if she discovered who the hell had given her that damned whisky, they'd get the sharp end of her tongue. She turned away and went into the ward, her carefully set smile belying her inner turmoil.

The men were definitely feeling better. They were all awake and grumbling about the lateness of their breakfast and the lack of a decent cup of tea. She was about to go to the kitchen to see what had caused the delay when Sarah and her sister entered the ward pushing clattering trolleys loaded with plates and vast tin teapots. As the native girls handed out the food and poured the tea, Becky left them to it and went to look in on her grandmother.

Gwyneth was also awake, her hair standing on end, her expression determined as she struggled to pull her clean trousers on over the thick bandage.

171

Becky rushed to her side. 'Let me help you, Gran,'

'You'll do no such thing,' she said through her tightly bound jaw. 'The last time someone dressed me I was five. Go and find something sensible to do and leave me be.'

'But it's silly to struggle when—'

'Go,' she said fiercely.

Becky knew when she was beaten. 'I'll go if you promise to eat your breakfast first and not try to walk home on your own,' she said sternly.

Gwyneth gave a deep sigh of aggravation and mumbled something under her breath which Becky suspected was none too polite.

Becky handed her the clean blouse which lay on a nearby chair and closed the door behind her. Gran was as obstinate and independent as a mule, and she wouldn't put it past her to make a bid for freedom the minute she was dressed – but short of actually locking her in, there wasn't much she could do about it.

The answer came in the bustling form of Louise Harper, who was approaching with a tray laden with porridge and scrambled egg – Gwyneth was on a strict soft-food diet. 'And how is Gwyneth this morning?' she asked cheerfully.

'Fighting fit,' she replied.

Louise's little face creased with concern. 'Oh dear,' she sighed. 'That usually bodes trouble. Is there anything I can do?'

Becky smiled. 'It would help if you kept an eye on her until I can walk her home,' she replied.

'Well, all right,' she said hesitantly, 'but you know what she's like, Rebecca, so don't leave it too long.'

Becky smiled and opened the door for her. 'Thanks, Louise,' she murmured. 'I'll be back as soon as I can.'

It didn't take long to discover that Mary and her family had already left for their tumbledown shack on the outskirts of town – which meant that Becky would have to go over there later to make sure she was keeping her cut foot clean and that the baby was all right.

But it would also give her a chance to hold an impromptu clinic to treat the sandy blight which seemed to affect most of the children and elderly there. Brought on by the dust, lack of hygiene and the ever-present sandflies, it was a painful affliction and often caused blindness if not treated properly with warm saline solution and special eye-drops.

It took quite a while for Becky to do the rounds of the ward and the other verandas, and to check on the men, who were voraciously eating their breakfast. As they all seemed perfectly well, she told them they could leave once they'd finished their meal, and then went back to Gwyneth.

'I'm perfectly capable of walking across the street,' she grumbled as Becky helped her down the steps a while later.

'I know you are, but just humour me, Gran.'

Gwyneth muttered under her breath and leaned heavily on her walking stick as she kept her weight off her damaged leg. 'I suppose you'll be wanting a cup of tea?' she said ungraciously as they finally reached her back veranda.

'I'd love one, but I really don't have the time,' Becky replied as her offer of help was refused and Gwyneth hauled herself up the steps and slammed through the outer fly-screen door.

'Ups-a-daisy, old girl,' shouted Coco from his cage. 'G'day, g'day.'

Gwyneth checked on the joeys in their pillowcases, sank into one of the rattan chairs and looked at the drifts of sand that were strewn across her garden and veranda. 'I see by the footprints in the dust that Danny has been over to look after the animals,' she said grudgingly. 'Tell him to come back this afternoon and I'll give him a couple of bob for his trouble.'

Becky nodded. 'I'll ask him to fetch your grocery order at the same time.'

Gwyneth's tone was thoughtful as she scooped a handful of seeds out of a nearby tin and filled Coco's bowl. 'It's good to see he's come to his senses at last,' she commented. 'Let's hope that's an end to it.' Her sharp gaze fell on her granddaughter. 'I suppose you'd better ask Ben round here for his tea,' she said briskly. 'If he's going to be a part of this family, then I want to get a proper look at him and make sure he's as reliable as his father.'

Becky shuddered at the prospect. Gwyneth was daunting at the best of times, but when she played the family matriarch to the hilt, she was impossible. 'Perhaps it would be better to leave it a bit,' she said hastily. 'He's very busy at the moment.'

She pushed through the screen door and, with a muttered promise to come back later, fled to the sanctuary of the hospital.

The ward and veranda were empty when she returned, but for Bert, who was refusing to leave his bed. He sat with his arms folded, his expression belligerent as Becky took his temperature and declared him fit to go home.

'Yeah? And how's that then?' he whined. 'Jake's shut me pub. I ain't got no home – and I still ain't feeling well.' He screwed up his face and rubbed his midriff. 'Me belly hurts something rotten.'

Becky was about to reply when Enid Harper appeared with a bucket of soapy water, a rubber tube and a suction pump. The expression on the older woman's face was one of determination and not to be dismissed lightly. 'If you're not well enough to go home, Bert,' she said in her strident voice, 'then you obviously need an enema. Roll on to your side and pull down your pyjamas.'

'You ain't coming near me with that thing,' he gasped in horror, clutching the sheet to his chin as he edged away from her.

'Come along now, don't be shy,' she boomed as she continued to advance on him, the rubber tube dangling from her hand. 'A good enema will sort things out, and you'll be feeling better in no time.'

'Reckon I was mistaken,' he gabbled, swinging out of bed and grabbing his clothes. 'Must have been that breakfast making me feel crook.'

Enid Harper watched with gimlet eyes as he hastily dragged his clothes on over his pyjamas and clamped his hat over his thinning hair. 'Well,' she said sternly, 'if you're sure.'

He darted round her, his gaze fixed on the dangling rubber hose and the bucket. Without another word he was out of the hospital and almost running down the street.

'Nothing like the threat of an enema to sort out malingerers,' said Enid with a smile of satisfaction. 'Right, now we've got rid of him, let's get on with cleaning up this hospital. The whole place looks like a sand dune – most unhygienic.'

Becky was grinning as she stripped the last of the beds and carried the linen into the laundry. They'd broken the mould when Enid and Louise had been made – but then it seemed that their generation of women was born tough and indomitable, and Morgan's Reach would not be the same without them.

Sandra was still in her nightclothes as she smoked one cigarette after another and flicked through an old magazine. She had been moody and restless all morning, and Jane was worried enough about Hugh without having to deal with her daughter-in-law's self-inflicted hangover and sullen expression.

She was on the point of telling the girl to either get stuck into some work about the place or come with her to the hospital when the call came in on the two-way.

'G'day, Jane.' The drawling voice came down the crackling line. 'This is Don Warrington out at Gilburn Station. One of me drovers has had a bit of a run-in with a bull. I tried the Flying Doctor but he's gone up to Borroloola, and the spare plane's out of action cos of last night's storm. Reckon we might need a bit of help.'

Jane closed her eyes and took a deep breath. 'Hugh's already out, but my son Terence is here. Is the injured man at the homestead?'

'Nah, he's out near Blackman's Creek. One of the trackers rode in this morning to tell me. I'll send him down to the main road to wait for Terence and show him the way.'

'Can't you bring him in?'

'Reckon he wouldn't last if we moved him,' he replied. 'The bull's horn ripped him in the belly. Would appreciate it if Terence could get here quick.'

'I'll arrange it now.'

'Terry's asleep,' said Sandra as she flung the magazine aside and stubbed out her cigarette in the overflowing ashtray. 'And I need him here. Why can't you go?'

Jane kept hold of her temper and eyed her daughter-in-law with little affection. 'I'm not a doctor, and if you could see what a bull can do with its horns, you would understand why that poor man's needs are far more urgent than yours.'

Sandra blinked at the sharpness of her tone. 'Terry's exhausted,' she said. 'And the weather's closing in again. It wouldn't be safe.'

Jane didn't even bother to reply as she headed for their bedroom and tapped on the door before going in. 'I'm sorry, Terry,' she said as she gently shook him awake. 'You're needed out at Gilburn Station.'

He groaned and sat up, his eyes bleary with sleep, his chin dark with stubble. 'What's happened?'

Jane gave him the details. 'I'll make some strong coffee while you get dressed,' she finished. She hurried back to the kitchen to find Sandra had already started on the coffee. 'Could you do some sandwiches as well while I go and pack his medical bag and check on the fuel in the . . .'

She let out a groan as she remembered Hugh had taken the hospital utility. 'He'll have to borrow mine,' she said. 'At least its fuelled up and there's emergency equipment and a stretcher already stowed in the back.'

Terence came into the kitchen still looking bedraggled, and Jane left hurriedly to fetch his bag from the hospital.

'I don't think you should go,' said Sandra, buttering rounds of bread and slapping thick slices of cold tinned meat between them. 'The weather's turning nasty again and you—'

He gulped down the scalding coffee. 'The man could be dying,' he said flatly. 'Bad weather or not, I have to go to him.'

'But it's dangerous,' she persisted, the tears shining in her eyes. 'Please, Terry, don't leave me.'

He finished the cup of coffee and poured the rest of the pot into a thermos flask before wrapping the sandwiches in a sheet of waxed paper and dropping them into the pocket of his jacket which he slung over his arm. 'I'll be back as soon as I can,' he said. 'Until then it wouldn't do you any harm to get dressed and lend Mum and Becky a hand.'

She folded her arms and looked sullen. 'So what I want doesn't matter?'

He reached for his bush hat and planted it over his tangled hair. 'It would if you weren't hungover and feeling sorry for yourself,' he said. 'Sort yourself out, Sandra,' he encouraged her, as he gave her the briefest peck on the cheek.

Before she could reply he'd opened the screen door and run down to meet his mother, who was loading his medical bag and a pile of clean blankets and sheets into her dusty ute.

'I'll radio in when I can,' he assured her after he'd checked the cans of fuel and water in the back.

'You take care out there,' said Jane. 'And don't worry about Sandra. I'll see she's right.' She stepped back as Terence reversed the utility out of the driveway and disappeared in a cloud of dust down the track which led to the main road.

'You don't have to worry about me,' said Sandra, who'd come to watch from the doorstep. 'I'm perfectly capable of looking after myself.'

'I'm sure you are,' said Jane briskly, 'and I certainly have more to worry about than a silly girl with a hangover. Get dressed, Sandra, and put all that wasted energy into something useful.'

Sandra folded her arms tightly about her waist and glared in defiance.

Jane returned that glare, determined not to back down. When Sandra gave a deep sigh and padded back into the house, Jane knew she'd won this short tussle of wills. But she also knew it was just the start of what could be a long drawn-out battle – not made any easier by the fact that Hugh and Terence were away and the weather was unreliable. She could only pray there were no more emergencies, and that they both returned safely.

The heat had risen all morning and the clouds were dark and tinged with red from the dust that still floated in the breathless air. Becky had enlisted the help of Django's brothers as well as Sarah's sister and some of Mary's older boys, and together they had shifted numerous wheelbarrows of sand from the floors and tipped them outside. No doubt it would be blown back in when the wind picked up, but that was just one of the vagaries of living out here and they were all inured to the inconvenience.

Becky had pulled the broad white blinds down over the verandas after Terry had driven away, and was sitting in the shade drinking a well-earned cup of tea when her mother appeared with a rather sullen-looking Sandra. 'You timed that well,' she said cheerfully. 'We've just finished.'

Jane's answering smile was wan. 'I'm sure I've shifted enough of that stuff to earn one day off,' she replied. 'When are you going to visit Mary and her baby? Only I thought Sandra might like to go along with you. I'm assuming you'll be running an eye clinic while you're there.'

By the look on her face Becky wasn't at all sure that Sandra wanted to do any such thing – or even if she wanted the woman with her, but she was careful not to let her doubts show. 'I'd be glad of the help,' she said instead. 'We'll be leaving in about half an hour.' She looked back at her mother. 'Have you seen Danny at all?'

'He went out early to sort out Gwyneth's animals,' said Sandra, 'and came back for breakfast. I haven't seen him since.'

'I saw him cycling past the house about two hours ago,' said Jane. 'He's probably up at the caves, or with Billy at the shacks. I shouldn't worry, Becky – he'll be home the minute he gets hungry again.'

Becky accepted that her mother was probably right and, as Danny had been behaving like any other little boy since his birthday, she wasn't unduly concerned. 'Well, if you see him while we're away, tell him Granny Gwyn has a couple of bob for him.'

'You're very careless with that boy of yours,' snapped Sandra. 'He disappears for hours and could be in all sorts of trouble, for all you know.'

Becky didn't rise to the bait. 'We might seem careless to you, Sandra,' she said evenly, 'but Danny is an Outback boy, and as knowledgeable about this place as any city urchin is of the streets of Sydney. Mum's right. He'll come home when he's ready.'

'Well, it all seems very slapdash,' Sandra retorted. 'If he was my boy, I'd want to know where he was, what he was up to and who he was with.'

Becky didn't see why she should justify her way of raising Danny to anyone, but it was her mother who brought the awkward conversation to an end. 'We do things differently out here,' she said pleasantly. 'Gwyneth raised her six children the same way as we did Terence and Becky. None of them came to any harm, and they grew up independent and resourceful – just as Danny will.'

Becky decided to change the subject. 'Come on, Sandra, you can help me put together everything I'm going to need for the eye clinic, and then we can get on before the weather closes in again.'

They were about to clamber into Becky's ancient utility when the roar of an approaching truck stilled them. 'That'll be Ben,' said Becky in delight as she hastily shut the ute's door against the dust he was kicking up.

He drew up beside them, red clouds billowing in his wake. 'I managed to get away for a few minutes while Jake minds the two-way,' he said as he jumped from the driver's cab. He tipped his hat at Sandra, but his warm smile was for Becky. 'I hear you've had quite a go down here,' he said.

'It's been interesting,' she replied, her face glowing with the pleasure of seeing him. They were only half aware of Sandra moving away to the shade of the veranda as they drew closer and looked into one another's eyes. 'I've missed you,' Becky murmured.

'I've missed you too,' he replied, his finger softly tracing the curve of her cheek and jaw. 'D'you reckon we could find a bit of time to ourselves once things get back to normal?'

She smiled up at him, loving the warmth in his eyes, the tilt of his lips and the yearning in his expression. 'Have you ever known normal to happen around here?' she teased him. 'But once Dad and Terry get back, and these storms blow themselves out, I reckon we might just manage some quiet time.'

His expression suddenly grew solemn and he scuffed his boot into the dirt. 'Becky, there's another reason why I came to see you,' he began.

She felt a stab of unease. 'What's the matter?'

'Well,' he said, his hesitance clear, 'it's probably nothing to really worry about, but I thought you should know.'

Her pulse began to race. 'Know what?' she asked sharply.

'Danny and Billy Blue have made some sort of camp in the caves.'

She laughed with relief. 'Is that all? I thought for a minute it must be something really serious.' She smiled up at him. 'I'm sure you made camps up there as a boy – I know Terry did. I shouldn't let it bother you.'

He still looked decidedly uneasy. 'I wouldn't usually take much notice, but this camp's a bit out of the ordinary,' he said in a rush.

He must have seen how her smile slipped and her eyes became wary, for he cleared his throat and hurried on, 'It's not a camp to play in, Becky. They've left bedding and food, made up a fire and . . . and left a note.'

Her mouth dried and her heart thudded painfully. 'What note?'

He pulled the folded paper from his shirt pocket and, after a momentary hesitation, handed it to her.

Danny's best hand-writing was in brightly coloured crayon and it filled the single page that had been torn from an exercise book.

This camp is for the soldier John Miller. If you want anything else we will be coming up every day. Please wait until we can talk to you. Yours sincerely,
Danny Morgan and Billy Blue.

She gave the note back and realised her hand was shaking. 'I wondered if all that talk about the mysterious stranger would affect him. But why make him a camp – why do they want to talk to him?'

She looked up at Ben, her eyes widening as an awful possibility dawned on her. 'Surely he doesn't think it's his father?' she breathed.

Ben shook his head and took her hands. 'Deep down, I'm sure he knows it's not,' he said. 'But he's a bright and inquisitive boy, Becky, always asking me and Jake about the war. I think it helps him to understand what happened to Adam, and I'm sure that's all he wants from this bloke.'

'Oh, God,' she breathed, 'I'd hoped he'd stopped all this talk of war. It's as if he's obsessed by it.'

'I'm sorry to trouble you like this, Becky, but I thought you'd want to know.'

She pulled herself together and stood on tiptoe to kiss his cheek. 'Thanks, Ben,' she murmured. 'You did the right thing. I'll talk to him tonight and try to make him understand that accosting strange men in caves is not the best idea. None of us knows who this John Miller is, or what he's doing wandering about in the bush.'

'I've got Jake on the case,' he assured her. 'He's put out a call to all stations to look out for Miller, but the man's probably harmless.'

'War does strange things to people,' she said. 'He could be up to anything.'

'I'll come back tonight and have a talk with Danny and Blue if that would help.'

'It would, thank you.' She smiled wanly back at him. 'What would I do without you, Ben?'

He brushed her forehead with his lips. 'I'm not planning on going anywhere,' he said softly, 'so I reckon we'll see this through together.' He reluctantly pulled away from her. 'I've got to get back, darlin', but if you need me, just call.'

'Will you keep an eye on the caves and send him home if he turns up there?

He nodded and tugged down his hat-brim. 'No worries. I'll do that.'

Sandra slowly descended the veranda steps and came to stand beside her as Ben drove back up the street and disappeared in a swirl of dust. 'Now that's what I call a real dish.' She sighed appreciatively. 'I hope you realise how lucky you are, Becky. Most girls would give their right arm to have a man like that chasing after them.'

Becky thought of her handsome, clever, sweet brother, who loved Sandra despite the nightmare she was putting him through, and had to bite down on a bitter retort. She opened the utility's door and climbed in. 'It's getting late,' she said flatly. 'If we don't leave now we won't have time to run the clinic and get back before dark.'

Ben quickly drove to all the places he used to haunt when he was a boy, but there was no sign of Danny or Billy, and none of the other kids had seen them either. Not that there were many about, for most of them lived on the stations and were kept busy helping out through the school holidays.

He had an idea and returned to town, stopping at Emily's little cottage beside the schoolhouse. She would often organise things during the holidays to keep the younger children occupied, and he was hoping the boys might be with her.

Ben had known Emily since he was a boy; she was the daughter of one of the northern station managers and had come to teach at Morgan's Reach during the war. She was on the plump side, with dark hair, brown eyes and the sweetest disposition. He found her hard at work in the kitchen, cooking up something that smelled delicious.

She pushed back her long hair from her forehead with the back of a floury hand and smiled at him as he came through the screen door. 'G'day, Ben. This is a surprise. I was expecting Jake.'

'Sorry, Em, he's up on lookout, but he won't be long.' He smiled back at her. 'Something smells good,' he murmured appreciatively. 'Jake's a lucky bloke.'

She flushed with pleasure and dipped her chin as she continued to knead the bread dough. 'My mum always said that the way to a man's heart is through his stomach,' she said shyly. 'Was there something you wanted, Ben?'

'I'm trying to track down Danny and Billy,' he said, his gaze falling on a batch of iced fairy cakes.

'They were here earlier,' she replied, handing him two of the little treats. 'Said they were going up to the caves and did I have any spare cake.' She smiled up at him. 'That's the second batch today. They took half the other one.'

'About what time was this?' he asked through a mouthful of deliciously light sponge and lemon icing.

She shrugged plump shoulders and wiped her hands on the apron which covered her cotton dress. 'About ten or eleven, I think.' She frowned. 'Why?'

'No real reason,' he replied carefully. 'I just wondered where they'd got to.'

She raised a fine dark brow and eyed him thoughtfully. 'I know Danny has a habit of going walkabout, Ben – but most boys do. He'll turn up, no worries.'

Ben plucked another cake from the plate, dodged her playful slap and left her to her cooking. As he headed for the utility truck he looked up at the darkening sky. It was unbearably hot, the clouds low and thunderous, the atmosphere heavy with menace. Flies buzzed and flitted about his face, but the only other sound he could hear was the rasp of his own boots on the gravel as he approached the truck and climbed into the furnace of the cab.

Slamming the door on the flies, he drove down the street, collected his boxes of supplies from Annie's and then headed for the relative shelter of the surrounding bush.

The engine whined and the cans and spare parts rattled in the back alongside the boxes of supplies as he negotiated the steep winding track to the top of the hill and finally pulled up by Eagle Rock. The cloud was thicker up here, clinging to the tops of the trees in a dark mist of red and grey and black.

He carefully clambered down to the caves and switched on the torch. The camp looked unchanged, but he saw there were four of Emily's little cakes tucked into a tin box alongside the rather stale bread, and another note which was similarly worded to the first.

He stood and thought about what he should do, and then decided he was probably making something out of nothing. He would keep an eye on the cave and, if John Miller did show up, then he'd have a talk with him and find out exactly what he was up to.

Returning to the house with the boxes of supplies, he found Jake and Django playing poker on the kitchen table as the hiss of static came through on the two-way. 'You'd better get down to Emily,' he said as he dumped the boxes on the side and beat the dust out of his hat. 'She's cooking something special for your tea, you lucky old bastard.'

Jake folded his hand of cards with studied nonchalance. 'Some of us have got it, and some ain't,' he said. 'Never mind, mate,' he added with a grin, 'not everyone's blessed with my good looks and charm.'

Ben and Django burst out laughing and threw the cards at him.

Jake shook his head good-naturedly and rammed on his hat as he headed for the door. 'Django will keep you company while I enjoy the comforts of the lovely Emily. Catch you poor saps later.'

Ben was still laughing as he pulled a bottle of beer out of the kerosene fridge. After he'd swallowed the first cold mouthful he began to relax. 'How you going, Django?'

He grinned, showing large yellow teeth, his face creasing as deeply as a dried prune. 'Bellyache all gone, boss. No alonga eat Bert's meat pie.'

Ben was about to reply when the two-way crackled into life. 'This is Jim Rider from Wallaby Creek Homestead calling Morgan's Reach fire chief. You there, Ben?'

Ben's mouth dried as he heard the note of panic and swiftly connected the call. 'I'm here, Jim.'

'We've got a bit of a situation out here, mate,' he drawled. 'Fire's broke out to the south of us and coming fast. It's a big bugger all right – gunna need every hand you can muster.'

11

Carey Downs was in mourning. The little girl had died in the night and, as Hugh had drawn the sheet over the tiny still figure, her mother had finally collapsed with grief. Big Mac's expression told of his own profound distress, but he'd squared his jaw and gently lifted Maeve from the bedside and carried her to the privacy of their bedroom.

Hugh had signed the death certificate as the wind howled around the house and the dust veiled the dawn. The sound of the other children crying and the mournful wails of the Aboriginal women who'd set up a vigil on the back veranda had merely deepened his depression. Big Mac's family had owned Carey Downs for five generations. They were the salt of the earth, tough and fearless, inured to the harsh conditions and all too familiar with the tragedies that could befall those living in such isolation. He knew he couldn't have done more – he'd known the child would die the moment he'd seen her. But that didn't stop him from feeling useless and defeated.

As the day waned and the wind dropped to a sigh Big Mac appeared on the veranda, the small home-made coffin cradled in his arms. The long procession which followed him to the station cemetery was testament to the abiding respect and sense of community that his family had engendered over the years, for the men and women who worked on Carey Downs and the outlying stations had arrived in trucks, on horseback and in wagons, the black trackers and jackaroos accompanied by their women and children. Even Bob Freeman and his family had come all the way from Wilga to pay their respects – and although relations between him and Big Mac were uneasy, they acknowledged one another with a terse nod.

The cemetery was a lonely place, set away from the homestead on the edge of the encroaching bush. Surrounded by a weathered picket fence, the leaning marble memorials and wooden crosses marked the resting places of those who'd lived and died on Carey Downs. And, as Big Mac stood at the graveside, the coffin in his arms, it was as if he was made of stone. The silent assembly watched as he lowered that small box into the ground, and knew by the set of his jaw that he was fighting to contain his grief.

Hugh found that his voice was rough with emotion as he read the service from the prayer book he always carried in the ute, and his heart went out to poor Maeve, who was inconsolable. Their four other children clung to one another, tears silently rolling down their faces as they learned the harshest lesson of all. Death didn't always come gently – and it could touch young and old alike.

As Hugh closed the prayer book, Big Mac once again took his little wife in his arms and silently carried her back to the house, his other children trailing behind him.

Bob Freeman and his family left for Wilga. They wouldn't be staying for the wake. But the rest of the gathering slowly moved away from the cemetery towards the cookhouse, where they began to help the Chinese cook and his son assemble the food and drink everyone had brought.

Hugh was aware of the ache in his chest as he dug his hands into his trouser pockets and watched the two native stockmen shovel the dirt over the coffin and place heavy stones on top to deter the dingoes. He took one of his pills and stood there for a long while after the men had left to join the muted wake at the cookhouse, his thoughts drifting like the sand that sifted through the cemetery. He'd seen death too many times, but it always touched him – especially when it was a child and, as he stood there, he finally let his tears fall.

He'd lost track of time, but as his tears dried and he gained control of his emotions he became aware of a distant sound that at first he couldn't identify. He looked around, noticing suddenly how dark it had become – and although there was very little wind, the dust clouds that moments before had been red-tinged were now grey and swirling.

His sharp intake of breath confirmed his greatest fear, for that wasn't dust surrounding him, but smoke.

Heart hammering, he raced across the stony ground to the cookhouse and began to pull frantically on the bell which hung outside. 'Fire! Fire!' he shouted.

People came pouring out of the cookhouse, the barns and the homestead. As one they followed Hugh's pointing finger – and as one they froze. The sky above the great sweep of bush that spread along the far southern end of Carey Downs was a broiling mass of black and grey, tinged orange with the flames that flickered in the canopy.

Big Mac was the first to move and, as he shouted orders, the men raced to obey him. He approached Hugh at a run. 'We've got to get the women and children out of here,' he said flatly. 'I'm putting you in charge.'

Before he could reply, Big Mac was already running back to the homestead, no doubt to alert the fire services. Hugh knew there was no time to waste. He turned to the women, who were still milling about outside the cookhouse. 'Round up your children and gather over by the trucks and wagons. Do *not* take off on your own. I'll be back in a minute.'

Without waiting to answer their frantic questions, he ran for the homestead. He found Maeve and her children gathered on the veranda alongside the native housemaids who were fearfully eyeing the distant blaze, their small children clutched in their arms. 'All of you, go with the other women,' he ordered.

'You can take the kids, but I'm staying,' said Maeve.

'You'll bloody well do as you're told!' roared Big Mac as he emerged from inside the house, his expression grim.

Maeve was all of five feet tall, but that small frame belied the inner steel that had served her well over the years of living in this isolated and dangerous place. 'Don't shout at me,' she snapped. 'This is my home and I'm not leaving.'

Big Mac glared at her, then, without warning, swung her off her feet and over his shoulder. 'I've lost enough today,' he rumbled. 'I ain't losing you too. Come on, kids.'

Hugh and the maids helped the children to follow him as he ran down the steps, his protesting wife beating her ineffectual fists against his broad back as he carried her across the clearing to the collection of cars, trucks and wagons and unceremoniously dumped her into the back of Hugh's ute.

'If she gives you trouble,' he growled to Hugh, 'you have my permission to bloody well tie her in.'

Hugh saw the fight go out of Maeve as she took in the distant smoke and flames and gathered her surviving children close to her. He turned to the three native housemaids who were hovering nearby with their own small children, and helped them up into the flatbed. Fastening the tailgate, he ignored the sudden tightening in his chest and rushed over to orchestrate the evacuation.

But there was no need, for the women had filled every cart, wagon, car and truck. Crammed in tightly, they and their children were clinging to the sides, the running boards and the tailgates. Several of the black stockmen's women were already astride the tough little stock horses, their children sitting in front and behind them, clutching whatever they could to stay on board.

Hugh looked round and saw his heavily pregnant niece, Millicent Cooper, surrounded by her four daughters. 'Come with me, Millicent,' he ordered.

'This baby's on its way,' she gasped as she doubled over in pain. 'I'll only slow you all down.'

Hugh swore under his breath and tried to make a grab for little girls, who were clinging fearfully to their mother. Realising he was wasting time, he followed Big Mac's example and swept her into his arms. As he carried her over to his ute, he was aware that the children were following – that the fire was closer – and that all the men could now be seen as small black silhouettes against the glow of flames.

He slammed the door on the utility, checked everyone was all right in the flatbed and stood on the running board seeking out Delilah. Her husband, Jimmy, was Big Mac's most prized tracker, and he knew she was just as gifted. 'Delilah,' he shouted. 'Where are you?'

'Here, boss,' she called as she turned her husband's skittish horse towards him.

'I need you to lead us out of here,' he said, his gaze flitting over the baby sleeping in a sling across her chest and the two wide-eyed children clinging to her waist.

'I do dat, boss,' she replied, stilling the horse with a tug on the reins. 'Alonga me quick, quick.'

Hugh nodded and turned towards the gathering. 'Keep close together, and follow me,' he yelled above the wailing of babies, the frightened sobs of small children and fretful whinnying of the horses. 'Any problems – send one of the riders up to let me know.'

It was a bit of a squash inside the utility cab, but that didn't matter. He turned the key in the ignition, rammed the gears into first, ignored the pain in his chest and Millicent's groans – and followed the slender figure on horseback into the darkening, smoke-laden wilderness.

Less than a hundred miles away, to the east of Carey Downs, Terence had turned off the main road and followed the tracker and his wagon to where the drovers had set up camp close to Blackman's Creek. It was a desolate place, the creek all but dry, the landscape naked to the sun which beat down remorselessly.

The injured man was lying under a canvas awning which had been tied to the desiccated remains of a fallen tree and held up at the front by two pronged bits of wood. The other two men had lit a fire under the billycan and were using their hats to keep the flies off the blood-soaked shirt that covered the wound. They introduced themselves as Paddy and Mike.

'Good to see ya, Doc,' the injured man groaned. 'The name's Ross.'

'G'day, Ross,' said Terence with a swift glance at the bloodied shirt. 'Don't try to talk, mate.' Ross was, he guessed, in his mid-twenties, with the weathered skin of a man who earned his living under the sun. His face was drawn and etched with pain, his breath shallow, and his skin had the dry heat of fever.

Terence opened his medical bag and took out a hypodermic and a phial of morphine. 'This will help ease the pain,' he reassured him, as he injected the muscled arm.

As Ross slipped into unconsciousness, Terence carefully cut away the shirt that was stiff with the man's blood. The gash from the bull's horn had almost ripped the man in two, and Terence surmised that Ross must have the constitution of an ox to have survived this long.

'Keep the flies off him while I prepare for surgery,' he said to the tracker. Turning to the two drovers, he started issuing orders, and before long the wagon had been pulled close to the makeshift tent so the awning could be lifted higher and provide more shade and room to manoeuvre; boiling water was poured into a kidney dish so Terence could wash his hands, and a large rubber sheet was very carefully spread on the ground beneath the injured man. In an effort to keep the dust away, the stretcher had been put into service as a windbreak, and the four kerosene lamps the tracker had brought from the homestead had been primed for when the light faded.

'I'm going to need help,' he said to the two drovers. 'Which one of you has the stronger stomach?'

'Reckon I do,' said Paddy, glancing at his younger offsider who had turned an interesting shade of green. 'I was a stretcher bearer in the army medical corps, so I'm used to it.'

Terence handed him the soap and nail brush. 'Good,' he said. 'You know the drill. Wash right up to your elbows and then don't touch anything unless I tell you,' he said firmly.

He handed the tracker one of his clean towels. 'I'll need you to keep the sweat out of my eyes, Sam,' he said, 'and the flies off the wound.' At the tracker's nod, he began laying out his instruments on the second clean towel he'd spread in the lee of the stretcher.

'Mike, you move the horses away from here and clear away their dung – it's attracting the flies – then keep the fire going. We're going to need more hot water.'

Once Terence had set up a drip for the anaesthetic, and everything was prepared to his satisfaction, he eyed the two men who were crouched with him beneath the awning. The tracker's expression was inscrutable, but he continued to move his hat back and forth against the buzzing flies as Paddy squatted on his haunches, his scrubbed hands held out to pass the instruments.

'Ready?' Terence asked softly. At their nods, he took a deep breath. 'Then let's get this done.'

The animal's horn had torn through muscle and soft tissue, and pierced the stomach, liver and intestines. He'd seen the same sort of wounds inflicted by mortar fire, and knew that even if he managed to repair the damage, it would be touch and go as to whether Ross would live.

But as Paddy quietly and efficiently passed him instruments and swabs, and the tracker continued to mop the sweat from his eyes and bat away the flies, Terence began to feel a spark of hope. Ross was young and fit, his heartbeat was regular and surprisingly strong, and as long as infection didn't set in, it was possible he would survive.

The gall bladder had been too badly gored to save, but Terence had managed to tie off all the bleeds, repair the tears in the stomach and liver and was carefully cutting away the damaged section of the intestine when Mike called softly from the other side of the wagon.

'There's a mob of people and animals coming this way,' he said. 'Can't make out who they are, but it looks like a fair number.'

Terence was concentrating hard on the task of clamping off the two ends of the intestine as he removed the damaged section. Dropping it into the kidney dish, he waited for Sam to mop away the sweat that was stinging his eyes and then took the threaded suturing needle from Paddy.

'Go and tell them to take a wide path away from us,' he ordered. 'There's enough dust already. And ask them if they have any spare drinking water,' he added. 'We're down to our last.'

The needle was the finest he had, and Terence concentrated hard as he carefully stitched the intestine back together. He held his breath as he removed one of the clamps and then the other. It was holding.

Terence let his breath out in a long sigh of relief and then glanced at the drip. 'Can you hook a fresh one up and then light a couple of the lamps, Paddy? We've got a fair way to go yet, and it's getting dark under here.'

As he eased his back and prepared to begin suturing the torn ligaments and muscles in Ross's midriff, he heard the sound of motors, the whinnying of horses, the barking of dogs and the lowing of cattle – and then the approach of a galloping horse. 'I told you to keep them away,' he said sharply.

'It's Jim Rider from Wallaby Creek,' said Mike, 'and he insists on talking to you.'

There was something in his tone that made Terence look up. 'Tell him I'm busy,' he snapped.

'Then you'd better get on with it, mate,' said Jim, his head appearing between the stretcher and the tarpaulin. 'There's a fire back there and it's heading this way faster than a bloody train.'

Terence looked over the other man's shoulder and beyond the cavalcade of trucks, horses, wagons and the scrub cattle that were being herded past by several dogs – through the dust they kicked up – to the distant horizon.

What he saw sent a chill to his very core, for above the bush canopy there swirled great plumes of smoke, and even at this distance, he could see the red glow of fire at its heart.

He looked back at Jim. 'How bad is it?' he managed.

'I've lost everything, and so have me neighbours. We're heading for Morgan's Reach, and I'd advise you to do the same.'

'This man can't be moved,' he said flatly. 'But we'd appreciate some drinking water.'

'I've got plenty spare you can have,' he muttered, 'but you're bloody mad to stay out here.'

As he rode off to fetch one of the large containers of water from the back of a ute, Terence regarded his three companions.

'I can't leave Ross,' he said quietly, 'but I don't expect you to risk your lives by staying here. If you want to go with Rider, then don't hesitate to say so.'

The three men looked at each other, and Paddy spoke for them all. 'Reckon we owe it to Ross to see him right,' he drawled. 'Do what you have to, Doc. But make it quick, can ya? Only that bugger's moving closer by the bloody minute.'

Terence was only partially aware of Rider returning with the container of water, and of the sound of his fleeing family and neighbours fading into the distance. He was delicately stitching sinew and muscle, one eye on the amount of anaesthetic dripping through into Ross's vein, his senses attuned to the man's breathing. The pulse was becoming slightly ragged, the heartbeat a little more laboured. He would have to hurry.

All four lamps were lit now, but the closed wound had been liberally swabbed with antiseptic and tightly bandaged. Ross's colour was better, but his pulse was more erratic than Terence would have liked, and his skin still felt feverish. 'We'll have to risk moving him and hope the stitches hold,' he murmured as he washed his hands and face and took a long drink of water.

'Then we'd better do it now,' said Mike, who had gathered the horses together and was standing like a statue beyond the makeshift shelter.

Terence and the other two men crawled out of the cramped space and stared at the inferno that was now less than five miles away. The smoke-filled sky was red with fire as tongues of flame began to forge rivulets through the clumps of spinifex that dotted the landscape.

'We'll put Ross in the back of the ute,' said Terence, snapping out of his horrified stupor. 'It'll be a less bumpy ride. Paddy, you sit with him and keep him sedated.'

The four of them carefully lifted the stretcher and carried it to the utility truck, where they jammed it in with bales of rope, the spare tyre, boxes of tools and the medical chest. Covering him with a blanket, Terence then placed his hat over the man's face to ward off the dust and handed his medical bag to Paddy.

Fastening the tailgate, he shook hands with Mike and Sam the tracker, thanking them for all they'd done, and then climbed behind the steering wheel.

As the tracker slapped the reins over the back of the draught horse and the wagon pulled away, Mike tipped his hat at Terence and Paddy and, with Paddy's horse on a leading rein, was soon lost in the rapidly gathering darkness.

Terence took one swift glance at the great sweep of fire that was now less than two miles away and turned the key in the ignition.

There was a whirr and a grinding cough – and then nothing. The engine was dead.

Sal was still in tears as she reached the top of the steep slope that led through the black basalt mountains to the miles of dirt track that would eventually take her back to Morgan's Reach.

The engine whined and complained as it struggled to get up the hill, the heavy tyres slipping and sliding over the shale. It was unbearably hot and the sweat rolled down her face and back, her hands slippery with it as she gripped the steering wheel and silently urged the utility to make it to the top.

As she breached the hill and passed between the high black walls of the mountain Sal sighed with relief and brought it to a standstill so she could take a long drink from her water-bag. But as she looked out from her vantage point at the panorama spread before her all thought of thirst and heartache fled.

The great horseshoe of fire curved from east to west, smoke billowing into the darkening sky as it devoured everything in its path. Behind it was a smoking, blackened wasteland where once there had been homesteads and farms, barns, outbuildings and animal pens.

As she climbed out of the utility and stared at the scene in horror she could smell the smoke, hear the birds rising in alarm, and felt the wind of their wings as they raced away from this voracious and deadly enemy. She turned and ran back to the end of the narrow pass and looked further west.

The fire had spread to Carey Downs and was advancing on Wilga Station and the smaller Gilburn – if it spread any further, it would reach Max's forest, and ultimately his cabin. And Max had no way of knowing what danger he was in, because he refused to have a two-way radio.

Her heart was pounding as she raced back to the utility and struggled to turn it around in the narrow track. But once she had, she put her foot down on the accelerator and, disregarding the damage she might do to herself or the ancient vehicle, drove as quickly as she could back to the glade.

She leaped out almost before the ute slewed to a halt. 'Max! Max, where are you? There's a fire. A big one, and it's coming this way.' She slammed through the door of the cabin to find it deserted. 'Max!' she yelled. 'Max, where are you?'

Running to the storage shed, she found that was also deserted, and there was no sign of his easel or chair – no sign of Brandy – or even the ponies. Her tears were of frustration and fear as she continued to call his name and heard only the echoes of her desperate cries coming back to her.

She clambered on to the rocks where she'd sat the other day, hoping that from here she might be heard more clearly. 'Max,' she screamed. 'Max, answer me, please. There's a fire. You're in danger.'

But as the sky darkened and the first wisps of smoke began to float towards her above the forest canopy, Sal's fear strengthened. 'Max,' she shrieked through her tears. 'Max, I'm not leaving you here to die. Please tell me where you are.'

After receiving Jim Rider's urgent call, Ben had alerted the nearest fire station to Wallaby Creek, which was several miles to the south of the small settlement, and sent an advance corps of volunteers to deal with it. Knowing his call would be heard by everyone within a hundred miles or so of Morgan's Reach, he nevertheless put out an emergency alert to warn them to be on standby in case they were needed.

But when he received the call from Big Mac he knew his troubles had only just started, and that he would need all the help he could get.

He put out an emergency alert for every fire station within reasonable distance to come and help – with two fires several hundred miles apart he simply didn't have the manpower to cope. Once he'd given the salient details, he checked the fire truck and water bowser, yanked on his service jacket, boots and helmet and drove as swiftly as the heavy load allowed down into Morgan's Reach, where Django and Jake would already be organising things.

Jake was doing his best, but the main street was crowded with every kind of vehicle as men streamed in from nearby stations to offer their help and the women hastily filled tucker bags and drinking-water cans while their children gathered together spades, shovels and old sacks. Jim Rider, his family, neighbours and farm workers had just arrived along with their cattle, horses and dogs, and it was absolute mayhem.

'We've got two fires,' Ben said quietly to Jake.

'Yeah, I heard,' he replied, his expression grim. 'I've sent another small group over to Wallaby Creek with two of the water bowsers, and am about to send a bigger one to Carey Downs. But it'll take them a fair while to get there, and I just hope they've sent some help up from Charleville and Quilpie.'

'They've promised they're on the way – but we have to move quickly. Big Mac says it's spreading fast, and if it gets to Wilga there's nothing to stop it tearing right through Warratah Forest – and we won't be able to do a damned thing about it.' He looked around. 'Where's Django?'

'Sitting by the two-way,' shouted Jake over his shoulder as he ran back to organise the volunteers.

Ben decided to get some first-hand knowledge of the fire, and looked around for Jim Rider. He found him by the stock pens, where his cattle were now milling about. 'How bad is it out there, Jim?'

'It's a big bugger all right,' he said laconically. 'Came ripping through without warning, and we just about escaped with our lives. Last I saw of it, it was moving north – could reach here before morning if something ain't done quick.'

Ben felt a chill of foreboding and was about to turn away when the other man grasped his sleeve. 'The young doc's still out there – refused to leave the bloke he was treating.'

Ben had heard the earlier call from Gilburn, and in the subsequent chaos had forgotten that Blackman's Creek was several miles east of the station on the other side of the main road, and directly in the line of fire from Wallaby Creek. 'How long ago was this? Was he alone?'

Jim scratched his bristly chin. 'About a couple of hours ago, and he was with three of Don Warrington's men.'

Ben thanked him and hurried to Jake's house, where Django was filtering the chatter on the two-way and trying to keep the channel open for emergencies only. 'Sorry, mate,' Ben muttered. 'I need to get through to Gilburn.' He reached for the dials, effectively cutting everyone off.

'Have your men come back from Blackman's Creek?' he asked Don's wife without preamble.

'Mike and our tracker came in about an hour ago, and Don's sent them down with the others to help Big Mac. They said Paddy stayed with the young doctor and they were on their way back to the hospital. Haven't they arrived yet?'

'Not yet,' he said tersely, and disconnected the call. 'Keep listening, Django, and keep in touch with me on the walkie-talkie. I'm going down to Wallaby Creek.'

He raced outside and ran straight into a wild-eyed, frantic Sandra. 'You've got to find Terence,' she shouted above the noise as she grabbed his coat.

'That's where I'm going,' he said as he tried to prise her clutching fingers from his sleeve.

'Then I'm coming too.'

'No,' he said firmly. 'You have to stay here.'

'You can't stop me. I have to get to Terence. He could be—'

'You will stay exactly where you are,' he said, straining to keep his exasperation under control. 'And if you want to help, then see to it these men have food and plenty of water to take with them.'

Ben left her on the boardwalk and ran towards the fire truck, which had a huge bowser fitted with over ten thousand gallons of bore water in it. He stood on the running board and waited for Charley Sawyer to clamber on to the back by the ladder with his four helpers, and then looked over the gathering of vehicles that were waiting for the signal to move out.

'Stay together and follow me,' he shouted.

As the convoy rumbled down the road and along the track which would lead them to the main road, Ben didn't see Becky come racing out of the house, or hear her frantic cries.

Bert Davenport watched the chaos through bleary eyes as he finished the bottle of whisky and reached for another. He had no stomach for fighting fires. The bastards could all burn in hell as far as he was concerned. And if the fire took Morgan's Creek – well, it served them bloody right.

He turned from the filthy window, staggered across the room and swept the empty bottles and abandoned glasses off the bar. No one had been near him since Jake had closed the pub, and his anger was such that if Sal had been here, he would have killed her. But as she wasn't, he took it out on the few sticks of furniture and the ornate heritage mirror behind the bar.

He took the greatest pleasure in shattering that mirror, for it had been in Sal's family for three generations, and his boots crunched satisfyingly over the broken glass as he staggered and swayed and viewed his handiwork with grim satisfaction. The bitch was welcome to the place. He'd had enough.

He took a swig of whisky and shook his head in an attempt to settle his vision as he walked out of the back door and into the paved yard. The last of the crates of beer and cases of spirits were packed into the flatbed of the truck which he'd fuelled this morning. Leaving the back door swinging open, he climbed into the truck.

By the time he'd finished the bottle of whisky it was almost dark – and although he would have preferred to sleep for a while, he knew it was wiser to get out of town while everyone was occupied. He started the truck and drove out of the yard. He didn't look back.

12

Becky watched the convoy leave the settlement, her fears rising by the minute. The day was closing in – the fires were spreading – and still there was no sign of Danny. She should have taken notice of Sandra – should have kept a closer eye on her boy – no one had seen him since late morning.

Fear and panic were growing sour in her throat and drumming in her heart as she ran down the street calling for him. She'd been up to the caves and back to the native camp to question Billy Blue more closely, but the boy had been adamant that the last they'd been together was at the caves, and that Danny had said he was going home to help his grandmother see to the animals.

Becky had then gone to Gwyneth's and to Emily's – had even got through to Amy on the two-way in case he'd decided to bike his way over to Killigarth. But even though Amy had driven almost all the way to Morgan's Reach in search of him, there had been no sign.

Becky had then checked outhouses, sheds, barns, stables and backyards – had been out to the stock pens, to the blacksmith's and had even plucked up her courage to look in the yard behind the pub. All to no avail. Danny had vanished.

She was on her way back to the house when she saw her mother hurrying towards her. 'Have you heard anything?' she asked with frantic hope.

Jane shook her head and wrapped an arm round Becky's shoulders. 'I think it's time we got Jake to put out a call on the two-way.'

'Oh, Mum,' she said tremulously, 'you don't think . . .'

'I'm not speculating on anything at this precise moment,' replied Jane, who was drawn and pale with worry. She hooked her hand through Becky's arm and they pushed their way through the knots of men and machinery that blocked the road to get to the police house.

Django was manning the two-way, the black walkie-talkie placed closed by. 'Jake's alonga Carey Downs,' he explained after they'd told him about Danny. 'I alonga look for boy, but I alonga here till boss get back.'

'I'll look after the radio,' said Becky quickly.

'You'll be needed at the hospital once the casualties come in,' her mother reminded her softly. 'And with your father and Terry out there . . . well, I won't be able to cope on my own.'

Becky was about to protest when Emily came bustling into the small room with the blacksmith's mongrel on a lead. 'I'll take over,' she said firmly. 'People are finding it hard to understand what Django's saying, and he'd be far more use as a tracker.'

'Aw, fair go, Miss Emily. Alonga me good talk English.'

'Just go,' she said in the firm tone that her more unruly students knew well.

Django recognised authority when he heard it, moved swiftly from his chair and grabbed his hat. 'Must talk Billy Blue first,' he muttered. 'Dat boy know tings, for sure.'

'But I've already spoken to him,' Becky began.

Django tapped the side of his nose. 'He talk betta me. No worries, missus. Django find boy, alonga home.'

*

John Miller had seen the boy on the bicycle at around two in the afternoon and had watched him pass along the main road from his hiding place in the valley, deep within the shadows of a stand of trees. He'd wondered at the time what the kid had been doing so far from anywhere and why he seemed to be in such a hurry, but as it was none of his business he'd tipped the hat back over his face and settled down to sleep through the hottest part of the day.

But, despite the weariness that sapped him of strength, sleep had eluded him, and after a restless hour he had given up on it. He'd sat there, his back pressed to the sturdy trunk of a paperbark, his legs drawn to his chest, his eyes closed beneath the broad brim of his hat. His conscience was troubling him.

The boy had been much too young to be on his own so far from civilisation, and he'd done nothing to stop him. Perhaps he'd been in trouble – perhaps he was running away from something. Either way, if it had been his son, he would have wanted someone to look out for him.

At the thought of his boy, who would be about the same age now, he'd taken a deep, trembling breath and drawn the tattered black-and-white photograph from his shirt pocket. He'd carried it through the rigours of training and into the jungle. It had been the only thing he'd managed to hide from his captors – the only tie to home – and a constant reminder of what he was fighting for and why he had to survive.

He'd looked at it and gently run his finger over the faded faces of his wife and child smiling back at him from that long-ago frozen moment of time. His sweat and the humidity of the jungle had almost obliterated their features, the creases and ingrained dirt making it difficult to see the details. But he'd known that his wife had worn her best cotton dress that day, and that the pretty comb that held back her hair was pink – and that there was a sprinkling of freckles across his five-year-old son's snub nose.

He'd just tucked the photograph safely back in his pocket when he'd heard the unmistakable sound of a utility coming down the road. He'd sat very still, safe in the knowledge he was camouflaged in the dappled shadows beneath the trees.

The utility was driven at speed, the single occupant intent upon the road ahead. There was a red cross painted on the side, and he'd wondered if there was an emergency of some sort further down the road – or if the man was looking for his son.

He'd glanced at his watch. Over two hours had passed since he'd seen the boy, but at that speed, the man in the utility would be sure to catch up with him soon. Feeling rather happier about things, he'd slid further down the tree trunk and fallen asleep.

The shadows were more profound beneath the forest canopy, making it dark and rather forbidding, and Sal was all too aware of the time passing. Her throat was almost raw from calling out, and she'd returned to the utility and leaned on the horn for minutes at a time to try to get a response from him. But there had been nothing.

She climbed behind the steering wheel and wondered frantically what to do. The forest stretched for hundreds of miles, and Max could be anywhere. To try to find him would be madness – the fire was obviously still raging – and soon she could become trapped here. Yet she couldn't abandon him.

'Oh, Max,' she whispered through her tears, 'where are you?'

The sharp bark brought her swiftly out of her misery and she opened the truck door to find Brandy running back and forth in what was clearly some agitation. 'What is it?' she asked as she climbed down and stroked his head.

Brandy barked and ran away from her. Barked again and ran back to whine and fidget and nudge her hand with his nose.

Sal realised then that Max must be in trouble, and that the

dog had heard her calling and come to her for help. She yanked on the spare boots she'd slung on the floor and grabbed the two water-bags and the powerful torch.

The dog whined and yipped and ran in circles as she scrambled to find the first-aid box in the mess on the back shelf and then slammed the door. 'Good boy, Brandy,' she murmured. 'Take me to Max.'

He rushed off and Sal tried to follow as quickly as she could over the rough ground and entangled tree roots and vines. The bright beam from the torch lit up the forest which should have been silent at this time of evening, but was alive with bird calls and the rustle and crash of fleeing animals. The fire had to be getting closer, for now she could smell the smoke.

She reckoned she'd been fighting her way through the bush for over an hour when Brandy came back, waited for her to catch up and was off again. 'Wait,' she shouted. 'Brandy, come back here.'

'Sal? Sal, what the hell are you doing here?'

Her heart thudded with relief, but his voice had sounded weak. 'Looking for you,' she shouted back. 'Where are you?'

As he kept calling to her, she followed the sound of his voice and pushed her way through the hampering branches, ferns and lantana that seemed determined to keep her from him.

As the torchlight revealed the two tethered ponies, Brandy appeared suddenly and barked once before disappearing down what looked like a sharp slope.

'I'm coming, Max,' she called as she shone the beam down and found that he was sitting awkwardly on the stony riverbed, his belongings scattered about him, his face covered in blood.

She slithered down the steep incline and, in her haste, almost went tumbling before she managed to break her fall by grabbing hold of a tree root. She found a foothold and carefully eased the rest of the way down, all too aware that it would do no one any good if she injured herself as well.

'I told you to go home,' he scolded.

'Well, it's a good thing I don't listen, then, isn't it?' she retorted as she handed him one of the water-bags and used her handkerchief to wipe away the blood so she could see where it was coming from.

She wanted to cry with relief, to hold him close and tell him how much she loved him – but there was little time to be emotional if they were to get out before the fire came through – so all she said was, 'You've got a nasty cut there, and a bump the size of an egg on the back of your head – but you'll live.'

'What the hell are you doing wandering about out here anyway?' he asked as she put a pad of gauze over the wound and bound it with a length of bandage.

'Looking for you, to warn you about the damned fire,' she retorted. 'I've been calling and calling for hours. Why didn't you answer me?'

'It was Brandy that heard you. I must have been knocked out when I fell.' He tried to move and couldn't disguise the flinch of pain. 'Could you look at my leg?' he asked. 'I think it might be broken.'

Sally's hands were shaking as she shone the torch on it. 'I really can't tell,' she replied. 'But it's swollen, so best to splint it before I get you out of here.'

'Don't fuss,' he said impatiently. 'Just give me your hand and I'll get out of here on my own.'

'If you're so clever, then why haven't you done it already?' she snapped back at him, her relief that she'd found him after the fear making her sharp.

She looked around, gathered up the large satchel which had spilled out sketchbooks, pencils and charcoal, rammed everything back in and picked up his walking stick.

Max slung the satchel over his shoulder and, grasping her arm, leaned heavily on his walking stick as he struggled to stand. His expression was grimly determined, but it was clear from the hiss of his breath and the way the colour drained from his face that he was in a lot of pain.

'You won't be able to climb up there,' she said as she eyed the slope. 'Is there somewhere that's not so steep?'

He shook his head. 'I tried coaxing the ponies down, but they didn't like the look of it either. You'd better leave me here to sort myself out, Sal. I can smell the fire now.'

'I'm not going anywhere without you,' she insisted as she grabbed a tree root and began to scramble back up the slope.

The two mares had been hobbled and couldn't run away, but they shied, stamped and shook their heads, making it difficult for her to grab hold of them. Selecting the sturdier of the two, Sal wound her fingers in her mane, unfastened the rope tied round her front legs and used it as a makeshift halter.

As the mare danced on her toes and flattened her ears Sal kept tight hold of her mane as she stood on a fallen tree branch and swung up on to her back.

'Good girl,' she crooned as she tried to calm the mare's fears and coax her down the slope.

'Come on, Betsy,' said Max softly from the riverbed. 'There's a good, brave girl. Don't be afraid.'

At the sound of their voices the mare seemed to find courage and she tenuously made her slithering, halting way down the slope – and soon they had reached the bottom. Sal had no rewards for her but a pat on the neck.

She turned to Max, who was lovingly stroking the mare's forehead. 'You can do all that when we've got out of here,' she said briskly. She cupped her hands. 'Put your good foot in there and I'll give you a leg-up.'

Max meekly did as he was told and smiled wanly down at her from the mare's back. 'I never realised before just how bossy you are,' he said.

'You ain't seen nothing yet,' she muttered. She looked up the slope at the other pony, who was watching them and whickering with concern. 'I'm going up for Molly. Then we can ride along the riverbed until we find a way out of here.' Without waiting for his reply, she once again clambered up the slope.

Molly was quite happy to have the hobble removed and to be coaxed down the hill. She snorted with pleasure as she rubbed noses with Betsy and they both stood calmly to see what would happen next.

Sal found a long piece of fairly flat wood and made a rough splint for Max's ankle, which she tied to his leg with the a roll of bandage from her first-aid box and fixed in place with a large safety pin. At least the bleeding from his head wound had stopped, but he'd have one hell of a headache later, if that bump was anything to go by.

'It's probably not wise to go back to the cabin. The fire might already have cut off that way out. Where does this river lead to?' she asked once she was satisfied the splint would hold.

'I've never explored it fully,' he said, 'but the old maps show it meanders north and finally ends up as part of Coopers Creek.'

Sal knew that Coopers Creek flowed into Lake Eyre to the far south-west, having passed through the Sturt Desert from Windorah and Longreach and its source somewhere south of Hughenden. 'That's one hell of a trek, Max. Are you sure there isn't another way out of here.'

'Only the way you came in.'

She turned her gaze to the sky and could see wisps of grey smoke curling above the treetops. 'I very much doubt we could get out that way now,' she said. 'We'd better get moving before we really get trapped.'

*

'Becky, there will be casualties coming in soon and I need you to stay strong and positive,' said Jane as they left the police house. 'Django will find Danny soon enough – he can't have got far since this morning, even if he has taken his bike.'

'I feel so useless, Mum,' she said with a quavering sigh. 'Sandra was right. I should have kept a closer eye on him and known where he was and what he was up to – and if anything should happen to him, I . . . I . . .'

Jane gripped her firmly by the arms and gave her a gentle shake. 'There's worry enough at the moment without you adding to it with talk like that,' she said firmly. 'Hugh and Terry are still out there, Sandra's on the verge of hysterics and I need you to stay strong and help me get through this.'

Becky looked at her mother through her tears, saw the lines of weariness and anguish in her lovely face and realised she was being selfish in her fear – forgetting that her mother was also frantic with worry. 'I'm so sorry, Mum,' she murmured. 'Of course I will.'

'That's my girl,' she replied, and softly kissed Becky's forehead. 'Come on – let's get back to the hospital and prepare for the rush. I've already got Enid and Louise on standby, and the girls are making up beds on the verandas.'

As they reached the steps to the hospital they were met by Gwyneth and an ashen-faced Frances Baker.

'Ma,' said Jane with a sigh, 'you should be resting.'

'I can't sit about doing nothing,' she said, the tight bandaging beneath her chin making it difficult to speak clearly. 'And I've brought Frances along to help. She's doing no one any good by moping about,' she added.

Frances eyed Gwyneth nervously and shuffled back towards the door. 'I can't help but worry about my boys,' she murmured. 'Wilga's right next to Carey Downs.' She fled inside, the screens clattering behind her.

'Ma, please go back home,' said Jane. 'You must rest that leg and—'

'I'll have long enough to rest when I'm six foot under,' she interrupted with a glare. 'There are always bandages to roll, equipment to sterilise and people to organise. I'm not completely useless, you know.'

Jane was about to reply when the sound of a truck coming up the track from the main road made them all turn. Their sighs of relief were audible, but before they could do or say anything, Sandra came flying down the street screeching like a banshee.

'Terry!' She just missed being knocked flat by the fast-moving utility as Terence swerved to a halt. 'Terry, I thought you were dead. Oh, God, I can't believe it.'

Terry just about managed to get out from behind the wheel as she clung to him and sobbed into his shoulder. 'Fair go, Sandra,' he muttered, his bashful glance sweeping over the spectators. 'Calm down, love.'

'But I've been frantic with worry,' she sobbed. 'Where have you been?'

'In the middle of nowhere,' he replied as he tried to prise her clutching hands from his sweaty blood-stained shirt. 'We would have got here earlier, but we had to push the flaming ute for about a mile to get her started.'

'Blood!' she shrieked, her eyes widening as she looked at his shirt. 'You've been hurt.'

'It's not mine,' he said, and firmly but gently pushed her away. 'I've got a patient to see to, Sandra. We'll talk later.'

'But I thought you were dead,' she sobbed, her voice high-pitched and on the point of hysteria. 'Can't you at least *pretend* you're pleased to see me?'

'For goodness sake, Sandra,' he hissed, aware that Paddy was watching this exchange with great amusement. He reddened to the roots of his hair as he caught the drover's eye. 'Let's get young Ross into a proper bed,' Terence said as he hurried to the back of the truck. 'I want to make sure those stitches are holding.'

As the two men carried the stretcher into the hospital, Jane and Gwyneth followed, but Becky held back for a moment to have a quiet word with the sobbing Sandra.

'He does love you, you know,' she said as she gave her a handkerchief and drew her away from the veranda. 'And of course he's pleased to see you, to be back home – but at moments like this his work has to come first.'

Sandra sniffed back her tears and made no reply as she refused to meet Becky's gaze.

'I know you've been worried – we all have – but now he needs our help, and the best way to do that is to stay calm and focused.'

Sandra sighed tremulously and folded her arms tightly round her waist. 'Of course I realise that,' she said flatly. 'I'm not stupid. But he could have said something kind. I'm a highly emotional, sensitive person, and can't help showing how I feel. We can't all be ice-cool and collected like your mother.'

'My mother is terrified at the moment,' Becky said fiercely. 'She just has more self-control and dignity than to make a drama out of it. Dad's still out there, Danny's gone missing, and until a few minutes ago we didn't know if Terry had come through the fire at Blackman's Creek. Pull yourself together, Sandra,' she snapped, 'and start behaving like an adult instead of a spoiled, needy brat.'

Becky turned away from her and ran up the steps into the hospital. Her fear for Danny and her anger at Sandra's stupidity had made her say more than she should – but the time had come to stop pussyfooting about. Sandra either shaped up or shipped out. Either way, at this moment, Becky didn't care.

*

Sandra slowly climbed the steps and sank into one of the wicker chairs. She felt as if the wind had been knocked out of her. She stared out to the street where a light burned in every window to combat the gloom and people were bustling back and forth to cater to the men who were still pouring in to help fight the fire.

Young and old, they all seemed to have something to do. They had a place in this tight-knit but far-flung community, and understood the parts they had to play. This was where Terence belonged – she could see that now. But if she and Terence had any chance of rescuing what they'd once had together, where could she fit in – and how?

She sat there feeling lost and very alone. She'd been raised in a city orphanage, and Terence was all she had. She didn't want to lose him. But life in this small settlement was alien to her, the people unsophisticated and as tough as their surroundings. Could she ever learn to understand them, to become a part of Morgan's Reach just as Terence and his family were?

Becky's sharp words came back to her, reminding her that it was not the first rebuke she had had that day. Did Terry and his family really see her as a demanding, wilful child who needed constant attention, and couldn't be trusted not to get drunk at the first sign of trouble?

She shivered despite the heat. It seemed they did. And it was a shocking awakening.

'My waters have broken,' groaned Millicent. 'You'll have to stop, Hugh.'

He flashed his headlights to signal to Delilah, and drew to a halt. When she turned back towards him, he climbed out of the utility. 'Millicent is about to give birth,' he said quietly. 'We'll transfer Maeve and the rest into the other vehicles and I'll stay here.'

'No good, boss,' she replied. 'Smoke come fast. Alonga no see track.'

'There's no wind, and with so much traffic passing through, the trail will be easy to follow in the headlights,' he replied firmly.

He quickly explained his plan to the others and, after a great deal of arguing and persuasion, managed to get them all squeezed into the other vehicles. Once that was done, he reached into the back of the utility for his medical bag and went to attend to Millicent.

Delilah led the long convoy away. They were soon out of sight, swallowed by the smoke-laden gloom and, as the sound of the engines finally faded, the silence closed in.

Millicent might only be in her mid-twenties, but she was an old hand at giving birth, for this would be her fifth. The labour was quick, and she dealt with it without fuss, lying stoically along the front bench seat of the utility as she pushed her baby out. He was a healthy size, with a good set of lungs.

Hugh dealt with the cord and the afterbirth, which came moments later, as Millicent calmly suckled her newborn son. 'I'm glad I've given William a boy at last,' she murmured. 'He feels a bit outnumbered with so many females about the place. I reckon William Hugh would be a fitting name. What do you think?'

'I think we'd better get going,' he replied as he tried to ignore the persistent band of pain in his chest and the ache in his jaw. 'The smoke's getting thicker, and I don't want to risk the wind getting up and wiping out the trail.'

Millicent eyed him sharply. 'Are you feeling crook, Hugh? Only you look the same colour as my mother-in-law's tasteless porridge.'

'Just got a touch of indigestion,' he assured her as he finished cleaning up and climbed back behind the wheel. He rubbed his

215

jaw and flexed his tingling fingers. 'You settle down and rest. We'll soon be in Morgan's Reach.'

The track was clear enough in the headlights, but as Hugh pressed the utility to a greater speed, he was finding it increasingly difficult to keep focused. The tight band of pain in his chest was constant now, the ache in his arm numbing his hand and reaching up into his neck.

He knew what was happening to him and tried desperately to ward it off – it was imperative he caught up with the column so he could signal for help. He had absolutely no idea where he was or how far it might be to Morgan's Reach.

13

Danny had decided he couldn't rely on the off-chance that the mysterious soldier might find his way to the caves, so had set out to track him down. He felt bad about not telling Billy Blue where he was going, but knew that his best friend was hopeless at keeping secrets, and he didn't want anyone to stop him. He'd filled a water-bag, made a couple of peanut-butter sandwiches to eat along the way, borrowed his grandfather's binoculars and set off on his bicycle while no one was looking.

It had been surprisingly easy to slip away from Morgan's Reach and, as the bicycle tyres hummed reassuringly along the tarmac road, he'd felt a surge of excitement. This was a proper adventure, for he'd never been this far on his own before – but it was a good, fairly straight road and he knew exactly where he was headed, so there was no danger of getting lost.

Having listened to Frank's story, and mulled it over for a while, he'd gone back early the next morning to question him more closely. Once he'd gleaned as much information as possible he'd returned home, found his great-grandfather's old maps and pinpointed the spot where the man had last been seen. From everything he'd heard, the man was definitely heading north and would soon come to Morgan's Reach – but was he planning on coming into town or to skirt around it?

He'd come to the conclusion that the man didn't want to be seen, so would probably go cross-country. Exactly where he might be headed was a bit of a problem, but he'd listened to Django's stories often enough to know that everyone left a trail, no matter how careful they were. If he could reach the railway cutting just the other side of the main track to Wilga, where Frank and Jim had met him, then he could begin his search and put his own tracking skills to the test.

Danny had cycled on as the sun beat down, the water-bag and binoculars bumping against his hip. After two hours he'd become hot and thirsty, his legs beginning to ache from the prolonged pedalling. He'd been tempted to stop for a while and rest, but he couldn't waste time; he needed to get as far from Morgan's Reach as possible before anyone noticed he was missing.

He felt guilty about worrying his mother. He loved her very much – but when you were just a kid no one really listened to you, and it was hard to make the grown-ups understand how important certain things were, and how necessary it was to see them through.

His rambling thoughts were interrupted an hour later by the unmistakable sound of a utility truck coming along the road behind him. Luckily it was still the other side of the long bend he'd just negotiated, so he had time to hide.

Jumping from the bicycle, he dragged it with him as he scrambled down the steep side of the run-off ditch. His heart was beating wildly as the utility came nearer and nearer, and he ducked even lower as it passed. The red cross on the white door and the man behind the wheel were all too familiar. Uncle Terry was out looking for him.

He stayed in the ditch until he was certain Terry couldn't spot him in the rear-view mirror, and then had a bit of a struggle to get himself and the bike back on to the road. His heart was still thudding, and the sweat was stinging his eyes. He'd have to be very careful from now on, because Terry might turn around and come back.

After a drink of water and a big bite out of a sandwich, he climbed back on his bike and continued on his way. He reckoned he had about another hour or two before he reached his destination, but he was beginning to wonder how he'd manage to track anyone once it got dark. The thought of being alone out here at night was a bit scary, and he wished then that he'd asked Billy to come with him.

He cycled on, growing increasingly more tired. He stopped again, finished the sandwiches and took another long drink as he surveyed his surroundings. It looked as if the road ahead was all downhill, so he could freewheel for a while and save his legs.

His hat blew off and dangled from the strap, buffeting his back as the bike sped down the hill and he gave a whoop of sheer joy. But when he reached the bottom and saw the long, steady climb ahead of him, he gave an inward groan. He'd only been this way before in the ute, and hadn't realised there were hills like this.

Undeterred, he climbed off the bike and began to push it. His calf muscles tightened and his knees began to ache as he plodded along, but he kept his gaze fixed to the ground, not wanting to be daunted by how much further he might have to go.

Danny was about halfway up when he heard the sound of many engines behind him and only just managed to throw himself and the bike into the bushes at the side of the road before they were drawing parallel. He pressed himself to the ground and watched in amazement as the fire truck and bowser rumbled past, followed by a huge convoy of more trucks pulling bowsers, utilities of every size and colour, cars and even a few horses and carts.

He knew what it meant and, as he remained hidden in the fronds and clinging vines on the side of the road, he realised he'd been so intent on his mission that he hadn't smelled the smoke before now.

Danny waited until he was sure the last car had passed, and was about to emerge from his hiding place when he heard a utility coming over the brow of the hill towards him. Hunkering back beneath the foliage, he saw it was Terry – but he wasn't alone now; there was a man sitting in the flatbed. Perhaps he hadn't been looking for him at all – if so, the coast would be clear.

He waited impatiently for the sound of the engine to fade and then came back out on to the road. The smell of smoke was really strong now and, as he pushed his bike up the hill, he wondered just how close the fire was.

He had a stitch in his side, and was out of breath and sweating as he reached the crest, but the sight before him wiped away his discomfort and froze him to the spot.

An enormous wall of fire stretched along the horizon for as far as he could see, with billowing clouds of smoke and flame rising hundreds of feet into the air to blot out the sky. He stared in horrified fascination and then reached for the old binoculars.

Taking them from the worn leather case, he adjusted the focus as Granny Gwyn had taught him and watched the fleeing animals bouncing and running across the empty pastures. Then he turned the focus on the fire itself, seeing how the red licks of flame shot skyward and the clouds tumbled and rolled like a stormy sea.

He bit his lip and wondered what to do. The fire was still a long way off, but getting to the railway cutting would mean having to cycle towards it. And fire was unpredictable – Ben Freeman had told him how a change in the wind could send it roaring back on you, and how the explosive elements in the eucalyptus trees could trigger even more fires. Perhaps it would be better not to risk it.

Danny felt a huge surge of disappointment, because he'd set great store in finding the mysterious soldier – and now the doubts over who he was would never fully be cleared up, his curiosity and longing never satisfied.

He was close to tears and he knuckled them away, angry at how childish he was being. And yet he was wise enough to know it was time to forget about the soldier, to be like his mate George Blake and accept that no matter how many questions he had, he would never know the answers – and that nothing could be changed by wishful thinking.

But before he turned away he couldn't resist taking one last look through the binoculars. The fire seemed a little closer now, and the convoy of trucks and cars were like tiny dots against that great tidal wave of flame and smoke. He noted that the sky was darkening over the horizon even though the sun still beat down on him here at the top of the hill. Was there another storm brewing – or was it just clouds of smoke? Either way, he knew better than to hang around to find out.

He took a long, slow sweep of the paddocks that spread between the rocks of Morgan's Reach and the fire. There were emus, kangaroos and wallabies racing across the valley floor, and those black pinnacles didn't seem very far away when viewed through the powerful binoculars. He knew he wouldn't reach home until long after dark – and that he would have to cycle like the wind to stay ahead of that billowing smoke.

Danny realised he was wasting time, and was about to head off when he caught a glimmer of something sparkling in the far distance. It winked from the shadows beneath a small stand of trees at the northern end of the valley, and he thought at first he must have imagined it. He was going to dismiss it, but curiosity made him focus the binoculars on the spot – and he saw it again.

He tried adjusting the binoculars, but whatever it was moving down there remained just too far away to be seen clearly. His pulse began to race as his imagination took hold and his thoughts ran helter-skelter. It definitely hadn't been the spark of fire – but it could have been an old tin can, or a bit of glass catching the sun. That thought didn't satisfy him, for cans and bits of glass didn't move about, and whatever was glinting down there was winking back at him at regular intervals.

He could hardly breathe in his excitement as a possibility began to take shape. The shadows were dappled, and if someone was lying in them dressed in camouflage, then of course he couldn't be seen clearly. But if it was the soldier, why hadn't he smelled the smoke? Why wasn't he hurrying away from that awful fire that seemed to be creeping closer by the minute? Surely he couldn't be asleep.

Danny chewed his lip in an agony of indecision. Maybe he was injured and couldn't run – maybe something terrible had happened to him and he was dead. And yet, Danny reasoned, if he was dead then what was moving down there, flashing that wink of light?

Danny rammed the binoculars back into the battered leather case, took a long drink of water and picked up his bike. He would go and find out for himself.

He decided it would be quicker to freewheel back the way he'd come and then find a way through the roadside bush to the wide valley where he'd seen that stand of trees. As he reached the bottom of the hill he realised it might not be so easy, for although he was now in the lowest part of the road, the bush on the valley slope clung to a steep rocky outcrop.

He paused, uncertain of what to do as he looked up the hill. The rocks were even higher there, the scrubby outcrop towering jaggedly over the valley. Heights didn't really faze him, and he was good at climbing – but that looked far too dangerous to tackle.

Danny gnawed on his lip again as his anxious thoughts whirled. The road beyond the hill snaked away from the valley in a series of sharp bends, and he would have to cycle almost to Morgan's Reach before he could find another way down. But it would take several hours, and he didn't have the time – not if someone was down there and unable to escape the rapidly approaching blaze.

Another quick look through the binoculars confirmed the tiny spark was still winking, but he still couldn't make out what exactly was there. It was very frustrating. But as he wondered what on earth to do, his anxiety became tinged with a rising doubt he couldn't ignore. The fire was at the southern end of the valley, the day was closing in as the smoke masked the sun and it would take some time to navigate his way down the rocks and then walk to that distant stand of trees. But if the soldier was down there – if he was injured – he couldn't just leave him.

Danny made up his mind and quickly hid his bike beneath the spreading fronds of a giant fern and scattered dried leaves and bits of twig over it to make sure it couldn't be seen from the road. Then he hitched the water-bag and binocular straps over his shoulders, pushed his way through the trees and bushes that clung to the craggy rocks and planned his route down.

His heart was thudding and he could feel the sweat trickling down his back as he carefully eased over the edge and found the first foothold. As he inched his way down, he had to force himself to keep a slow but steady pace. It was vital that he didn't try to rush, for although this outcrop wasn't as high as the other, it was still steep, and the rocks were proving to be unstable.

What he hadn't counted on was the large and deadly king brown snake which suddenly appeared from a hole beneath the thick root he was clinging to. The flat head and forked tongue were inches from his hand, the eyes evil as it poised to strike.

Danny gave a cry of terror and let go of the root. His feet slipped, and before he knew what was happening he was plummeting down the rock face. He tried to grab at anything at all to break his fall, but he was going too fast.

As he hit the unforgiving ground of the valley floor the breath was knocked out of him – and he knew no more.

Hugh's vision blurred. The pain was a vice in his chest now, and he was fighting to breathe. He couldn't seem to keep the utility in a straight line – and when the tree loomed in front of him, he used the last of his strength and wits to swerve away from it and stamp on the brake.

As the agony ripped through him and his heartbeat thundered in his ears he was dimly aware that the engine had stalled and that someone was calling his name. But he couldn't see – couldn't speak – for he was enveloped in a world of darkness and pain.

Millicent had been keeping a wary eye on him ever since they'd set out again. Despite Hugh's assurances to the contrary, she'd known something hadn't been right and had braced herself for whatever might come. So, when Hugh had narrowly missed that tree and swerved to a skidding halt, she'd been prepared. She'd clutched the baby to her chest with one hand and clung to the door with the other, her feet pressed resolutely against the floor.

But her heart was racing in fear as Hugh slumped over the

steering wheel, making the horn sound. She held her baby close and squeezed her eyes shut in an attempt to muster some sort of calm. She had to be strong – had to think clearly – and she couldn't do that if she let fear overwhelm her.

The continuous blare of the horn finally brought her to her senses, and she tenderly wrapped her newborn son in her cardigan and laid him at her feet. Then she yanked on the handbrake and eased Hugh back from the steering wheel. The sudden silence was deafening.

His face was grey but for the blue tinge around his lips. The only sign of life was the rapid pulse beating in his neck. 'Can you hear me, Hugh?' she asked tentatively.

He gave a sort of groan and his lids fluttered to reveal the whites of his eyes.

Millicent knew a heart attack when she saw one – her father had gone the same way – and she also knew she needed to get Hugh to the hospital as quickly as possible if he was to have any chance of pulling through.

Reasoning that Hugh must have known he had a heart problem, she swiftly went through his pockets and found a small bottle of pills. She had absolutely no idea what they were, but it was logical to assume he'd been carrying them for just such an occasion. She slipped one under his tongue and hoped she was doing the right thing.

He gave a groan and his eyelids fluttered again as she eased his torso towards her until he was almost lying in her lap. 'It's all right,' she soothed. 'I'll get us home.'

The smoke was thick and choking as she opened the passenger door and clambered down. Hugh was a dead weight, but Millicent was used to dragging stubborn sheep about at shearing time and she made quick work of getting him on his side along the bench seat, his knees drawn to his chest so she had room to climb behind the wheel.

Once this was accomplished she undid the top buttons of her dress, picked up her baby and carefully placed him against her breasts before fastening the buttons again and tightening her belt. The loose cotton bodice made a perfect sling and he would be warm there, and far safer than rolling about on the floor.

She could hear the roar of the fire now and it terrified her, but she knew that if she panicked all would be lost – and her baby and Hugh needed her to get them to safety. She slammed the passenger door shut, refusing to even think about the dangers her husband, William, must be facing as he fought the fire, but thankful that her other children were with the convoy that must surely be close to safety by now.

Climbing behind the steering wheel, she turned the key in the ignition. She could only pray that the wind wouldn't get up – for in the gathering gloom and swirling smoke she had absolutely no idea where she was, and if the track was obliterated they would all perish.

Beyond Blackman's Creek the great leviathan of flame and smoke roared before them, its fiery breath searing their faces and heating their sweat. Sparks flew as the oily eucalyptus pods exploded and rivulets of flame raced along trunks and branches to devour and destroy. The smoke stung their eyes, was acrid in their mouths and stifling in their noses despite the kerchiefs they'd tied over them. And, as they struggled to beat back the slow but ever-determined advance of those flames, it felt as if they were fighting the fires of hell itself.

Ben had quickly ordered the men to position the bowsers at equal distances along the line of the fire, not only to try to extinguish the flames, but to soak the ground in front of them and protect the axe-men as they chopped down the trees in the fire's path. The youngest volunteers then cleared them away and chased down any trickle of flame that might be reaching for the mulga scrub and clumps of spinifex that grew across the valley floor.

The hardiest of the volunteers had been ordered to dig a deep trench that was wide enough to stop the flow of flame. It was slow, gruelling work, for the heat was intense, the smoke disabling and the ground as solid as iron.

Ben mopped the sweat from his face as he took a moment's rest. The water from the bowsers was making the smoke so thick it was hard to breathe at all, but to his experienced eye it seemed they were at last beginning to make a bit of headway. He peered through the swirling smoke to the youngest volunteers, who were still working at clearing the felled trees. Their youth and enthusiasm meant they stood a chance of holding this beast at bay.

He blinked the stinging sweat and grime from his eyes and actually grinned as he saw Pete and Mark Baker, the reverend's twins, enthusiastically beat out two rivers of flame that were heading for quite a large clump of very dry grass. They'd certainly proved themselves today – as had every man here.

Ben pulled the kerchief back over his nose and resumed digging. He was working alongside Charley Sawyer, who was swinging the pickaxe with ease, his great arms moving like a metronome as the rock-hard earth yielded to his assault. The other men might not have been built like Charley, but they too seemed to have got into a rhythm and the trench was growing rapidly.

The roar and crackle of the fire, the ringing of axes against wood and the shouts of the men almost drowned the voice that came over the walkie-talkie that Ben had attached to his belt. Stepping away from the work, he turned his back on the fire and sought the meagre shelter of a nearby truck to get out of the heat.

'Ben Freeman,' he said tersely.

'We're going to need more help over here,' came Jake's shout. 'The homestead's gone and the fire's spreading towards Wilga. I've had five casualties already and don't reckon we can hold it back much longer.'

'Have you heard from the other fire stations?'

'Like you, we've got men from Quilpie, Charleville and Thargomindah working to the south of the fire – but we can't hold it back this side without more help.'

Ben glanced towards the distant black rocks of Morgan's Reach and then back over his shoulder to the smoke that was still billowing, and the flames that were voraciously devouring the last line of trees. 'I'll get through to Blackall, Barcaldine and Windorah again and see what's keeping them. I can't spare anyone here just yet.'

'Righto. But make it quick, mate.'

As Jake cut the connection, Ben got through to Emily who was still manning the two-way back in Morgan's Reach. 'Any word on how soon we can expect relief?'

'They're on their way, and should be with you very soon,' the schoolteacher replied. 'I told them to divide up so both fires can be dealt with at the same time. I hope I did the right thing.'

'Yeah, you did. Thanks, Emily.' He was about to end the call when he had a sudden thought. 'Where's Django? Did he go with Jake to Carey Downs?'

'Um, he's . . . Well, he's gone tracking,' she replied warily.

'What!?' Ben's jaw tightened in fury.

Emily cleared her throat. 'Danny's gone missing,' she said in a rush. 'No one's seen him since this morning, and Becky's frantic.'

'Bloody hell,' hissed Ben. 'That's all we need.' He took a deep breath. 'Keep me posted, Em – and if Django does find him, lock the little bugger in Jake's cell until I get back. That boy needs a serious talking to.'

'I can't do that,' she gasped. 'Rebecca would have a fit.'

'At this moment I have more important things to worry about,' he snapped and, without waiting for her reply, he cut the connection and returned to digging the trench.

But the knowledge that Becky must have searched all the usual places for Danny and not found him meant she had to be at her wit's end by now, and it made him regret his bad-tempered reaction. Django was one of the best trackers in the district and would find the boy, he was sure of it – and yet the thought of Danny alone out here with two fires raging, the day closing in and all the dangers that could befall such a youngster filled him with dread.

The nightmare was one he'd had many times, and although he was desperately trying to wake from it, it held him prisoner – just as he had been a prisoner on that terrible day.

They had been on reconnaissance and, as the only officer available at the time, he'd been seconded from his usual duties to accompany them. The native village had been hidden deep in the jungle, and he and his men had approached it warily, for the Japs were known to be in the area and often used villages like this to spring a trap. But all looked quiet and undisturbed, the small, brown-skinned men and women going about their daily tasks as their children splashed and played in the nearby river.

There had been a whispered debate over whether they should quietly circle around the village and head for battalion headquarters, which were still two days' trek away, or stop awhile to eat and rest. They'd been patrolling this jungle for over two weeks and everyone was suffering from the damp heat, the plaguing mosquito bites, torrential downpours and cold, tasteless rations.

The consensus was that the natives hated the Japs as much as they did and would welcome them with open arms – but there was also the very real danger they would bring to the village if they were discovered there. The Japs had no compunction against killing women and children, and taking the men to use as slaves.

He'd listened to the arguments going back and forth and felt uneasy about putting those gentle people at risk just because his men were tired and in need of decent tucker. He was about to order everyone to back off and take the long route back to headquarters when a small boy emerged from the surrounding jungle and began to chatter excitedly at him.

He and his men were soon surrounded by eager children, wary warriors carrying spears and curious women who smiled shyly as they put their graceful hands together and bowed their heads in welcome. His doubts as to the wisdom of what they were doing still nagged at him, but it seemed he was in a minority of one, so when the little boy put his hand in his, he let him lead him into the village.

He could see it in his dream – and could hear little Hakim's piping voice so clearly it was as if he'd been there hours before, not several years ago. The thatched longhouse was at the centre of the village, for this was where everyone ate and slept. Built high on thick poles to avoid flooding from the river, the only access to the single room was a bamboo ladder. Neat reed shutters covered the many windows, and intricate carvings decorated both sides of the doors.

He and his men were made welcome with bowls of fish and rice that the women brought from the campfire as their menfolk tried to communicate with hand signals and role play and their children tinkered with brass uniform buttons and watches, shrieking in delight as they touched the bristled chins and whiskers of these strange-looking foreigners.

They had stayed longer than intended, for the company was

pleasant, the children enchanting and the rice wine potent. In this small oasis it was easy to forget their reasons for being here and the dangers that always lurked in the steaming jungle that surrounded them.

Hakim was about seven or eight – it was hard to tell because the natives were all tiny compared to the hulking great Australians who sat around their campfire – and he'd singled him out as someone who could do magic with a bit of string. He was trying to fathom out how to emulate the intricate twists and shapes in the cat's cradle when the jungle seemed to explode with movement and noise.

Responding on instinct, he pushed the boy and his mother to the ground and shielded them with his body as he grabbed his rifle and fired into the line of Japanese soldiers who had appeared and were advancing on the village.

But the village was surrounded, the native spears useless against the hail of enemy bullets – and he didn't hear the footsteps behind him until it was too late. He half turned, saw the butt of the rifle coming swiftly down towards his head and didn't have time to defend himself.

When he came to, he discovered that two of his men lay dead and that he and the other battered and bloodied survivors of his group had each been tethered hand and foot to the man next to him. His vision was blurred and it felt as if his head had been cracked in two, but as the fog finally lifted from his bleary eyes and his senses returned he wished he'd remained in oblivion. For the scene before him was blood-chilling.

The fearless little native warriors had fought valiantly to protect their families, but their spears and pangas had been no match for the bullets and bayonets, and the headman and his warriors lay dead alongside the women, the elderly and young babies they hadn't been able to protect. The terrified survivors, women and children, were being herded up the bamboo steps and into the thatched wooden longhouse.

In his sleep he knew what was coming and moved restlessly as he tried to shy from it – to break the shackles that bound him to that moment. But the images had been etched deep into his memory and they returned full force.

The Jap soldiers had kicked away the bamboo ladder and were now throwing lit sticks from the communal fire up into the dry thatched roof and in through the doorway. Making a competition of it to see who could throw the most accurately, laughing about it, admiring their handiwork as the flames grew and the black smoke rose above the jungle canopy.

He moaned in his sleep, his legs kicking out as his hands clenched. He could feel those tight ropes holding him back – could hear the women screaming as they clutched their children and begged for mercy – could see Hakim clinging to his mother, his little face contorted with fear as they leaned out of the window and implored their new friends to help.

He'd urgently strained against the ropes and cursed his captors. But their bonds were too tight and there was nothing he or any of his men could do. He was not the only one who wept with frustration and horrified anguish as they were forced to watch this wicked slaughter of innocents.

The longhouse was now consumed in the flames, the screams were fewer – and the last he saw of Hakim was his pathetic small arm reaching through the window in desperate supplication. And then even that was gone.

The sickening stench of roasting flesh mingled with the suffocating smoke and the fetid stink of the jungle – and, in that moment, he'd known he would never be free of that smell, or of the memories of that evil day.

He woke suddenly, jolting upright, fighting to breathe as tears of anguish streamed down his face. Still trapped in the

dark clutches of his nightmare he blindly sought the light –
redemption – freedom.

But the light was a fiery red glow in the darkening sky, the
smell of smoke was filling his nostrils, and he could still hear
the screams of a small boy calling for help.

14

Sal and Max had been riding along the almost dry river bed for hours, but still the sides were too hazardous for the ponies to climb. They had stopped to let them drink from the shallow pools that lay in the deeper, more sheltered parts of the river and rested while they cropped at the grass before moving on again.

Brandy had no difficulty in running up and down those precipitous banks, and dashed back and forth, nose to the ground, tail going like a windmill as he followed the scents of the animals that burrowed in the undergrowth.

Max could see that Sal was tiring but, as usual, she was being stoic, keeping up a stream of bright chatter in an attempt to make light of their situation and boost their morale. But he could hear the quaver in her voice, had noticed the way she kept glancing over her shoulder, and knew she was frightened.

He was frightened too, but not for the same reason. Sal was depending on him to get her to safety, and he hadn't been totally honest with her when he'd said there was nothing much wrong with him.

It hurt every time he breathed, and he suspected he'd cracked a rib or two when he'd fallen on that hard gravel. His head was pounding, his vision was blurred and a spear of agony shot up his leg every time Betsy slipped on the uneven shale. He was fighting the nausea and the ever-increasing darkness that filled his head – and was finding it almost impossible to stay on the mare's back. Yet he knew he couldn't give in to it. Knew he had to keep going until his precious Sal was safe.

'Max, look,' she said excitedly some time later. 'There's a dip in the bank.'

He tried to focus on where she was pointing, but the bank seemed to be shifting and swaying, the trees blurring into a kaleidoscope of mixed hues. 'You lead the way,' he murmured. 'Betsy will follow Molly without any trouble.'

'Max? Max, you look terrible. What is it?'

He couldn't bear to see such love and concern in her expression and hurriedly looked away. 'I'm fine,' he said brusquely as he blinked the cold, stinging sweat from his eyes and took a firmer hold on the rope halter.

'Well, you don't look it,' she replied. 'Come on, follow me, and as soon as we get out of this damned river bed, you're going to rest.'

He couldn't afford to rest, didn't dare lie down and give in to the throbbing, urgent need to sink into the oblivion that threatened to overwhelm him. He dipped his chin and tried to take deep, even breaths to combat the faintness, but each breath seared like a knife in his side.

Yet he kept going – kept tight hold of the halter and Betsy's mane and almost bit through his lip to stop from crying out as the mare scrambled up the slope, jolting his ribcage.

'Right, that's it,' said Sal forcefully. She slid off Molly's back and rushed to Max's side. 'Let me help you down, Max. You need to rest, and I want to check that head wound. It's bleeding again.'

'There isn't time,' he rasped. 'We have to head east and get closer to the main road. I'll rest then.'

'But, Max,' she protested, 'you're crook and—'

'Just do as you're told for once, Sal,' he hissed, and before

235

she could reply, he'd turned Betsy's head to the east and was plodding away from her. He had no fear that she wouldn't follow, and within minutes he heard Molly trotting along behind him.

'Do you have any idea of where we are?' she asked as she drew alongside, his satchel and the water-bag swinging from her shoulder. 'Only it's getting darker by the minute, and soon we won't be able to see anything.'

Max had always possessed an inner compass and knew exactly where to find east – but as the sky darkened and they reached scrubland where the surrounding trees grew more sparsely, the stars would become visible. 'Look up, Sal,' he said through gritted teeth. 'Orion and Venus will always guide you.'

'I don't need the stars when I have you beside me,' she said, giving the sky a scant glance. 'Max, I really do think we ought to stop. I'm worried about you.'

'Later,' he replied, his breath hissing as Betsy suddenly swerved from some imaginary danger in the bushes and danced on her toes. He held tightly to the mare's halter, soothing her with his voice as he fought to quell the pain. Betsy had sensed there was something wrong with the man on her back, and that had spooked her.

'You're frightening me, Max.' Sal put out her hand and touched his arm. 'Please let's stop. We've come a long way, and I can't smell the fire any more. You need to rest.'

'Soon. I promise,' he muttered. He glanced up at the sky, but Orion was just a blur, the bright Venus and Sirius fading in and out of focus – he was running out of time.

The mare was still skittish, her ears flicking back and forth as she shied from every noise and shadow, but Max used the last of his rapidly ebbing strength to guide her on through the trees and around the vast termite mounds. It was dark now, their only light coming from the stars and the quarter moon, but the trees were thinning, and soon, very soon he would be able to rest.

Sal seemed to realise he didn't need her to fuss or chatter, and she rode beside him in fretful silence until they finally emerged from the trees and took stock of where they were.

'I recognise that fancy windmill,' she said. 'John Blake had it brought up all the way from Melbourne just before the war. We must be on Killigarth land.'

Max felt an overwhelming sense of relief that his darling Sal would now be safe. But his head felt as if it had been cleaved by an axe, the thudding pain driving into his neck and spine like a sledgehammer. 'The homestead isn't far,' he managed as he pointed towards a low rise several hundred yards away. 'Get help.'

'I'm not leaving you,' she replied.

Max closed his eyes and curled into the agony as sweet oblivion finally claimed him. He felt nothing as he slithered from the mare's back and crumpled to the ground.

Sal threw herself to her knees beside him, the satchel and water bottle flying from her hands as she frantically searched for a pulse. It was thready and uneven, his skin was cold and clammy and the bandage round his head was soaked with his blood.

'Max,' she sobbed as she stroked his face and tried to rouse him. 'Max, my darling, please wake up.'

Brandy whined and licked his hand, snuffling against him and nudging him with his nose.

But Max didn't respond.

'Stay and look after him,' Sal ordered the dog. 'I'm going to get help.' She jumped back on to Molly, startling the mare into a skittering dance.

Sal dug in her heels, urging her into a gallop – and beyond the rise and still some distance away she could now see the low huddle of sprawling buildings. But there were no lights gleaming in the darkness, and no sign of movement but for the shifting cattle in a nearby pen and the furious barking coming from the kennels.

'Come on, Molly,' she urged the mare. 'There has to be someone there who can help us.'

But as the mare galloped past the seemingly deserted native quarters, bunkhouses, barns, sheds and cookhouse, there was no reply to her frantic calls.

She brought Molly to a skidding halt outside the homestead, leaped off her back and crashed through the screen door on to the veranda. 'Is anybody here?' she shouted. 'I need help.'

The only reply was the continued cacophony of barking coming from the kennels.

She yanked open the inner screen door and entered the homestead. Surely Amy must be at home looking after George? 'Amy?' she called. 'Amy, are you there?'

But even as she called, she could see the remains of a meal still on the table and all the signs of a hasty departure. The whole of Killigarth must have gone south to help fight the fire.

She stood in an agony of indecision. There were no trucks or vehicles of any sort outside, so she couldn't get Max back to Morgan's Reach that way. And she certainly couldn't risk trying to get him back on Betsy. But she had to do something – and fast.

The old-fashioned two-way stood in the corner by the large stone fireplace. Sal ran to it and began to pedal it into life. 'This is Sal Davenport calling the hospital at Morgan's Reach,' she said once it was fully charged. 'Doctor Hugh, this is an emergency.'

A woman's voice she didn't recognise came down the line. 'Doctor Hugh isn't available, and Doctor Terence is in theatre. What sort of emergency do you have – and where are you?'

Sal frowned. She'd only been away from Morgan's Reach a matter of days. Who was this woman – and who the hell was Doctor Terence? She shook off these insignificant irritations. 'Max has collapsed and I can't rouse him. He's losing a lot of blood from a head wound. You have to send someone quick.'

'Where exactly are you?'

'Killigarth Station, but Max is in the bush about a mile away, close to that newfangled windmill.' She pedalled faster as her sense of urgency increased. 'Please, whoever you are, send help quick. He's very badly injured.'

'I'm Mrs Terence Morgan, and the minute my husband is out of theatre I'll give him your message.'

'How long will that be?'

'Not too long now,' the other woman soothed. 'Perhaps you could give me some idea of Max's injuries, so Terence can be prepared?'

Sal was perspiring and her heart was racing as she carried on pedalling and gave the irritatingly calm woman at the other end of the line all the salient details she knew. 'I have to get back to him,' she finished breathlessly. 'We'll be by the windmill.' She didn't wait for a response and cut the connection.

Racing back into the kitchen, she hunted out clean cloths that would do for bandages, two small bottles of antiseptic and a wad of cotton wool. Then she filled an abandoned water-bag to the brim and, after a slight hesitation, also took the half-bottle of brandy that was on the dresser. As she ran back towards the front door she snatched up two blankets and a cushion from a couch and tied everything in a bundle before clattering through the screens.

Molly was standing by the steps, happily munching the withered remains of several pot plants. She clearly didn't like the noises Sal was making, or the way she tried to grab her mane, for she rolled her eyes and, with a snort of displeasure, skittered off.

'Molly, get back here,' yelled Sal, the tears of frustration running down her face as she set off after her.

Molly tossed her head and flicked her tail, then kicked up her heels and headed in the opposite direction at a fast gallop.

Sal knew when she was beaten. She tightened the knot on the bundle, slung it over her shoulder and broke into a stumbling run across the clearing. 'Let him be all right,' she muttered as she ran. 'Please, please let him be all right.'

Gwyneth had set Frances Baker to work in the kitchen making piles of sandwiches and endless cups of tea. She kept an eye on her as well as on the native girls who were ironing the fresh linen while she sterilised the medical instruments and rolled bandages in preparation for the next influx of patients.

They'd had a busy afternoon, with men coming in with burns, smoke inhalation, heatstroke and exhaustion – as well as a multitude of accidents caused by the misuse of axes and other sharp objects. It was quite like old times and, despite the fact she couldn't move about too easily, and it was a damned nuisance not being able to talk properly, Gwyneth felt useful.

But beneath that stoic facade she was a profoundly worried woman. They'd heard nothing from Hugh since the day before, and all they'd been able to gather from Big Mac's terse calls on the two-way was that Hugh was leading the women and children away from Carey Downs in convoy for Morgan's Reach.

But that was hours ago – and by the sound of it the fire was getting out of hand – reaching ever closer to Warratah Forest, and to Sal and Max.

As for Danny, there had been no sighting of him since this morning – and no word from Django since he'd left town in search of the boy. The thought of her beloved great-grandson all alone out there in the dark made her heartsick. But Gwyneth knew she wasn't alone in her anxiety, for it showed in her granddaughter's face and in Jane's – and in the way they kept busy, as if by doing so they wouldn't have to think about anything but the task at hand.

She admired their strength and fortitude in the face of such awful fear, and was trying to follow their example in the hope that she wouldn't let the side down by collapsing under the weight of her own dread, and yet her stoicism was about to be put to the test in the cruellest of ways.

She was precariously balancing a tray of teacups on one hand as she headed for the kitchen when she heard Sal's voice over the two-way. As the import of what the girl was saying sank in, the world seemed to tilt and the dirty crockery slid from the tray and crashed to the ground. 'Dear God,' she breathed. 'Not Max too.'

The room began to spin, and she would have fallen in a dead faint if not for the strong hands that gently eased her down to sit on the floor.

'Put your head down,' said Sandra, 'and try to take deep breaths while I get you some water.'

Gwyneth did as she was told and fought off the nauseating, swirling darkness that was threatening to overwhelm her. When Sandra placed the glass of water to her lips, she drank gratefully before pushing it away. 'Thank you,' she muttered. 'So silly of me. Please don't fuss.'

'I saw your face when that girl was talking to me over the two-way,' Sandra said as she squatted beside her. 'You went quite white. Is she a relative?'

Gwyneth shook her head and grasped Sandra's arm urgently. 'Where's Terry? He has to get to Max before it's too late.'

'He's still in theatre,' replied Sandra with a frown. 'Come on, let's get you off the floor and into a chair where you can rest for a bit. You've been on the go all day – it's no wonder you fainted.'

Gwyneth allowed her to help her to her feet and then tottered to a nearby chair. She sank into it gratefully. 'Go and tell Terence to hurry up. He must help Max.'

Sandra folded her arms. 'I can't disturb him when he's operating, you know that, Gwyneth.' She relaxed a little and gave her a tentative smile. 'You seem awfully worried about this Max. I'd have thought your real priorities would be Danny and Hugh. They are family after all.'

'Max *is* family,' Gwyneth said flatly. 'He's my son.'

Millicent gripped the steering wheel and peered through the swirling smoke, her gaze fixed to the headlights which illuminated the many ruts and hoof-prints left by the cavalcade.

She had been living on Carey Downs for eight years, but she had no idea where she was. Even in daylight one bit of track looked much like any other out here, and she'd always been very careful to use only the main route in and out of the property, but in the smoky darkness the landscape had become completely alien, and she could only assume that Delilah was following some traditional path known only to her people.

She glanced across at Hugh. He hadn't stirred since she'd taken over the driving and as far as she could tell there had been no further attacks. The fact that she could hear his ragged breathing was something of a consolation. At least it meant he was still alive.

The baby began to squirm against her, his hungry mouth searching for her nipple, and she held him there with one hand while she carried on steering with the other. It felt as if she'd been driving forever, but her watch told her it had been less than two hours – and still there was no sign of the convoy.

There was a headache lurking behind her eyes, she desperately needed a pee and was very thirsty, but the water-bag was on the back shelf and she didn't have a hand free to reach it. And she didn't dare stop, for she was suddenly all too aware of how the trees on either side of the utility were beginning to rustle and sway.

She battled on, the headache worsening as she concentrated on those two beams of light and the tracks that would lead them out of here. But the wind was picking up, and eddies of dust were now softly but inexorably erasing all sign of the convoy's route.

Brandy looked up as Sal returned. He whined softly and wagged his tail before returning to his vigil, his bottom resting on the satchel, nose lightly pressed to on Max's chest.

'Good boy,' she murmured. Sal stroked his head as she knelt down, rescued the satchel and began to gather up the contents that were strewn across the ground. Stuffing everything back and snapping the lock, she turned her attention to Max.

He hadn't moved while she'd been gone – and although his colour was ghastly, at least he was still breathing. But his ashen face was cold and clammy to the touch, his fingers not responding as she took his hand and held it to her tear-streaked cheek. 'Help is coming, Max. Hold on, darling. Please hold on.'

She eventually sniffed back her tears and wrapped Max in the blankets, then carefully put the cushion beneath his head and rolled him on to his side. She didn't like the look of that blood-soaked dressing, but it was drying, which meant the bleeding must have stopped. Deciding it would be better not to disturb it, she turned her attention to his leg and gently untied the splints and bandage.

The torch batteries were running down, but as the weakened beam flickered and stuttered, she managed to examine the swelling round his ankle. It looked much worse, but there was no glimmer of bone, so perhaps it was only sprained. She eased off his boot, and using some of the drinking water and cooling antiseptic to soak the bandage, she wrapped it loosely again and refitted the splints.

'Try to drink some water, Max,' she murmured as she very carefully raised his head and put the nozzle to his slack lips. But the liquid spilled down his chin, ran into the hollow of his neck and soaked his shirt.

Remembering how she'd once kept the runt of a litter of puppies alive, she drenched one of the clean cloths she'd found in Killigarth's kitchen with water, added a few drops of brandy and squeezed the liquid into Max's mouth drip by drip and saw him swallow.

Encouraged, she tried to do it again. But this time it just dribbled down his chin. Frantic to do something to help him, she wetted his lips and then cleaned away the smears of blood that had trickled down his face.

Brandy whined and licked his lips as if he too was thirsty.

'Go and drink from the trough,' Sal ordered quietly, pointing towards the windmill. 'Go, Brandy. Water.'

The dog rushed off, and Sal heard the splash as he jumped into the trough, the furious lapping at the water and the unmistakable sound of him shaking himself once he'd climbed out again. He returned, still wet, and nestled down beside Max.

Sal realised there was nothing more she could do now but stay with him and wait for help. So she lay alongside them both, her arm protectively over Max's midriff in the faint hope he might realise she was there – and take comfort and strength from it.

She must have fallen asleep, because when she next opened her eyes the moon was on the wane, and the windmill's long shadow had crept right across the clearing. Molly had returned and the two mares were dozing beneath the trees while Brandy was whining and licking Max's face.

She came fully awake and sat up. Max wasn't breathing.

As the dog continued to whine and snuffle at Max, she searched frantically for a pulse. But there was nothing. Max's skin was cold and as pale as marble in the moonlight, his eyes staring blankly up into the night sky. He'd left her.

The tears were coursing down her face as she took him in her arms and held him close to her heart. 'Oh, Max, my love,' she whispered against his lifeless cheek as she began to rock back and forth. 'If only . . . If only . . .'

The sorrow was too deep for words and she held him, hoping with all her heart that somehow he would now know how deeply she loved him.

Danny had opened his eyes to discover it was night – but it was a strange kind of darkness, for it was tinged with red and filled with thick, choking smoke. In that first moment he'd wondered where he was and how he'd got here – and then he remembered.

He sat up quickly, feeling a bit shaken, but still in one piece. But the smoke was really thick, blinding him, making him cough. It was then that he realised he was in deep trouble.

'Help!' he cried. 'Help me. I'm over here!' His voice sounded very small and thin, and the smoke was smothering him, but he kept calling in the hope that John Miller might hear him.

But there was no reply.

Danny trembled with fear as he crouched low in the fallen boulders beneath the cliff. He had no idea how long he'd been lying here, or how close the fire might be. And the soldier could be miles away by now. He had to get away from the fire – had to find his way home – but the smoke was so thick he couldn't see more than a few feet in front of him.

'Help! Help!' he screamed. 'I'm over here by the rocks.'

The smoke coiled and rolled like a great grey sea and, as Danny fearfully peered into its heart, he saw something slowly take shape.

It was the silhouette of a man – a tall man in a broad-brimmed slouch hat and long army coat. His features were masked by the smoke – but his voice was deep and reassuring as he walked towards him. 'It's all right, son. I'm here. You're safe now.'

Danny's heart was pounding. 'Daddy? Daddy, is that really you?'

15

The bowsers had run out of water so Ben had sent them over to the nearest borehole to fill up again. It took almost two hours before they arrived back, and in that time there were four more casualties, who then had to be driven back to Morgan's Reach.

Ben couldn't really spare the manpower even though he knew there were several hundred volunteers beating back the fire to the south, and many more were doing the same over at Carey Downs. But as darkness fell and the flames continued to leap skyward, it didn't feel as if they were making much headway.

He and the men who worked beside him were soaked through with bore water and sweat, their faces blackened by the smoke and ash, their muscles aching and tight as they trampled through the charred debris on the forest floor and pushed back the fire.

The trench was finished, though it probably wouldn't be needed now, and the diggers had been ordered to chop down the trees that were still burning to clear the way for the firefighters. Ben had sent the youngsters to act as runners, delivering much-needed drinking water to the firefighters when they weren't needed to drive casualties to the hospital. Everyone was exhausted although he'd ensured that young and old were regularly sent to rest, have a cuppa and something to eat before they returned to the fray.

He blinked the sweat from his eyes and peered through the thick smoke at the convoy of trucks that were now entering the valley. 'At last,' he breathed. 'Come on, Charley, you've earned a rest, mate. We've got company.'

'I'll rest when this bugger's out,' the blacksmith grunted in reply as he swung the axe to fell a blazing tree that groaned and collapsed back into the inferno.

'Just watch what you're doing, mate. A tired man gets careless.' Ben could tell Charley wasn't listening, so he wiped the sweat and grime from his face and hurried away to welcome the new arrivals.

The fire chief from Windorah was a big man in his fifties who'd seen it all before. 'G'day, Ben,' he boomed as he jumped out of the leading truck that towed an enormous bowser and shook Ben's hand. 'Sorry we couldn't get here sooner, but this old bitch only does twenty miles an hour on a good day.' He glanced towards the fire, hitched up his trousers, and grinned. 'And I reckon this ain't a good day.'

'Good to see you, mate,' he replied as he flexed his fingers and tried to get some life back into them after that vice-like grip. 'We should have this thing licked now you're here with extra bowsers.'

The man from Windorah was still grinning as he slammed a meaty hand on Ben's shoulder. 'No worries, mate. We'll put her out for you, and then get over to Carey Downs – they've got a real bastard to deal with by all accounts.' He turned away and began to bellow orders to his men.

As Ben smiled ruefully and eased his bruised shoulder he watched the four bowsers line up next to his, and within minutes the jets were soaking the long line of men who were still hacking at the trees and beating back the flames. He began to breathe more easily, for beneath that heavy onslaught of water the flames were dying, the roar of the fire and the crackle of flame finally falling silent.

Ben contacted Jake on the walkie-talkie. 'How's it going over there?'

'Better now we've got some help from Windorah and Blackall. The blokes from Charleville and Quilpie say they're making some headway to the south of us. But Big Mac got himself badly burned. Silly bugger was trying to race the fire and get the gas canisters and stores of kerosene out of the barn when the whole thing blew hell west and crooked.'

'But he's all right, isn't he?'

'He'll live,' said Jake, 'but the Chinese cook's dead, and two others won't make it either. I've sent nine casualties back to the hospital, and can't afford to lose any more. How is it at your end?'

'We're winning now we've got help. Once I'm sure it's dowsed enough to keep just a small working party here, we'll be on our way.'

'Glad to hear it,' said Jake, and cut the connection.

Ben took a long drink of water and grabbed a rather stale-looking sandwich from the nearby tucker box. The fire was definitely ebbing. The bowsers were inching southward as the men on the ground continued to chop down trees and beat the flames into submission with shovels and sacking and anything else they could lay their hands on. Deciding that the big man from Windorah had everything under control for the moment, he reached again for the walky-talky.

'Any news of Danny?'

'Django called in about an hour ago,' replied a weary-sounding Emily. 'He reckons Danny must have gone along the main road, heading your way, because he found his bike under some bushes about ten miles north of Goff's Siding.'

'What the bloody hell was he doing out there?'

'I have no idea,' she retorted crossly. 'Django said he was following his tracks, that's all. I'm not a flaming mind reader.'

He scrubbed his face with his free hand. 'Sorry, Em. I didn't mean to shout at you.'

'We're all at the end of our tethers, Ben. I'll tell you the minute I get any news. How's Jake?'

'He's fine – we just spoke. I'll be going over there as soon as it's safe to leave here.'

'Tell him to be careful and not play the bloody hero. I want him back in one piece.'

Ben grinned. 'Yeah, I'll do that, Em. Over and out.' He was clipping the walkie-talkie back on to his belt when he saw the big fire chief from Windorah striding towards him.

'I've just had word from the blokes working the south side of this fire,' he said without preamble. 'They think they found what started it.'

They'd all supposed that the fire had been caused by a lightning strike, and Ben waited anxiously as the other man took a long drink of water and smeared the sweat from his face.

'There's a burned-out car and the remains of a petrol can about seven or eight yards away from it. Some damned fool must have left their bloody car in the middle of a stand of trees – hot exhaust probably started the fire. The bloody car must have blown up, because they found the wreckage of a door and a wheel several hundred feet away on the other side of the road.'

'Bloody hell. Was anyone in the car?'

The big man shook his head, his expression grim. 'But there was a body about three miles away. Couldn't tell who it was – burned to a crisp. They're taking it back to the hospital morgue at Charleville.'

Ben had seen what fire could do to the human body and he shuddered at the memory of blackened limbs and arched spines, the skeleton forever frozen into a grotesque and macabre carving. If, as he suspected, the dead man proved to be Reverend Baker, then his wife must be kept from visiting that morgue at all cost.

'I'm going with you,' said Gwyneth.

'No, you're not,' said Terence. 'I can get things done much more quickly if I don't have you to worry about.'

'He's my son. I have a right to be there.'

Terence took a deep breath and ran his hands through his hair. 'Killigarth is at least an hour's drive away, and you've been on your feet all day. I don't want you keeling over as well.'

'I do *not* keel over,' she retorted stoutly – conveniently forgetting her fainting fit earlier. She rose from her chair and glared at him. 'Come along,' she snapped. 'We're wasting time.'

'Gwyneth, it really isn't wise,' said Sandra. 'Terence will treat him and bring him back soon enough, and then you can have a nice long visit with him.'

She ignored Sandra and hooked her hand into the crook of Terence's arm. 'Help me down the steps. I'll wait for you in the ute.'

'I didn't even know Uncle Max was alive, let alone living locally,' he said as he gave in with a sigh and steadied her down the steps and along the path.

'Just goes to show you don't know everything, young Terence. Now get a move on.'

Her expression was grim as she watched her grandson run back into the hospital. She always got her own way in the end – but she was dreading what she might find when they got to Killigarth.

*

Rebecca was as surprised as her mother to learn that the reclusive and rather mysterious Uncle Max had turned up injured at Killigarth Station with – of all people – Sal Davenport. But once Granny Gwyn and Terry had left the hospital to go to find him, she had pushed all thought of him and Sal to the back of her mind and thrown herself back into work.

She was like an automaton, refusing to rest, to eat or even think, knowing that if she stopped she would go mad with worry over Danny and her father, and she had to stay strong – not only for herself, but for her mother.

Amy Blake had come in some time before with George and her mother to offer help and support while their menfolk went to fight the fire. Amy had been her usual sympathetic and sweet self, offering comfort and understanding. But neither she nor George could shed any light on where Danny might be.

Becky found great solace in her friendship with Amy, for although they rarely managed to spend time together because of the distance between them, their bond had never weakened. They'd known one another since childhood, had shared the joys of falling in love, been bridesmaids at each other's weddings, given birth to their sons within the same year – and grieved together when they were widowed. They both had loving families, but it was to each other that they turned in times of trouble, knowing they would find true understanding.

Once the hospital got busy and Rebecca was needed on the ward, Amy had hustled George off to the hospital kitchen, where she got him drying the dishes for Frances Baker and laying supper trays while she orchestrated the cooking of the evening meal and the making of endless cups of tea.

The casualties had begun to come in thick and fast, and not just from the fire. The tension was at breaking point among the women in Morgan's Reach, and accidents were inevitable. Annie O'Halloran had tipped over a pot of boiling water

252

and badly scalded her arm; another woman almost severed a finger as she was hurriedly trying to open a can of corned beef, and two more had sustained fairly serious injuries while attempting to calm a horse that had taken great exception to being harnessed into the supply dray.

But the injuries among the firefighters were more serious and Terry had been in theatre for most of the day before he'd had to leave with Gwyneth. Sandra had proved to be a godsend, working efficiently and quietly, always ready with a kind word, the right instrument and sensible suggestions. Becky didn't know how or why Sandra had made the swift transformation from spoiled brat to dependable nurse, but they were all grateful for it – and hoped it would last.

As Big Mac was driven in by one of the Baker twins, it was clear he would bear the scars of his fiery encounter for the rest of his life. 'Where's my wife?' he rasped as the smoke-blackened youth helped him up the steps.

'Maeve's on her way,' Becky soothed. 'Try to relax, Mac. You'll do her no good if you make your condition worse.'

Angry blisters covered one side of his face, his hair, lashes and brows were all but gone, and his shirt had been burned into his chest and back. They sat him on the examination table and Becky and Jane got to work, carefully cutting away the charred shirt and dowsing the awful burns in warm saline water.

'She should be here by now,' he said through gritted teeth as they soaked away the remnants of his shirt. He swung a meaty arm to shoo them off him. 'I've got to go and find her,' he said, struggling to get off the table.

'You'll do no such thing,' said Rebecca, pressing his uninjured shoulder firmly back. 'She and Dad are probably coming in right now, and you need to get these burns treated.'

'But I've got to get back to the fire. Bob Freeman's running things, and I don't trust him not to make off with my scrub cattle.'

'Bob Freeman has better things to do than nick your cattle,' insisted Rebecca. 'He wants that fire out as much as you do, so give it a rest, Mac, and keep still.' She nodded to her mother, who had prepared a hypodermic.

As the needle slipped into his arm and Jane slowly depressed the plunger, Big Mac's eyelids fluttered and he went limp.

'I just hope to God they *are* on their way,' muttered Jane as she propped him on his uninjured side so she could continue to cut away the big man's clothing to get to the rest of his burns. 'They're certainly taking their bloody time about it.'

Rebecca eyed her mother sharply. Jane rarely swore, and it was a measure of the strain she was under. 'I expect we'll know soon enough when they get here,' she replied, trying hard not to think of Danny all alone out there in the darkness – lost, perhaps injured – frightened, hungry – in danger from the fire.

'Stop it, Becky,' murmured Jane, giving her hand a gentle squeeze. 'Thinking the worst won't bring them home any quicker.'

Becky blinked away the tears and forced herself to keep her hands steady as she bathed Big Mac's burns. 'I know, but . . .'

As if on cue there was a shout from the street. 'They're back! They're back!'

Becky and Jane looked at one another, hope gleaming in their eyes. 'You go,' said Jane. 'It might be Django and Danny.'

She didn't need telling twice, and ran out of the examination room and straight into Frances, who was hysterically trying to stop her son from going back to the fire.

'Let him go, Frances,' she said as she pushed past in the narrow corridor. 'They need every hand they can get out there, and your boy has proved today that he's man enough to join them.'

254

Without waiting for Frances's reaction, she ran out on to the veranda to find that it was quite dark now, and a warm wind was blowing the dust along the street.

Her initial response to the scene was one of mixed emotions. It hadn't been Danny and Django who'd come back, but at least one of her family had made it home safely. For Delilah was perched regally on her stock horse, her children clinging to her as she lead the Carey Downs convoy into town.

But as she watched the townspeople welcome the long cavalcade of wagons, horses, cars, lorries and utes, she could see no sign of the white hospital utility. Dread chilled her as she ran down the steps and caught up with Delilah, who was swinging down from her horse. 'Where's Dad?'

The Aboriginal girl frowned as she turned back and regarded the untidy gathering which had followed her through the bush and into town. 'Missus Milly alonga have baby,' she muttered. 'Doc say along me, quick, quick. We alonga give good track 'im follow.'

'That's the last of the convoy, Delilah,' Rebecca replied, her voice tight with fear and tension as the wind ruffled her hair. 'He's not there, which means he's still back on the track somewhere – and the wind's getting up.'

'I alonga get 'im. Take kids.' She dumped the baby in Rebecca's arms and nudged the two toddlers towards her. 'Go Missus Becka,' she told them firmly. 'Mum alonga back soon.' With that she stuck her bare foot in the stirrup, swung up into the saddle and urged the sturdy little mount into a gallop.

The baby started howling and the two small girls looked up at her with wide tear-filled eyes and trembling chins. Rebecca knew that if she didn't do something quickly, she'd have three screaming children on her hands. 'Come on,' she said, jiggling the baby in her arms and holding out her free hand. 'Reckon you might like a couple of bickies and some milk?'

'Me drink 'im cordial,' said the eldest child. 'Yeah, me too,' piped her sister.

'Let's go and see if we've got any.' She felt them gripping her wrist as they slowly negotiated the steps, and the memory of how Danny used to do the same thing when he was small almost broke her resolve not to cry.

'I'll take care of this lot,' said Sandra as she reached for the squalling baby. 'Go and have a cup of tea and a chat with Amy out on the back veranda. You've done enough for a while.'

Rebecca saw how tenderly Sandra took the baby into her arms, and how sweetly she smiled at the two bewildered little girls and held out her hand to them. She felt a tear slowly roll down her cheek as Sandra led them towards the kitchen. She must have been a wonderful mother – how cruel Fate had been to take away her own little boy.

The tears continued to flow as she sank into a veranda chair and prayed fervently that Danny would come home.

He could just make out the boy's face through the smoke and see the hand reaching out to him. For an instant he was back in Malaya and it was Hakim who needed rescuing. He blinked away the memory and focused on the scared little boy who looked up at him with such hope and joy.

'Daddy? Is that really you?'

His heart thudded and his mouth dried as he looked into those trusting eyes and tried not to let the boy see how deeply he'd been affected by his question. 'I've just come to help you,' he said quietly. 'I ain't your daddy.'

'But you look like him,' the boy stuttered, the tears glistening in his eyes.

He stepped through the smoke that floated between them and squatted down. 'We soldiers all look alike in these coats,' he said, his gaze taking in the grazes and cuts and the bruising on the boy's arms. There was also a trickle of blood oozing through his short brown hair. 'It looks like you've had a bit of a fight with that big rock, mate,' he said. 'Mind if I take a look at the damage?'

'I'll be right,' he replied with more than a hint of bravado.

'I'm sure you will,' he murmured as he checked the boy's cut. He'd obviously fallen from that rock ledge and hit his head on the way down, but it was a glancing blow and the wound wasn't deep. 'Reckon all your brains are still in there,' he said with a smile, 'but you'll have a bonzer lump to show off to your mates tomorrow.'

'You're John Miller, aren't you? I'm Danny. Danny Jackson, and my dad was a soldier, just like you.'

'Was he now?' he replied as he kept his expression neutral and examined Danny's limbs and ribs for any breakages.

'Yeah, and my mate George's dad was a soldier too. His name was John Blake.'

His heart was thudding and his hand wasn't quite steady as he dabbed at the head wound with the cleanest part of his handkerchief. 'Is that so?' he said.

'Yeah,' said Danny with a sniff. 'But John Blake and Dad didn't come back.' He looked up, his eyes wide and bright with unshed tears. 'I thought you might be my daddy, you see,' he added wistfully.

'Now why should you think that, Danny?'

'I heard Frank's story about you,' he said, his voice hitching, 'and when I saw you coming out of the smoke I thought you might be Daddy coming to help me.'

His little voice was so plaintive it struck his heart, and he wanted to take him into his arms and rock away all the anguish that was clearly coursing through him. 'My name is John Miller,' he said instead, his own voice rough with emotion, 'but I'm sure your daddy is watching over you right now. Perhaps he even sent me to find you.' He gave the boy a reassuring smile. 'I don't believe in ghosts and spirits and things like the black fellas do, but I've been having some funny dreams lately,' he finished.

'Me too,' he sniffed.

'Now, Danny, we've got to get out of here. The fire is under control now, but all this smoke isn't doing either of us any good.' He regarded the boy solemnly. He was very pale. 'It looks like you're a bit shook about, mate. Can you walk, d'you think?'

'I climbed down that rock, didn't I?' he retorted, his chin lifting in defiance despite the wariness in his eyes as he glanced away towards the fire. 'Reckon I ain't a baby. Course I can walk.'

He held out his hand and helped Danny to his feet. He saw the last of the colour drain from his face and his eyelids flutter and caught him as he fainted. Cradling him to his chest, he looked down at the pale, freckled face, his thoughts and emotions in turmoil – and then he picked up his kitbag and strode back into the smoke towards the dark pinnacles of Morgan's Reach.

Django had been tracking Danny all afternoon. It hadn't been hard once Billy Blue told him he'd been fascinated by Frank's stories and had even mentioned going to Goff's Siding to see where the mysterious soldier had been.

He'd followed the trail of tyre treads in the soft earth at the side of the round, and the discarded crusts of peanut-butter sandwiches – found where he'd hidden in a storm ditch, and eventually discovered the bike in the undergrowth.

But the overhang of rock had worried him, for it was clear that someone – or something – had dislodged a tree root and the earth clinging to it. He'd spent a while searching for other tracks, but there were none, and he had to assume Danny had hidden the bike deliberately and tried to climb down the rock face. What could have made him do such a stupid thing baffled

Django, for the boy was usually very aware of the dangers out here and knew his limitations.

Django was an old man, but he was light and nimble still, and he'd carefully begun to clamber down when he'd heard an unmistakable sibilant hiss and the dry rasp of snakeskin on rock.

He'd frozen, wide-eyed and terrified, as the king brown slithered out of the hole in the dirt and slowly meandered away from him. One bite and he would be dead within a heartbeat.

He'd waited until the snake was out of sight, praying to the Ancestor Spirits that the creature had brought no harm to Danny. Then he'd cautiously made his way down to a narrow ledge where, through the swirling black smoke of the dying fire, he had a reasonably good view of the valley floor beneath the rock.

He'd heard the boy's calls before he caught sight of him, and had been on the point of answering him when he saw the man emerge from the smoke. He'd quickly turned off the walkie-talkie and squatted down on the ledge, safe in the knowledge he wouldn't be seen in the smoky darkness.

He listened to them talking and smiled. This John Miller might tell Danny that he didn't believe in ghosts, but there was little doubt in Django's mind that this man had been sent by the Ancestor Spirits to save Danny, and free him from the things that troubled him.

He watched Miller carry him away and, when they were lost in the smoke, he quickly climbed down from the ledge. He had no fear that the boy would come to any harm, but he was curious as to what Miller was going to do now.

As he stood in the swirling smoke and listened to Miller's boots brush through the dry yellow grass he smiled again and silently began to follow him.

16

Millicent was now terrified. She could no longer see the tracks, the headlights barely penetrated the thickening smoke and, as she turned off the engine, she could hear the deep breath of fire blowing with the wind through the trees.

She glanced across at Hugh, who was still comatose on the seat beside her, and then through the rear window. There was a red glow in the smoke now and, with a moan of dread, she held her sleeping baby close, squeezed her eyes shut and began to pray.

The sharp rap on the window made her jump and she screamed.

The dark face and wild eyes regarded her through the glass. 'Missus Milly. Alonga quick, quick. Fire come.'

Millicent's heart was pounding and her hands were shaking as she wound down the window. 'Thank God,' she shouted above the wails of her startled baby. 'I thought we were going to be burned alive.'

'You die you alonga stay,' said Delilah sharply. 'Come me now.'

As Delilah disappeared into the smoke Millicent ignored the screaming baby squirming against her breasts, turned the key in the ignition and switched on the headlights. She could now see the tracker's wife astride the horse, her arm waving impatiently for her to follow.

Millicent was trembling and the sweat was soaking through her dress as she gripped the steering wheel and pressed her foot on the accelerator. She'd always regarded herself as a tough, strong woman who could handle anything life threw at her – but now she was on the verge of collapsing with dread.

The fire was too close, Delilah had kicked the horse into a fast trot and kept disappearing into the swirling smoke and the petrol gauge was showing almost empty.

She gritted her teeth and put her trust in God and Delilah to get them all out of here.

Gwyneth's jaw was hurting and her knee was throbbing. She suspected it was her own fault she was in such discomfort, for she'd ignored everyone's advice as usual and had carried on regardless of her injuries. But she was made of stern stuff, and a bit of pain wasn't going to stop her getting to her injured son.

Terence had driven north towards Killigarth Station in almost complete silence, and Gwyneth wondered if that was because he was tired and needed to concentrate or because she'd made him cross by insisting upon coming with him. Either way, the journey was quite pleasant on this empty road, with the clear bright stars overhead and the sprawling pastures gilded by the waning moon.

But her thoughts weren't really on the scenery; they were on Max and the awful fear that lay heavy in her heart. But as the utility tyres hummed on the tarmac, she determinedly put her dread aside and let the memories flood back.

She and Rhys had only been married four months when it became clear she was going to have a baby. Although Gwyneth really didn't mind what sex it might be, she knew Rhys was hoping for a son.

The labour had been long and painful, and she could tell by Rhys's expression that he was getting worried. He'd tried to persuade her to return home to her parents in Brisbane for the birth, but she'd insisted upon having her baby at Morgan's Reach, just like all the other women. After all, her husband was the community doctor, and if she couldn't trust him to deliver her safely, then no one else would.

The baby had finally arrived with a squall of defiance, his little fists waving angrily about as if he wanted to fight the world. Rhys's face was a picture as he cut the cord and held his son, and Gwyneth fell in love with him all over again – so glad that he'd got his wish. And then the pains had come once more, and the urgent need to push – and before Rhys could draw breath she'd given him a second son.

Gwyneth blinked away the tears as she remembered that moment. They had both shed tears of joy as Rhys gently placed her twin boys in her arms. 'Two precious gifts you've given me today,' he'd murmured as he kissed her. 'You are my darling, my treasured wife, and I will love you forever.'

And he had loved her, right up to the moment he'd died – and it was at times like these that she missed him the most. Yet she'd always felt he was with her, watching over her, waiting patiently for her to join him, and that had sustained her through the darkest days.

She sniffed back her tears and gave a watery smile as she stared, unseeing, out of the window. Hugh and Maximilian were very grand names for such small babies, but Rhys had chosen them and she hadn't wanted to spoil that heady moment. It was a different story when her next baby had arrived, and she'd argued fiercely against the stuffy-sounding Aurelia, insisting upon calling her Bethany.

Gwyneth felt the twist of disappointment that always accompanied her thoughts of Bethany. She should have let Rhys have his way with her name too. Bethany conjured up an image of someone sweet and soft – the exact opposite of her daughter. Aurelia would have been far more appropriate.

'What's the matter, Gran? Are you feeling unwell?'

She blew her nose rather forcefully. 'Not at all,' she retorted. 'I was just remembering the day Max and your father were born – and thinking about your Aunt Bethany.'

'I've heard of her, of course, but I don't remember her at all,' Terry replied, his gaze fixed on the track.

'You wouldn't,' she said with a sniff. 'She was a larrikin, with a terrible temper and a wilful way about her. She left home at sixteen for the bright lights of Sydney and never came back – and I confess I didn't miss her. She was nothing but trouble from the moment she was born.'

She saw Terry's shocked expression and realised she'd been rather too forceful in her condemnation of her daughter. 'I speak as I find,' she said with a sigh, 'and if Bethany were here she wouldn't be offended. She and I never got on.'

'That's so sad,' murmured Terry.

'It's a fact of life,' she replied. 'Just because you're a mother doesn't necessarily mean you have to like your children when they get past the baby stage.' She blew her nose again. 'But at least she did something right in the end,' she said. 'My granddaughter turned up here a few years ago, and she's proved to be a strong, fearless, hard-working young woman who I'm proud to say bears absolutely no resemblance to her mother.'

He gave a low whistle. 'And who is this paragon of virtue I never knew existed until today?'

'Millicent Cooper. She's married to William who manages the sheep on Big Mac's place. You'll meet her soon enough if you stick around. Her fifth baby's due any minute.' She chewed her lip thoughtfully. 'It's strange and rather wonderful how life seems to go in circles. We all come back to our roots one way or another, don't we?'

'Becky and I were talking about that the other day,' he said. 'I suppose it's in our nature to discover who we are and where we belong.' He shot her a teasing glance before negotiating the dirt track that would lead them to the homestead. 'Though I don't ever remember you wanting to go back to Brisbane – or Wales.'

'Hmph. There's nothing for me in Brisbane – and I never fitted in there anyway. As for Wales, I hardly remember it. I was seven when my parents brought me to Australia.' She folded her hands in her lap. 'No, this is where I belong. I don't need anywhere else.'

'Perhaps that's why Uncle Max came back?'

'Maybe,' she agreed. 'He was always the quiet one; artistic, gentle and perfectly happy with his own company as long as he was free to roam in the bush. He went off to work in the city to try to drum up some interest in his paintings, but I don't think he was happy there – and then the war came and he was sent to Gallipoli and Flanders. He was never the same after that.'

'But Dad must have taken part too. How come he wasn't affected?'

'Oh, he was,' she said. 'He just never speaks of it.' She sighed. 'All men are changed by war – even you, Terence. But Max suffered from what we now know was shell shock. He came home for a short while and then went wandering. It was several years before we heard from him again, but he'd found his refuge at last, and was contented to live a solitary life out in Warratah Forest.'

Terence concentrated as the utility bounced and jolted along the rutted track that was as hard as iron. The homestead and station buildings were a low huddle on the horizon now. They were almost there. 'If he was living like a hermit in the bush, how on earth did he meet Sal Davenport?'

Gwyneth chuckled softly. 'Sal has always confided in me,

and I knew she needed to find the same sort of peace as Max so, without telling her that he was my son, I sort of pointed her in the vague direction of his cabin and let Fate do the rest. She's an artist too, you see – and a gentle soul under all that make-up and tough attitude.'

'Strewth, Gran. I'm learning things tonight I would never have imagined.'

'Yes, well, you can't always tell a book by its cover, Terence,' she said with some asperity. 'People are complex beings, and what you see doesn't always tell the full story. Start unravelling the layers and you might often be surprised by what you find.'

She fell silent for a moment. 'Take Sandra for instance,' she continued. 'I've misjudged her completely,' she admitted. 'She's clearly a troubled young woman who has lost her way – but after today I do believe she has some good qualities – and they need to be nurtured, Terence.'

He smiled at her wearily and patted her hand. 'I'm glad you feel that way, Gran. I've always loved Sandra, you know, and of course I'll do all the nurturing she needs.' He climbed out of the utility to open the heavy five-bar iron gate.

As they drove through it they could see the windmill silhouetted against the sky – and as they got nearer they could see two ponies cropping the grass in the deep shadows beneath the trees.

Gwyneth had always been blessed with excellent vision and, as the headlights illuminated the scene, the dread returned. Sal was lying on the ground next to the still figure wrapped in blankets, and the red setter's muzzle was resting on Max's chest.

Terence kept the lights on as he drew the utility to a halt, grabbed his medical bag and climbed out. 'Stay there, Gran. I'll be back for you in a minute.'

Gwyneth opened the door and struggled down as Terence hurried off. She winced as she jolted her knee and had to lean heavily on her walking stick as she tried hard to calm her racing heart and dispel the fear that they might be too late.

But as she slowly approached the small gathering and looked down at her beloved, troubled son, she knew it was over.

Sal's wan little face was streaked with tears as she got to her feet. 'He's gone, Gwyneth. He's left us.'

Gwyneth opened her arms and held the sobbing girl as Terence knelt by the still figure wrapped in blankets and closed Max's eyes for the last time. She closed her own eyes and prayed that at last her boy would find the peace he'd so yearned for.

She let Sal cling to her and cry and, when she felt the storm was ebbing, she smoothed back the wild hair and cupped her face. 'He'll always be with us, Sal,' she soothed, her own voice wavering with emotion. 'Max will live on in our hearts, and in our memories, guiding you and giving you the strength to find your true destiny.'

Sal nodded and smeared away her tears. 'I know, but it hurts too much, Gwyneth. I can't bear the thought of never being with him again – and there was so much I wanted to say to him – so many things . . .'

'I know, Sal,' she crooned into her hair. 'And I understand. He was my son and I loved him dearly – but I regret that I didn't have time to say goodbye to him.'

'Your son?' Sal's eyes widened in her tear-streaked face. 'But why didn't you or Max ever tell me?'

Gwyneth patted her cheek. 'You didn't really need to know, and it wouldn't have changed anything, would it?' she asked softly.

Sal was silent for a moment and then she shook her head. 'I loved him, Gwyneth. It didn't matter who he was.'

Gwyneth held her as she cried, and when her sobs had

266

finally stuttered to a stop she gently withdrew her embrace and coaxed her to round up the ponies and collect her things. While Sal was occupied, she approached Terence. 'Was it the head wound?' she asked as she regarded the blood-soaked bandage.

'I suspect the injury produced a blood clot in his brain, and that was the end really. It would have been very quick, Gran. He wouldn't have suffered. But I can't tell you any more until I've done an autopsy.'

Gwyneth shook her head vehemently. 'There'll be none of that,' she said firmly. 'Max is gone and there's nothing we can do about it. He'll be buried with dignity, and all in one piece.'

Terence bowed his head. 'It's all a bit irregular,' he said, 'but I suppose it won't matter in the circumstances.'

She looked down at her son, the tears blinding her as she cursed the useless legs that were stopping her from kneeling at his side and gathering him to her. 'Would you please carry Max over to the utility? We need to take him home now.'

The dog growled as Terence gathered Max into his arms.

'It's all right, Brandy,' soothed Sal. 'We won't hurt him. Come on, boy. You can ride in the back with him.'

Terence gently laid Max on the utility flatbed and the dog immediately jumped in and sat beside him, one paw protectively resting on Max's chest as he continued to growl.

Gwyneth looked at her son's pale, lifeless face and felt her heart contract with sorrow. He'd endured so much during that awful war, had isolated himself from all who loved him – except for Brandy, who'd given him loyalty and companionship, and Sal, who perhaps had brought him some joy. How fitting it was that he should die here with them both by his side, at peace beneath the trees and with the sound of the dawn chorus which had sustained him through his lonely life.

She touched his cold cheek and brushed back the long tangle

of tawny hair as tears rolled down her face. 'Rest in peace, son, and know that you were always loved,' she whispered.

There was hardly a woman in Morgan's Reach who wasn't frantic with worry – and those who didn't have a husband, father, brother or son fighting the fire knew someone who was. In this far-flung community, where silly squabbles and old enmities could so easily flare up, for once there was harmony. For everyone mattered in this desperate fight for survival.

Amy had put George to bed in the isolation room and gone to relieve Emily. Her lonely vigil by the two-way had lasted for over twelve hours and she was almost incoherent with weariness and worry. Sandra had made sure Delilah's children were fed and changed before she put them to bed in cots next to George, while Jane and Louise Harper organised more beds on the back veranda.

The dead had been brought in on the back of a wagon and taken straight to the church, where Frances Baker and Enid Harper respectfully washed their bodies, covered them in clean white sheets and laid them out on the altar steps. They hadn't known quite what to do about the Chinese cook, who was no doubt a heathen – but as he'd lost his life fighting for Carey Downs, he was treated the same as all the others.

Everyone was expecting more casualties, for although the fire had been quenched at Blackman's Creek, the news from Carey Downs wasn't good. The inferno had spread through the western boundaries of Wilga and was heading rapidly towards Warratah Forest.

Becky was trying hard not to think about the people she loved and the danger they were in as she dealt with the cuts and bruises the women and children had sustained while riding in the backs of utilities across the rough ground from Carey Downs. She knew from Emily that Django had picked up Danny's trail, but there'd been no further news – and it had been over two hours since Delilah had gone back to find her father. As for Ben, she could only glean from the gossip of those coming into Morgan's Reach that he was still out there with Jake and the hundreds of volunteers, battling to keep the fire out of Warratah.

Becky was on the front veranda having a cigarette and a cup of tea when she saw Amy running down the street towards her. Her pulse began to race as she dropped the cigarette in the tea and pushed through the screen door, her mouth drying with fear. 'What is it? What's happened?'

'It's all right,' panted Amy. 'Django's found Danny. He's safe.'

Becky felt her legs trembling and she made a grab for Amy to stop herself from falling down. 'Thank God. Where is he? I have to go to him.'

Amy shook her head, her dark curls flying about her face. 'Django said you must wait until he brings him home.'

'But why? Why can't I go and fetch them both?'

Amy steered her back up the steps and on to the veranda, pushing her down into a cane chair. 'I know how you must be feeling – I would be the same if it was George. But Django was very clear when he said Danny was safe. He's keeping an eye on him, Becky – and when Danny's ready to come home he'll bring him straight back.'

She twisted her hands in her lap. 'I don't understand,' she said fretfully. 'Why does he need watching – why can't he just bring him straight home?'

Amy sat down beside her and put an arm round her shoulders. 'Danny is with someone called John Miller, and Django reckons—'

Rebecca sprang from the chair. 'I don't care what Django reckons,' she snapped. 'None of us knows who the hell this John Miller is and I don't want him anywhere near my son!'

'But Django seemed so certain,' said Amy, her brown eyes glistening with unshed tears. 'Please, Becky, you . . .'

Jane had overheard this exchange and now she came through the inner screen door with a clatter and turned Rebecca to face her. 'If Django is keeping an eye on Danny, then no harm will come to him,' she said firmly. 'You must trust him.'

'But I don't understand,' said Rebecca. 'Why is he making such a mystery out of everything? Who is this Miller? Why does he trust him with my little boy?'

Jane turned to a distressed Amy. 'What did Django say exactly?'

'He said Danny was safe with Miller, and that he reckoned they should be given time so that Danny can talk to him and perhaps finally come to terms with his father's death.' The tears sparked in Amy's eyes as she turned back to Rebecca and took her hand. 'I'm sorry, Becks, but I think he's got a point.'

Rebecca gnawed at a fingernail, her doubts and fears making her unable to think clearly. Then a sudden thought struck her and she looked back at Amy and her mother. 'Did Django say where they were?' she asked sharply.

'It doesn't matter where they are,' said Jane before Amy could reply. 'We know he's out of danger and that Django will keep an eye on him.'

She firmly drew Becky off the veranda and into the hospital. Standing in the dimly lit corridor, Jane cupped her face in her hands. 'Danny's clearly gone to a great deal of trouble to find this Miller, so give him the chance to speak to him,' she said softly. 'He'll come home soon, darling – and then you can find out all about it.'

Becky could see that her mother was right – but it still didn't make it any easier.

*

'You didn't have to carry me,' said Danny gruffly. 'I'm not a little kid.'

'I couldn't just leave you lying there, now, could I?' he replied as they sat wrapped in blankets on the cave floor above Morgan's Reach, and waited for the billy to boil. 'You passed out cold, mate.'

'Bloody hell,' Danny breathed.

He raised an eyebrow. 'Does your ma let you cuss like that, Danny?'

Danny reddened, shook his head and dipped his chin into the folds of the blanket. 'She'd give me a clip round the ear,' he admitted. 'But I didn't think it mattered as there ain't no silly girls about.' He looked up at him slyly. 'I bet you swear when you're with your mates. My dad did.'

'Reckon you're right,' he replied as he stirred the tea leaves in the billy and breathed in the fragrance. 'Tell me about your dad, Danny. What can you remember about him?'

Danny looked down from the cave to the trickle of water that splashed over the rocks into the stream that disappeared among the trees. 'His name was Adam Jackson, and he was big and strong, with brown hair and eyes just like mine. He had a really loud laugh and used to sing when he was shaving in the morning.' He wrinkled his nose. 'Mum said he had a voice that could break glass, but I liked it – it made me feel good inside.'

He watched the different expressions flit across Danny's face and heard the longing in his voice, but he said nothing as he poured the tea into the tin mugs and added some sugar.

'My dad was a vet – the best vet in Sydney. The bloke we've got here is a grumpy old man who lives way out of town and charges everyone too much.' He looked over his shoulder at him. 'I was very proud of my dad,' he said, before heaving a deep sigh and returning to watching the water. 'He used to play games with me after tea, and sometimes we'd go camping in the bush and we'd play Cowboys and Indians and eat bush tucker.'

'He sounds like a bonzer dad,' he said through a throat that was tight with emotion. 'You must miss him.'

'Yeah, I do. He was my best mate.' Danny knuckled away a tear and then shuffled back from the cave mouth and faced him. 'How come you knew about this place? Are you from around here?'

He blew on the hot tea, playing for time. 'Reckon I know lots of places like this,' he said quietly. 'Where there's water and a spring there are usually rocks and caves. It wasn't hard to find.'

'Why didn't you take me back to Morgan's Reach?'

'I wasn't sure if that was where you lived,' he replied. 'You were out cold, remember, and we hadn't had the chance to get properly acquainted. Besides, I'm a stranger here,' he added, 'and it would have caused a fuss if I'd turned up carrying you like that.'

Danny's eyes sparkled. 'Are you on the run?' he breathed. 'Are the police hunting for you? Is that why you've been hiding?'

He smiled and shook his head. 'I'm just a bloke minding me own business and trying to get from one place to another. I prefer my own company, that's all.'

Danny eyed him thoughtfully as he picked up the tin cup and blew on the hot tea. 'George said his dad was a bit like that. John Blake was a drover, and liked being out in the bush with the black fellas.'

'You can learn a lot from the black fellas, Danny. That's no bad thing.'

Danny grinned. 'That's what my dad said – and he knew all about bush tucker and finding wild honey.' His expression became more serious as the memories flooded back. 'He promised we'd visit his dad's big cattle station over to the east. But that was before the war, and now Grandpa Jackson has sold up and gone to live in Darwin with my auntie.'

'Perhaps when you're older your mum will take you there on a visit.'

Danny's shrug made him wince. 'Mum says we can't afford to go such a long way,' he mumbled. His gaze fell on his slouch hat which was sitting between them on the cave floor, and his expression lightened. 'That's the same insignia as my dad's,' he said. 'You were in the 8th Division, weren't you? Did you go to Malaya too?'

He realised this was a loaded question which must be answered carefully, and as truthfully as possible. 'A lot of men went to Malaya,' he hedged, 'but I wasn't there very long. Spent most of my war in Burma and Thailand.'

'What's the jungle like? Is it really hot, and are there monkeys and things? Was it exciting?'

The pain in his gut was like a grinding fist, but he didn't want Danny to see him taking pills, so he put down the cup and reached for the tin of tobacco and his rolling papers. 'War isn't an adventure, Danny – it's cruel and bloody and terrifying. The jungle is a dangerous, hot, nasty place with swamps full of leeches, and spiders that can kill you within minutes. The Nips come at you without any warning, bomb your camps, set up mantraps and shoot anything that moves. I saw a lot of good men die in Malaya.'

Danny dipped his chin, the tea forgotten. 'My dad was working in the field hospital at a place called Melaka when it was attacked. Mum showed me the letter from his commanding officer, but with so many bodies, how could he be so certain it was my dad that died?'

'We all wore identification tags,' he said softly. 'There would have been no mistake if he'd been on base.'

Danny blinked away his tears. 'But what if they *were* mistaken? What if Dad had been taken prisoner and no one knew where he was? What if he'd come home and lost his memory – and was trying to find me?'

He reached out and gathered the boy to his side. 'Is that why you thought I was him when I found you under that rock?' he asked, his voice rough with emotion.

Danny nodded. 'I really wanted it to be him, and you looked just like him at first.' He lifted his chin and appraised him. 'You've got brown eyes, but your face is a different shape and all lined and wrinkled – and your hair is much lighter and thinner than Dad's. In fact, you look much too old to be my dad.'

He didn't dare show how deeply the boy's innocent evaluation had hurt him, so he gave him a hug and then eased him away. 'Drink your tea before it gets cold,' he said. 'It'll be light soon and time to take you home. Your ma will be worried sick.'

'I don't want to go home,' muttered Danny. 'I want to stay here with you and talk about my dad and Malaya and the war. Ben and Jake were in Africa and Europe, Mum doesn't know anything and you're the only person who doesn't talk to me like a kid.'

He lit the cigarette and leaned back against the ledge of rock that ran down one side of the cave. The boy was bright and inquisitive, and there was a vulnerability about him which tugged at his heart, for he clearly needed some answers. But he knew he would be treading a very fine line with Danny. To tell him everything would be a mistake, perhaps give him false hope. But to lie to him would be a betrayal.

'John? Please can I stay with you for a little while longer?'

He looked into the boy's eyes, saw the yearning there and knew he couldn't abandon him to the uncertainties that obviously plagued him. 'Only if you drink that tea before it gets cold,' he said with a sigh.

17

The battle at Blackman's Creek had been won – but the war was not yet over on Bob Freeman's Wilga. The men had been fighting the fire for over eighteen hours now and everyone was exhausted, faces blackened into anonymity by the smoke and ash, lungs burning and eyes streaming. But the wind was gusting and the inferno was still raging against the pale dawn sky, devouring homesteads, barns and outbuildings, roaring across the empty plains like a great broiling fiery sea.

Ben continued to hack down trees to clear a firebreak while he kept an eye on the bowsers and the hundreds of volunteers that kept pouring in. So many of them were young and green when it came to firefighting, and although there was a hardened core of experienced men, he knew all too well how easily accidents could happen when over-enthusiasm and tiredness took over.

The heavy hand clamped on Ben's shoulder, making him jump. 'Give me the axe, son. I'll take over here while you get some rest.'

Ben tightened his grip on the axe, unwilling to hand it over. His father had aged within the past few hours, his usually rugged and ruddy face grey and lined with weariness and anguish. 'I need someone to take over one of the bowsers,' he said. 'Young Pete Baker has been on his own for too long.'

Bob Freemen raised bushy brows and his eyes twinkled.

'Send an old man to do a boy's work, eh? Give the old fella a bit of a rest?'

'That's about it, Dad,' said Ben. 'Mum would never forgive me if you dropped dead from a heart attack – and I have to say you look crook enough to keel over at any minute.'

Bob glowered at him and pushed back his sweat-stained hat. 'I'm as strong and fit as any man here – and this is my property. I have a right to defend it.' He gave a deep sigh and surveyed the smouldering barns and stock pens, the charred remains of the cookhouse and the tool sheds. 'What's left of it,' he murmured.

'At least you got the stock out in time,' Ben replied. 'And the homestead's still standing. Where's Mum?'

'I sent her and your sisters off with the other women and kids to Morgan's Reach. Didn't want to have to worry about them as well as everything else.' He looked back at Ben. 'D'you reckon we'll beat this bastard?'

Ben looked up at the pearl-grey sky beyond the palls of smoke and leaping flames and saw the ominous thunderheads of black cloud that were building up to the east. 'If the wind changes and those clouds are carrying rain, then we'll have a better chance of getting it under control more quickly,' he replied.

'And if they don't?'

Ben eased the tight muscles in his neck and shoulders and gave a sigh. 'Then we keep going for as long as it takes.'

Bob clamped his hand on Ben's shoulder once more and nodded. 'Reckon that boy might need a rest. I'll take over the bowser.'

Ben watched his father stride away until his sturdy figure was swallowed up in the rolling smoke. The Freemans had worked Wilga for four generations – they had battled fire, flood and drought to make this place the success it was, and he was damned if he was going to let this bitch of a fire destroy his heritage.

He grasped the axe and was about to continue chopping down an ironbark when he heard a shout of warning from up the line.

The ancient she-oak towered above Charley and the young black jackaroo, its diadem of blazing leaves and branches showering sparks down on their heads as it slowly and majestically began to lean towards them. The two men froze.

Every man close by was shouting at them to run – yelling at them to get away – even rushing to try to drag them to safety.

Charley and the boy suddenly snapped out of their trance and took to their heels – tiny figures dwarfed by the giant tree trunk and spreading branches that were coming ever nearer.

But the impetus of the heavy crown increased the speed of the fall – the blazing branches catching Charley and the youth in mid-stride, pinning them to the ground. They began to scream and struggle as the flames voraciously started to feed.

Ben and the others raced towards them, chopping away the branches, shouting for water, smothering the flames with earth and shovels and bits of sacking, desperate to get them out alive. They were sweating and straining to lift the heavy branches as the flames licked at their clothes and hair and the two men continued to scream.

'Get that bloody bowser over here,' Ben yelled to the man beside him before returning to help beat out the flames.

Charley was within reach now, but his leg was trapped and the flames were blackening his clothes. 'It's all right, mate,' Ben gasped as he kept hacking at the branches. 'We'll get you out.'

The great gush of water almost knocked the rescuers off their feet. Smoke and ash blinded them as they quickened their frantic pace and continued to try to cut the men out. Both men had stopped screaming now, and the dreadful silence only made the rescuers work harder.

But the flames were dying, sizzling beneath the onslaught, and finally they could reach the two men.

It took six of them to lift Charley out and carry him to safety, for he'd fainted and was a dead weight. The young jackaroo was much lighter, and Ben scooped him up and ran towards the first-aid station they'd set up several hundred yards away from the fire.

Yet, as he laid the boy on the stretcher next to Charley, he could see how badly he'd been burned and knew that he was dead. He pulled the sheet over the slender, charred body, muttered a quick prayer and turned to see how Charley was.

Paddy had been put in charge of the first-aid station. He'd been in the medical corps during the war, and had given Ben the salient details of what had happened with Terence over at Blackman's Creek. 'Reckon he'll live,' he said as he checked Charley's pulse and began to cut away the blacksmith's shirt and trousers. 'He won't look too pretty for a while, but he got off lightly compared to that poor little bugger.' He glanced across at the shrouded figure and then returned to Charley.

Ben took a long drink of water and blinked the stinging sweat from his eyes as he regarded the three other badly injured men who were waiting to be taken to Morgan's Reach for treatment. 'I'll go and find Mark Baker and get him to bring the truck. We need to get these men to hospital,' he murmured.

'I'll give this one a jab of morphine to knock him out for the journey,' said Paddy. 'Don't fancy young Mark's chances of keeping him still once he wakes up. The bloke's built like a flaming outhouse.'

'I'll send Mark's brother along with him. The pair of them need a bit of a breather, and I expect their mother will be glad to see them.'

Paddy plunged the hypodermic in Charley's meaty arm,

soaked a clean sheet in a bucket of fresh water and pulled it over him. 'That should stop the dirt getting into the burns and keep them moist,' he said.

He looked up at Ben as he wiped the sweat from his face. 'Any news on whose car that was? Only, I hear tell, it could be the reverend's body they found.'

'We don't know anything for certain,' replied Ben, 'and I'd appreciate it if you didn't say anything in front of the twins.'

The little Irishman nodded. 'We've kept it quiet so far, but I reckon it won't be too long before someone lets it slip.'

Ben had a fair idea that Paddy liked nothing better than a bit of gossip. 'Just don't let it be you,' he warned. 'Those boys have worked as hard as any man here; they deserve to be told something like that in private.'

'I was only saying,' protested Paddy.

'Well, don't,' snapped Ben as he turned away and went in search of food. He couldn't remember the last time he'd eaten anything decent, but the cooks from the surrounding stations had got together and there was now a tucker wagon parked well away from the fire, which offered beef stew, fresh bread and soup.

But as he walked wearily towards the wagon he realised something had changed. He stood and looked around him, wondering what it could be. And then, as he understood what it was, his face split into a broad grin.

The wind had miraculously changed direction. Now it was blowing towards the thousands of miles of barren sand and rock to the west. The fire could be beaten, for nothing could survive the Simpson Desert.

Gwyneth was so tired she'd actually fallen asleep on the journey home. She opened her eyes and looked about her in bleary confusion as Terence drew the utility to a halt – and for a blessed second she had no memory of why she was sitting in a truck at the break of dawn. And then she remembered and sorrow almost overwhelmed her.

'Come on, Gran,' said Terence softly. 'Let me help you inside.'

For once in her life she didn't have the energy to argue and, as he steadied her up the hospital steps, she felt as old as Methuselah. She saw Jane come out to welcome her and reached for her hand. 'Is there any news of Hugh?'

Jane shook her head and told her about Danny and Django.

Gwyneth gave a deep sigh tinged with both relief and sadness. 'I've brought Hugh's brother home,' she said wearily. 'I hope he gets back soon, because he'll want to say goodbye to him.'

She saw Jane glance through the screens to the tethered ponies and the truck where Sal was now sitting next to the shrouded figure that was still being guarded by the red setter. 'He was already gone before I could get to him,' she said. 'All we can do now is give him a decent funeral.'

'I'm so sorry, Gwyneth,' said Jane. 'You've been through too much these past hours. Come in and I'll find you a bed so you can rest. Rebecca and I will lay him out.'

Gwyneth shook off her hand. 'I'll sleep when I know Hugh is safe,' she muttered. 'As for Max, I'll prepare him. I'm his mother, and it's the last thing I will ever be able to do for him.'

Terence gave a sigh of impatience. 'Gran, you're exhausted. I'm sure we can—'

She glared at him furiously. 'You will respect my wishes, Terence. Take Max to my house and put him on my bed. I'll come over when I've had a cup of tea and something to eat.'

As Terence went in search of a stretcher to carry Max, Gwyneth tucked her hand in the crook of Jane's arm and nudged her towards the kitchen. 'Make me a cuppa, dear, and while I'm drinking it you can tell me what's been happening since I've been away.'

Brandy trotted alongside them as Sal and Sandra helped Terence carry the stretcher across the street and into Gwyneth's bedroom. It was gloomy and cluttered like the rest of the house, with large old-fashioned dark furniture that made the room seem very small. They laid Max gently on the thick eiderdown that covered the ornately carved four-poster bed and Sal had to restrain the dog as it tried to climb up beside him.

'We'll leave you to have a few minutes with him before Gran comes over,' Terence said gently. 'And don't worry about the ponies. I'll put them in the field behind the forge and see that they're fed and watered.'

Sal gave him a wan smile as she nodded her thanks and, as they left the house, she let her breath out in a long trembling sigh. She felt as if she hadn't drawn breath since discovering that Max was dead and, as she sat in the bedside chair and looked down at him, the tears began to flow again.

Brandy whined and pawed at her knee. His eyes – as tawny as Max's – were liquid with sorrow.

'I know,' she murmured, stroking the animal's silky ears. 'We're both going to miss him, aren't we? He was such an important part of our lives – the only person who really mattered to either of us. How are we ever going to carry on without him?'

She reached for the lifeless hand and kissed the fingers that had wielded a paintbrush and palette knife with such skill – fingers that were roughened from chopping wood and building a cabin – fingers that would no longer caress her cheek and calm her fears.

Sal sat holding his hands as the clock solemnly ticked away the minutes. At the sound of Terry's voice calling to Gwyneth to wait a moment so he could help her across the street, she rose from the chair.

Folding his hands together on his chest she lovingly smoothed back the tangle of hair from his forehead, her soft kiss feeling the chill of death that now possessed him. 'Goodbye, my darling,' she whispered. 'I'll look after Brandy and the horses – and one day we'll be together again.'

She turned from the bed and surveyed the room. Fading photographs in tarnished silver frames jostled for space on top of the dressing table and chests of drawers, alongside empty bird-seed packets, foggy glass jars of dubious-looking creams, squashed tubes of toothpaste – and incongruously, a man's shaving brush and cut-throat razor.

It was a far cry from the clean lines and uncluttered space of the cabin in the woods, but she had a feeling that Max belonged here – that it was right that he'd come home in the end.

She hitched his satchel over her shoulder. 'Come, Brandy,' she murmured as she slipped her belt through his collar. 'I know you hate walking on a lead, but I'm going to need you to help me face Bert, cos I bet he's not out there fighting the fire, but lying stinking drunk in the bar.'

She took one last, longing look at Max and left the house. It was now almost five in the morning, and although the sun was up, it was hidden by thick black scudding clouds. The wind was cooler, as if it was coming from the sea in the east, and she felt a small spark of hope. Perhaps the wind and those dark clouds would bring the rain and put out the fire.

She hurried down the street, relieved it was still too early for most people to be about. The last thing she wanted was to have to talk to anyone. But as she reached the pub she saw the notice that had been nailed across the front door.

'CLOSED UNTIL FURTHER NOTICE.' It had been signed by Jake on behalf of the Queensland Police Authority, so it was official.

'Bloody hell,' she muttered. 'What on earth's been going on here?'

She felt a swift stab of hope that Bert might have finally drunk himself to death – and then immediately felt ashamed. Bert was a bastard, and life would be much better without him – but it was wicked to wish him dead.

She took a firmer hold on the makeshift lead and headed towards the back of the pub. The big wooden gates were standing open and Bert's truck had gone. She frowned. Bert was a coward and it was unlikely he'd have joined the others in fighting the fire. But where could he have gone? The next pub was over a hundred miles away, and if he wanted a drink, then the back room and bar held enough booze to sink a battleship.

She cautiously approached the back door, which was creaking back and forth in the rising wind. Bert was crafty and mean, and perfectly capable of setting a trap. Perhaps he'd hidden the truck and was lying in wait for her, drunk and beyond all reason.

'Stay close, Brandy,' she murmured.

The dog seemed to understand and pressed himself to her legs, his lips drawing back in a snarl.

Sal warily stepped into the back room and almost gagged from the awful smell. Flies were swarming in great black drifts and there were maggots squirming in the remains of rotting meat which had been left on the chopping board. More rotten food lay amid spilled bags of flour and sugar, and an army of ants was vying for the spoils with beetles and tiny bush mice.

She gave a yelp of fright as an enormous rat shot out from under the heavy wooden table, blood dripping from its whiskers. She jumped in terror as it ran over her feet and into the yard. Brandy snapped his teeth, missing the creature's long tail by inches.

Sal pulled on the belt. 'You don't want to eat them,' she muttered, still shaking with fright. 'You'll catch something horrible.'

Wary of disturbing any more rats, or of being ambushed by Bert, she kept the dog close and headed down the narrow passage. The storeroom didn't smell, but it had been ransacked. Empty beer crates lay on their side next to smashed bottles of whisky and rum, and the crates that should have been full of bottles of spirits were missing.

She hoisted the heavy dog into her arms and picked her way through, her boots crunching the broken glass as she headed for the bar.

She froze in horror at the scene of absolute devastation. There wasn't a stick of furniture unbroken, not a brass railing that hadn't been torn from its moorings around the dark polished oak bar, or a bottle left whole. The bar itself had been deeply scored, and in places it looked as if someone had taken a sledgehammer to it. But it was the ruined mirror that made her want to cry, for it had been in her family for four generations and had hung behind the bar for almost a hundred years. Now it was in a thousand pieces, the beautiful ormolu frame reduced to a splintered wreck.

Sal couldn't bear to look at it any longer. She turned away from the wreckage and, still carrying the dog over the glass, headed for the stairs.

The Dog and Drover had eight bedrooms, which opened on to the broad first-floor veranda that overlooked the street. They did good trade during round-up time, or when drovers and shearers needed a bed for the night after a heavy drinking session. These rooms were still as she'd left them, but when she entered the room she shared with Bert, her gaze flew to the ransacked drawers, the open, empty safe and the jewellery box that lay on the bed.

She set the dog and satchel down and reached for the little velvet box where she'd kept the few precious bits and pieces her grandmother had left her. Everything was gone but for a cheap necklace of coloured glass. It was only then that she noticed the mangled photographs that lay scattered on the floor. Bert had taken the silver frames as well.

She sat there, cradling the jewellery box, deep in thought as the dog sniffed around the room and explored the almost empty wardrobe. Bert had been handsome and charming when she'd met him, and she'd gone against all her parents' warnings and married him anyway. She'd soon come to regret that terrible mistake, and was no stranger to Bert's ugly temper and mean ways, but until today she hadn't realised how much he must have hated her. Hated the pub too – because it had never been his.

Her parents had never approved of Bert, and they were determined to protect her as best they could by signing the pub over to her when they retired. The deeds had been lodged with a Sydney lawyer under the strict instruction that only Sal could redeem them – it had been vital that Bert didn't get his hands on her legacy. And although he'd knocked her about and tried to make her turn it over to him, she'd stood firm and continued to defy him. It was her only defiance. He'd forced her to give in to everything else.

Sal finally got off the bed and reached for the cardboard suitcase that sat on top of the rickety wardrobe where the empty coat hangers told their own tale. She began to pack her few clothes, and when she'd finished, she gave Brandy a drink of water and then shut him in the bedroom.

Going back downstairs, she ignored his whines and reached for her apron. She needed something to do to stop her from thinking about Max's funeral and Bert's betrayal – and as Bert had done his best to destroy her pub and leave her with nothing, she would do her damnedest to scrub it clean and have it open again before the end of the day.

Rebecca was almost dead on her feet as she slumped in the veranda chair and smoked yet another cigarette. The hours had flown, the casualties kept coming in and it seemed as if she'd been on her feet for at least a week.

She smiled wearily as she thought of how Enid and Louise had clucked over Charley when he'd been brought in. They'd been like two mother hens, and had obviously forgiven him for owning such a reprobate mongrel. His burns hadn't been as bad as Mac's, and he would soon recover, but both big men had had to be sedated to stop them from leaving.

Terence came out on to the veranda and slumped into the nearby chair. 'I feel as rough as you look,' he said through a vast yawn. 'I can't remember when I had a decent eight hours' sleep.'

'Neither can I,' she replied drily. 'How's Ross getting on?'

'The stitches seem to be holding, but the next twenty-four hours will be crucial. Once this fire's out, he'll need to be flown to Brisbane. Operating on him in those conditions was risky to say the least, and with such major internal injuries it's wiser to have him in a fully equipped modern hospital.'

She shot him a wry glance. 'Are you suggesting this place is a bit behind the times, Terry?' She gave him a wan smile. 'Tut-tut. Whatever would Dad and Gran say?'

'I expect they'd agree with me if they were being honest,' he said on a sigh. He looked at his watch and then up at the sky. 'Where the hell has Dad got to anyway? Delilah's been gone for hours.'

She was about to reply when Sandra came through the screen door and handed them each a cup of fragrant coffee.

'Compliments of Annie O'Halloran. She thought it might help keep us all awake.'

She sat down next to Terence and lit a cigarette. 'I've smoked too many of these damned things today,' she muttered through the smoke. 'Almost makes me wish I could give them up.'

'We've had too much of everything,' replied Rebecca as she stubbed out her own cigarette and breathed in the aroma of the coffee. 'Too many cigarettes, too much worry, too many people needing our help.' She gave a weary chuckle. 'But definitely not enough sleep.'

She sipped the hot and fiercely strong coffee, which had lots of sugar in it and very little milk. If this didn't wake her up, nothing would. She looked out to the street, wondering where on earth Danny and Django were, and how much longer it would be before they came home.

She'd been thinking a lot about Django's message to Amy, and she was fairly certain now that the Aboriginal elder knew more than he was letting on. Why else was he so certain that Danny was safe with Miller? Did he know him? Was Miller local after all? That reasoning was certainly logical – but even so, the man's determination to make a mystery out of himself didn't make sense. She finally gave up speculating. Her brain was sluggish, she was tired to the very bone and nothing made sense any more.

'Oh, my God, look,' breathed Sandra.

They turned as one and slowly got to their feet as they stared at the strange sight that was emerging from the track that led to the main road.

Delilah was riding the stock horse, with Millicent Cooper wedged in front of her, her newborn baby wrapped in a cardigan sling over her chest. The horse was pulling a travois, and lashed to the wooden slats was a man.

'Mum! Mum! Delilah's back and she's got Dad.'

Terence and Sandra were already down the steps and racing to help Millicent down from the horse and check on Hugh when Jane hurried on to the veranda.

Her face was ashen as she took in the scene. 'Oh, God,' she breathed through trembling fingers. 'He's not dead, is he?' Before Becky could reply or stop her, she'd slammed through the outer screen and was flying across the street.

Rebecca raced after her. Hugh's colour was as ashen as her mother's, his breathing laboured. But his eyelids fluttered and he groaned as they quickly untied the vines that lashed him to the travois and gently transferred him to the stretcher Enid Harper had brought.

'What happened, Millicent?' Rebecca asked sharply as they hurried up the steps and into the hospital.

Millicent clutched her baby to her chest as she stumbled along beside them. 'He's had a heart attack,' she panted, 'but he passed out and hasn't had another seizure since. I found some pills in his pocket and gave him one. I hope I did the right thing, Becky,' she puffed as she struggled to keep up. 'I tried to get him back to you as quickly as possible, but I lost the track, the ute ran out of fuel and we had to make that to get him home.'

'Thanks, Milly – and thank you too, Delilah,' said Jane hurriedly over her shoulder as she took the bottle of pills and helped Terence with the stretcher.

'Yes, thanks, Millicent, you did really well,' said Sandra as she firmly steered her and the wide-eyed Delilah away from the theatre door and guided them towards the kitchen. 'You and the baby will need to be checked over now, and then you can rest.'

'Reckon I could sleep for a week,' Millicent muttered ruefully. 'I don't suppose you know if my William and the kids are all right?'

'The children are asleep in our makeshift nursery. Gwyneth has checked on them a couple of times and they're fine,' she reassured her. 'But there's not been much news coming in from Wilga, so we have to assume that as he's not come in as a casualty, he must be all right.'

She handed a relieved but exhausted Millicent over to Louise, who'd proved to be the less daunting of the spinster sisters, and then turned to Delilah. 'None of them would have made it if it weren't for you, Delilah. You're the bravest person I know – and your babies are the most beautiful little ones I've ever had the privilege of looking after.'

Delilah looked bashful and stared at the floor. 'Doc alonga betta now 'im 'ere. Doc make my fella Jim good – me want good him too.' She raised her chin, her tawny eyes drooping with weariness. 'Me alonga babies now, missus. Sleep.'

Sandra led the way to the isolation room, which had become a nursery during the past twelve hours. There were eight cots in there now for the smaller ones, and George was sharing the bed with two other boys of the same age, topped and tailed like sardines in a tin.

She was about to suggest that Delilah could sleep on one of the truckle beds they'd got out of storage when the girl gently picked up her baby, tucked it into the sling she'd made from a scarf and then softly woke her two toddlers.

'You can all stay here. We have spare beds,' Sandra said in a hurried whisper so as not to disturb the other sleeping children.

'Me alonga go dream with Auntie Sarah,' she replied. 'Better dere.'

Sandra nodded, although she would have loved to play with the little girls again and hold the enchanting baby for a while longer. There were tears in her eyes as she watched the regal black girl walk down the corridor, her baby at her chest, the two little girls clinging to her narrow hips. Delilah was not only brave and serene, but very, very lucky.

She turned away and headed back along the corridor. If Hugh needed an operation, it would be unethical for Jane and Becky to assist – and Terry couldn't manage on his own. She sniffed back her tears, tamped down the treacherous thought of how good a glass of whisky would taste right now and pushed through the doors into the small theatre.

18

The hours of battling the fire were beginning to take their toll, especially on the older men, and Ben watched with concern as Sean O'Halloran dropped his axe and staggered away from the blaze as if he was drunk. The Irish storekeeper managed just a few steps and then he stopped, swayed and toppled like a felled tree, his face hitting the ground with a resounding thud.

Ben raced over to him, fearing he'd been knocked unconscious or had suffered a heart attack. But Sean was fast asleep, his resonant snores puffing up the dust.

'It looks like someone's had enough,' he said with a smile as Jake came hurrying over to see what had happened. 'Help me get him to the first-aid station.' They carried the slumbering Sean across the clearing and left him with the injured and exhausted. He'd given his all and would be taken back to Morgan's Reach on the next wagon.

Jake wiped the grime and sweat from his face as they headed for the tucker wagon. 'I envy him,' he muttered. 'Reckon I could sleep for a week – and I'm half his age.'

Ben nodded as they fetched tin plates of food and began to eat voraciously. 'The oldies are certainly showing their metal,' he agreed through a mouthful of delicious beef and gravy. He glanced across and saw his father driving the bowser back from the borehole. Bob Freeman hadn't stopped for more than a few minutes during the past eighteen hours, and by the looks of him, he didn't intend to rest until Wilga was safe.

'At least with the wind changing direction we can get this bugger beat,' muttered Jake. 'Hitting it on both sides and keeping it contained should send it straight into the desert.' He looked up at the scudding clouds. 'Rain would help,' he said wryly.

Ben was about to answer when he saw something that silenced him. He stared in astonishment as the willy-willy spun across the clearing and neatly plucked a blazing ball of tumbleweed from the edge of the inferno which it carried up into the air. Sailing across the clearing like a flying saucer, it flew several hundred yards and dropped on the roof of the homestead.

'Bloody hell,' hissed Jake. 'Here we go again.'

Ben was already running towards it. 'Get the bowser over here,' he shouted over his shoulder.

He ran up the steps, stood on the veranda railings and scrabbled for purchase on the guttering. Hauling himself up, he could see the tumbleweed had rolled down the roof and into the guttering by the stone chimney. Flames were already sprouting from the dead leaves which had gathered in the gutter, and the wooden tiles were beginning to char.

Ben suddenly realised that in his haste to get up here he had nothing to beat out the flames. But he crawled towards the spitting, blazing ball of tinder-dry weed anyway and reached out his gloved hands. Grabbing the fireball, he tossed it over the side and watched it sputter out beneath Jake's boot.

He turned back to examine what damage it had done to the roof. The tiles had been badly charred and could still burst into flame at any moment. He could feel the heat even through the heavy gloves as he yanked the affected ones loose and slung them into the clearing.

'Look out,' shouted Jake.

But his warning was too late and Ben was almost knocked from his perch by the powerful jet of water. Drenched and unable to maintain his grip on the now slippery roof, he began to slither towards the guttering. His heavy boots crashed down on it, ripping the metal channel away from its moorings as his fingers desperately sought a hold.

And then he was falling.

He landed on his back with a thud on to something soft, but his breath was punched from his lungs and found he couldn't move.

'Get off,' shouted Jake. 'I can't flaming breathe.'

Ben heaved a great gulp of air and blinked the sweat from his eyes as he attempted to get to his feet. But it seemed his body was still in shock from the fall and refusing to obey him. He lay there like a beached whale as Jake wriggled and squirmed to get from under him and his father continued to hose down the homestead.

'Bloody hell, mate,' Jake gasped as he finally managed to get free. 'Next time you decide to take a dive off a roof, find someone else to land on.'

Ben grabbed his hand and managed to get to his feet as the torrent of water continued to batter them. He was still winded, but at least the soft landing meant no bones were broken. 'Stop whingeing like a Pom, Jake,' he panted, 'and tell Dad to take that flaming bowser somewhere else.'

The jet of water stopped abruptly, and without a word of apology his father drove the bowser away. But as Ben doubled over, hands on knees to try to get his breath back, he heard more warning shouts coming from across the clearing.

He shook his head, blinking away the muck and water in his eyes and stared in horrified fascination as an army of willy-willies went spiralling merrily over the ground, picking up more blazing tumbleweed, bits of fiery twig and fallen leaves, swirling them up into the air and carrying them before the wind.

The youngsters were chasing after them with whoops of excitement, competing with each other to catch and smother them.

Bob Freeman and the big man from Windorah brought this game to an end by shooting down the whirling fireballs with jets of water as if they were on a firing range.

Ben grinned at Jake. 'It's like the gunfight at the O.K. Corral,' he said, 'only with giant water pistols instead of six-guns.'

He looked around him and noticed how the atmosphere had lightened after this moment of fun. His dad and the man from Windorah were laughing uproariously, the boys were wearing great big grins despite looking like drowned rats and everyone's humour and energy seemed to be restored. They would see this thing through.

Hugh opened his eyes and looked at his family in confusion. 'What happened?' he asked, his voice sounding strangely muffled.

'You had a minor heart attack,' said Jane, her lovely face grey with weariness and anxiety. 'Milly and Delilah brought you in an hour ago.' She took his hand. 'Terry said you were lucky this time, Hugh, but it's a strong warning that you've been doing too much and must take it easy from now on.'

'How's the baby? Are he and Milly all right?'

Her grip on his fingers tightened and her expression became very serious. 'They're absolutely fine,' she said, 'but I want you to promise you'll do as you're told and never scare me like this again.'

He realised he was wearing an oxygen mask and dragged it

from his face so he could speak properly. 'I'm sorry, Jane,' he rasped through a dry throat. 'I didn't do it on purpose.'

Jane's blue eyes became steely. 'But you knew you weren't well, didn't you? Millicent found these in your pocket.' She rattled the small brown bottle of pills in front of him. 'I'm a nurse, Hugh. I know what these are for, so don't even think about arguing with me.'

Hugh felt bruised and battered and certainly in no mood to argue with her. The pills had helped ease the pain in his chest over the past few months, and he'd only used them sparingly – but he silently admitted that he'd known for some time that this heart attack was waiting to happen – and he had young Millicent to thank for her quick thinking and courage. 'Don't fuss,' he said as he put the mask back on. 'I'll be right soon enough.'

'You'll be right if you listen to Mum's advice for once,' said Terence as he checked his pulse and adjusted the drip that was attached to a needle in his arm. 'It's time you slowed down, Dad, and took things easy.'

'You've seen what it's like here,' he muttered. 'How can I?'

Terence placed his hand on his shoulder and gave it a gentle squeeze. 'I'll think of something. Don't worry about it now.'

'We're all just so glad you made it back in one piece,' said Becky, who was also looking tired and drawn. 'You must have been very close to that awful fire, and we were worried sick.'

'Is it out? Where's Danny?'

She gave him a weary smile. 'Danny's safe, and Ben reported in to say the fire at Wilga is now under control. Delilah's gone to stay with Django's family until she can go back to Carey Downs, and Millicent's children are asleep in the nursery. She's had all the necessary checks and is now tucked up with her baby on the ward. So you can stop worrying about everyone and start concentrating on getting yourself well.'

Hugh closed his eyes and sighed with relief. Everyone was all right. He could rest now.

But then he heard his mother's voice in a heated, whispered argument before she determinedly ordered everyone out of the room. It seemed he would not be allowed to sleep just yet.

The tap of her walking stick heralded her approach, and he regarded her with concern as she sat down. She looked troubled – seemed to have aged since he'd seen her last, to have shrunk and become bowed by the weight of all that had happened.

He battled against the drugs that were making him drowsy and took her hand. 'I'm sorry I gave everyone a fright,' he managed. 'Go to bed and rest, Ma. I'll be right soon enough.'

Her expression was solemn as she looked back at him. 'There's something I have to tell you, Hugh,' she said softly. 'It's about Max.'

When she finally fell silent he closed his eyes and felt the trickle of hot tears course down his face. He'd been the elder brother by only five minutes, but he'd always felt responsible for Max. There had been a vulnerability about him, a dreamy gentleness that Hugh had understood must be protected – although Max had been perfectly capable of standing up to the bullies and getting involved in scraps like any other boy.

And yet, despite their different characters and talents, they'd shared the special bond that only twins could understand. And then they had gone to war – and Max's gentle soul had been all but destroyed.

Hugh felt his mother's soft touch as she wiped away his tears, and he knew how hard this must be for her. He groped again for her hand and held tightly to it as he remembered Max the last time he'd seen him.

It had been at his lovely cabin in Warratah Forest on Hugh's biannual visit there. Max had seemed to be at peace with his world at last – had become almost a part of his beautiful surroundings as he spent his day foraging and painting, repairing and maintaining the cabin, and tending his animals. Hugh had almost envied the tranquillity and freedom his twin had found, but Max's solitary existence was also a lonely one, and Hugh couldn't imagine going through life without Jane and his family at his side.

'No mother should have to bury her son,' said Gwyneth. 'It's in the wrong order of things.' She gave a deep, trembling sigh. 'Do you want to see him before the funeral? Say a last goodbye?'

Hugh shook his head, for he preferred to remember his brother alive and glowing with health, his eyes glinting with some wry humour, his long hair drifting over his shoulders as he brought life and colour to a blank canvas. 'But I want to be at the funeral,' he said. 'When is it?'

'There's been no sign of Reverend Baker, and so the pastor from Blackall is on his way down. Max isn't the only one to be laid to rest, and we're hoping to have the service before the day is over.'

She blew her nose and took a deep breath as if to fortify herself. 'Big Mac has ordered that his Chinese cook be buried on Carey Downs once the fire's out – Wi Ling's son will see to it that it's done according to Chinese custom. The young Aboriginal boy will be tended to by his people after the sun goes down.'

Hugh was battling to stay awake, and his eyelids fluttered.

'I'll leave you to rest for now,' murmured Gwyneth as she released his hand and tucked it beneath the sheet. 'When it's time, I'll get Terence to hunt out that old wheelchair so you won't have to walk to the church.'

He wanted to tell her he was perfectly capable of walking that short distance, to protest against the idea of being wheeled about like some ancient invalid, but the spark of protest died as sleep finally claimed him.

*

The two enormous groups of firemen and volunteers who'd been working both sides of the fire were now joined as one. The line of bowsers kept up a constant stream of drenching water as over four hundred men slowly and determinedly trampled the ashes into the ground and continued to beat at the flames, which were now dying out.

As the final licks of flame were dowsed and the burning embers flickered and died, the men knew they had won. But they were too exhausted to celebrate and could only stare in stunned horror at the devastation.

Ben stood beside his father and Jake as they surveyed the miles of scorched earth which seemed to reach to the distant horizon. They looked across the fried debris of the forest floor to the blackened skeletons of barns, homesteads and shearing sheds – to the shrivelled remains of seared tree-stumps and trampled anthills – and on to charred sentinel trees and the cremated bodies of the animals that hadn't managed to escape.

Ben turned to his father and they shared weary, relieved smiles. 'Reckon we're done here at last,' he said.

His father's hand clamped on his shoulder. 'I reckon we are, son, but there's a lot of hard work to do if we're ever gunna get the place right again.'

A great clap of thunder made them jump and everyone looked skyward to the dark thick clouds. The wind was suddenly cooler, the clouds looming low over the land.

Ben felt a spatter of something cold on his face – and then another – and another. He began to laugh as the heavens opened and the rain pelted down. 'Better late than never,' he shouted to Jake over the steady drumming of the cloudburst. He slapped him on the back. 'Come on, mate. We'd better get out of here before we drown.'

The man calling himself John Miller looked up from the cave to the thickening clouds that glowered above the tree canopy. The wind had changed direction, and he thought he could scent rain in the air. The fire would soon be out and the men would be returning to Morgan's Reach. It was almost time for him to disappear again.

Danny had finished his tea and eaten all of the little iced cakes as he'd bombarded him with questions. He had answered as truthfully as he could, but as the birds piped their lovely music and the wind tossed the top of the trees, he felt a strange sense of peace. His decision to keep his survival secret had been the right one. Death was hard enough to understand and accept when you were as young as Danny and George, and to give any child false hope only to dash it away again would be too cruel – and ultimately very selfish.

He'd tried to ignore the gnawing pain in his gut, but it had become too demanding and he reached into his pocket for the small bottle of morphine pills. The doctor had warned him not to take too many at a time, but he slipped two into his mouth and swallowed them down with the last of the cold tea.

'Are you crook?' asked Danny with a frown. 'You don't look too good.'

'I've just got a bit of indigestion,' he replied, rubbing his chest. 'Nothing for you to worry about.'

'My grandpa gets that,' muttered Danny. 'He takes pills every morning, but I'm not supposed to know, cos he says it will worry Grandma Jane.' He gave a deep sigh and poked a stick through the ashes under the billycan. 'Grown-ups are really complicated, aren't they?'

'I reckon they are,' he replied softly. 'But then boys can be complicated too. I know I was when I was your age.'

Danny regarded him thoughtfully. 'Did you hate your gran kissing you, and people patting you on the head, and your mum coming into your room when you didn't want her to, even though you like it when she kisses you goodnight?'

He smiled as the pain began to ease. 'All of that and more. I didn't like girls either, and hated doing homework after school, and having to wash.'

Danny shot him a broad grin of acknowledgement. 'Girls are silly, aren't they?'

'You'll learn to appreciate them when you're older,' he replied with a soft smile.

Danny wrinkled his nose. 'It's better when it's just me and Billy and George. Girls just complicate things and want to take over.'

'I suppose you and your mates come up here all the time,' he said thoughtfully as he tried to steer the conversation back to more important things. 'Is that why you made this camp?'

'George thought it was a stupid idea, so me and Billy made it on our own. We hoped you'd find it, so we could talk to you. That's why we left a note and food and everything.'

'Yeah, I saw the note. Tell me about your mates, Danny.'

'Billy's Django's grandson – he's the tribe elder – and he's got red hair. George can't get over here much cos he lives out at Killigarth Station, but our mums are best friends, so he sometimes comes to stay a couple of nights in the school holidays. George likes reading and is a bit serious sometimes, but he's a good mate. We both go to St Martin's in Brisbane. Billy goes to Miss Emily's school.' He dropped the stick into the embers and watched it catch light. 'Billy never had a dad, and now me and George don't either,' he finished softly.

'How long is it since your mum got that letter from your dad's commanding officer?' he asked quietly.

'Three years.'

'That's a long time,' he replied. 'Do you *really* believe he's coming back?'

Danny was silent for a long while and then gave a tremulous sigh. 'Not really. Not any more. But sometimes I just have to come out here and think about him. It's as if he's closer here, and I can talk to him. I like wandering out in the bush.'

'What does your mum say when you go walkabout like that?'

Danny reddened and refused to look at him. 'She cries a lot, and sometimes she gets really cross.'

'And what about your mate George?' he asked. 'Does he go looking for his father too?'

Danny shook his head. 'George and me fell out about it, cos he knows his dad's never coming back, and it upsets him. He said I was stupid not to believe what all the grown-ups have been telling me.' He chewed his lip.

He regarded the boy evenly. 'Why do you think he's so sure about that, when you're clearly still secretly hoping your dad will come back?'

'Dunno,' said Danny, with a slight shrug that made him wince. 'But he and his mum had to go to Brisbane to get a special medal from the army – and they wouldn't have given her that if they thought he was still alive, would they?'

'I suppose not,' he agreed. 'What about your dad? Did he get any medals?'

Danny nodded. 'Three. We've got them in a special box with all his letters and Mum's favourite photographs. She calls it our special memory box.'

'Your mum must really have loved your dad,' he murmured.

Danny balled his fist and kept his chin tucked into the blanket. 'Yeah, she did. But I know she likes Ben Freeman now, cos I saw them kissing.'

He threw the stub of his cigarette into the small fire and scrubbed his face with his hands. 'Three years is a long time, Danny. Your mum is doing the right thing by trying to start again.' He saw the boy's fists and the stubborn set to his mouth. 'Don't you like this Ben Freeman? Is he a bad man, do you think?'

Danny continued to look surly. 'He's all right,' he said grudgingly. 'He's the fire chief, and he lives up there in that cabin he built.' He relaxed his fists. 'I've been up to the top of the tower and looked right over the trees through his binoculars. He lets me wear his fire helmet and drive his ute sometimes too,' he finished.

'So he's not all bad then?'

Danny pulled a face and shrugged. 'Mum wouldn't like him if he was a complete drongo, I suppose. But he'll never be my dad.'

'I doubt very much if he's ever considered trying to take your father's place,' he replied, 'but he sounds like a good man, and if your mother likes him enough to kiss him now and again, then I reckon you should accept that.'

'I don't want her kissing anybody,' he hissed. 'She's my mum, and dad wouldn't like it.'

'But your dad isn't here,' he said evenly. 'He's been dead for three years and your mother shouldn't have to spend the rest of her life mourning him just because you refuse to accept the truth.' He looked across the small fire at the bowed head. 'Do you want her to spend the rest of her life being sad and alone, Danny?'

Danny's eyes were swimming with tears as he looked back at him. 'I don't want her to be sad,' he whispered. 'But if she likes Ben, I'm afraid she'll forget all about Dad. She's already put the memory box away, so I can't go through it.'

He reached for Danny's hand. 'Perhaps that's because she finds it too painful to always have it around,' he said softly. 'Grown-ups hurt too when someone they love dies. We find it almost impossible to believe we will never see them again, or hear their voice – but it's what we must accept. They've left us, and there is absolutely nothing we can do about it. But they live on in our memories, Danny – and in your mother's heart there will always be a place for your dad, whatever the future might hold.'

'But it's so hard,' Danny sobbed as he threw himself against him.

He let him cry out his pain and had to blink back his own tears as he held the boy and waited for the storm to pass. War and death caused so much anguish, affecting everyone, regardless of their age, touching their lives and colouring their futures. There were so many questions he wanted to ask the boy, for he hungered for every small detail of the lives that were being lived without him – but despite the yearning, he held his tongue. Such questions might give him away.

He sighed deeply. The past was another country, and he was as guilty as Danny in wishing the clock could be turned back. They were learning harsh lessons today, but he had a feeling that this chance to talk and to explore their darkest thoughts would sustain them both for what lay ahead.

He closed his eyes and rested his chin on Danny's head. He knew where his own future lay, but Danny had his whole life in front of him. It was vital the boy was made to understand that nothing could be achieved by constantly looking back.

The boy eventually stopped sobbing and he gave him a hanky to blow his nose. Once he was calm again, he looked deep into his eyes. 'I know it's hard to accept that he's gone, Danny, but people like your dad and John Blake died fighting for your freedom to live your life the very best way you can.'

He took the boy's hand and maintained his steady gaze. 'They died for your right to grow up in a world free of war. They died so you could live. And that is a precious gift you must never turn your back on. The past is gone, Danny. The future is yours, and your mother's, and it's time to accept that.'

He smiled and softly nudged his fist against Danny's small chin. 'Make your father proud, Danny, and fulfil his dreams for you by growing up into the strong, brave man that he hoped you'd be.'

Danny was silent as he digested this. Then he nodded and sniffed back the last of the tears. 'I never thought about it that way before,' he said finally. 'Do you think Dad is watching us from up there?'

John looked out from the cave and up to the sky, where the clouds were still threatening rain. 'The Aborigines have a belief that the souls of the dead are taken up into the heavens on a special boat and once they've sailed across the Milky Way they are turned into stars. And those stars are our guardians, watching over us and waiting until it is our turn to join them.'

Danny sat and looked at the sky for a long while. 'Django told me that story,' he said finally. 'But he's a black fella, and they believe in all sorts of strange things.' He regarded him evenly. 'Do *you* believe my dad's up there?'

He nodded as he answered truthfully. 'Oh yes. He's there, and when the sky is clear and you can see the millions of stars up there, you'll find one that's winking right at you to let you know he can see you. Then one day, when you're an old, old man, you'll take that boat ride along the Great White Way and be with him again.'

Danny chewed his lip as he mulled this over. Then he shrugged off the blanket and got to his feet. 'Mum will be really worried,' he muttered. 'I'd better get home now.'

'I'll come with you as far as the edge of the trees. Then I must be on my way too.'

'But I want you to meet my mum, and my mates George and Billy.'

He shook his head. 'Not this time,' he replied. 'Perhaps another day if I'm passing this way again.' He smiled at Danny and resisted the urge to push back the lick of hair that was flopping in his eyes. 'I reckon you've done enough climbing for one day. How about I give you a piggyback ride down these rocks?'

Danny giggled and waited for him to squat down so he could clamber on to his back.

'Hold on tight, and wrap your legs around my waist. Are you ready?'

Danny laughed. 'Yeah,' he shouted. 'Let's go.'

He felt his light weight on his back and the warmth of his skinny arms around his neck. It had been a very long time since he'd carried a boy on his back, and the memories were almost too hard to bear.

He determinedly concentrated on the job in hand and began the descent, his army boots finding the nooks and crannies in the rocks until they'd reached the bottom. Then he continued to carry Danny through the trees until he reached the large natural pond which lay only a few yards away from the dusty main street.

Danny slid to the ground. 'I'll never forget you, John Miller,' he said shyly.

'And I'll never forget you either, Danny Jackson.' He solemnly shook the boy's hand and, after a moment of silence in which they looked into one another's eyes, Danny turned away and slowly headed for his home.

He stood there long after the boy had gone, and then finally began to retrace his steps through the trees. He'd left his kitbag in the cave and needed to rest a while before he completed his final task. Then he would leave Morgan's Reach behind him for the very last time and begin his own journey along the Great White Way.

He smiled to himself as a dark shadow flitted amid a thick stand of ironbark. 'He's on his way home, Django,' he said. 'You can stop following me now.'

The black man emerged from behind the tree and eyed him thoughtfully. 'You still alonga you black fella ears and eyes I teach 'im,' he said gruffly. 'We hear you with spirits long time. Why you no alonga home like other white fellas?'

He smiled at the man who had taught him so much about bushcraft. 'The spirits are calling me, Django. They sing every day now, and soon I must go with them.'

'Spirits sing alonga you?' Django's tawny eyes seemed to penetrate to his very core as he regarded him for a long moment and then unerringly placed his dark hand against his midriff. His expression was sorrowful as he slowly nodded. 'Spirits sing. You alonga them soon, soon.'

He returned his steady, understanding gaze and then bowed his head in respect. 'Now you know why I didn't come home,' he murmured. 'Watch over them for me, Django.' At the other man's nod, he grasped his hand. 'Goodbye, old friend.'

Django watched as he turned away. The rain began to spatter through the trees and finally drew a fine curtain between him and the man he'd been proud to call friend, and he felt a great sorrow. His friend was already walking with the Ancestor Spirits – he could see them guiding him to where they must sing their final song and gather him up to take him on that last starry journey through the sky.

Django began to softly intone the ritual mourning song as the rain pattered down through the trees. When he had completed the last note, he turned away and headed for the street. He would keep his friend's secret.

19

The flow of casualties had slowed to a trickle, the walking wounded had returned home if they could, and apart from three or four of the more serious cases who must remain, the hospital was now quiet and almost deserted.

Amy had taken George over to Gwyneth's to help her feed and water the animals, Terence and Sandra were snatching a few quiet moments on the back veranda and the spinster sisters had gone home for a well-earned rest. The pastor from Blackall had arrived and would stay with Frances Baker, for the funerals were planned for later that afternoon.

The news that the fire was out was a huge relief to everyone and, although some had lost loved ones, and others had been deprived of their homes, the general consensus was that things could have been far worse if the widespread community hadn't come together when it most mattered.

It was now mid-morning and Becky was pacing the veranda, looking out frequently for any sign of Danny. Her nerves were shredded, and as the hours had ticked by since hearing Django had found him, the waiting became ever harder to bear.

She peered through the screens again and, as the rain began to fall, she saw the small figure ambling down the street as if he'd just been away for five minutes. Her heart leaped with joy. 'Danny,' she shouted as she pushed through the screen door, flew down the steps and raced towards him.

Danny's dirty little face split into a wide grin as he quickened his step. 'Mum! Mum, it's all right.'

Becky fell to her knees, gathering him to her and holding him tight, her kisses and tears smothering his grubby face as the rain softly fell on them. 'I was so frightened,' she said. 'I thought I'd lost you.'

'Fair go, Mum, I was with John Miller and—'

'I know. Django told me. But that was hours ago.' She looked at him through her tears and touched the cuts and bruises on his face and arms. 'You've hurt yourself,' she breathed. 'What happened?

'I fell off a cliff,' he said with a touch of bravado. 'John cleaned me up a bit, and it doesn't hurt.'

She wondered what on earth he'd been doing on a cliff in the first place, but it didn't matter for now. She had him home – questions were for later. She softly flicked back the damp hair from his eyes. 'I love you so much, Danny. Please don't ever run away again.'

He wrapped his arms round her neck and pressed his face against her cheek. 'I love you too, Mum, and I'm sorry I made you cry. I promise I'll never go off again without telling you first.'

His promise sounded heartfelt, and she was certain he meant it right this minute, but would he forget it in a while and disappear again? She had to trust that he wouldn't, but from now on she would keep a much closer eye on him.

Ignoring the rain that was now teeming down and soaking them both, she held his precious little body close and thanked God for keeping him safe. 'You've been gone for so long, Danny,' she said. 'Where were you – and why didn't Django bring you back like he promised?'

Danny wriggled from her close embrace and regarded her with a frown as she slowly got to her feet. 'I haven't seen Django since the day before yesterday,' he replied. 'John brought me back.'

Becky was confused by this, but she said nothing and peered through the rain to the end of the street. There was no sign of Miller or Django. 'I don't see him,' she said.

Danny looked up at her, his little face solemn. 'He has to go somewhere else. But he said if he was coming this way again, he'd visit us.' He slipped his small hand into hers. 'He's a bonzer bloke, Mum. He was in the 8th like Dad and John Blake, and even went to Malaya for a bit before he was sent to Burma. You'd like him.'

Becky eyed him thoughtfully. 'I'm sure I would,' she murmured. 'Perhaps he'll come back one day and I can thank him for looking after you.'

The rain was cool and refreshing after the oppressive heat, but they were both soaked through, and Becky began to lead him back towards the hospital. 'You went looking for him, didn't you?' she asked carefully. 'To ask him questions about the war.'

At his reluctant nod she pulled him to her side to reassure him, but her pulse was racing at the thought of what must have been going through her son's head to do such a thing. 'And do you feel better about things now?'

They had reached the steps leading up to the hospital veranda, and Danny came to a standstill and looked up at her. 'I know Daddy won't ever be coming back now,' he said with a hitch in his voice. 'But it's all right, Mum. John explained things, you see, and from now on I'm gunna be the best boy I can, and make Dad proud.'

Becky had no idea what the mysterious John Miller might have said to her son, but it seemed to have worked. 'Your dad was always proud of you, Danny. And I'm sure he's watching over you, knowing that you'll be a fine young man one day.'

Danny nodded thoughtfully and then brushed his wet hair from his eyes and broke the moment of solemnity with a huge grin. 'I'm starving,' he said. 'Can I have a bacon sandwich?'

Becky felt the tension drop away and she laughed. 'As it's such a special morning, you can have whatever you want.' She looked up to see Granny Gwyn, Terence and Sandra waiting for them, their smiles and tears speaking of their profound relief and delight at having him home again. 'But it might have to wait a bit,' she added softly. 'It looks like you're about to have a welcome-home party.'

After Danny had been hugged and kissed by everyone, he was given dry clothes, checked over by Terence and then taken to see his grandfather while Jane made him a doorstep sandwich.

Hugh had managed to smile at him and ruffle his hair before going back to sleep again, and Danny had had to accept it could be a while before he and his grandfather could share their adventure stories and compare notes.

Rebecca watched as he drank the cup of cocoa and ate the enormous bacon sandwich which dripped grease and tomato sauce down his clean shirt. He'd had a big adventure, and she would probably never learn all the details of what had passed between him and the mysterious John Miller, but it didn't really matter. Her little boy was home.

As his eyelids drooped with weariness and he sagged against her she rescued the remains of the sandwich from his lap and carried him into the now-deserted isolation room. He was fast asleep even before she'd pulled the sheet to his chin.

Terence drew Sandra into his embrace as they sat in the swing-seat on the back veranda and wearily watched the rain turn the backyard into a quagmire. 'It's been one heck of a few days,' he murmured, 'and I couldn't have done half of it without you.'

She snuggled closer. 'We're a good team, aren't we?'

He softly kissed the top of her head. 'Yes, we are.' He let the easy silence fall between them, relishing this quiet moment of togetherness. 'I do love you, you know,' he said some moments later. 'And I'm sorry I haven't always been the husband you needed.'

She shifted within his embrace and lifted her head so she could look up at him. 'You have nothing to apologise for,' she said firmly. 'It's me who should be saying sorry.'

'Sandra, you . . .'

She pressed her finger to his lips and drew back, her expression earnest. 'I lost my way after Michael died,' she admitted, 'and thought I could deaden the pain and guilt by drinking. I realise now how stupid that was – how thoughtless and demanding it made me. But at the time it seemed to be the only way to get through each day.'

His soft heart went out to her. 'Oh, darling,' he sighed.

She dipped her chin. 'I wasn't well, Terry, I can see that now, and the drink was just making it worse.'

'You don't have to explain, my darling girl. I did understand, really I did.'

She put her soft hand on his cheek. 'I haven't been fair to you, Terry. And I'm so sorry. Michael's death should have brought us closer together, but I felt so guilty at not being able to nurse him back to health that I needed someone to blame.' She looked down again. 'But of course neither of us was at fault. I can see that now.'

He drew her closer and tucked her head into his neck so she couldn't see the tears in his eyes. 'At least we had the chance to love him for a little while,' he murmured. 'And he'll always be in our hearts.'

She nodded and he could feel the dampness of her tears on his shirt.

'Do you think you could bear staying on here for a while

longer?' he asked tentatively. 'Only Dad will have to retire now he's been so ill, and this place has to be kept running.'

She eased from his embrace, took the handkerchief from his pocket and determinedly wiped away her tears. 'Of course it must,' she said firmly. 'The people here depend on it.'

'So you think you're ready to stay with me and help out? You've already seen how chaotic it can be. Do you think you could cope?'

She gave him a watery smile. 'If you mean can I go without a drink for more than a few days without falling off the wagon – then yes. I won't lie to you and say it'll be easy, because I know it won't. But these past two days have shown me how good it can feel to be doing something useful again – and to be a part of a real community. I'm willing to give it a go if you are.'

He felt a great wave of love for her as he drew her back into his embrace. 'You won't regret it, Sandra, I promise.'

She softly kissed his lips. 'Let's just take things one day at a time, Terry. The road ahead of us will probably be rocky, but as long as we have each other we'll get through.'

Her head was once again on his shoulder, her hand resting above his heart that was full to bursting. They had come through the worst and, with Sandra by his side, they would conquer the world – or at least conquer the trials and tribulations of running a bush hospital in the middle of nowhere.

It was now mid-afternoon and the squall of rain had passed. Jane saw Hugh's eyelids flutter and reached for his hand. 'I'm here,' she assured him.

He looked back at her and struggled to be rid of the oxygen mask. But his fingers were clumsy and he had to yield to her insistence that it stayed in place. 'I'm sorry, Jane,' he sighed. 'I didn't say anything about those pills because I knew you'd only worry.'

She eyed him sternly. 'You realise you'll have to retire now, don't you?'

He wasn't foolish enough to think he could carry on under such pressure any more, but he still recoiled at the thought of the hospital having to close. 'I'll take it easier from now on, I promise,' he hedged.

She leaned her elbows on the bed and took his hands. 'You will concentrate on getting better and leave the work to Terry,' she said firmly. 'We've had a long talk about things, and he's agreed to stay.' She smiled. 'He's already thinking of how to improve the place and get more help.'

Hugh frowned. 'How's he going to do that?'

'As you know, the Flying Doctor Service has small medical stations all over the Outback that supply nurses and doctors. Terry thinks Morgan's Reach would be an ideal location for just such a station, and he's going to write to Reverend John Flynn to see if he agrees.'

Hugh thought about the legendary man who'd founded the service way back before the First World War. 'But he's an old man now. Terry shouldn't bother him with our staffing problems.'

'He might be old, but he's still very much at the helm,' said Jane, 'and I'm sure he'll be able to offer some sort of solution.' She tucked the sheet in and switched off the light, plunging the shuttered room into dusky darkness. 'Don't worry about it all now, Hugh. Just rest and let the young ones get on with things,' she said softly. 'We've done our bit,' she added as she kissed his cheek. 'It's their turn now.'

He caught her hand as she was about to turn away. 'I don't want to go to a bungalow on the coast,' he said urgently.

She grinned at him. 'I know you don't. But once you're on the mend and our children are settled in their new lives, we can take long, leisurely holidays and see a bit of Australia. We'll always have Morgan's Reach to come home to when we've had enough.'

Hugh smiled as Jane softly closed the door. She was the best wife any man could wish for, and it seemed the future of the hospital at Morgan's Reach was in capable hands. He relaxed into the pillows. His work was over now, and he could look forward to spending more time with her – perhaps they could even celebrate his next birthday at Alice Springs. He'd always wanted to go there.

Sal had stoked the old copper boiler into life so she had hot water, then swept and scrubbed and scoured almost every inch of the back room and bar. There hadn't been much she could do about the ruined furniture, but as men usually preferred standing at the bar while they drank, she didn't think it mattered. As for the brass railings, she would get one of the men to fix them later.

Once she'd laid traps for any lingering rodents and cleared all the glass away, she'd let Brandy come downstairs. The dog had followed her about as she'd made a swift inventory of what was left in the way of drinks and had happily trotted along beside her as she'd gone over to Annie O'Halloran's, explained the situation and persuaded her to help restock the bar and organise the food for the wake.

Annie had been in a generous mood, relieved that her husband had come home in one piece and was happily snoring in the back room leaving her to get on with things. She and Sal came to an arrangement whereby Sean would take over running the pub while Sal took a break, the cost of the drinks and food recouped from the takings. Sean was yet to learn of these arrangements, but Annie assured Sal that he'd do as he was told, and that she'd be in charge of the food until Sal was ready to take over the reins again.

314

Sal was exhausted by the time she'd accomplished all this, and she returned to the pub ready for a long hot soak in the bath. But as she traipsed up the stairs and entered the bedroom, her gaze fell on Max's satchel. Sinking on to the bed, she unfastened the clasp and pulled out the sketchbook which he'd always refused to show her.

Her hands trembled and the tears rolled down her face as she turned each page and discovered just how deeply he'd loved her. For on every page he'd caught her likeness and drawn it with such tenderness that it shone from every line and curve. Here she was sitting by the fire in the cabin, Brandy at her feet while she read a book. And this one was drawn while she'd slept – the next while she sat in the grass beneath the trees with the ponies – and the last where she'd been perched on the rock, watching the storm.

She closed the book and held it to her heart. He had loved her deeply and truly, but had never had the courage to expose his secret and tell her. 'Oh, Max,' she whispered through her tears. 'If only we could have been brave enough to say what was in our hearts. How different things might have been.'

Rebecca was dozing in the chair at Danny's bedside when they were both startled awake by the deafening blare of car and utility horns outside.

Danny was out of bed and throwing open the shutters as she tried to clear the fog of exhaustion and sleep from her sluggish mind. 'Look, Mum,' he shouted. 'They're all coming back from the fire.'

Becky flew to the window, her pulse racing with relief and excitement. She looked out eagerly to discover that the rain had stopped, but the main street was awash and the long straggle of utilities, lorries, fire engines, bowsers, cars and horse-drawn wagons was splashing through the red mud. The danger was passed. Ben had come home.

'Let's go, Mum,' said Danny as he tugged her hand. 'I wanna see the parade.'

Becky ran with him to the veranda where the rest of the Morgan family had gathered with Amy and George to welcome the heroes home.

The men looked exhausted and bedraggled but, as the residents of Morgan's Reach poured into the street to join in the celebration, it seemed their spirits were still high, for there were shouts of victory and the ringing of laughter as they were swamped by their friends and loved ones.

As the two boys ran out into the street, Becky put her arm round Amy and grinned in delight. 'That's what I call a real sight for sore eyes,' she said, all tiredness banished.

'It certainly is,' Amy replied, her gaze trawling the length of the cavalcade until she caught sight of her father and brothers. She waved to them as her mother rushed to greet them, and then turned back to Rebecca.

'Danny doesn't seem to have come to any harm, despite his adventures. But is he really all right?'

Becky nodded. 'He's come through a sea change and is finally thinking more clearly. I have the mysterious John Miller to thank for that – and I wish he was here so I could thank him.'

Amy grinned. 'I think there's someone else who needs your attention more at this moment,' she said, her expression mischievous. 'Isn't that Ben over there?'

Becky flew down the steps and up the street to where Ben had parked the fire truck and bowser outside the police house. She flung herself into his arms and almost knocked him off his feet as she smothered his black-streaked face in kisses.

'Whoa there, Becky,' he laughed. 'Give a bloke a chance to catch his breath.'

They swayed, laughing in one another's arms, heedless of the mud and of everyone around. 'Welcome home, Ben,' she said softly as his arms wrapped round her and he held her close.

'Does this mean I'm allowed to kiss you in public now?' he asked with a twinkle in his eye.

She laughed up at him as she cupped his filthy face in her hands and felt the rough bristles on his chin. 'Only if you want to,' she teased.

He gave a soft groan. 'Of course I want to,' he breathed. His kiss was tender and sweet, growing in intensity as they clung to one another. The rest of the world faded away, leaving them in their own cocoon of happiness where little else mattered.

They finally drew apart, breathless and stunned by the depths of their feelings as they looked into one another's eyes. 'Danny's all right?' he asked. At her nod, he embraced her again. 'We'll take it slow,' he assured her, 'but from now on you're my girl, and I don't care if the whole bloody world knows it.'

Becky snuggled against him, warmed by his love and understanding and the deep sense of being where she belonged. They had come through the firestorm and, although it might still take time before Danny was ready to accept Ben into his life, Becky could already sense that things would be much better from now on.

Jane had been checking on Hugh again when she heard the cavalcade coming down the track. Quietly leaving him to sleep, she'd tiptoed to the door and closed it behind her, planning to watch the fun from the hospital veranda. But as she reached the screen she was startled to see Bob Freeman striding very determinedly towards her.

'Whatever's the matter, Bob?' she asked as he crashed through the screen door and stomped across the veranda.

'I've come to have a word with Big Mac,' he growled as he took off his hat and slapped the dust from it against his meaty thigh.

'He's asleep,' Jane said quickly.

'Then I'll wake the bugger up,' he rumbled.

Jane put her hand against his muscled arm. 'Please, Bob. Don't cause trouble. Not here.'

'I'm not here to cause flaming trouble,' he replied as he gently but firmly lifted her from her feet and set her down away from the door. Before Jane could do anything to stop him, Bob was clumping down the corridor towards the ward.

Jane scurried along behind him, but he was as big as a house and obviously fully determined to get to Big Mac. 'He's in the isolation room,' she said before he could disturb the whole hospital. 'But I know what you and Mac are like when you get going, and I will *not* stand for that sort of carry-on in my hospital. Is that understood?'

Bob looked down at her and nodded.

Jane quietly opened the door to the isolation room, and before she could stop him, Bob was approaching the bed.

'The wife reckoned I oughta come and see if you're right,' he growled.

'You needn't have bothered,' replied Big Mac, who was bound almost head to foot in special burn bandages.

Bob eyed the dressings and drips thoughtfully. 'Yeah, that's what I said you'd say, but you know what women are like.'

'Well, now you've had a good look, why don't you clear off and leave a bloke to get some rest?'

'You're a miserable old bastard at the best of times, Mac, but I reckon I gotta thank you for what you done today.'

'Reckon you done good as well, you thieving galah – and when I get outta this flaming bed I'll be counting every one of my clean skins to make sure you haven't nicked any.'

'And I've got enough to do clearing up my place, without worrying about a few scrawny cattle.'

The two men glared at one another as Jane stood uncertainly in doorway.

Big Mac was the first to look away. 'What's the damage, Bob?'

'Flaming fire went right through, mate. Sorry, there ain't much left of either of our places. We've rounded up all the cattle and sheep and sent them up to Killigarth until we've got some grass to feed 'em – and before you start sounding off, your stock has been separated from mine.'

Big Mac had a ghost of a smile on his lips. 'Thanks, mate.'

'No worries,' muttered Bob as he tugged on his hat. 'Hope you get better soon, mate. Catch ya later.'

'You can bet the house on that, you bloody old crook,' retorted Mac with a chuckle.

Jane stepped aside as Bob Freeman strode out of the room with a big grin plastered across his face. She would never understand men – especially these Australian men who lived out in the Never-Never, for they were definitely a breed of their own.

Gwyneth had been forcibly reminded of Rhys's passing as she'd washed and changed into a rusty-black dress that had seen better days and only came out of mothballs for funerals. A dark straw hat and sensible walking shoes completed her outfit, and she'd placed her prayer book on the dresser next to her black lace gloves.

She'd sat in her shuttered kitchen, the rough-hewn coffin on the table beside her, the single candle flickering in the gloom, and listened to the noisy arrival of the firefighters and their equally noisy welcome. She'd been glad that everyone was back, but hadn't had the energy or heart to go outside, for the events of the past twenty-four hours had taken their toll.

She'd remained there in the candlelight as the clock ticked away on the wall, Coco screeched from the back veranda and Wally snored in her lap. The shouts had finally faded and all was quiet as the community sobered itself for the funeral.

Her gaze had drifted repeatedly to the coffin as she waited. There were always spare coffins in the shed behind Charley Sawyer's forge, for death could strike at any time, and it was best to be prepared. But how could one possibly be prepared when it was a son who had been struck down so cruelly?

'It's time, Gran,' said Terence softly as he walked into the kitchen followed by Amy Blake's three hulking brothers and the rest of her family.

Gwyneth gently lifted Wally from her lap and snuggled him into the dog basket under the table. Then she rose from her chair and placed her hand softly on top of the coffin for a moment and then turned away to pick up her gloves and prayer book.

As the four men shouldered Max's coffin and carried it out of the front door and along the path, she saw a distressed Sal waiting by the gate with Brandy. 'Come, my dear,' she murmured. 'Give me your arm. We'll see this through together.'

There were three drays waiting in the street, each harnessed to a black horse that had been groomed to a gleam. Black plumes had been attached to their crownpieces, and the men who sat at the reins lifted their hats in respect as all three coffins were solemnly loaded on to the drays.

Gwyneth nodded to the other mourners and steeled herself for what was to come. The whole town had turned out, their numbers swollen by the firefighters, those who'd come in to help and the families of the other two dead men. There would be gossip, for most of them would never have heard of Max, let alone known that he was her son.

She patted Sal's hand, knowing that her presence beside her

would also make her the subject of speculation. 'Don't mind them,' she advised softly. 'What they think doesn't matter.'

Sal nodded and tightened her grip on Brandy's shiny new lead as the rest of Gwyneth's family gathered behind them and the cortege slowly moved off and trundled down the street.

There was a heavy silence as men raised their hats, women bowed their heads and wide-eyed children followed their progress. Gwyneth kept her gaze focused on the coffin, glad to have Sal's support as they accompanied their beloved Max on his last journey.

The service was over and the elderly minister from Blackall had followed the rest of the mourners to the pub, where Annie and Sean O'Halloran were trying to keep pace with the demands of their thirsty customers.

Gwyneth had told the rest of her family to go on ahead while she had a few minutes with Sal. She tucked her hand into the crook of the girl's arm so they could cross the rough ground of the graveyard to the wooden bench that stood beneath a drooping pepper tree. Once they were seated, they sat for a while in silent contemplation of the newly dug mounds of earth.

'I didn't realise you were going to open the pub so soon,' said Gwyneth.

'It's not out of lack of respect,' she replied, 'but I needed something to do to take my mind off things. Bert tried his best to ruin me, but knowing Max has given me the strength to fight back. He'll never beat me again.'

'You've said that before,' Gwyneth reminded her.

'It's different this time. Bert has gone, and I doubt any of us will see him again.' She stroked Brandy's head as he rested his soft muzzle on her knee. 'I'm going away for a while,' she said, 'and I've asked Annie and Sean to take over until I come back.'

'You're going back to Max's cabin, aren't you?'

Sal nodded. 'If it hasn't burnt to the ground I'll stay there until I've come to terms with things. You see, I need to decide what to do next. Max's agent seems to think I have a real talent and it would be a sin to waste it. But I'm not ready yet to commit myself to anything.'

Gwyneth took her hand. 'Then take my old utility, go back to Warratah Forest and take your time to heal,' she advised. 'The answers will come eventually – and when you're ready, you'll feel stronger and more confident to walk a new path.'

Sal's smile was tremulous as she helped Gwyneth to her feet and they began to stroll away from the cemetery and down the street. 'Thanks for everything,' she said. 'You've been such a dear, wise friend.'

'I'm much older than you, so of course I'm wiser,' she retorted. 'There's no need for all this soft talk, Sal. We know each other too well.'

Sal helped her up the steps and Gwyneth plumped down in her favourite veranda chair. 'I'll sit here awhile and keep an eye on things,' she said. 'The ponies will be looked after, and the keys to the ute are on the kitchen dresser. Go and find your future, Sal, and when you're ready, you can come back and tell me all about it.'

Gwyneth was weary and saddened by all that had happened, and she sat there deep in thought long after Sal had driven away. But as she settled into the cushions with Wally at her feet in his basket and Coco in his cage beside her she became aware of the noisy activity down the street and her formidable strength and avid curiosity returned.

There was always something to watch in Morgan's Reach and, with so many people milling about, things could prove to be even more interesting than usual.

*

He'd returned to the cave and gathered up his belongings while the rain thundered down through the trees. But he'd reasoned that it could be some time before Ben Freeman returned to his house above the cave so had huddled into his greatcoat, taken another pill and fallen asleep.

He'd been snapped awake by the sound of motor engines and the tooting of horns coming from the valley and had known it was time to leave. The ashes in the fire had gone cold, and so had the billy tea. He'd thrown the dregs away and stuffed the billy and tin mug into his kitbag. But as he'd rolled up the blankets he'd found the old pair of binoculars that Danny must have left behind.

The glass was cracked in one side, the strap broken, the outer casing scratched and battered. He'd thought long and hard about what to do, and then had dropped them in his deep coat pocket. Danny would get them back when he'd finished with them.

Then, with a deep sigh, he'd steeled himself for the long walk through the bush.

It had stopped raining now, but the music of the bush continued to play as he walked beneath the dripping trees. Birds sang in the sweet, fresh air, and insects hummed and buzzed and ticked as his boots scuffed through the leaves that carpeted the bush floor. The scent of wet earth and eucalyptus rose to greet him and, as the hillside steepened and he had to ease his pace, his boots scraped against the hidden black rocks that were so sacred to Django and his people.

He'd been walking for about an hour, circumventing Morgan's Reach until he was high above the northern end of the broad main road. The effect of the pills was already wearing off and, as he came to a large flat rock that jutted out from the hillside, he sat down to rest. He could see right down the main street quite clearly, for a broad firebreak had been cut through the trees, and a beam of late sunlight glinted in the puddles and on the roofs.

The trees threw deep shadows over the slab of rock and he had no fear of being seen by anyone down in the town. Slipping another pill into his mouth, he swallowed it and then waited for it to numb the pain as he sat very still and watched the people of Morgan's Reach gather at the churchyard.

It looked as if the whole town had turned out, and knowing how close these tightly knit communities were, he could almost be certain that every homesteader and station owner within several hundred miles would be down there after such a battle against their common enemy. Old enmities would have been set aside and new friendships forged – and in the ashes of the fire new shoots would grow to continue the rhythm of life's circle.

The funeral cortege was now moving slowly down the street, and he guessed it must be for the men who'd lost their lives in the fire. He pulled the binoculars from his greatcoat pocket and scanned the street. It was a bit out of focus through the cracked lens, but he persevered, yearning to find those much-loved faces among the crowd.

But there were too many people, too many faces he couldn't see because they were turned away from him. He hissed in frustration and tried to adjust his view as the service came to an end and the gathering began to disperse. This was his one chance – and it seemed he would miss it.

And then he saw her, and his heart missed a beat. She was standing arm in arm with another young woman and they were talking and smiling at one another. He would have recognised her anywhere – and even from this distance he could see that she was as beautiful as he'd remembered. His heart thudded painfully as he watched her laugh, and his longing to cry out to her had to be swiftly stifled.

The keening was deep in his throat as the two boys ran up to them. This was what he'd longed for; this was all that he'd hoped to achieve. He drank in the sight of them together – beautiful mother and precious son – his wistful gaze following their every movement as they began to walk away from the churchyard.

He silently willed them to stop again so he could prolong this treasured moment. But they kept on walking and were all too soon out of sight. He closed his eyes, etching the scene into his heart as he wept silent tears for what might have been.

Sometime later he tucked the boys' note into the binocular case and left it perched on the rock where it could easily be found. Then he hitched the kitbag over his shoulder and walked away from Morgan's Reach, the warmth of his loved ones' smiles chasing away the chill of the night.

The pain in his belly was growing stronger and soon it would defeat him. But he took another pill, determined to reach the distant place in the bush known only to the Aborigines. There would be no marker above his final resting place, and the dust of his earthly body would be carried on the wind to become as one with the great open plains that he loved so well.

John Blake lost track of time, but as the rain began to fall again and the darkness closed in, he felt strengthened by the knowledge that he'd achieved what he'd set out to do – that Amy and his son George were happy – and that he could now die in peace.

THE END

TAMARA
McKINLEY

Ocean Child

1920

Lulu Pearson, a young and talented Tasmanian sculptress, finds herself in London in the wake of the Great War. The future is looking bright until Lulu learns she has inherited a racing colt called Ocean Child from a mysterious benefactor, and she must return to her homeland to claim him.

*

Baffled by the news, Lulu boards a ship to Tasmania to uncover the truth, but it seems a welcome return is more than she can hope for. Unbeknownst to Lulu, more than a few fortunes ride on Ocean Child's success – it seems everyone from her estranged mother to the stable hands has a part to play, and an interest in keeping the family secrets buried.

TAMARA McKINLEY

Undercurrents

1894

The SS Arcadia sets sail from Liverpool, carrying Eva and Frederick
Hamilton – a young married couple determined to make a new start in an
exciting new frontier: Australia. But as the ship nears its destination,
it goes down in an unexpected storm.

*

Years later, Olivia Hamilton makes the same journey, hoping to learn
more about her mysterious origins. As Olivia draws closer to discovering the
truth about her past, she realises that, like Eva Hamilton all those years ago,
this could be a journey with unexpected consequences.